Traitors, Kings, and the Big Break

Traitors, Kings, and the Big Break
Copyright © 2008 by Lamp Post, Inc.

Library of Congress Cataloging-in-Publication Data
Lee, Young Shin.
Traitors, kings, and the big break / story by Young Shin Lee ; art by
Jung Sun Hwang ; edited by Brett Burner and J.S. Earls.
    p. cm. -- (The Manga Bible ; v. 4)
 ISBN 978-0-310-71290-9 (softcover)
 1. Bible stories, English--O.T. Kings, 1st. I. Hwang, Jung Sun. II.
Burner, Brett A., 1969- III. Earls, J. S. IV. Title.
  BS551.3.L428 2008
  222'.5309505--dc22

                            2008007655

Requests for information should be addressed to: Grand Rapids, Michigan 49530

This book published in conjunction with Lamp Post, Inc.; 8367 Lemon Avenue, La Mesa, CA 91941

Series Editor: Bud Rogers
Managing Art Director: Merit Alderink

Printed in the United States of America

09 10 11 12 13 14 /DCI/ 10 9 8 7 6 5 4 3 2

Traitors, Kings, and the Big Break

1 Kings–2 Kings (part 1)

Series Editor: Bud Rogers
Edited by Brett Burner and JS Earls
Story by Young Shin Lee
Art by Jung Sun Hwang

ZONDERVAN.com/
AUTHORTRACKER
follow your favorite authors

FIRST KINGS

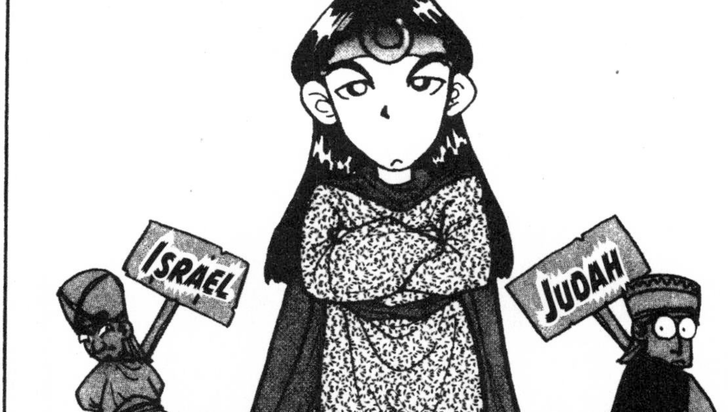
ISRAEL
JUDAH

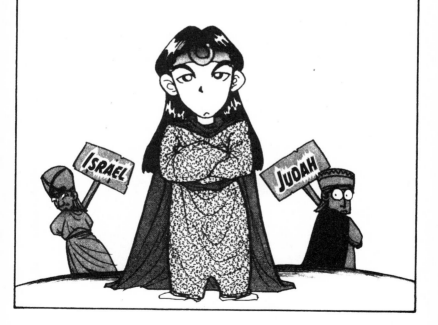

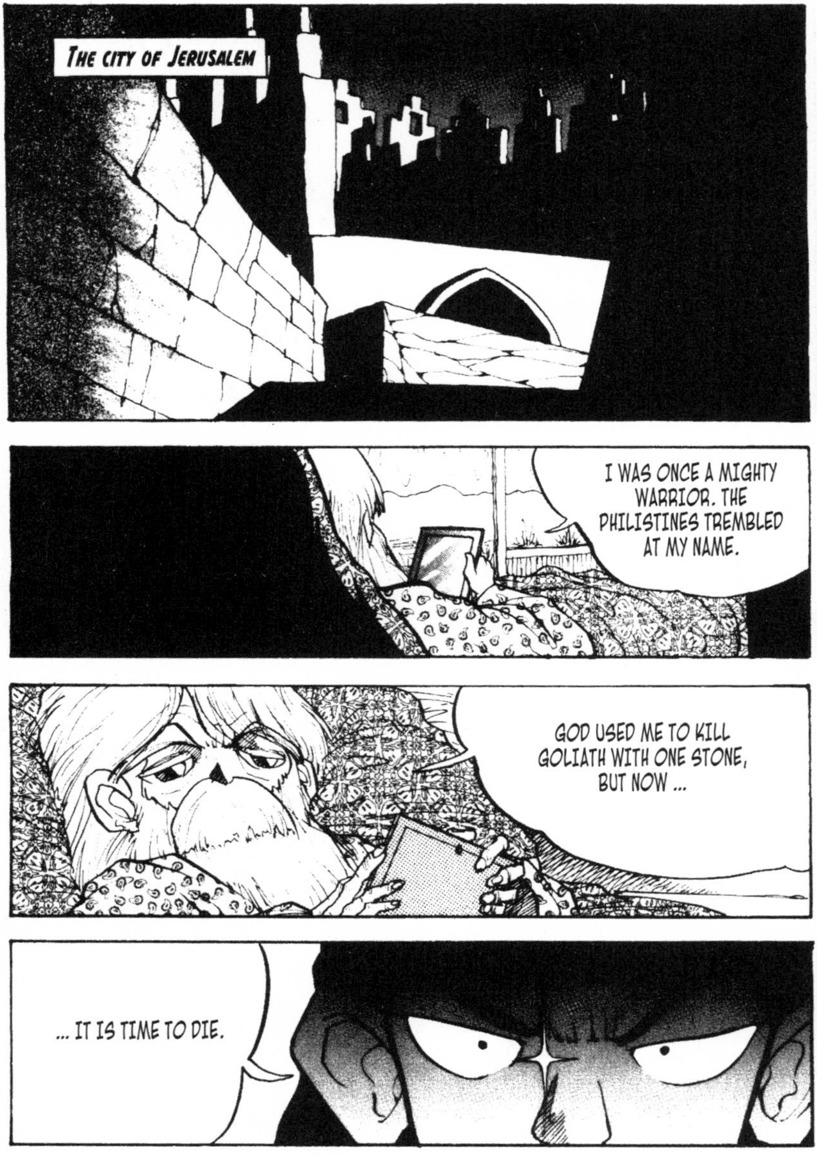
THE CITY OF JERUSALEM
I WAS ONCE A MIGHTY WARRIOR. THE PHILISTINES TREMBLED AT MY NAME.
GOD USED ME TO KILL GOLIATH WITH ONE STONE, BUT NOW ...
... IT IS TIME TO DIE.

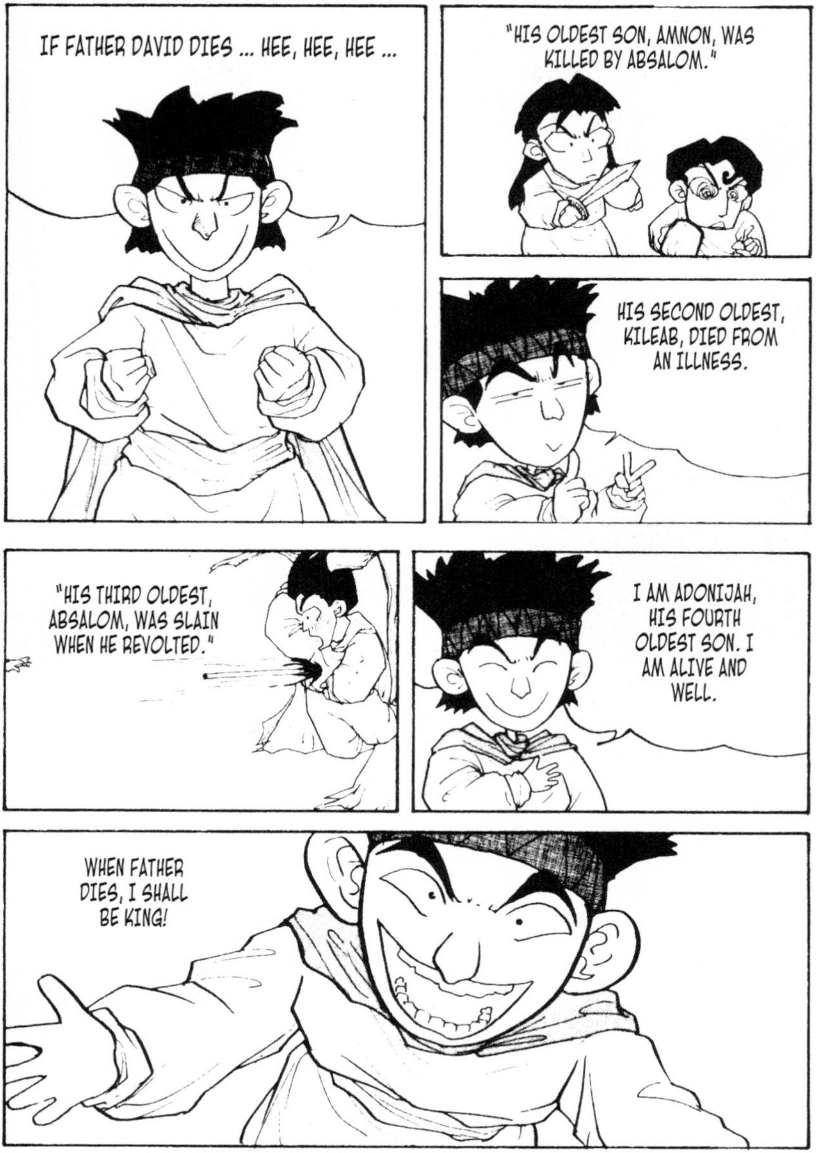
IF FATHER DAVID DIES ... HEE, HEE, HEE ...
"HIS OLDEST SON, AMNON, WAS KILLED BY ABSALOM."
HIS SECOND OLDEST, KILEAB, DIED FROM AN ILLNESS.
"HIS THIRD OLDEST, ABSALOM, WAS SLAIN WHEN HE REVOLTED."
I AM ADONIJAH, HIS FOURTH OLDEST SON. I AM ALIVE AND WELL.
WHEN FATHER DIES, I SHALL BE KING!

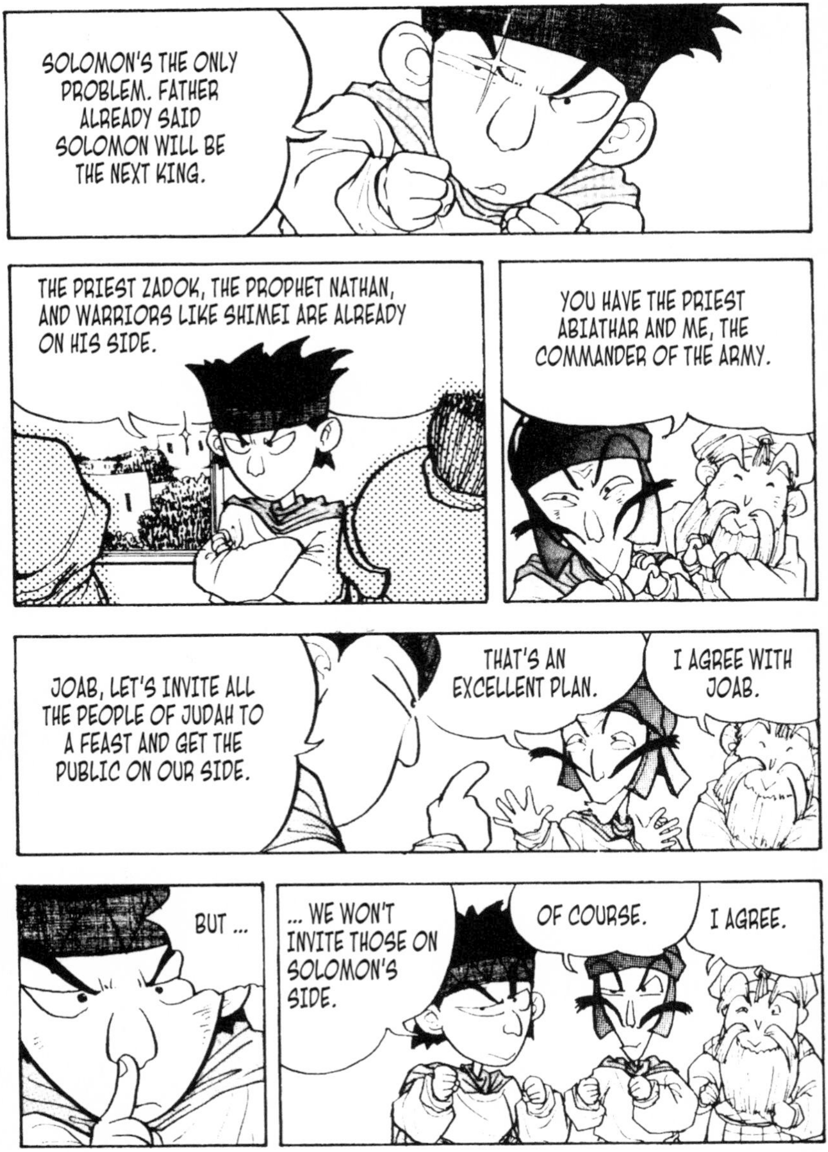
SOLOMON'S THE ONLY PROBLEM. FATHER ALREADY SAID SOLOMON WILL BE THE NEXT KING.
THE PRIEST ZADOK, THE PROPHET NATHAN, AND WARRIORS LIKE SHIMEI ARE ALREADY ON HIS SIDE.
YOU HAVE THE PRIEST ABIATHAR AND ME, THE COMMANDER OF THE ARMY.
JOAB, LET'S INVITE ALL THE PEOPLE OF JUDAH TO A FEAST AND GET THE PUBLIC ON OUR SIDE.
THAT'S AN EXCELLENT PLAN.
I AGREE WITH JOAB.
BUT ...
... WE WON'T INVITE THOSE ON SOLOMON'S SIDE.
OF COURSE.
I AGREE.

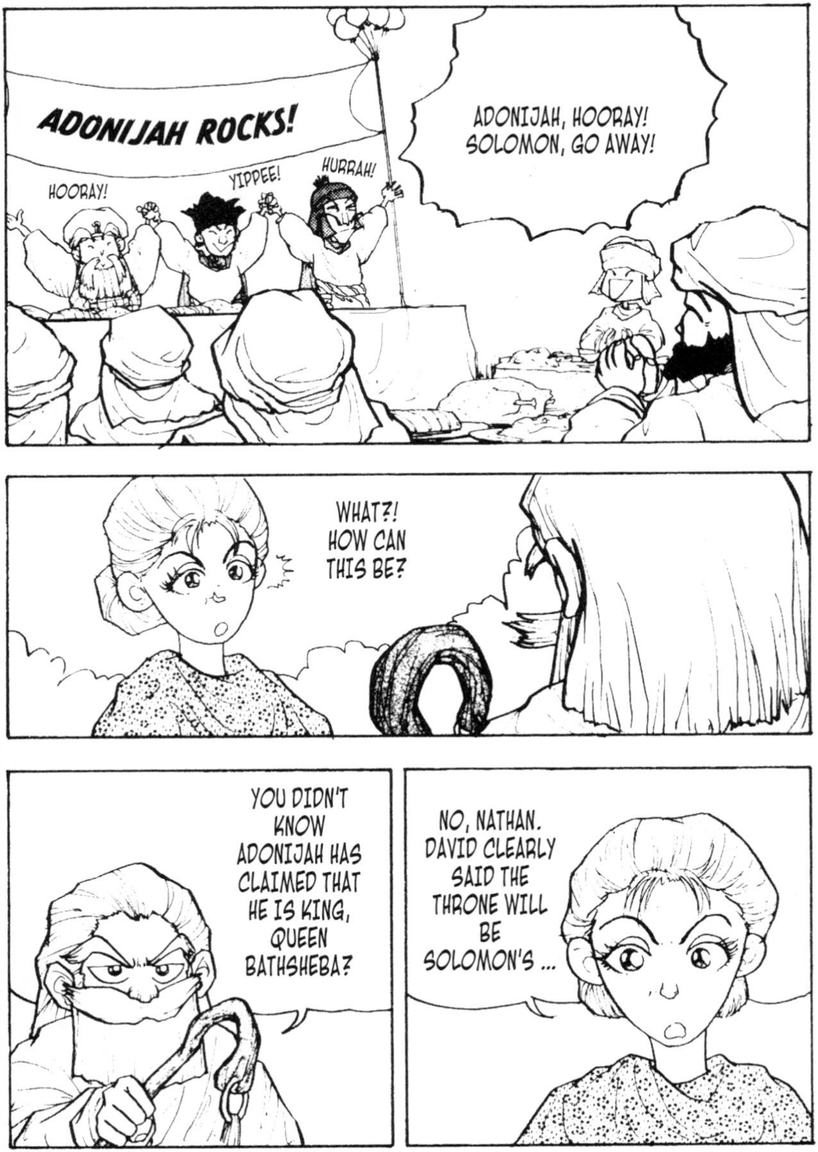
ADONIJAH ROCKS!
HOORAY!
YIPPEE!
HURRAH!
ADONIJAH, HOORAY! SOLOMON, GO AWAY!
WHAT?! HOW CAN THIS BE?
YOU DIDN'T KNOW ADONIJAH HAS CLAIMED THAT HE IS KING, QUEEN BATHSHEBA?
NO, NATHAN. DAVID CLEARLY SAID THE THRONE WILL BE SOLOMON'S ...

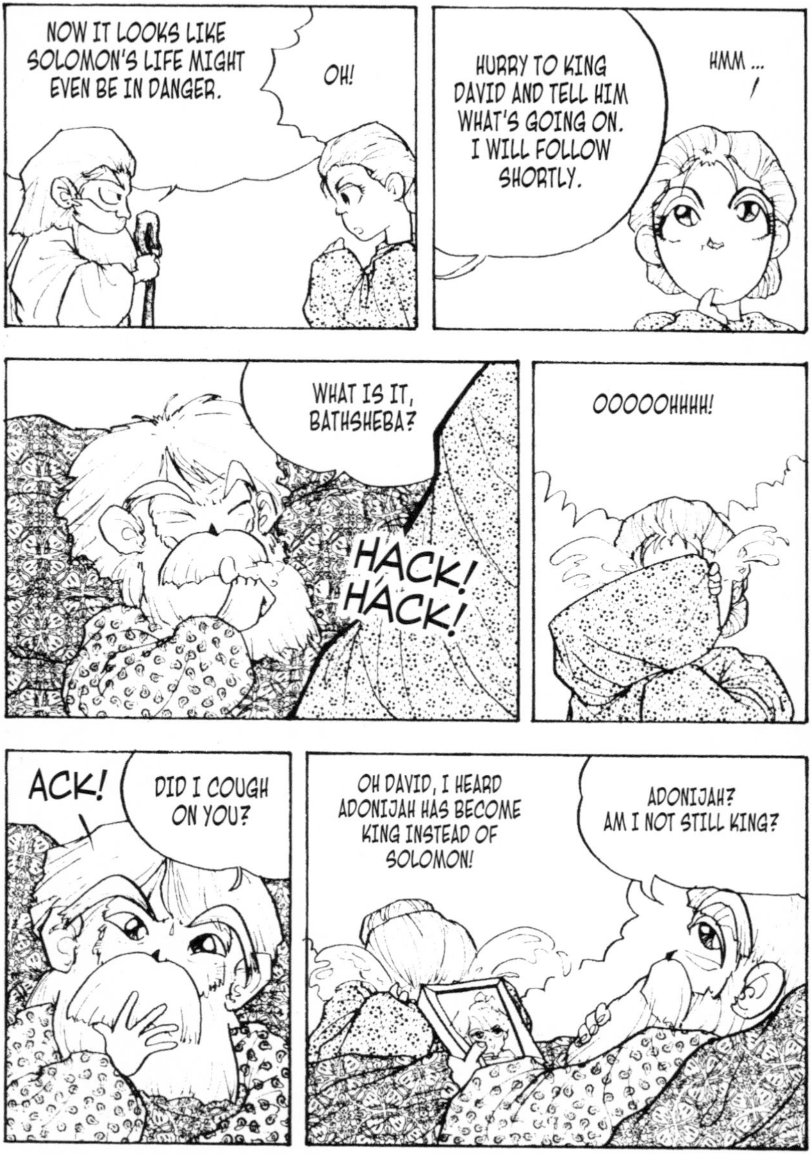
NOW IT LOOKS LIKE SOLOMON'S LIFE MIGHT EVEN BE IN DANGER.
OH!
HURRY TO KING DAVID AND TELL HIM WHAT'S GOING ON. I WILL FOLLOW SHORTLY.
HMM ...
WHAT IS IT, BATHSHEBA?
HACK! HACK!
OOOOOHHHH!
ACK!
DID I COUGH ON YOU?
OH DAVID, I HEARD ADONIJAH HAS BECOME KING INSTEAD OF SOLOMON!
ADONIJAH? AM I NOT STILL KING?

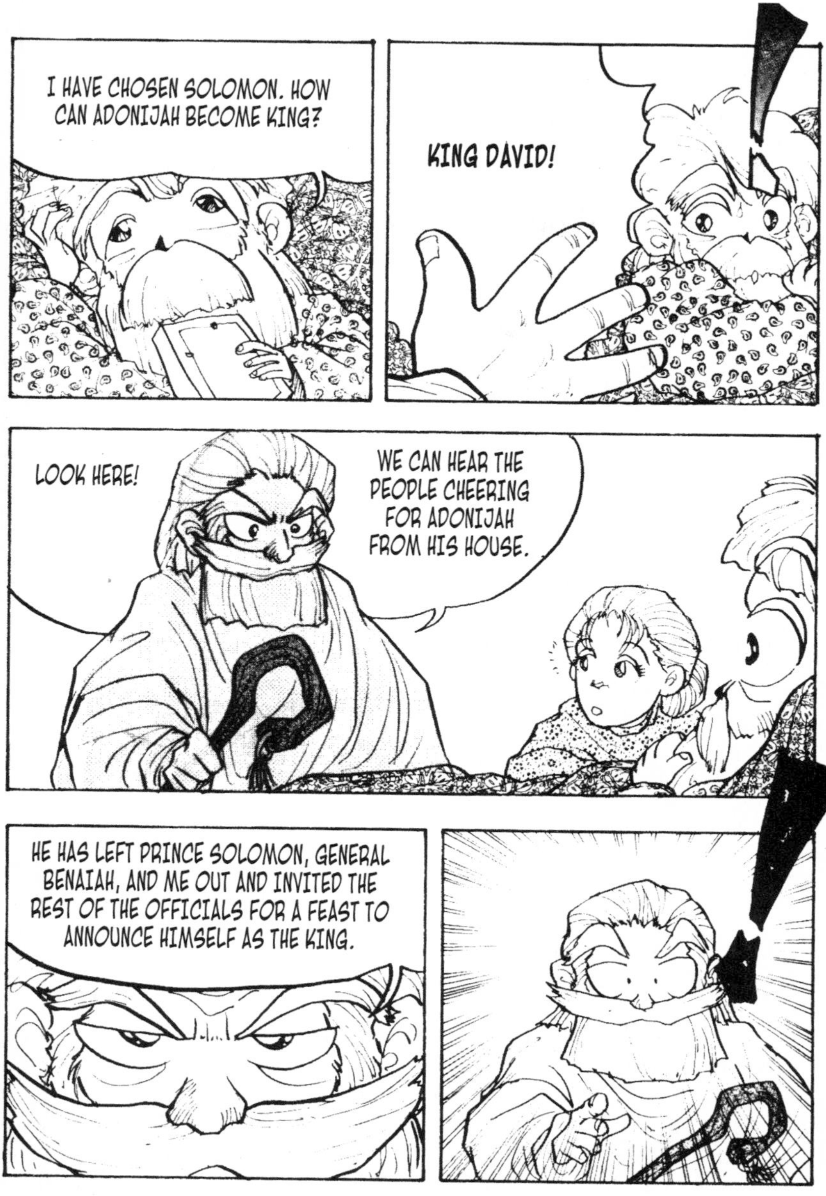
I HAVE CHOSEN SOLOMON. HOW CAN ADONIJAH BECOME KING?
KING DAVID!
LOOK HERE!
WE CAN HEAR THE PEOPLE CHEERING FOR ADONIJAH FROM HIS HOUSE.
HE HAS LEFT PRINCE SOLOMON, GENERAL BENAIAH, AND ME OUT AND INVITED THE REST OF THE OFFICIALS FOR A FEAST TO ANNOUNCE HIMSELF AS THE KING.

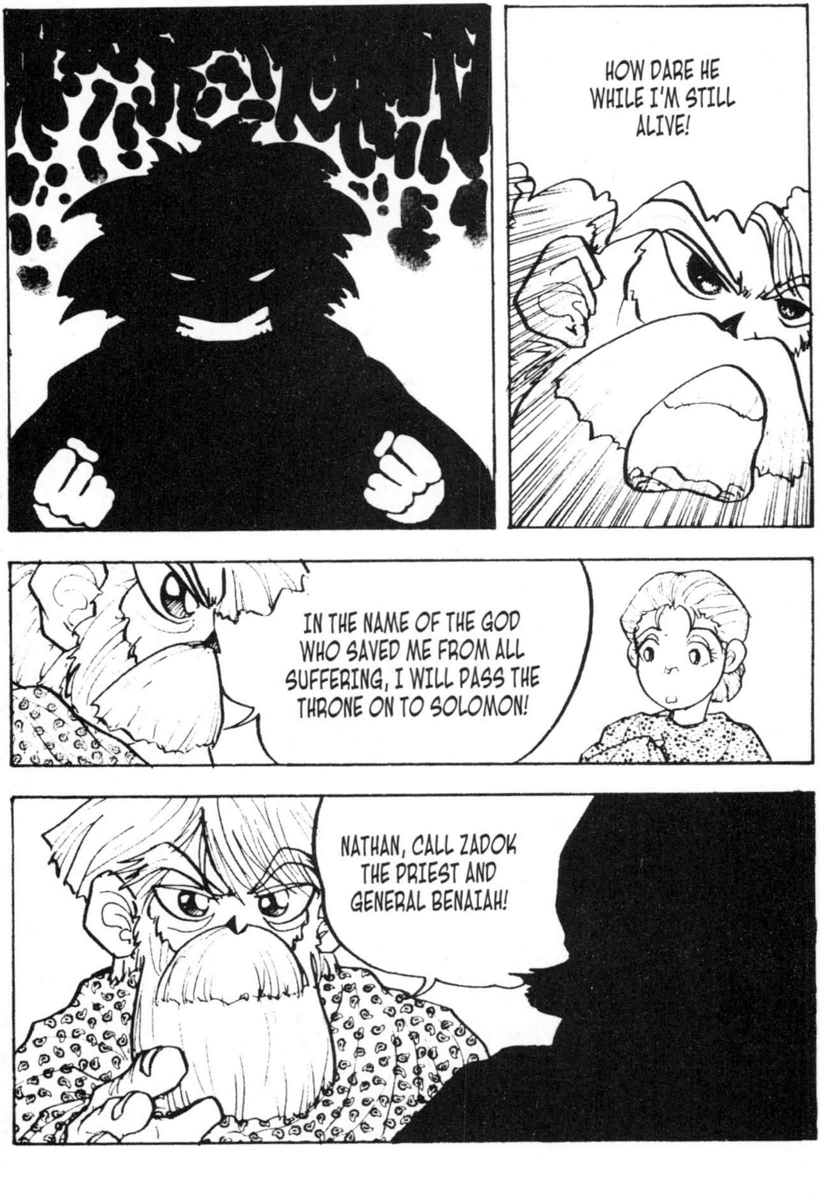

HOW DARE HE WHILE I'M STILL ALIVE!
IN THE NAME OF THE GOD WHO SAVED ME FROM ALL SUFFERING, I WILL PASS THE THRONE ON TO SOLOMON!
NATHAN, CALL ZADOK THE PRIEST AND GENERAL BENAIAH!

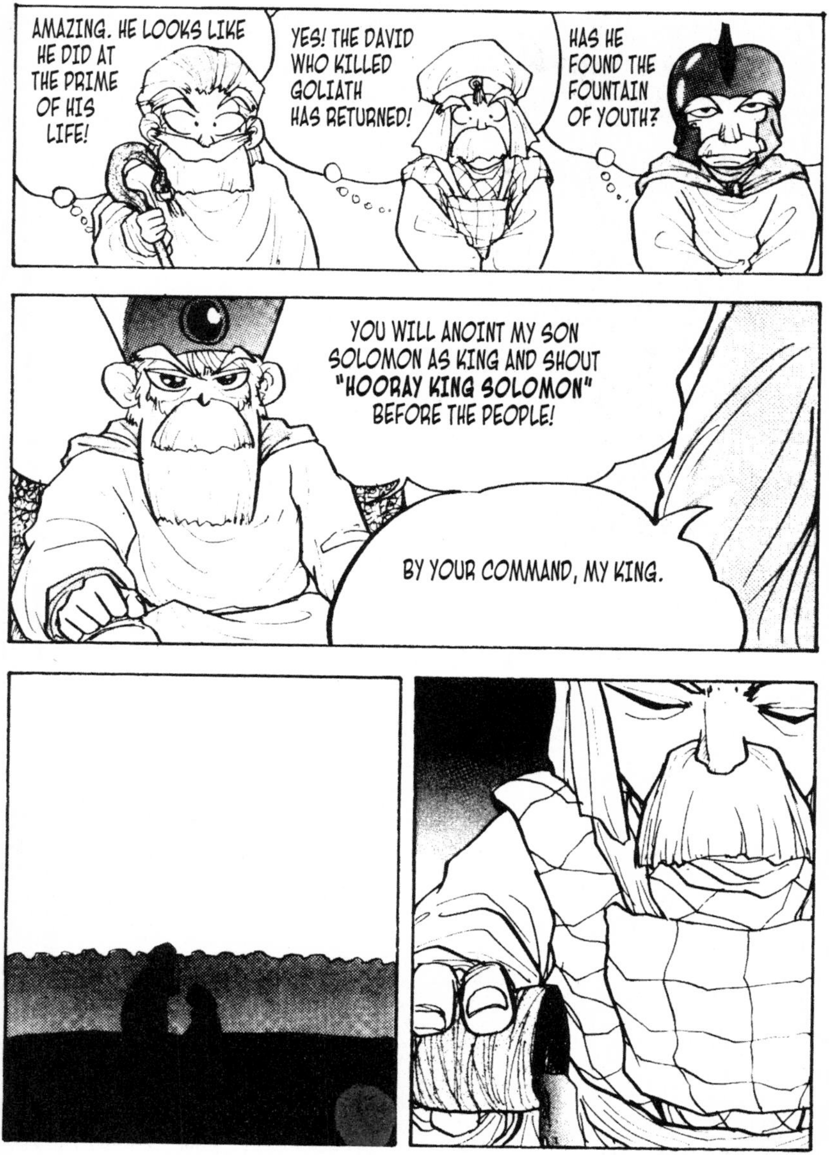
AMAZING. HE LOOKS LIKE HE DID AT THE PRIME OF HIS LIFE!
YES! THE DAVID WHO KILLED GOLIATH HAS RETURNED!
HAS HE FOUND THE FOUNTAIN OF YOUTH?
YOU WILL ANOINT MY SON SOLOMON AS KING AND SHOUT "HOORAY KING SOLOMON" BEFORE THE PEOPLE!
BY YOUR COMMAND, MY KING.

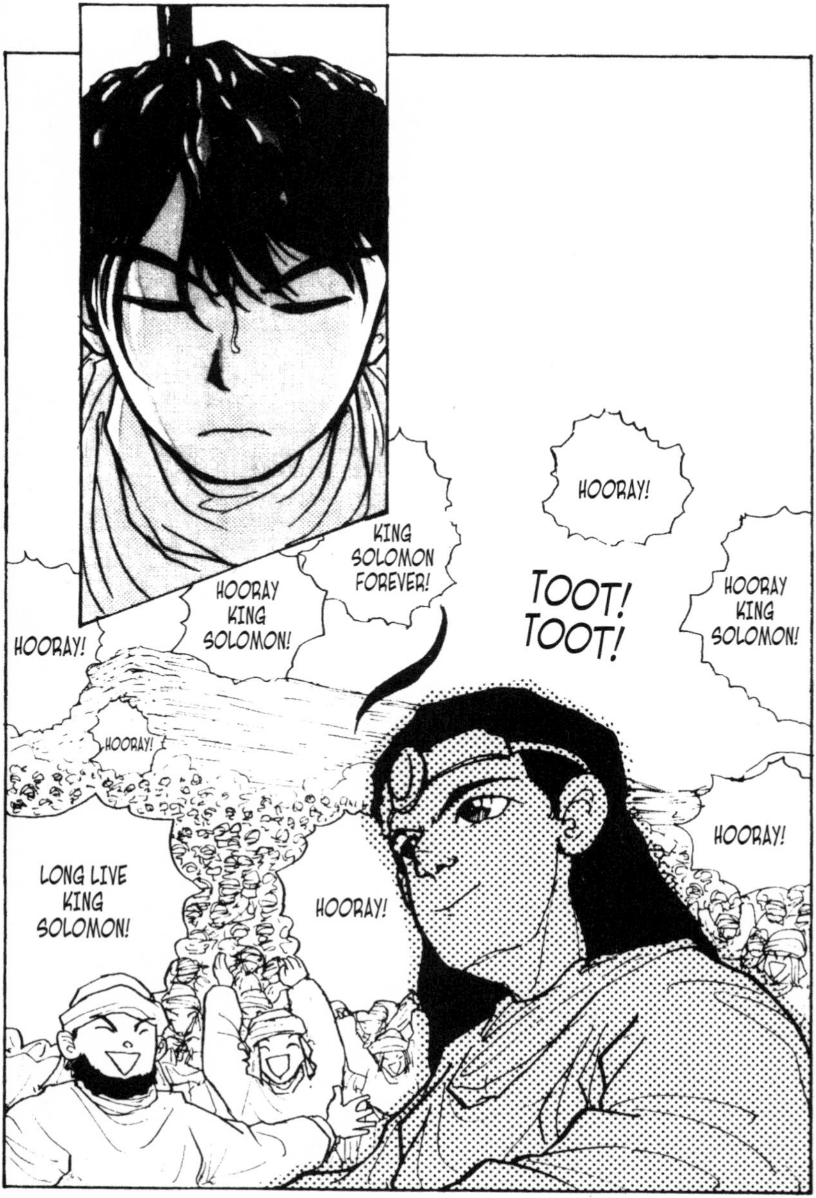
HOORAY!
KING SOLOMON FOREVER!
HOORAY KING SOLOMON!
TOOT! TOOT!
HOORAY KING SOLOMON!
HOORAY!
HOORAY!
HOORAY!
LONG LIVE KING SOLOMON!
HOORAY!

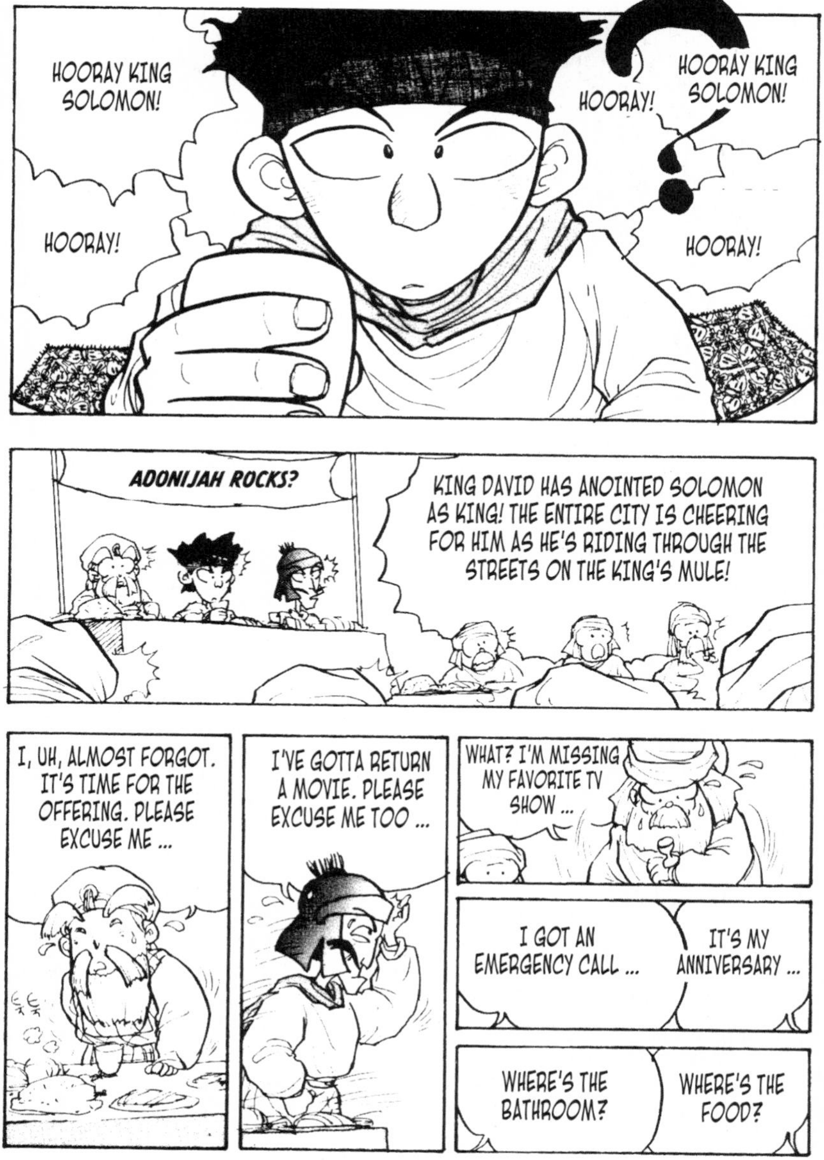
HOORAY KING SOLOMON!
HOORAY!
HOORAY!
HOORAY KING SOLOMON!
HOORAY!
ADONIJAH ROCKS?
KING DAVID HAS ANOINTED SOLOMON AS KING! THE ENTIRE CITY IS CHEERING FOR HIM AS HE'S RIDING THROUGH THE STREETS ON THE KING'S MULE!
I, UH, ALMOST FORGOT. IT'S TIME FOR THE OFFERING. PLEASE EXCUSE ME ...
I'VE GOTTA RETURN A MOVIE. PLEASE EXCUSE ME TOO ...
WHAT? I'M MISSING MY FAVORITE TV SHOW ...
I GOT AN EMERGENCY CALL ...
IT'S MY ANNIVERSARY ...
WHERE'S THE BATHROOM?
WHERE'S THE FOOD?

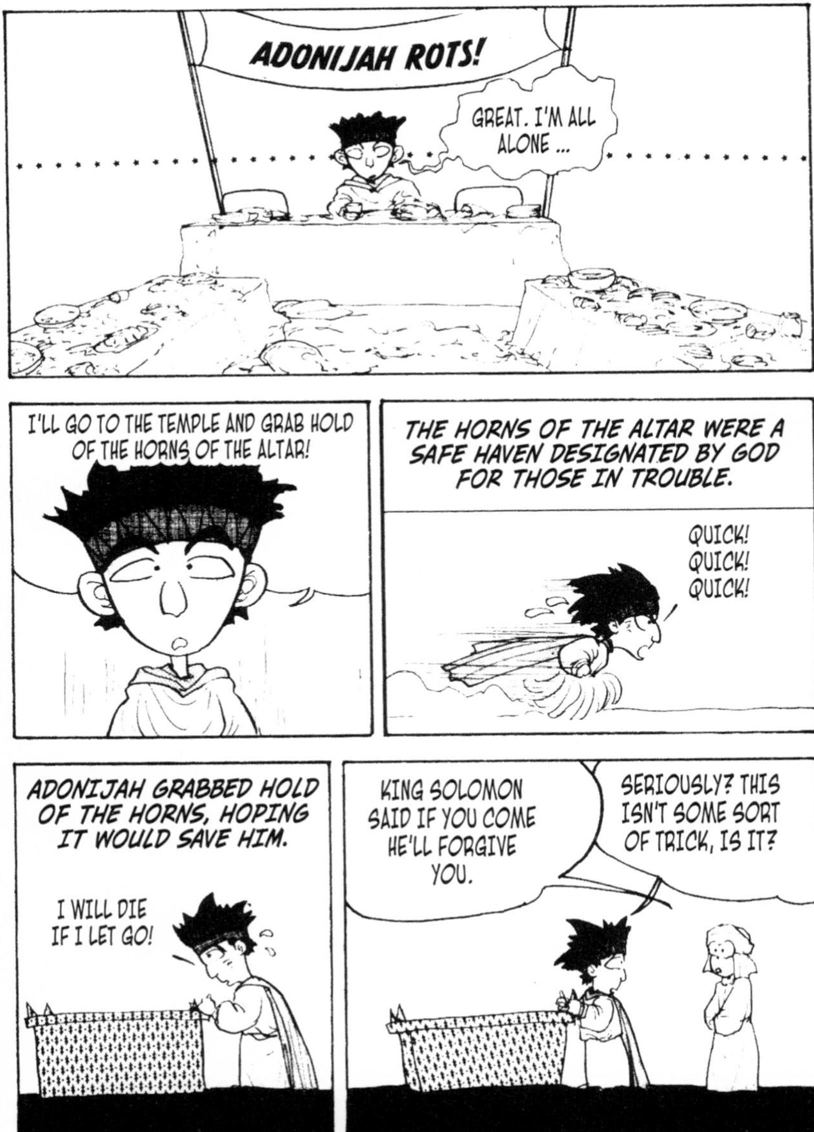

ADONIJAH ROTS!
GREAT. I'M ALL ALONE ...
I'LL GO TO THE TEMPLE AND GRAB HOLD OF THE HORNS OF THE ALTAR!
THE HORNS OF THE ALTAR WERE A SAFE HAVEN DESIGNATED BY GOD FOR THOSE IN TROUBLE.
QUICK! QUICK! QUICK!
ADONIJAH GRABBED HOLD OF THE HORNS, HOPING IT WOULD SAVE HIM.
I WILL DIE IF I LET GO!
KING SOLOMON SAID IF YOU COME HE'LL FORGIVE YOU.
SERIOUSLY? THIS ISN'T SOME SORT OF TRICK, IS IT?

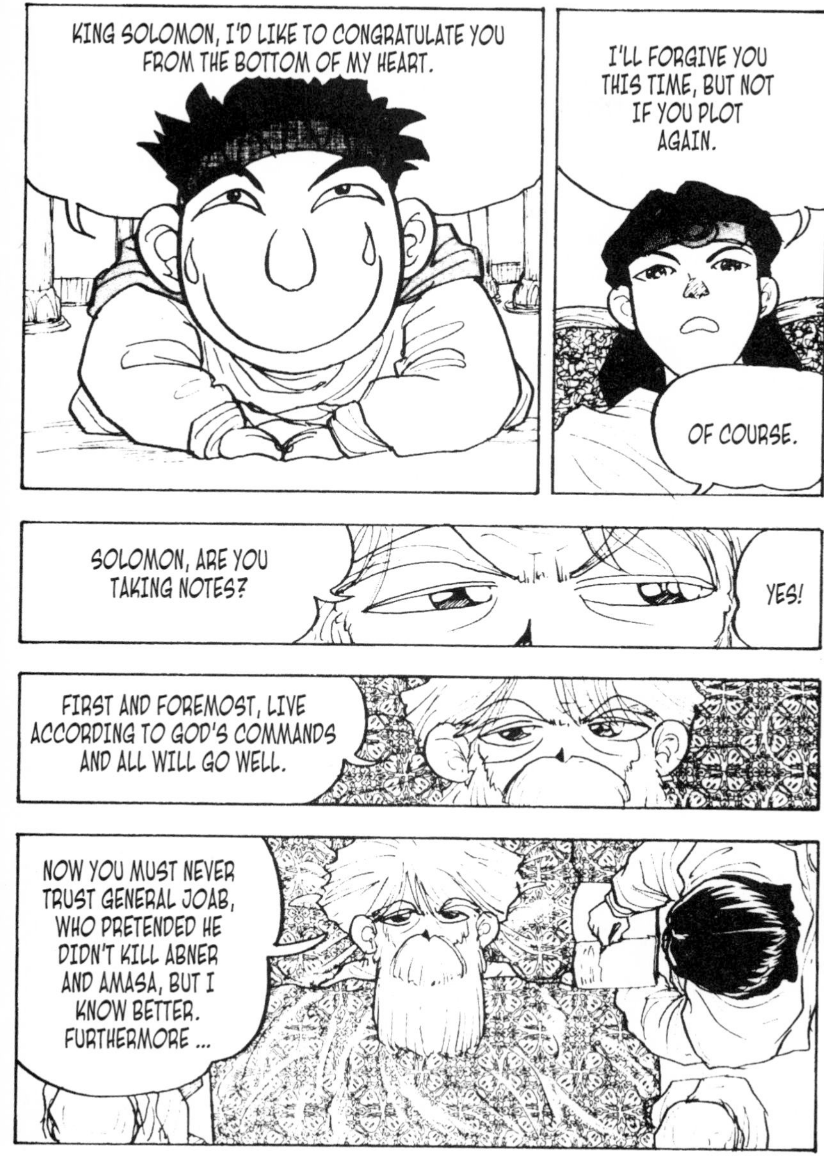
KING SOLOMON, I'D LIKE TO CONGRATULATE YOU FROM THE BOTTOM OF MY HEART.
I'LL FORGIVE YOU THIS TIME, BUT NOT IF YOU PLOT AGAIN.
OF COURSE.
SOLOMON, ARE YOU TAKING NOTES?
YES!
FIRST AND FOREMOST, LIVE ACCORDING TO GOD'S COMMANDS AND ALL WILL GO WELL.
NOW YOU MUST NEVER TRUST GENERAL JOAB, WHO PRETENDED HE DIDN'T KILL ABNER AND AMASA, BUT I KNOW BETTER. FURTHERMORE ...

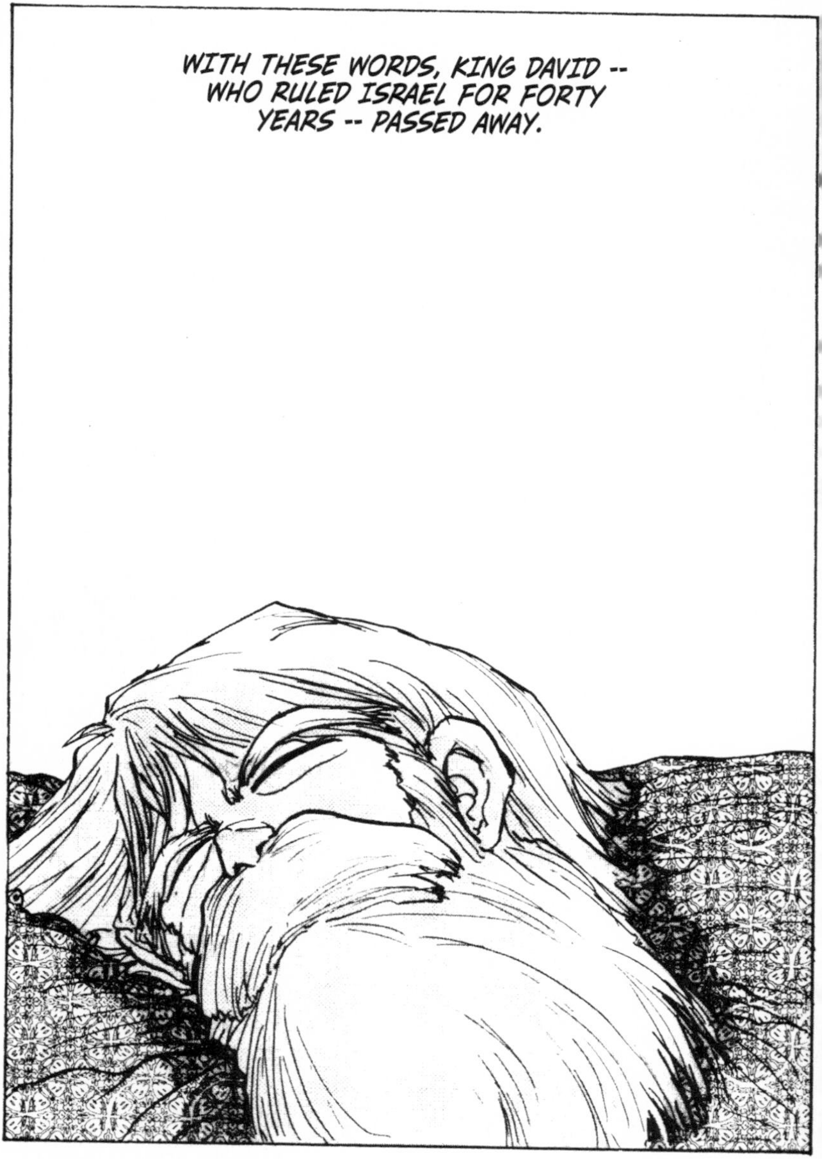
WITH THESE WORDS, KING DAVID -- WHO RULED ISRAEL FOR FORTY YEARS -- PASSED AWAY.

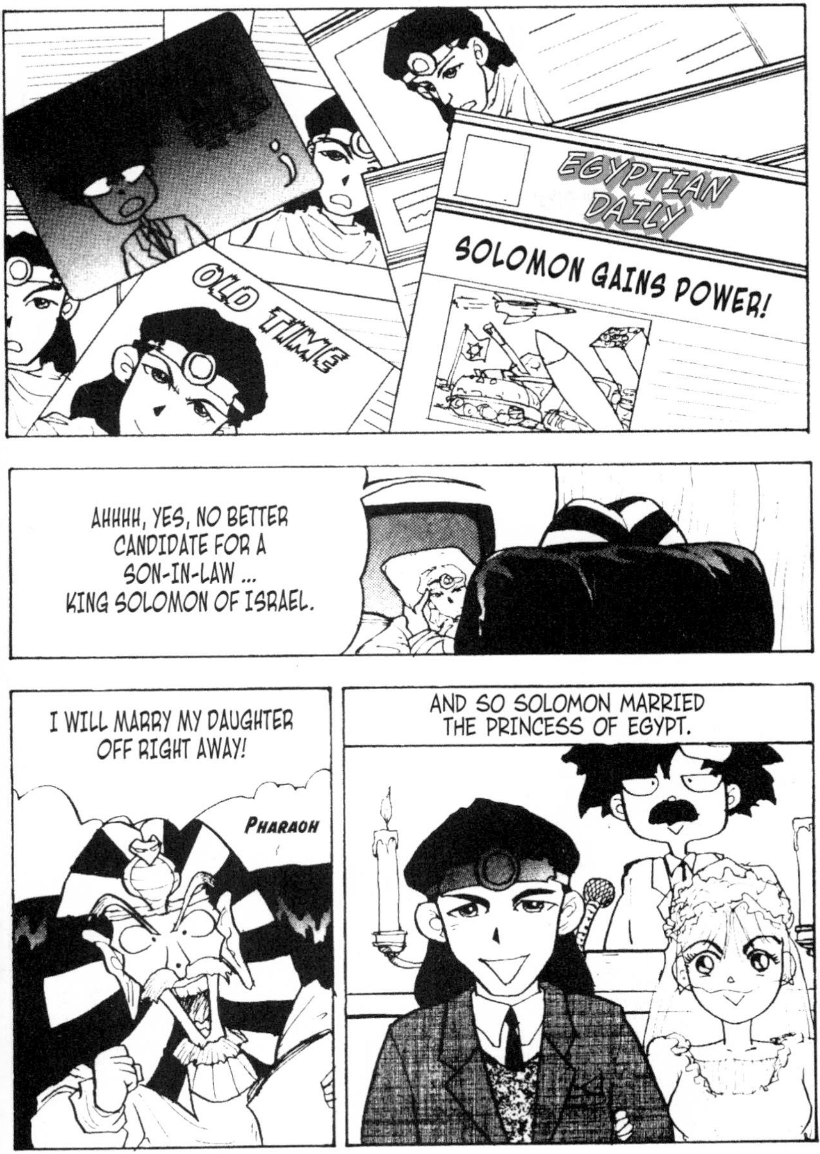
EGYPTIAN DAILY
SOLOMON GAINS POWER!
OLD TIME
AHHHH, YES, NO BETTER CANDIDATE FOR A SON-IN-LAW ... KING SOLOMON OF ISRAEL.
I WILL MARRY MY DAUGHTER OFF RIGHT AWAY!
PHARAOH
AND SO SOLOMON MARRIED THE PRINCESS OF EGYPT.

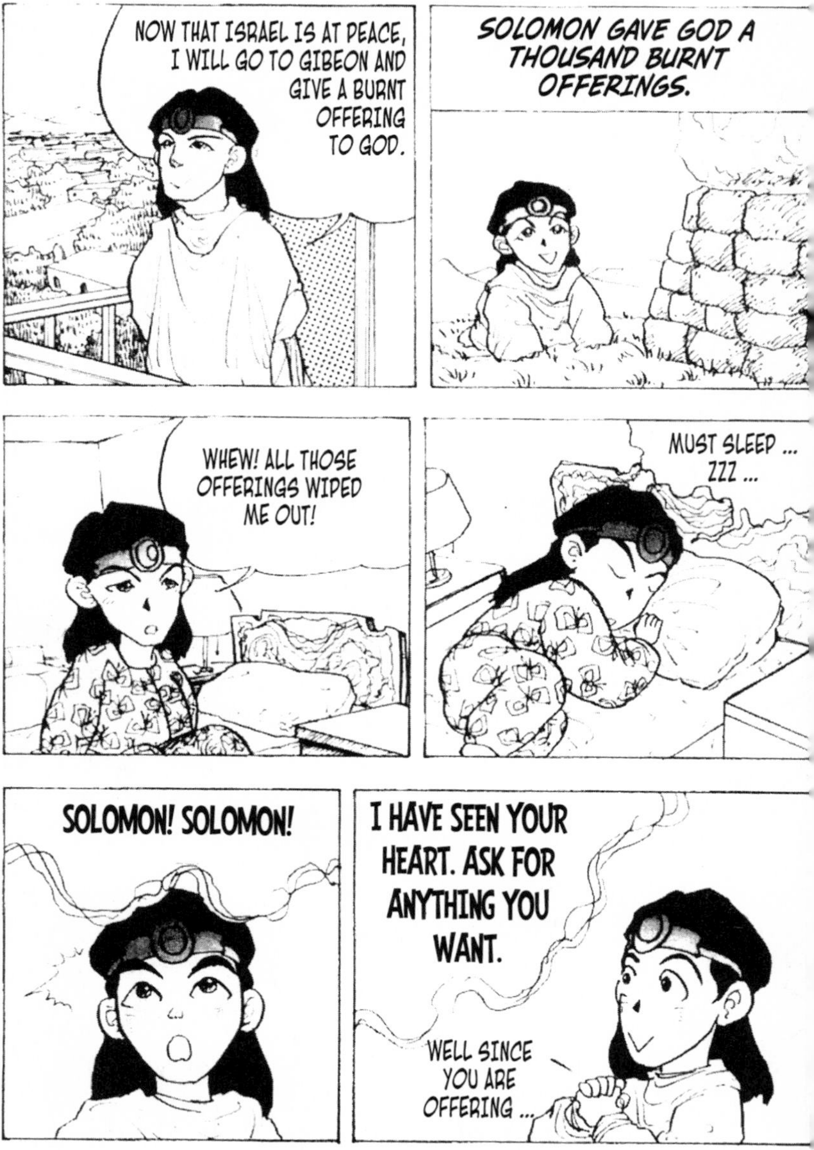
NOW THAT ISRAEL IS AT PEACE, I WILL GO TO GIBEON AND GIVE A BURNT OFFERING TO GOD.
SOLOMON GAVE GOD A THOUSAND BURNT OFFERINGS.
WHEW! ALL THOSE OFFERINGS WIPED ME OUT!
MUST SLEEP ... ZZZ ...
SOLOMON! SOLOMON!
I HAVE SEEN YOUR HEART. ASK FOR ANYTHING YOU WANT.
WELL SINCE YOU ARE OFFERING ...

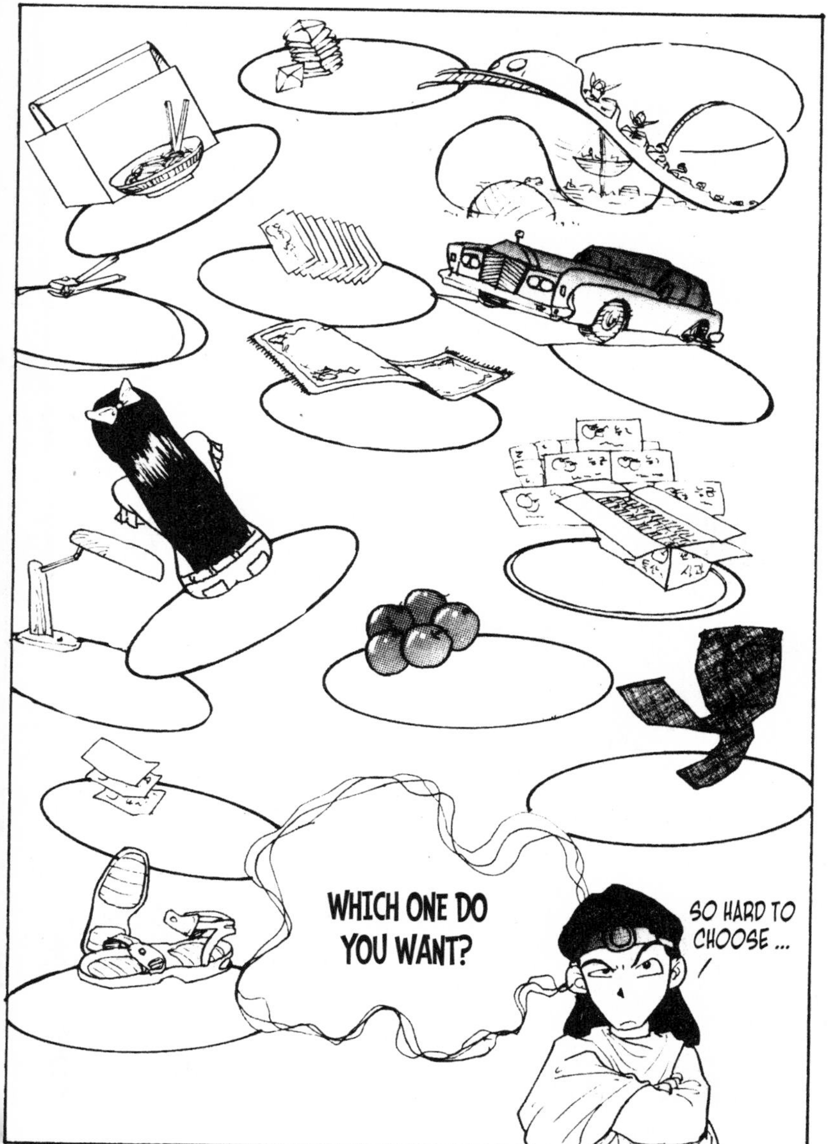
WHICH ONE DO YOU WANT?
SO HARD TO CHOOSE ...

YOU HAVE SHOWN GREAT KINDNESS TO MY FATHER, DAVID, BECAUSE HE WAS FAITHFUL AND RIGHTEOUS. YOU HAVE CONTINUED THIS KINDNESS AND HAVE GIVEN HIM A SON FOR HIS THRONE ...

SO WHAT DO YOU CHOOSE?

THINK ...
THINK ...

I'M HERE AMONG YOUR CHOSEN PEOPLE, A NATION TOO NUMEROUS TO COUNT OR NUMBER.

I'M GIVING YOU TO THE COUNT OF THREE.

THINK ...
THINK ...

I'VE GOT IT! GIVE ME A DISCERNING HEART TO GOVERN YOUR PEOPLE AND TO DISTINGUISH RIGHT FROM WRONG.

YOU HAVEN'T ASKED FOR LONG LIFE, WEALTH, OR FOOLISH THINGS -- I WILL DO WHAT YOU HAVE ASKED.

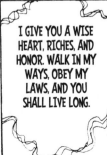

I GIVE YOU A WISE HEART, RICHES, AND HONOR. WALK IN MY WAYS, OBEY MY LAWS, AND YOU SHALL LIVE LONG.

HUH ... WAS I DREAMING?

ONE NIGHT, SOMETHING HAPPENED THAT WOULD TEST SOLOMON'S WISDOM ...

ZZZZ, ZZZZ

A WOMAN TOSSED AND TURNED IN HER SLEEP ...

ZZZZZZZ, ZZZZZZZ

OOF!

WHA--? WHERE ...?

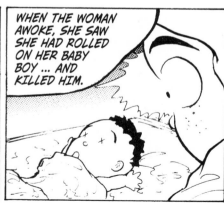

WHEN THE WOMAN AWOKE, SHE SAW SHE HAD ROLLED ON HER BABY BOY ... AND KILLED HIM.

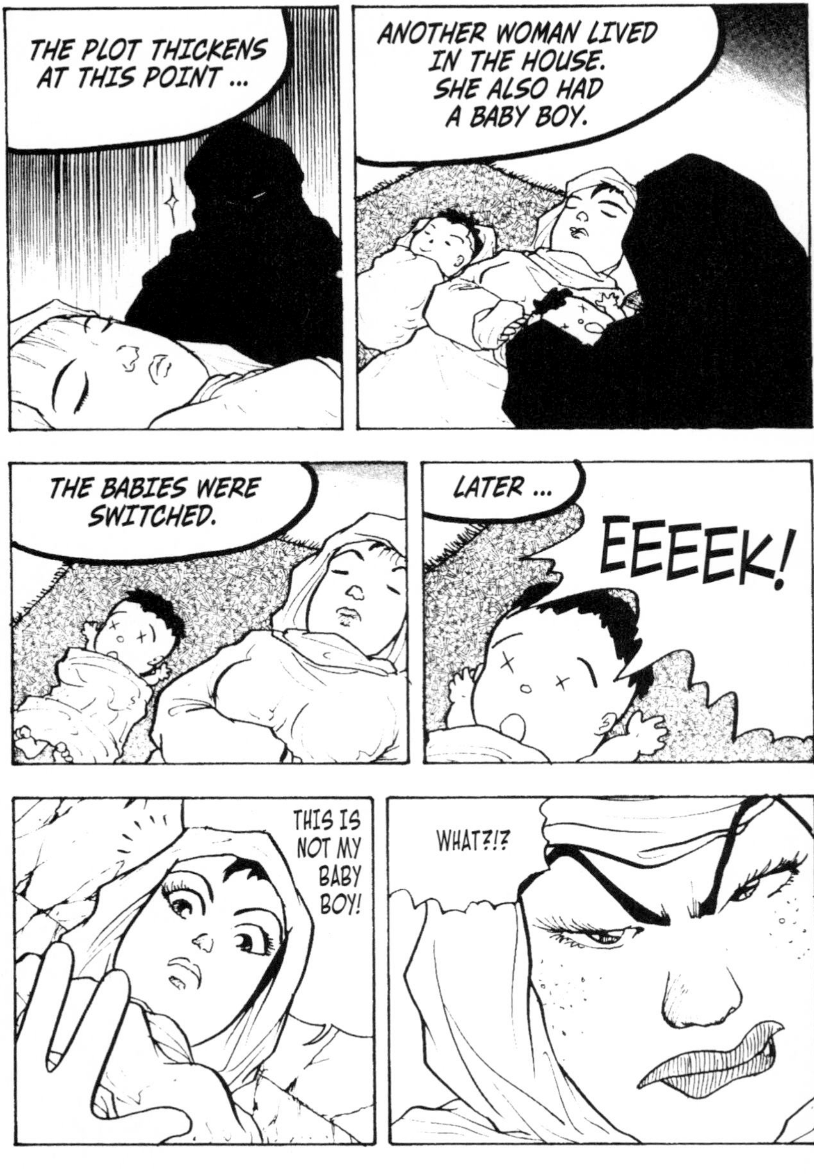
THE PLOT THICKENS AT THIS POINT ...
ANOTHER WOMAN LIVED IN THE HOUSE. SHE ALSO HAD A BABY BOY.
THE BABIES WERE SWITCHED.
LATER ...
EEEEK!
THIS IS NOT MY BABY BOY!
WHAT?!?

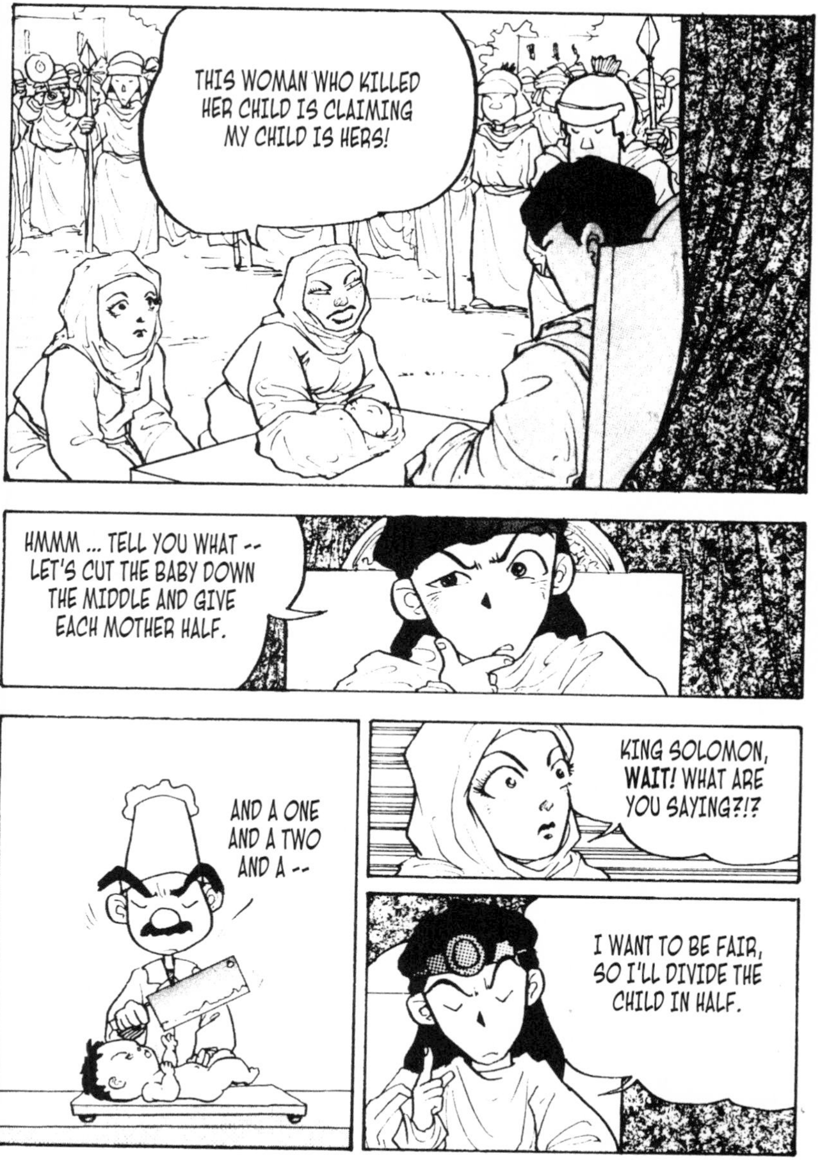
THIS WOMAN WHO KILLED HER CHILD IS CLAIMING MY CHILD IS HERS!
HMMM ... TELL YOU WHAT -- LET'S CUT THE BABY DOWN THE MIDDLE AND GIVE EACH MOTHER HALF.
AND A ONE AND A TWO AND A --
KING SOLOMON, WAIT! WHAT ARE YOU SAYING?!?
I WANT TO BE FAIR, SO I'LL DIVIDE THE CHILD IN HALF.

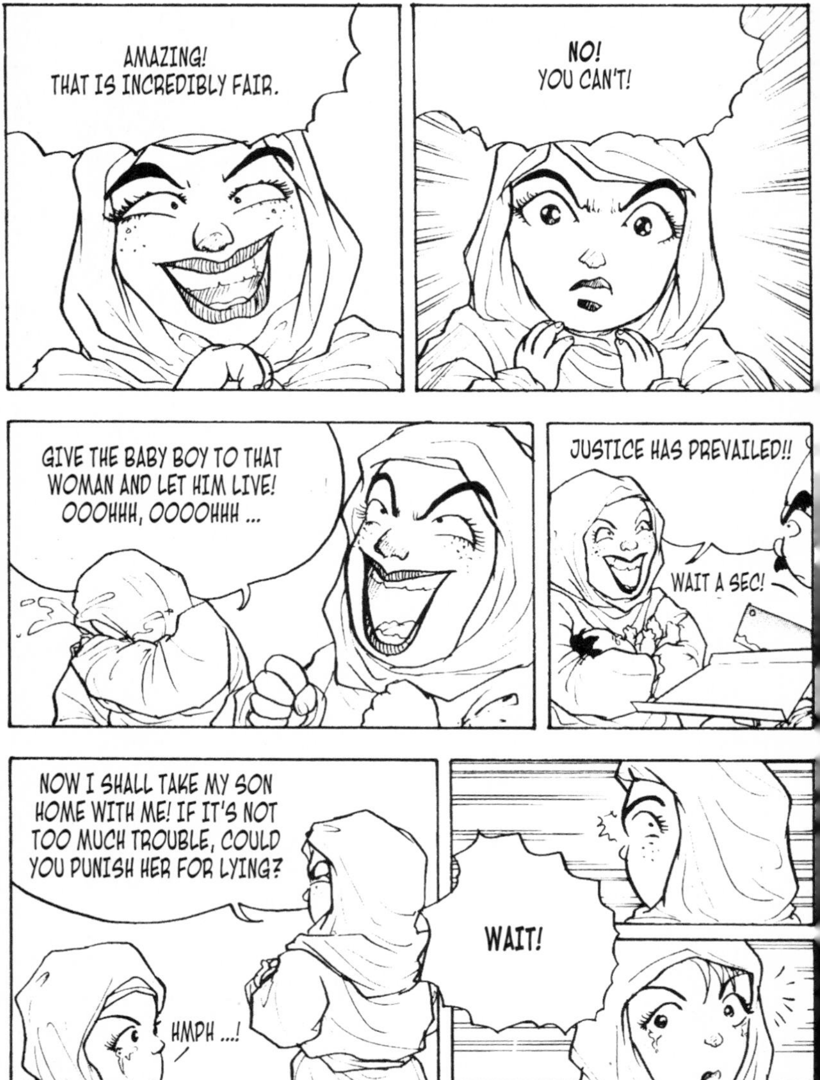
AMAZING!
THAT IS INCREDIBLY FAIR.
NO!
YOU CAN'T!
GIVE THE BABY BOY TO THAT WOMAN AND LET HIM LIVE! OOOHHH, OOOOHHH ...
JUSTICE HAS PREVAILED!!
WAIT A SEC!
NOW I SHALL TAKE MY SON HOME WITH ME! IF IT'S NOT TOO MUCH TROUBLE, COULD YOU PUNISH HER FOR LYING?
HMPH ...!
WAIT!

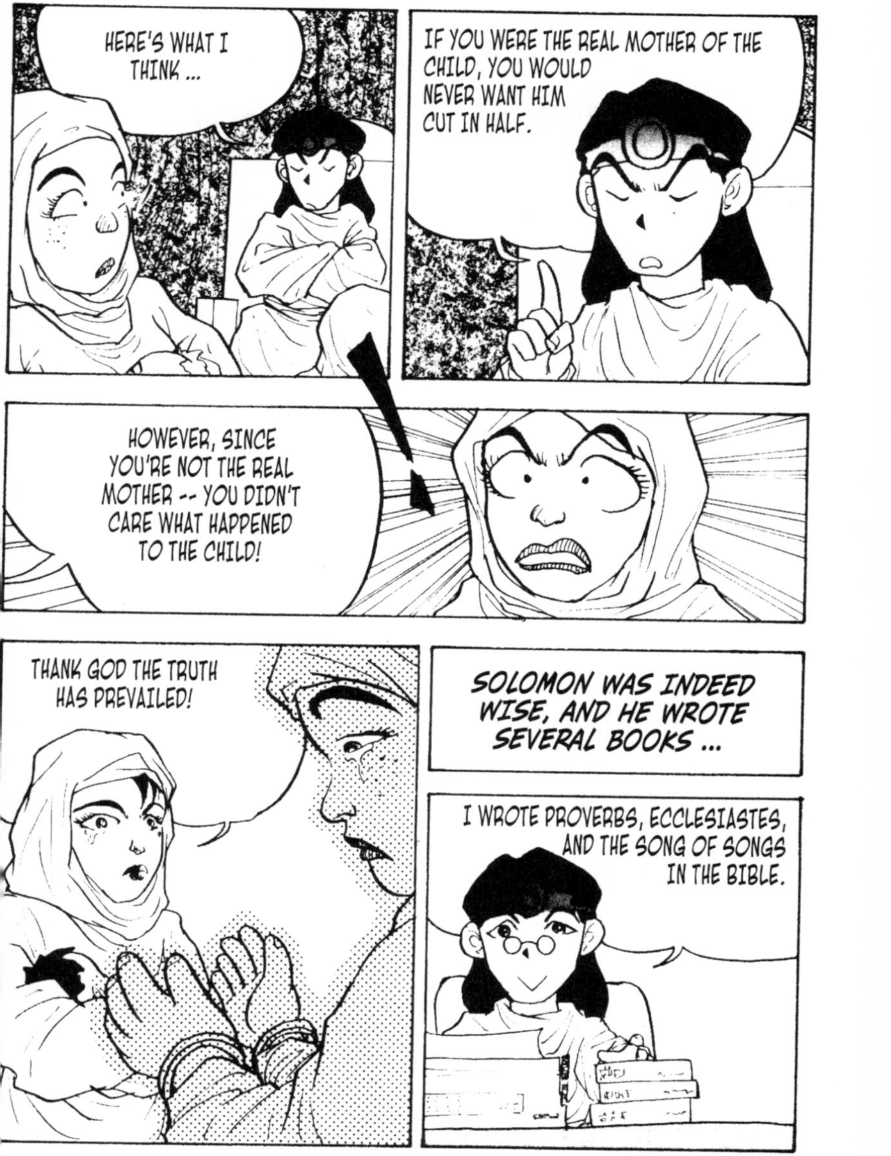
HERE'S WHAT I THINK ...
IF YOU WERE THE REAL MOTHER OF THE CHILD, YOU WOULD NEVER WANT HIM CUT IN HALF.
HOWEVER, SINCE YOU'RE NOT THE REAL MOTHER -- YOU DIDN'T CARE WHAT HAPPENED TO THE CHILD!
THANK GOD THE TRUTH HAS PREVAILED!
SOLOMON WAS INDEED WISE, AND HE WROTE SEVERAL BOOKS ...
I WROTE PROVERBS, ECCLESIASTES, AND THE SONG OF SONGS IN THE BIBLE.

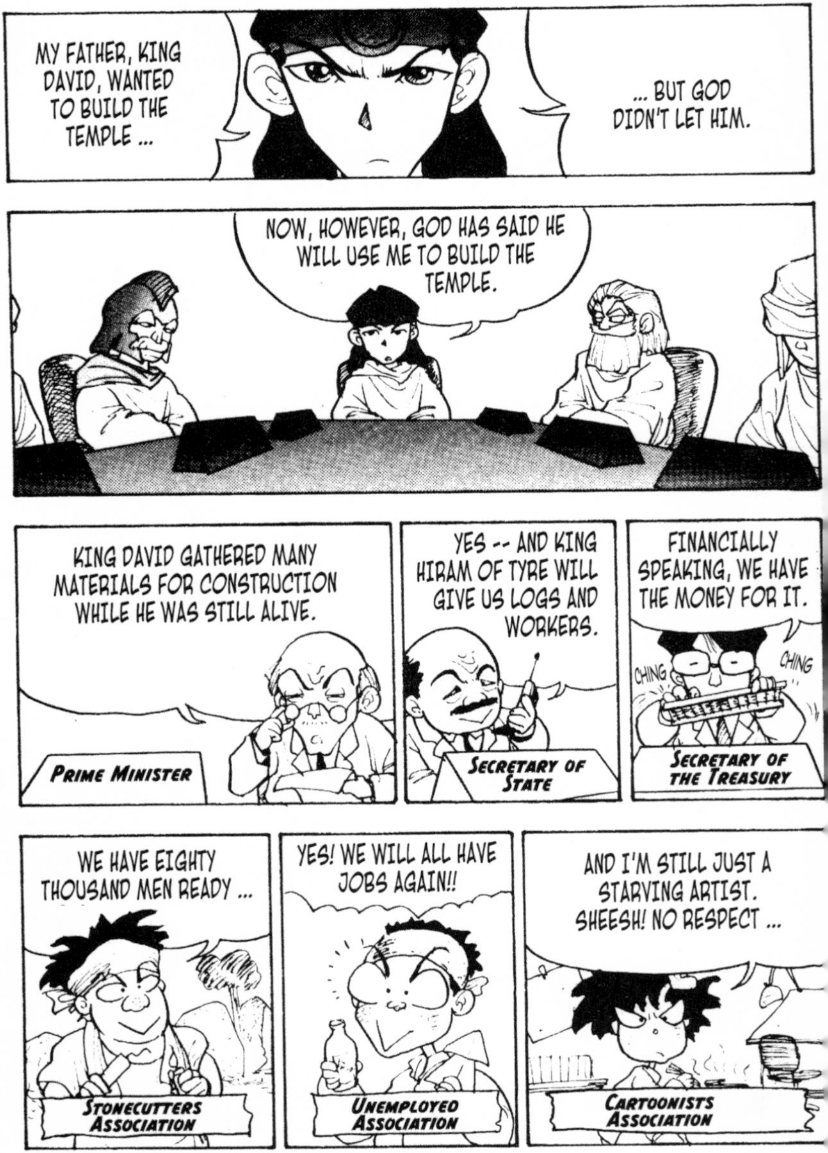
MY FATHER, KING DAVID, WANTED TO BUILD THE TEMPLE ...
... BUT GOD DIDN'T LET HIM.
NOW, HOWEVER, GOD HAS SAID HE WILL USE ME TO BUILD THE TEMPLE.
KING DAVID GATHERED MANY MATERIALS FOR CONSTRUCTION WHILE HE WAS STILL ALIVE.
PRIME MINISTER
YES -- AND KING HIRAM OF TYRE WILL GIVE US LOGS AND WORKERS.
SECRETARY OF STATE
FINANCIALLY SPEAKING, WE HAVE THE MONEY FOR IT.
CHING
CHING
SECRETARY OF THE TREASURY
WE HAVE EIGHTY THOUSAND MEN READY ...
STONECUTTERS ASSOCIATION
YES! WE WILL ALL HAVE JOBS AGAIN!!
UNEMPLOYED ASSOCIATION
AND I'M STILL JUST A STARVING ARTIST. SHEESH! NO RESPECT ...
CARTOONISTS ASSOCIATION

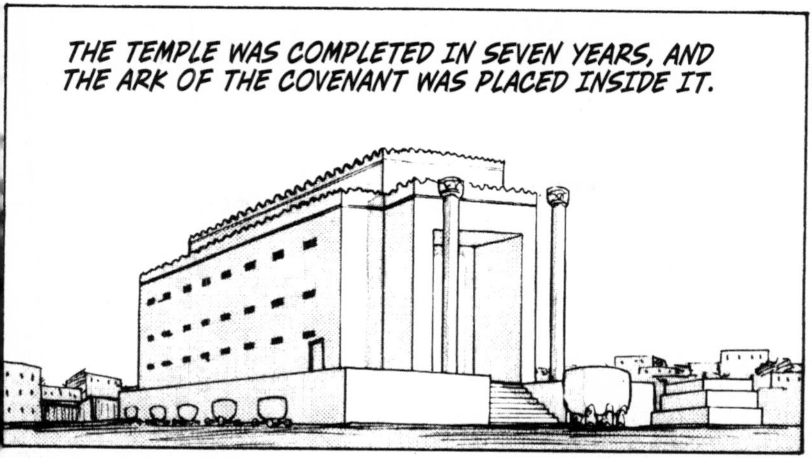
THE TEMPLE WAS COMPLETED IN SEVEN YEARS, AND THE ARK OF THE COVENANT WAS PLACED INSIDE IT.

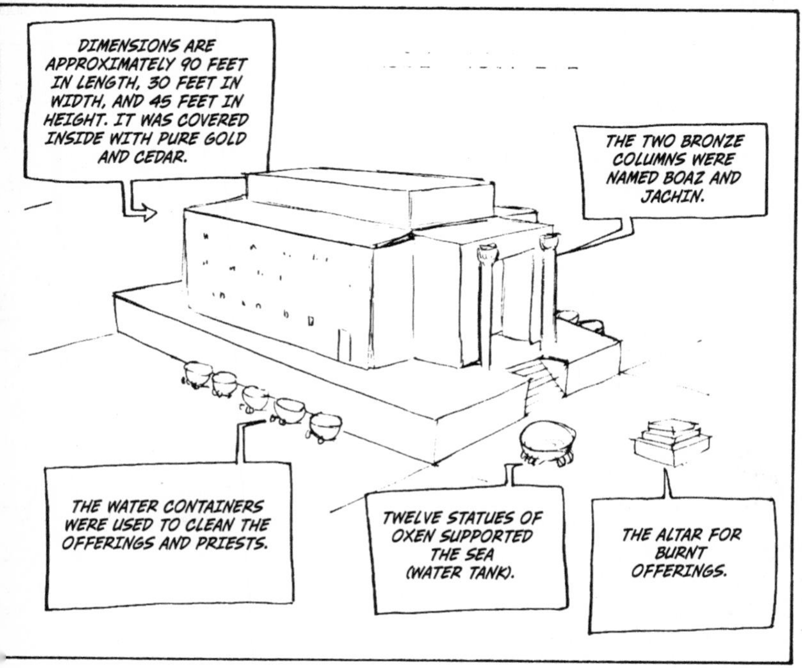
DIMENSIONS ARE APPROXIMATELY 90 FEET IN LENGTH, 30 FEET IN WIDTH, AND 45 FEET IN HEIGHT. IT WAS COVERED INSIDE WITH PURE GOLD AND CEDAR.
THE TWO BRONZE COLUMNS WERE NAMED BOAZ AND JACHIN.
THE WATER CONTAINERS WERE USED TO CLEAN THE OFFERINGS AND PRIESTS.
TWELVE STATUES OF OXEN SUPPORTED THE SEA (WATER TANK).
THE ALTAR FOR BURNT OFFERINGS.

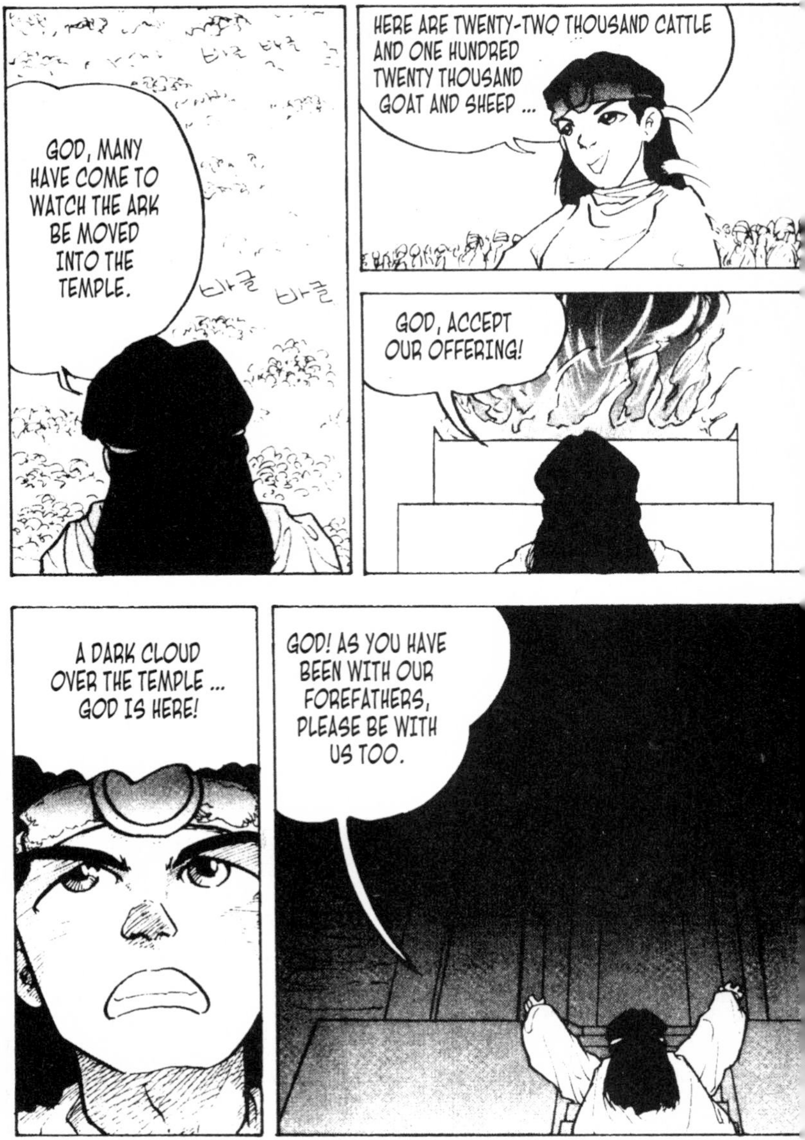
GOD, MANY HAVE COME TO WATCH THE ARK BE MOVED INTO THE TEMPLE.
바글 바글
HERE ARE TWENTY-TWO THOUSAND CATTLE AND ONE HUNDRED TWENTY THOUSAND GOAT AND SHEEP ...
GOD, ACCEPT OUR OFFERING!
A DARK CLOUD OVER THE TEMPLE ... GOD IS HERE!
GOD! AS YOU HAVE BEEN WITH OUR FOREFATHERS, PLEASE BE WITH US TOO.

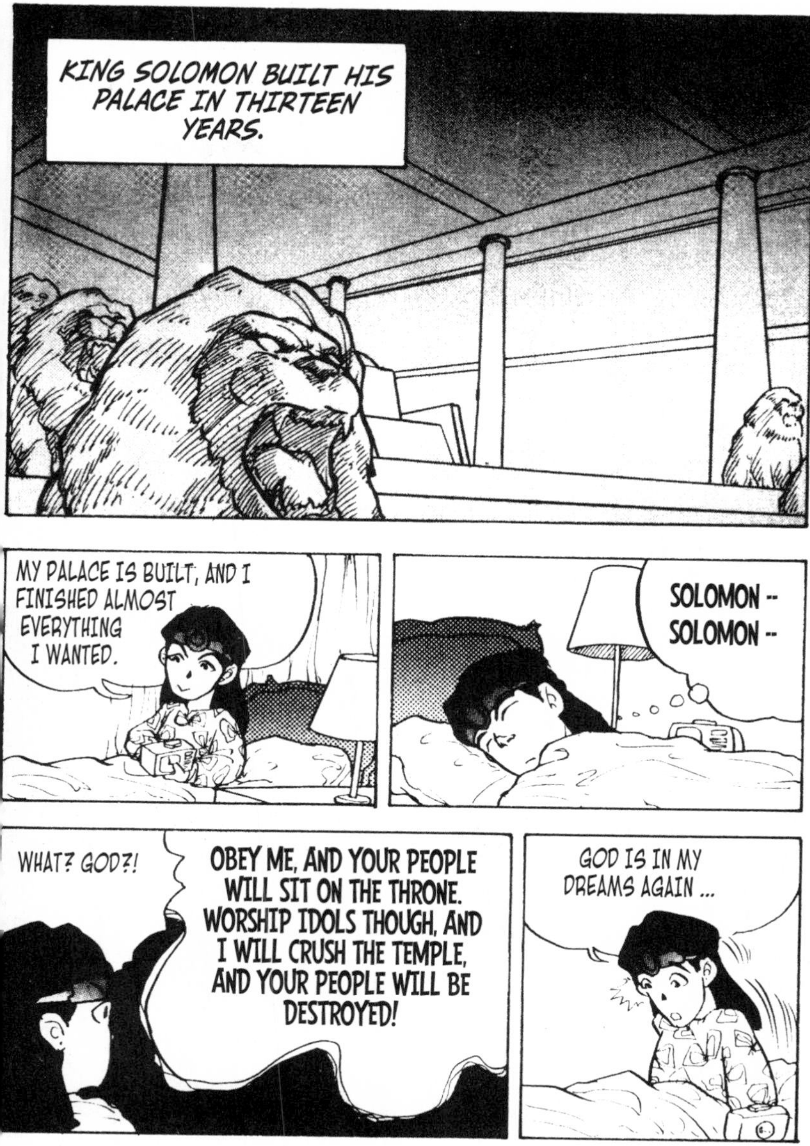
KING SOLOMON BUILT HIS PALACE IN THIRTEEN YEARS.
MY PALACE IS BUILT, AND I FINISHED ALMOST EVERYTHING I WANTED.
SOLOMON -- SOLOMON --
WHAT? GOD?!
OBEY ME, AND YOUR PEOPLE WILL SIT ON THE THRONE. WORSHIP IDOLS THOUGH, AND I WILL CRUSH THE TEMPLE, AND YOUR PEOPLE WILL BE DESTROYED!
GOD IS IN MY DREAMS AGAIN ...

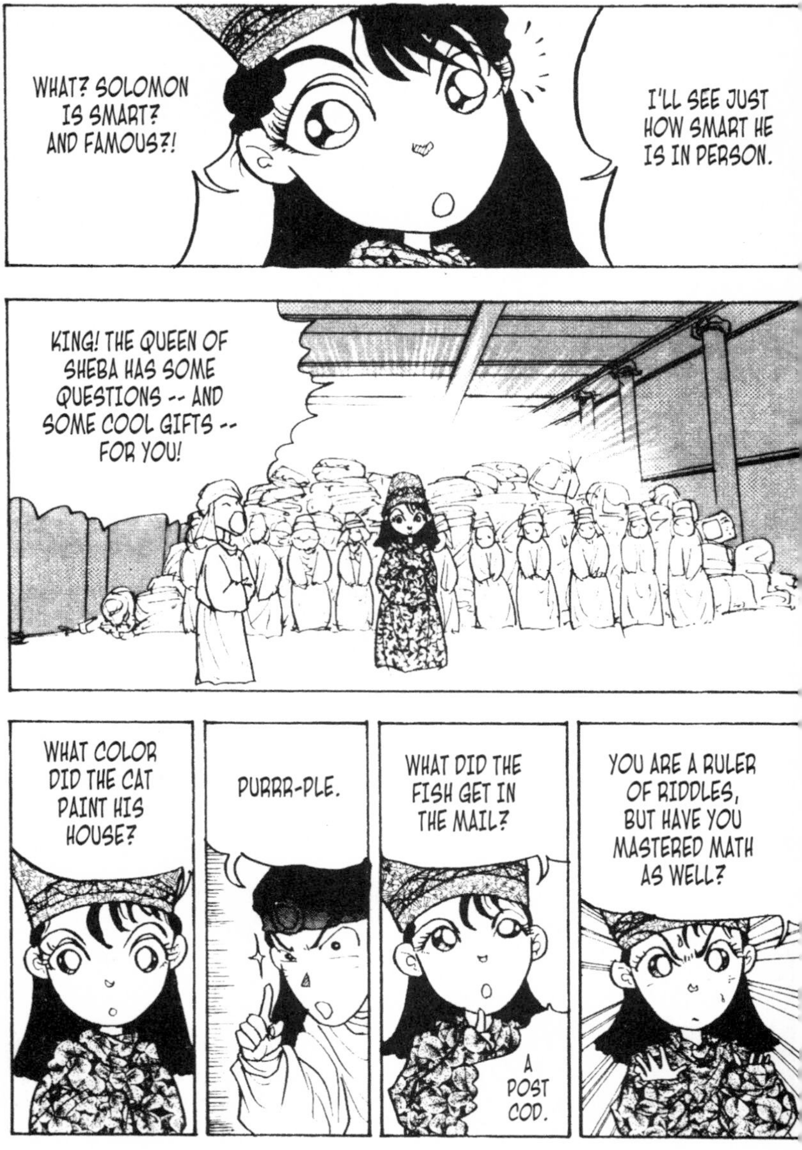
WHAT? SOLOMON IS SMART? AND FAMOUS?!
I'LL SEE JUST HOW SMART HE IS IN PERSON.
KING! THE QUEEN OF SHEBA HAS SOME QUESTIONS -- AND SOME COOL GIFTS -- FOR YOU!
WHAT COLOR DID THE CAT PAINT HIS HOUSE?
PURRR-PLE.
WHAT DID THE FISH GET IN THE MAIL?
A POST COD.
YOU ARE A RULER OF RIDDLES, BUT HAVE YOU MASTERED MATH AS WELL?

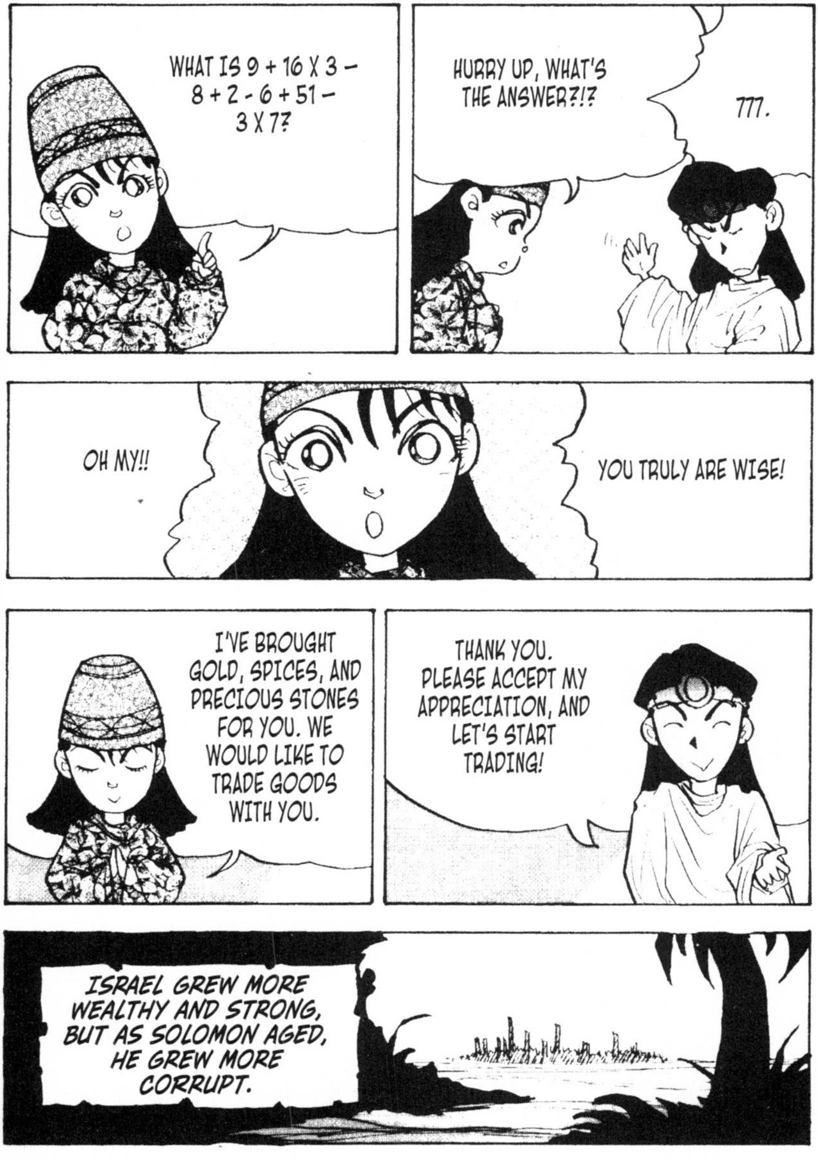
WHAT IS 9 + 16 X 3 – 8 + 2 - 6 + 51 – 3 X 7?
HURRY UP, WHAT'S THE ANSWER?!?
777.
OH MY!!
YOU TRULY ARE WISE!
I'VE BROUGHT GOLD, SPICES, AND PRECIOUS STONES FOR YOU. WE WOULD LIKE TO TRADE GOODS WITH YOU.
THANK YOU. PLEASE ACCEPT MY APPRECIATION, AND LET'S START TRADING!
ISRAEL GREW MORE WEALTHY AND STRONG, BUT AS SOLOMON AGED, HE GREW MORE CORRUPT.

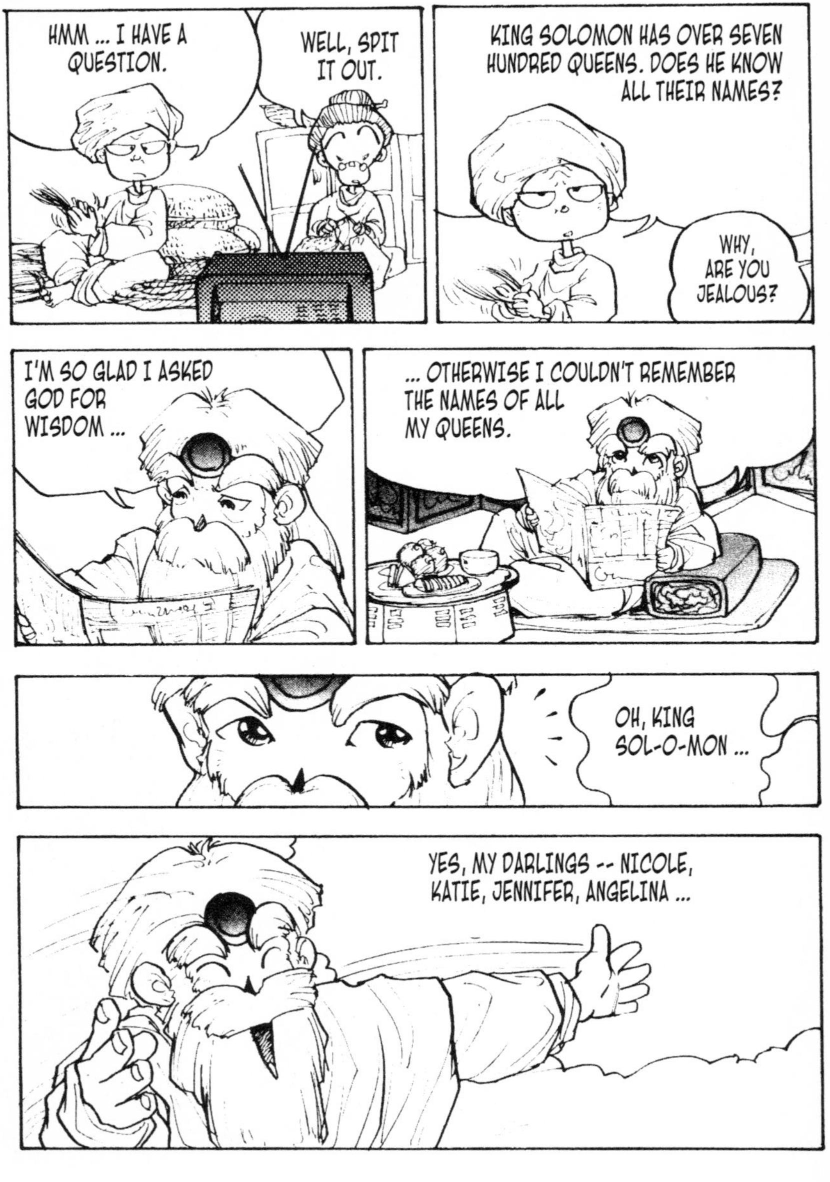
HMM ... I HAVE A QUESTION.
WELL, SPIT IT OUT.
KING SOLOMON HAS OVER SEVEN HUNDRED QUEENS. DOES HE KNOW ALL THEIR NAMES?
WHY, ARE YOU JEALOUS?
I'M SO GLAD I ASKED GOD FOR WISDOM ...
... OTHERWISE I COULDN'T REMEMBER THE NAMES OF ALL MY QUEENS.
OH, KING SOL-O-MON ...
YES, MY DARLINGS -- NICOLE, KATIE, JENNIFER, ANGELINA ...

AAHH ...

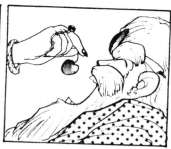

CHOMP! GULP!

WOULD YOU LIKE ANOTHER GRAPE?

THIS LITTLE PIGGY WENT TO MARKET ...

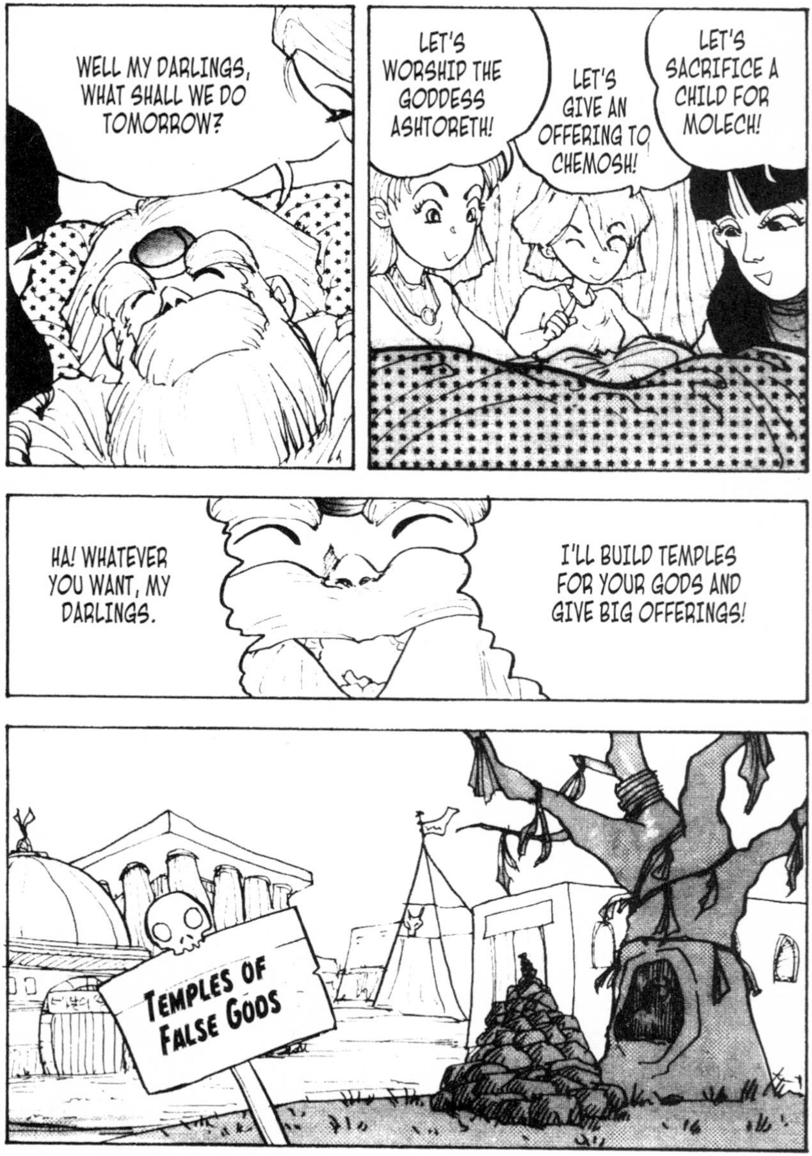

WELL MY DARLINGS, WHAT SHALL WE DO TOMORROW?
LET'S WORSHIP THE GODDESS ASHTORETH!
LET'S GIVE AN OFFERING TO CHEMOSH!
LET'S SACRIFICE A CHILD FOR MOLECH!
HA! WHATEVER YOU WANT, MY DARLINGS.
I'LL BUILD TEMPLES FOR YOUR GODS AND GIVE BIG OFFERINGS!
TEMPLES OF FALSE GODS

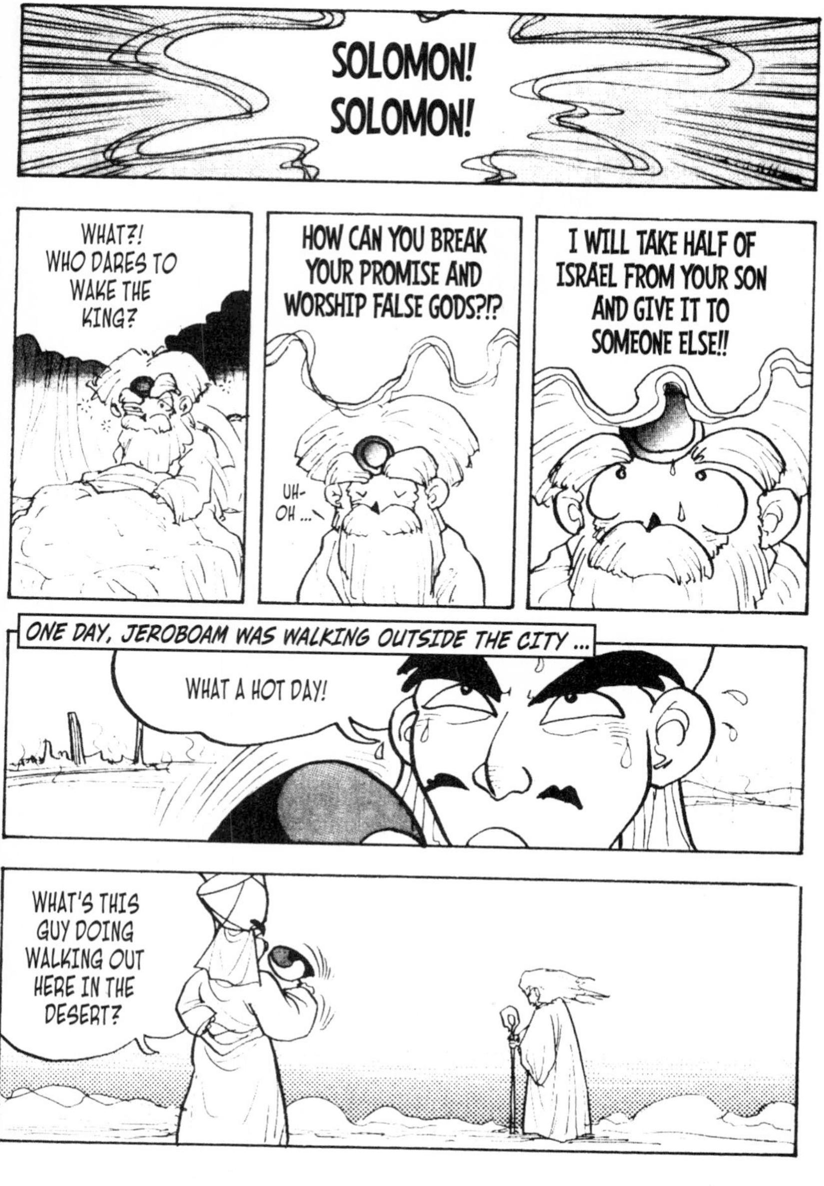
SOLOMON!
SOLOMON!
WHAT?! WHO DARES TO WAKE THE KING?
HOW CAN YOU BREAK YOUR PROMISE AND WORSHIP FALSE GODS?!?
UH-OH ...
I WILL TAKE HALF OF ISRAEL FROM YOUR SON AND GIVE IT TO SOMEONE ELSE!!
ONE DAY, JEROBOAM WAS WALKING OUTSIDE THE CITY ...
WHAT A HOT DAY!
WHAT'S THIS GUY DOING WALKING OUT HERE IN THE DESERT?

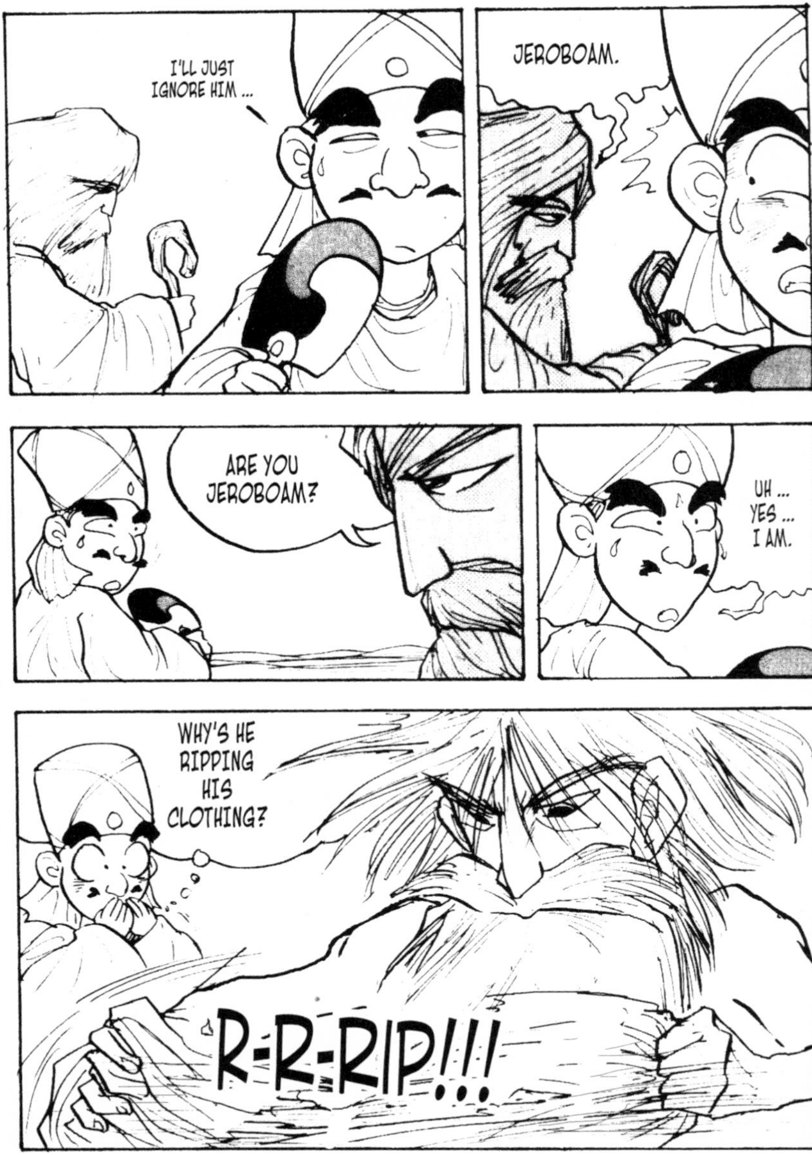
I'LL JUST IGNORE HIM ...
JEROBOAM.
ARE YOU JEROBOAM?
UH ... YES ... I AM.
WHY'S HE RIPPING HIS CLOTHING?
R-R-RIP!!!

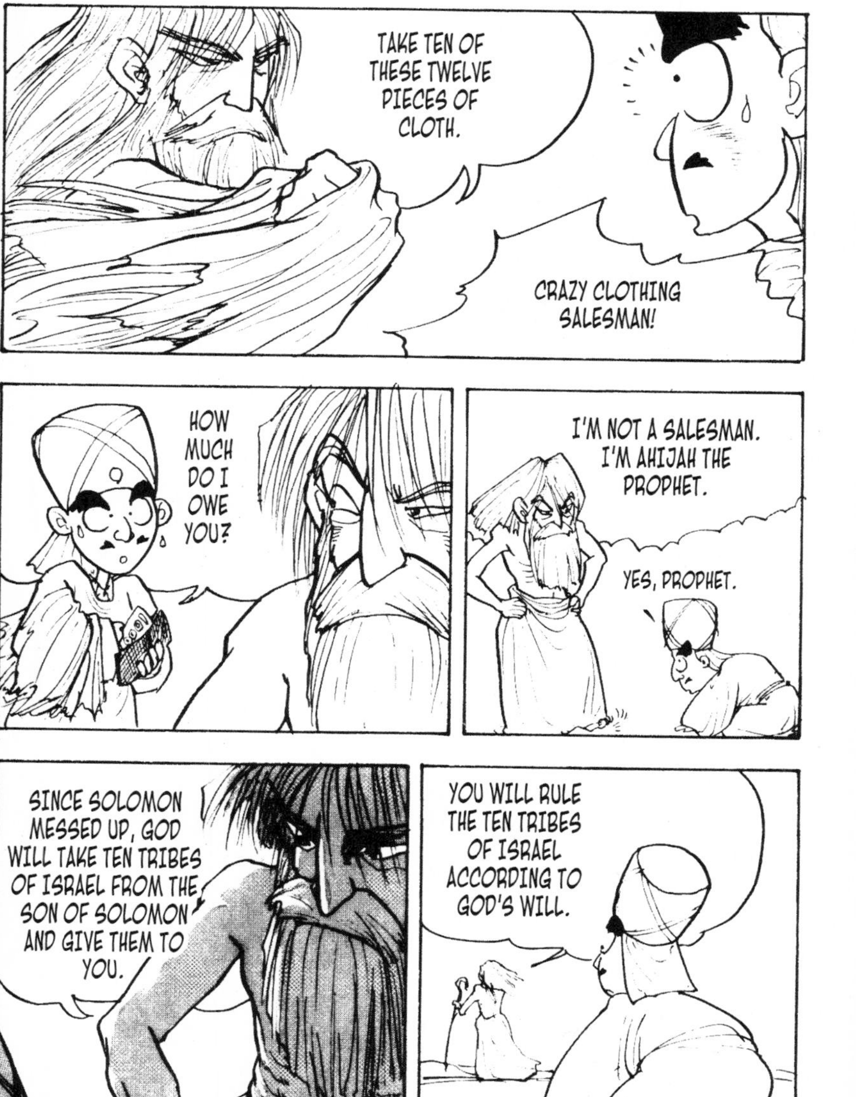
TAKE TEN OF THESE TWELVE PIECES OF CLOTH.
CRAZY CLOTHING SALESMAN!
HOW MUCH DO I OWE YOU?
I'M NOT A SALESMAN. I'M AHIJAH THE PROPHET.
YES, PROPHET.
SINCE SOLOMON MESSED UP, GOD WILL TAKE TEN TRIBES OF ISRAEL FROM THE SON OF SOLOMON AND GIVE THEM TO YOU.
YOU WILL RULE THE TEN TRIBES OF ISRAEL ACCORDING TO GOD'S WILL.

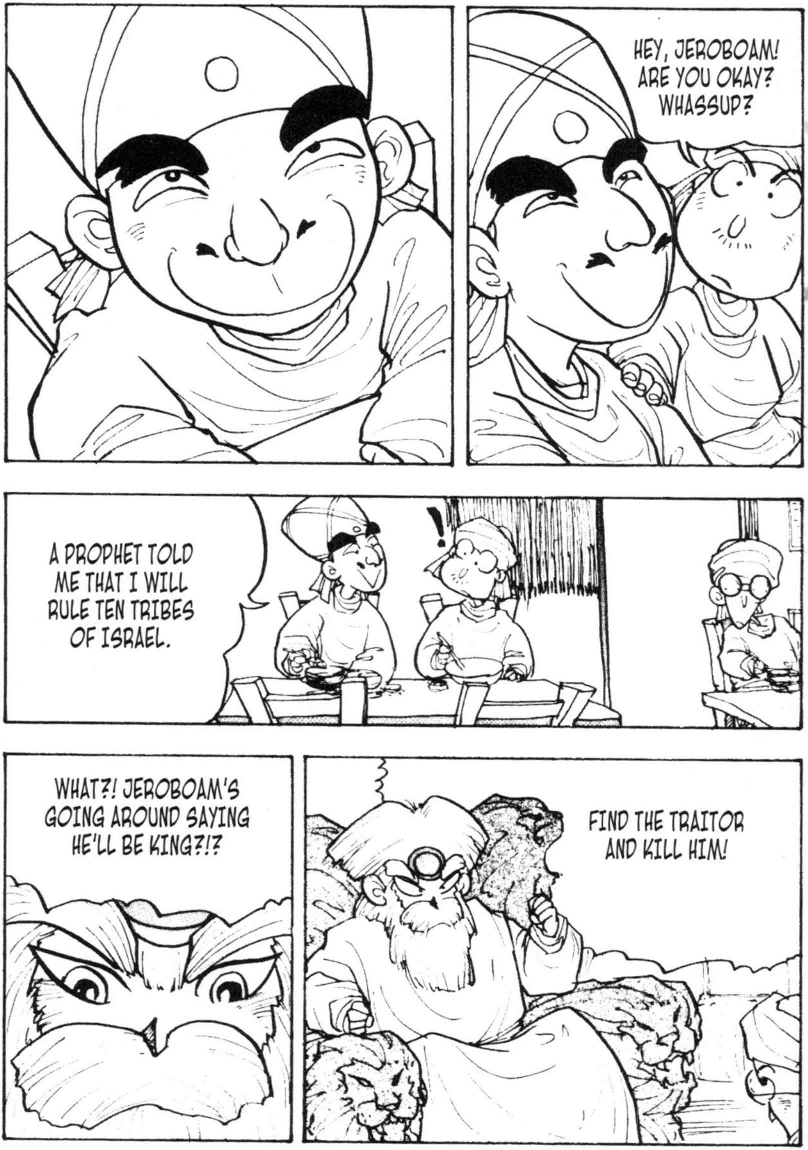
HEY, JEROBOAM! ARE YOU OKAY? WHASSUP?
A PROPHET TOLD ME THAT I WILL RULE TEN TRIBES OF ISRAEL.
!
WHAT?! JEROBOAM'S GOING AROUND SAYING HE'LL BE KING?!?
FIND THE TRAITOR AND KILL HIM!

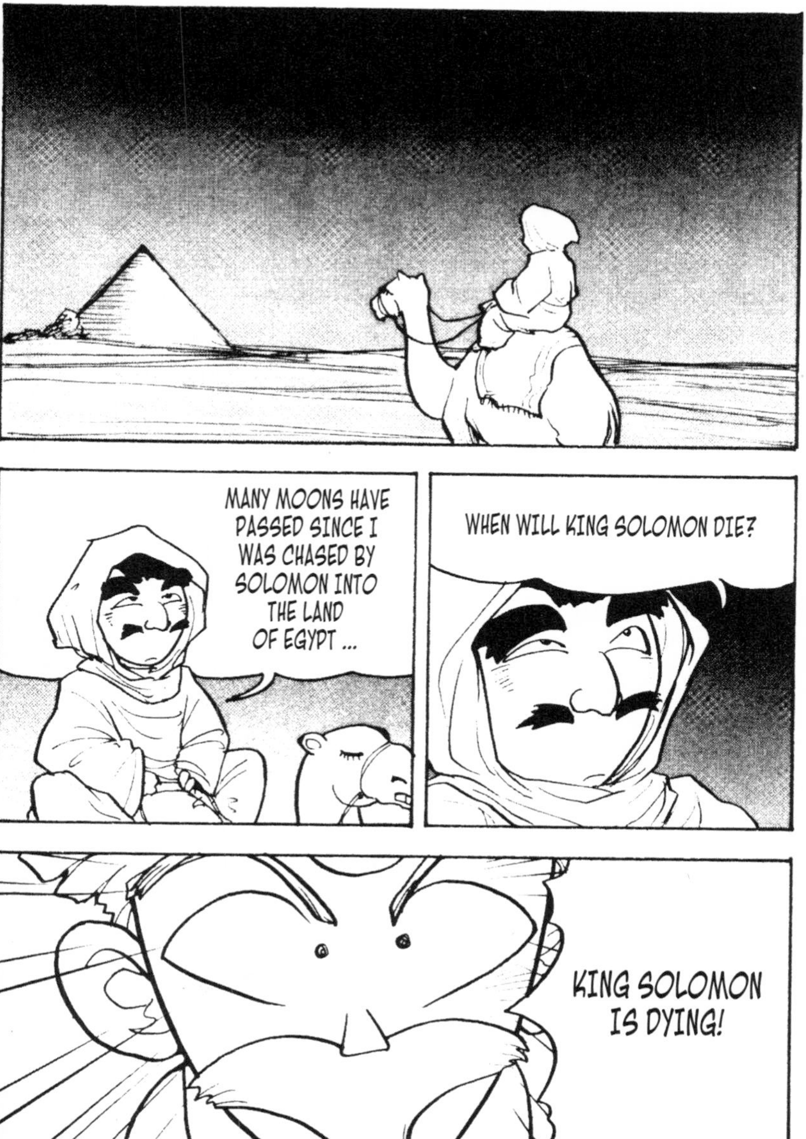
MANY MOONS HAVE PASSED SINCE I WAS CHASED BY SOLOMON INTO THE LAND OF EGYPT ...
WHEN WILL KING SOLOMON DIE?
KING SOLOMON IS DYING!

MY SON REHOBOAM,
YOU SHALL RULE
ISRAEL ...

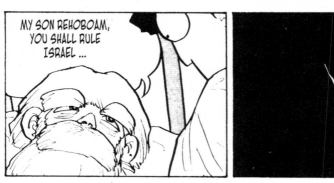

WHEN SOLOMON DIED, THE PEOPLE OF ISRAEL CALLED FOR JEROBOAM AND WENT TO THE NEW KING TOGETHER.

REHOBOAM, WE WILL SERVE YOU AS KING IF YOU CUT THE TAXES AND HEAVY LABOR.

UM, ER, WELL -- LET'S TALK AGAIN IN THREE DAYS.

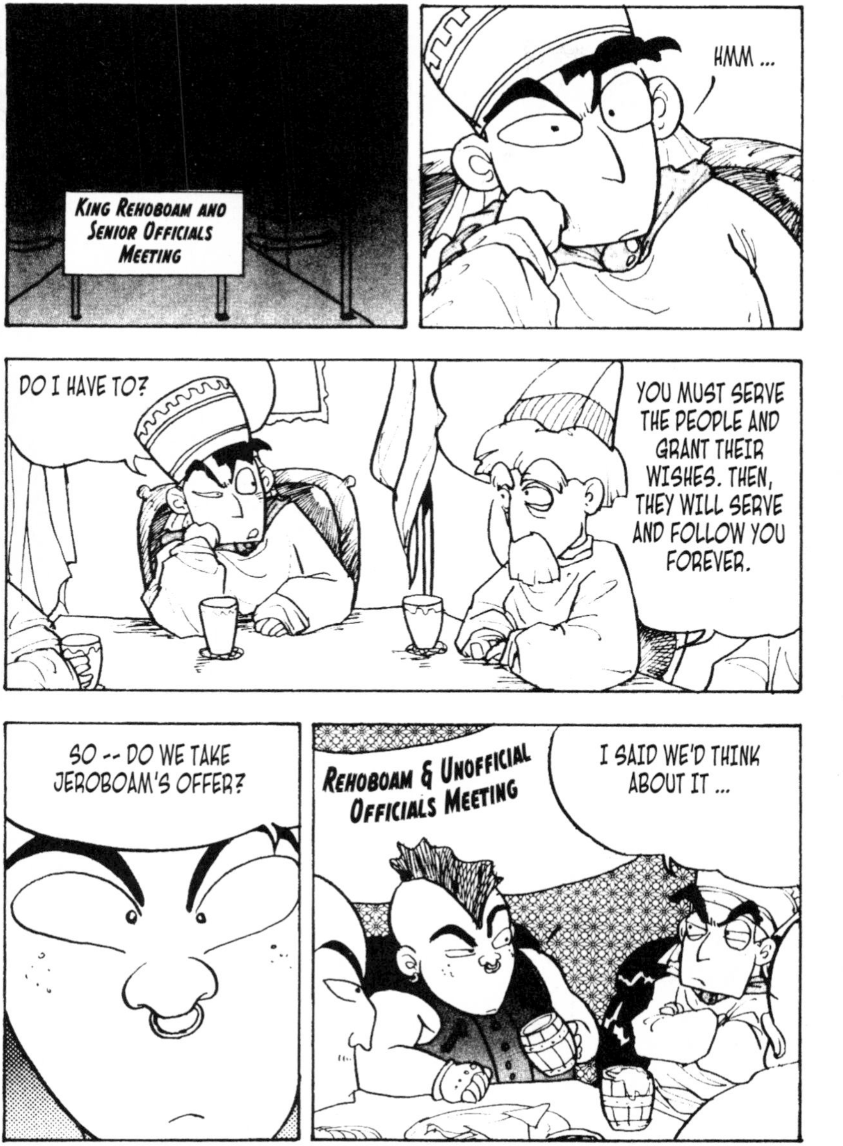
KING REHOBOAM AND SENIOR OFFICIALS MEETING
HMM ...
DO I HAVE TO?
YOU MUST SERVE THE PEOPLE AND GRANT THEIR WISHES. THEN, THEY WILL SERVE AND FOLLOW YOU FOREVER.
SO -- DO WE TAKE JEROBOAM'S OFFER?
REHOBOAM & UNOFFICIAL OFFICIALS MEETING
I SAID WE'D THINK ABOUT IT ...

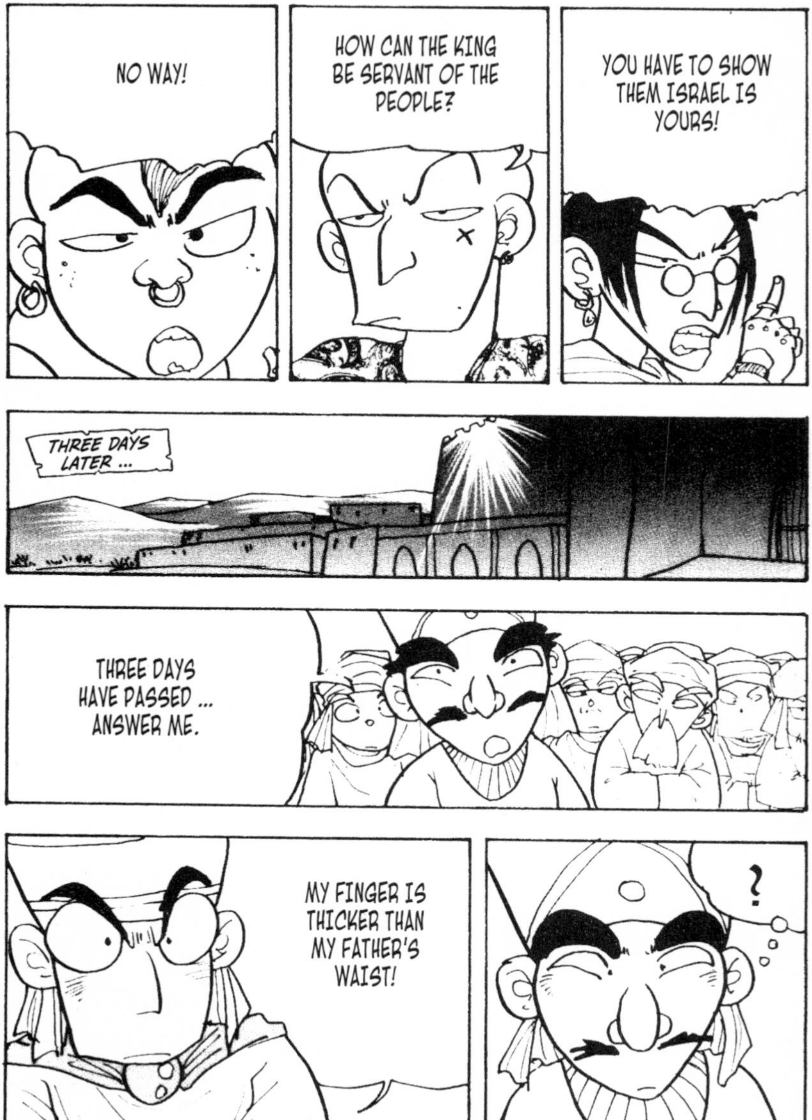
NO WAY!
HOW CAN THE KING BE SERVANT OF THE PEOPLE?
YOU HAVE TO SHOW THEM ISRAEL IS YOURS!
THREE DAYS LATER ...
THREE DAYS HAVE PASSED ... ANSWER ME.
MY FINGER IS THICKER THAN MY FATHER'S WAIST!
?

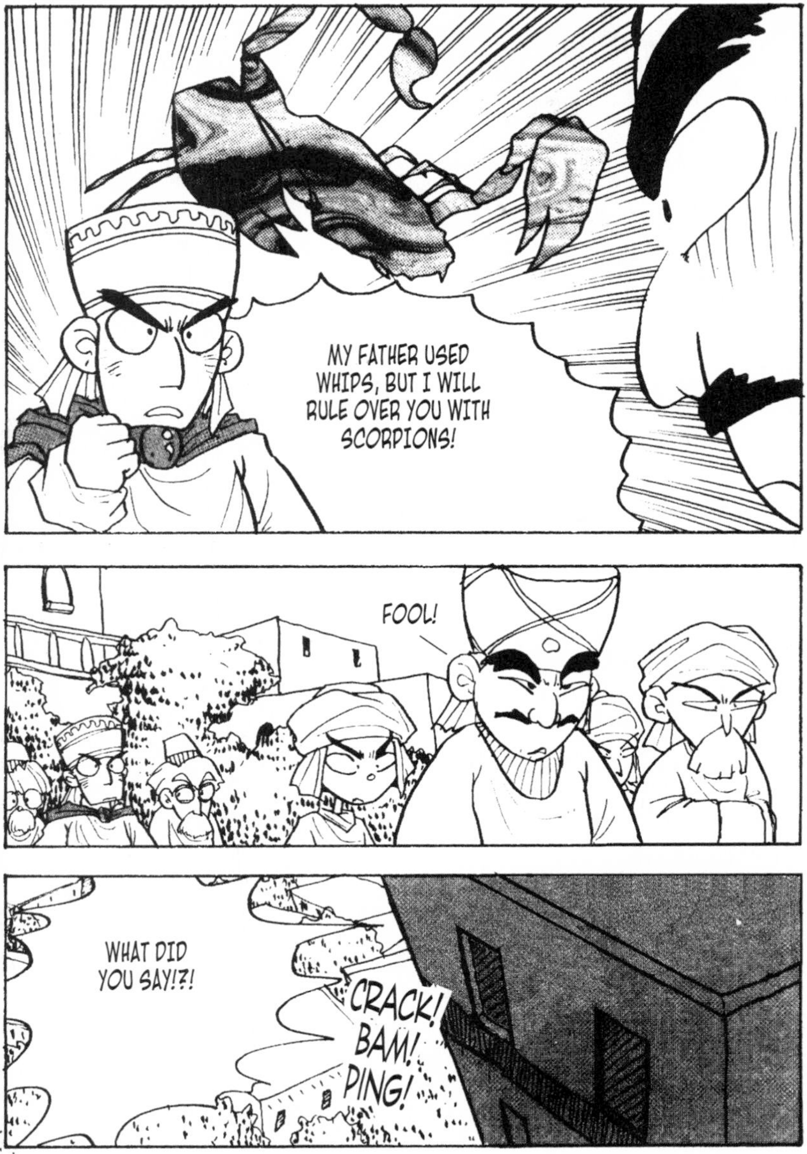
MY FATHER USED WHIPS, BUT I WILL RULE OVER YOU WITH SCORPIONS!
FOOL!
WHAT DID YOU SAY!?!
CRACK! BAM! PING!

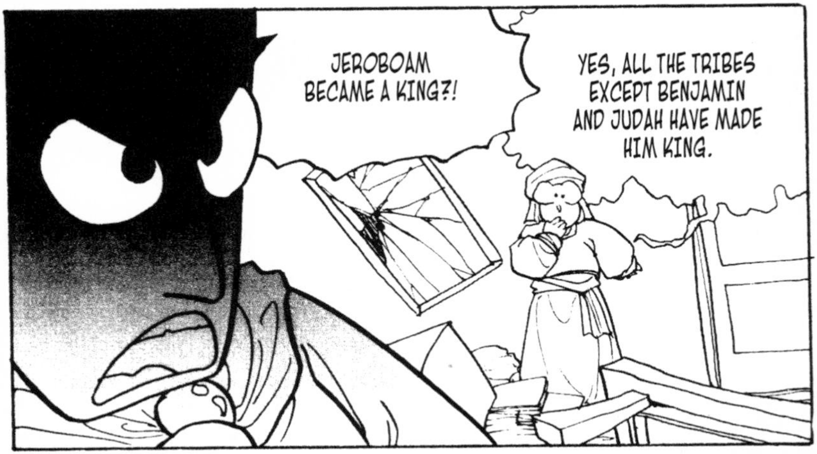
JEROBOAM BECAME A KING?!
YES, ALL THE TRIBES EXCEPT BENJAMIN AND JUDAH HAVE MADE HIM KING.

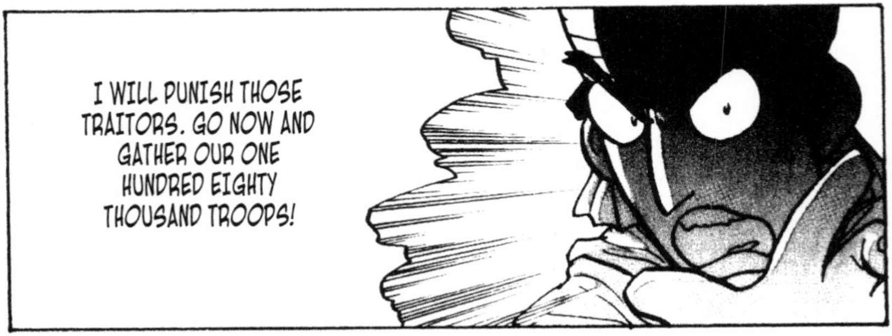
I WILL PUNISH THOSE TRAITORS. GO NOW AND GATHER OUR ONE HUNDRED EIGHTY THOUSAND TROOPS!

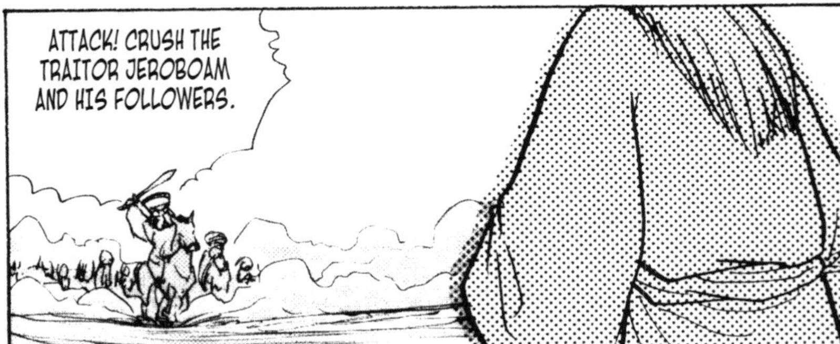
ATTACK! CRUSH THE TRAITOR JEROBOAM AND HIS FOLLOWERS.

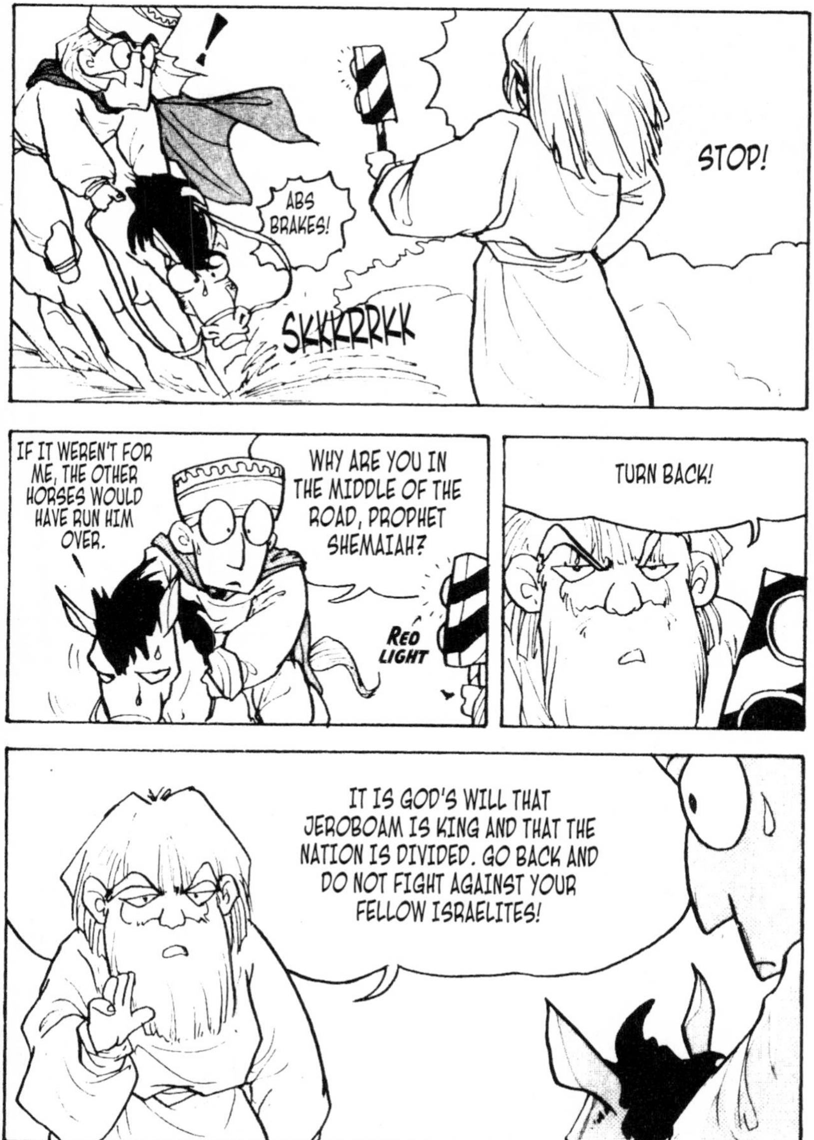
STOP!
ABS BRAKES!
SKKKRRKK
WHY ARE YOU IN THE MIDDLE OF THE ROAD, PROPHET SHEMAIAH?
IF IT WEREN'T FOR ME, THE OTHER HORSES WOULD HAVE RUN HIM OVER.
RED LIGHT
TURN BACK!
IT IS GOD'S WILL THAT JEROBOAM IS KING AND THAT THE NATION IS DIVIDED. GO BACK AND DO NOT FIGHT AGAINST YOUR FELLOW ISRAELITES!

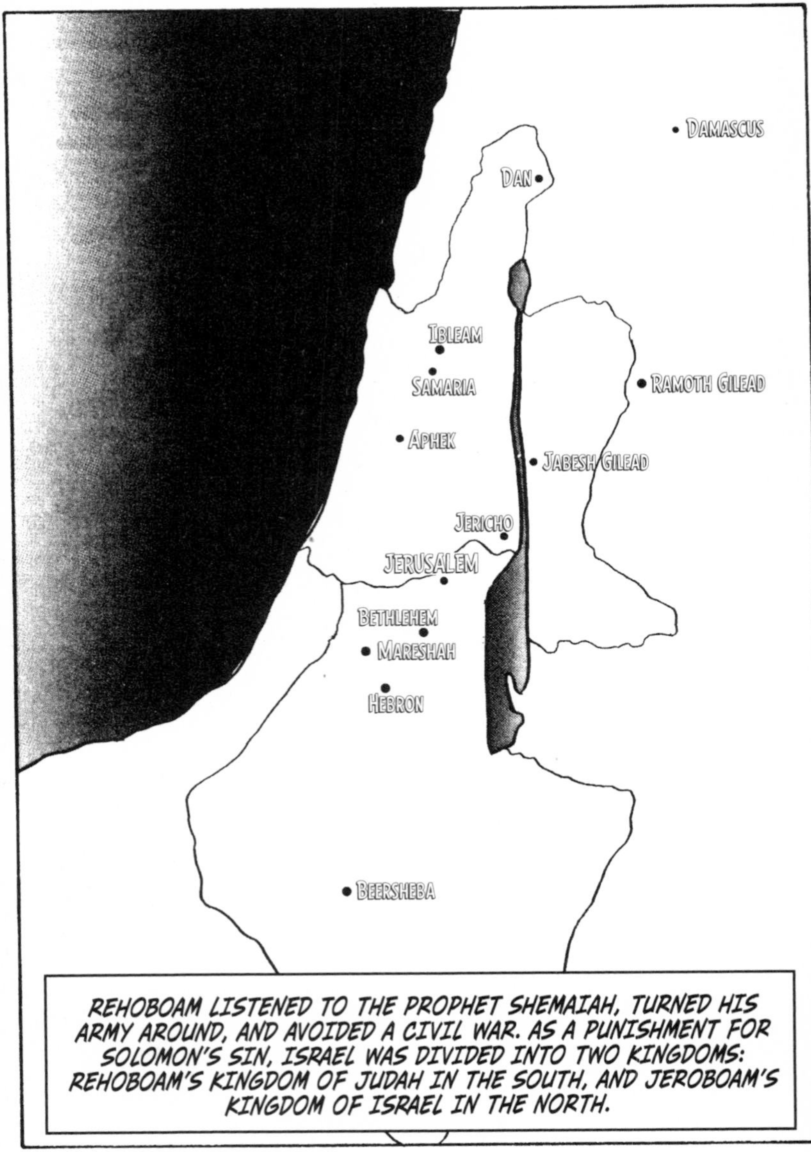
DAMASCUS
DAN
IBLEAM
SAMARIA
RAMOTH GILEAD
APHEK
JABESH GILEAD
JERICHO
JERUSALEM
BETHLEHEM
MARESHAH
HEBRON
BEERSHEBA
REHOBOAM LISTENED TO THE PROPHET SHEMAIAH, TURNED HIS ARMY AROUND, AND AVOIDED A CIVIL WAR. AS A PUNISHMENT FOR SOLOMON'S SIN, ISRAEL WAS DIVIDED INTO TWO KINGDOMS: REHOBOAM'S KINGDOM OF JUDAH IN THE SOUTH, AND JEROBOAM'S KINGDOM OF ISRAEL IN THE NORTH.

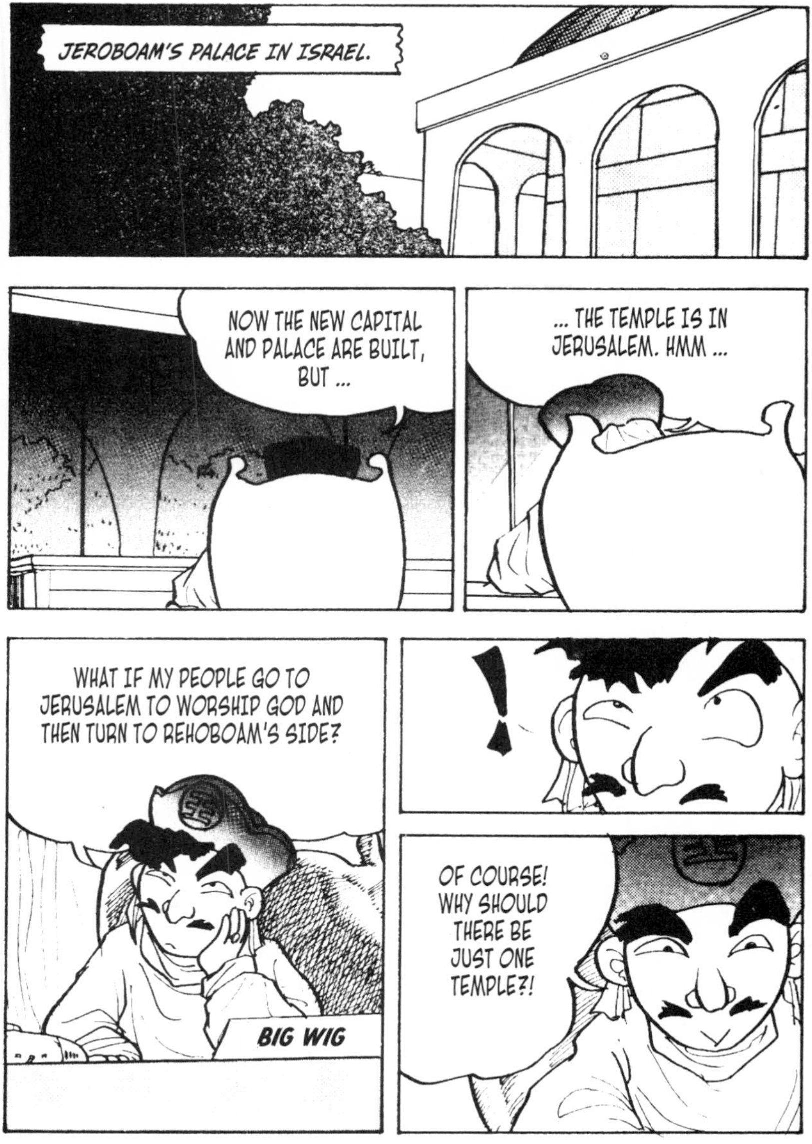
JEROBOAM'S PALACE IN ISRAEL.
NOW THE NEW CAPITAL AND PALACE ARE BUILT, BUT ...
... THE TEMPLE IS IN JERUSALEM. HMM ...
WHAT IF MY PEOPLE GO TO JERUSALEM TO WORSHIP GOD AND THEN TURN TO REHOBOAM'S SIDE?
BIG WIG
!
OF COURSE! WHY SHOULD THERE BE JUST ONE TEMPLE?!

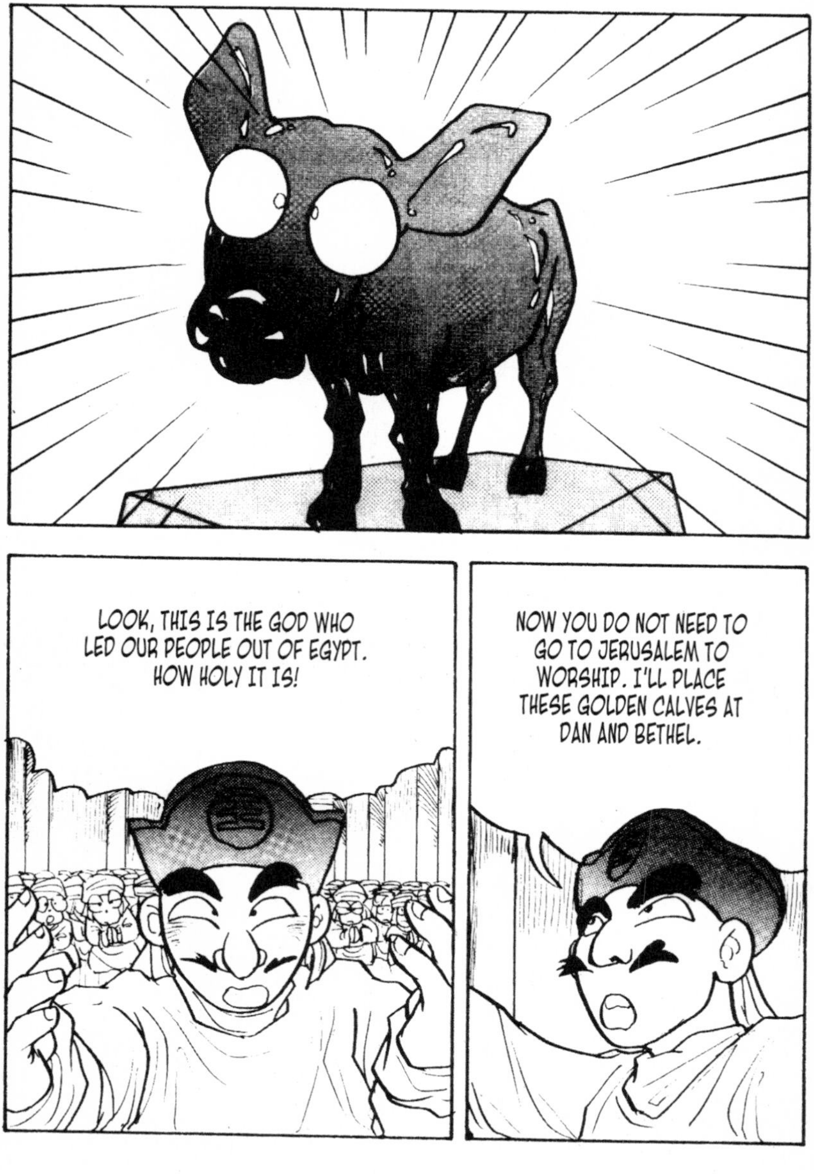
LOOK, THIS IS THE GOD WHO LED OUR PEOPLE OUT OF EGYPT. HOW HOLY IT IS!
NOW YOU DO NOT NEED TO GO TO JERUSALEM TO WORSHIP. I'LL PLACE THESE GOLDEN CALVES AT DAN AND BETHEL.

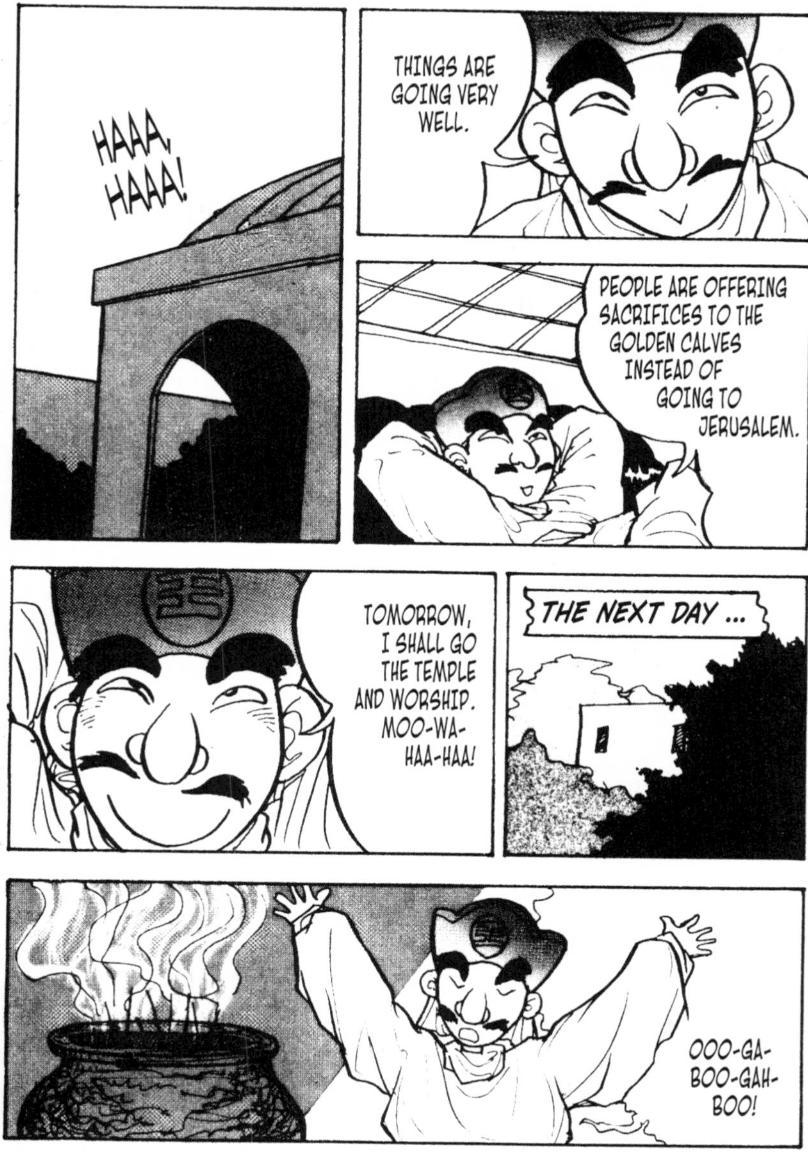
HAAA, HAAA!
THINGS ARE GOING VERY WELL.
PEOPLE ARE OFFERING SACRIFICES TO THE GOLDEN CALVES INSTEAD OF GOING TO JERUSALEM.
TOMORROW, I SHALL GO THE TEMPLE AND WORSHIP. MOO-WA-HAA-HAA!
THE NEXT DAY ...
OOO-GA-BOO-GAH-BOO!

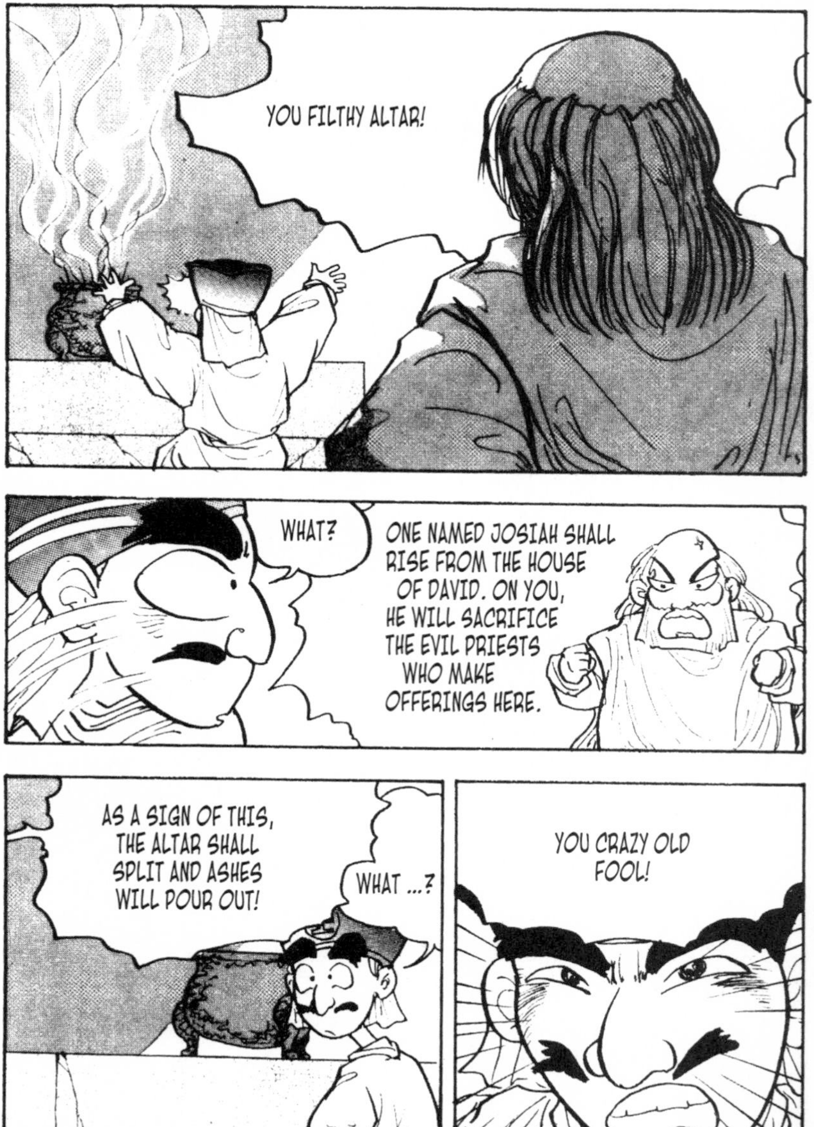
YOU FILTHY ALTAR!
WHAT?
ONE NAMED JOSIAH SHALL RISE FROM THE HOUSE OF DAVID. ON YOU, HE WILL SACRIFICE THE EVIL PRIESTS WHO MAKE OFFERINGS HERE.
AS A SIGN OF THIS, THE ALTAR SHALL SPLIT AND ASHES WILL POUR OUT!
WHAT ...?
YOU CRAZY OLD FOOL!

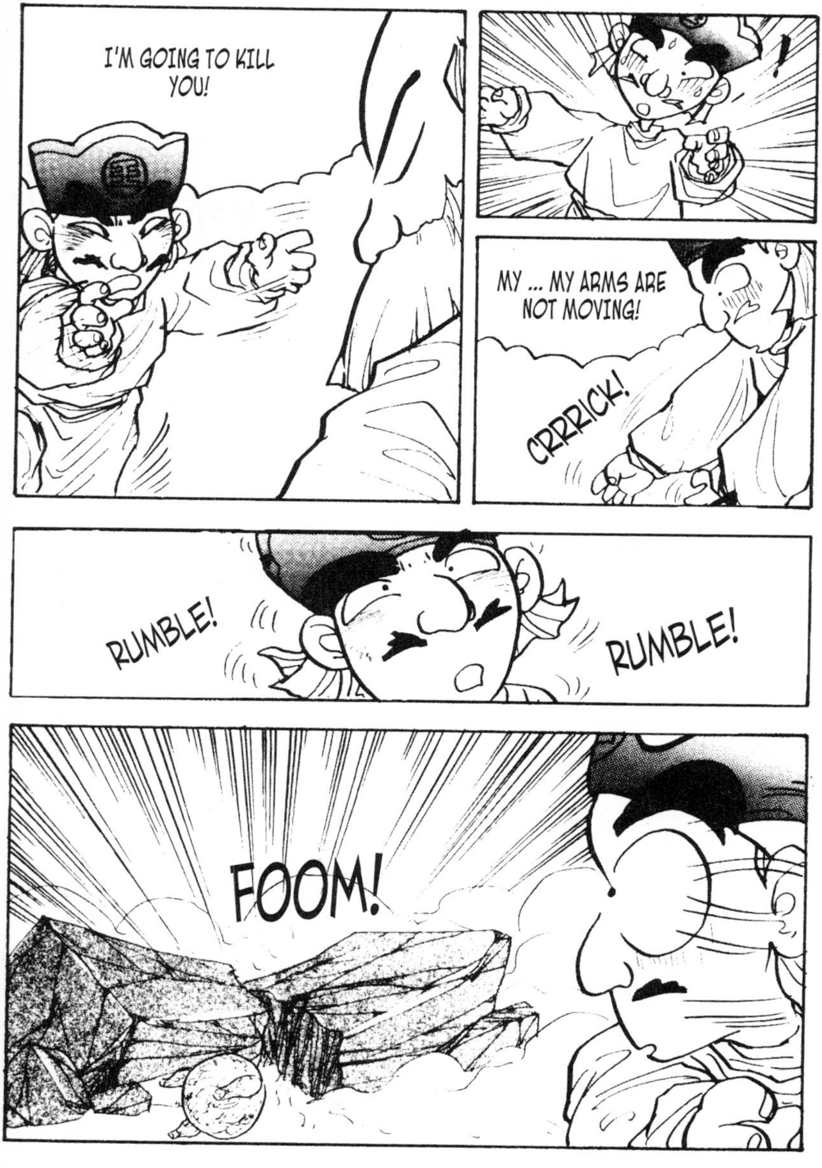
I'M GOING TO KILL YOU!
!
MY ... MY ARMS ARE NOT MOVING!
CRRRICK!
RUMBLE!
RUMBLE!
FOOM!

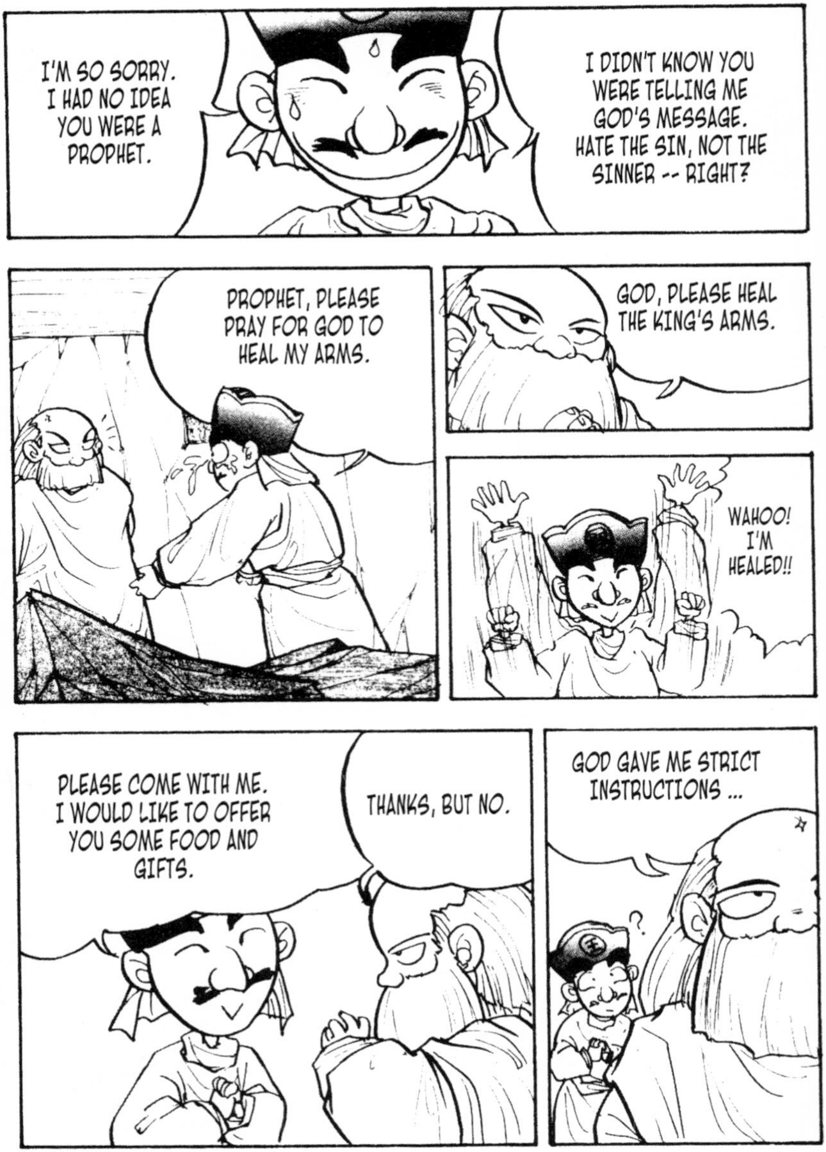
I'M SO SORRY. I HAD NO IDEA YOU WERE A PROPHET.
I DIDN'T KNOW YOU WERE TELLING ME GOD'S MESSAGE. HATE THE SIN, NOT THE SINNER -- RIGHT?
PROPHET, PLEASE PRAY FOR GOD TO HEAL MY ARMS.
GOD, PLEASE HEAL THE KING'S ARMS.
WAHOO! I'M HEALED!!
PLEASE COME WITH ME. I WOULD LIKE TO OFFER YOU SOME FOOD AND GIFTS.
THANKS, BUT NO.
GOD GAVE ME STRICT INSTRUCTIONS ...

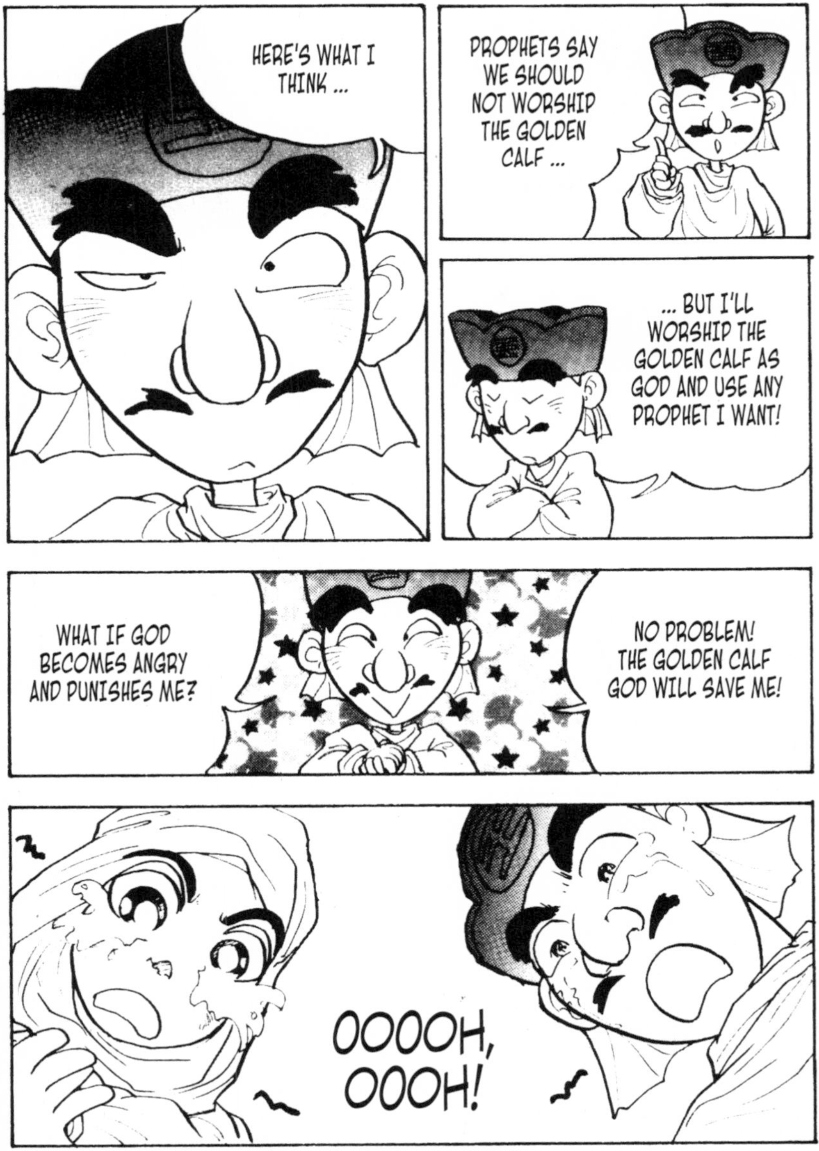
HERE'S WHAT I THINK ...
PROPHETS SAY WE SHOULD NOT WORSHIP THE GOLDEN CALF ...
... BUT I'LL WORSHIP THE GOLDEN CALF AS GOD AND USE ANY PROPHET I WANT!
WHAT IF GOD BECOMES ANGRY AND PUNISHES ME?
NO PROBLEM! THE GOLDEN CALF GOD WILL SAVE ME!
OOOOH, OOOH!

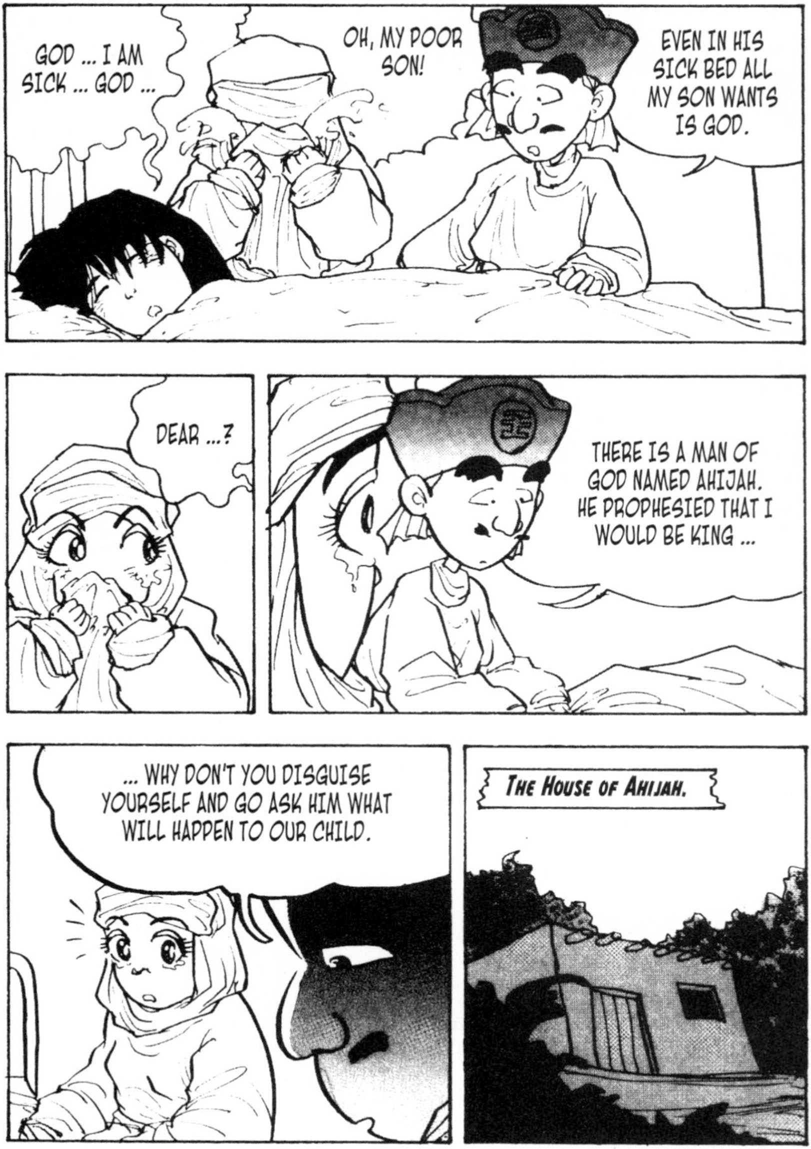
GOD ... I AM SICK ... GOD ...
OH, MY POOR SON!
EVEN IN HIS SICK BED ALL MY SON WANTS IS GOD.
DEAR ...?
THERE IS A MAN OF GOD NAMED AHIJAH. HE PROPHESIED THAT I WOULD BE KING ...
... WHY DON'T YOU DISGUISE YOURSELF AND GO ASK HIM WHAT WILL HAPPEN TO OUR CHILD.
THE HOUSE OF AHIJAH.

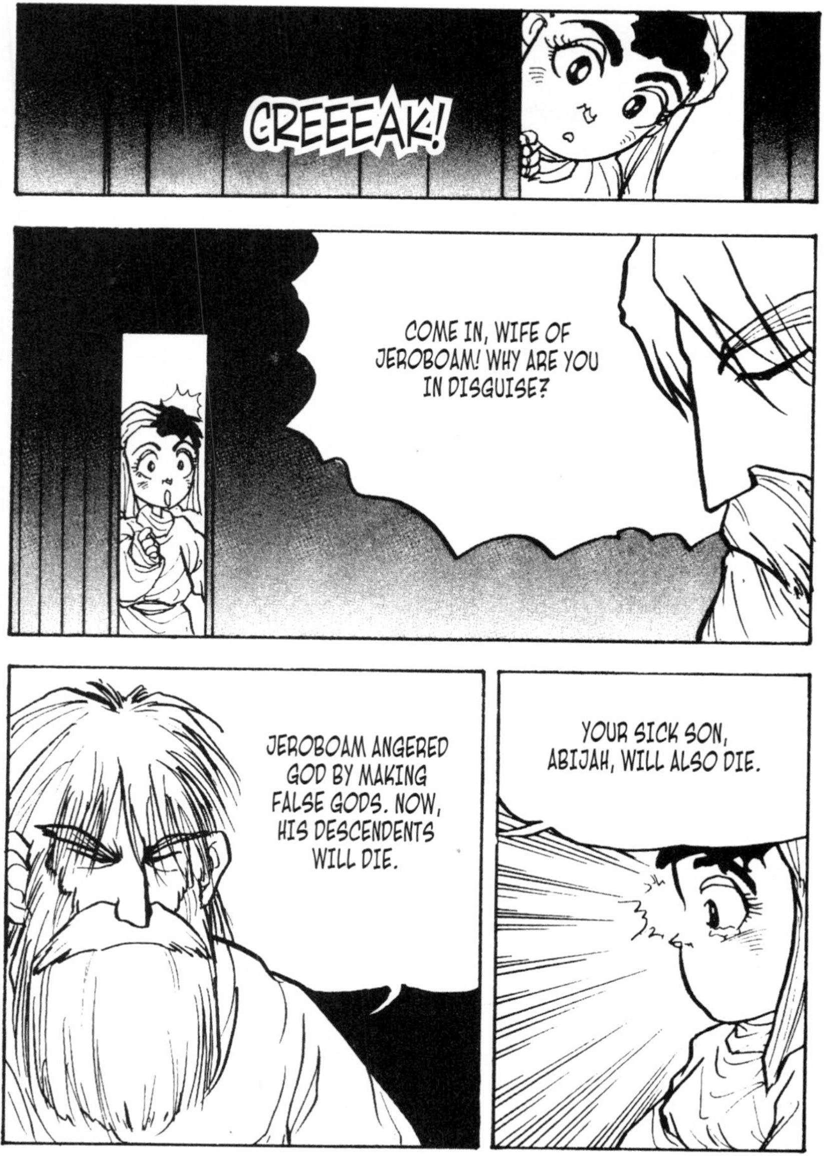

CREEEAK!
COME IN, WIFE OF JEROBOAM! WHY ARE YOU IN DISGUISE?
JEROBOAM ANGERED GOD BY MAKING FALSE GODS. NOW, HIS DESCENDENTS WILL DIE.
YOUR SICK SON, ABIJAH, WILL ALSO DIE.

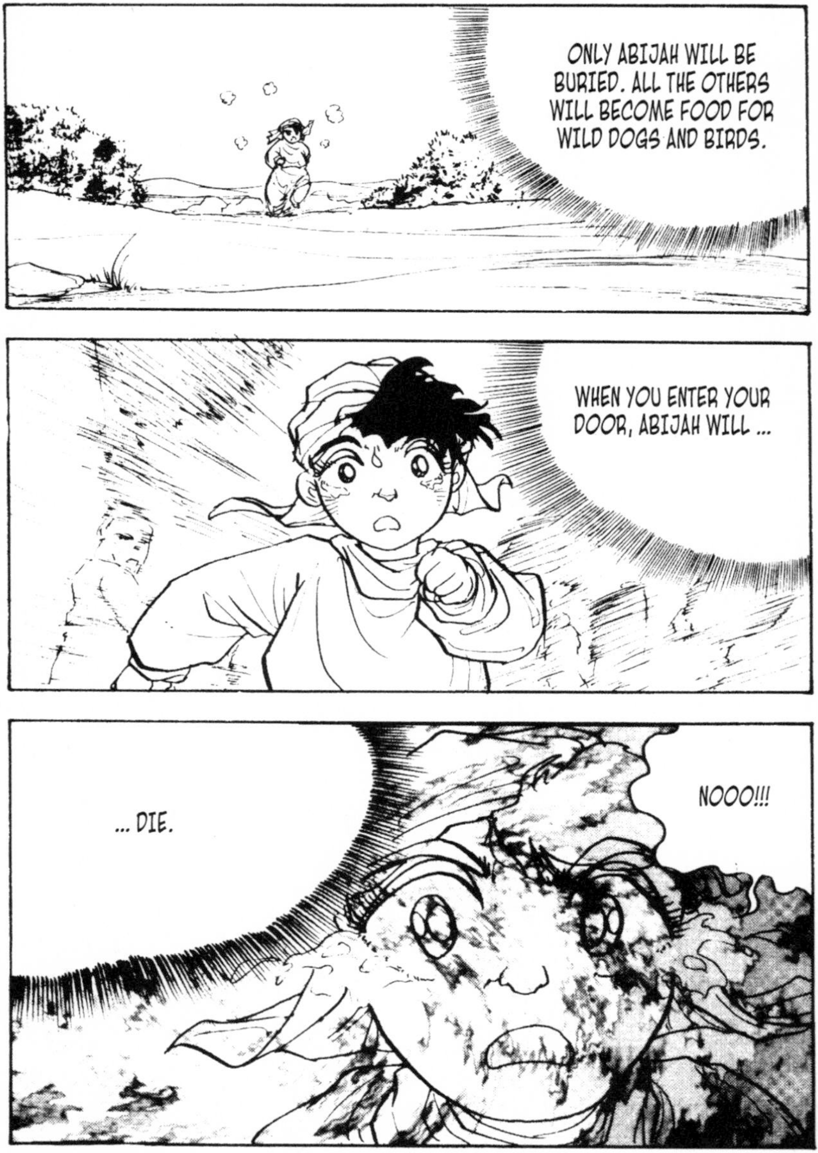
ONLY ABIJAH WILL BE BURIED. ALL THE OTHERS WILL BECOME FOOD FOR WILD DOGS AND BIRDS.
WHEN YOU ENTER YOUR DOOR, ABIJAH WILL ...
... DIE.
NOOO!!!

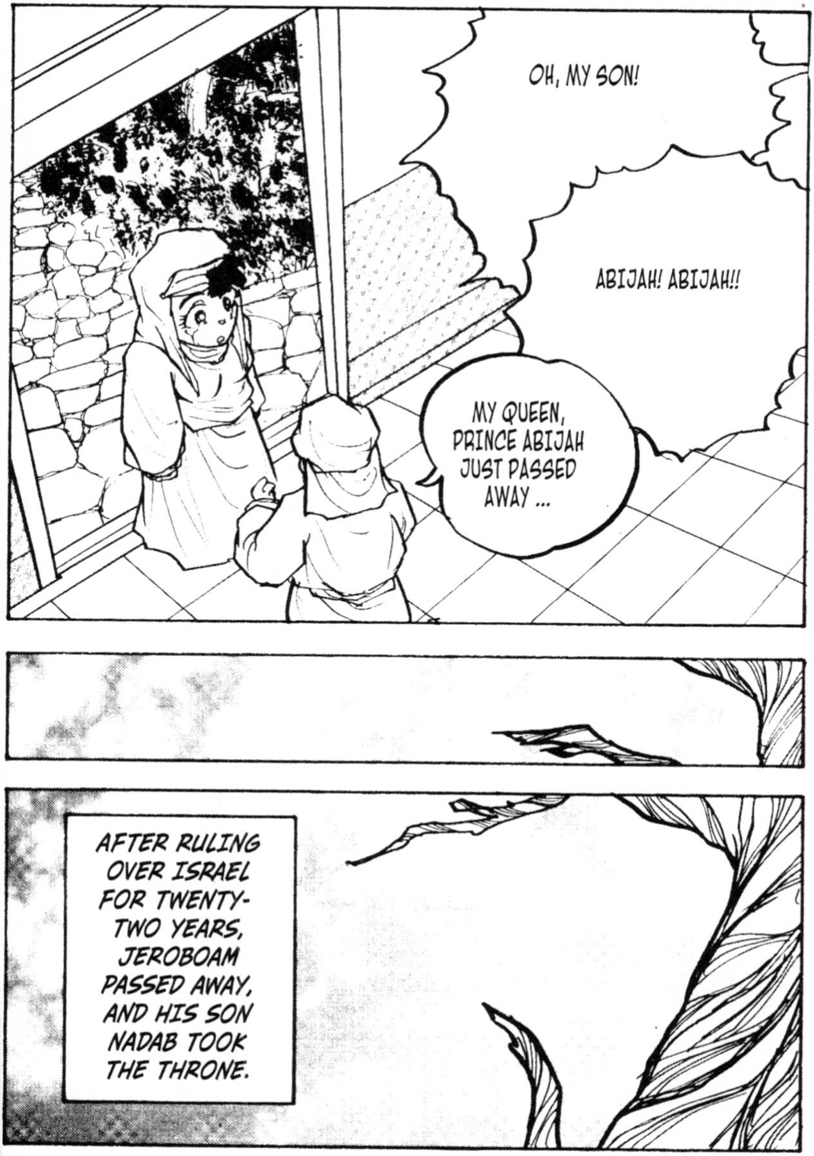
OH, MY SON!
ABIJAH! ABIJAH!!
MY QUEEN, PRINCE ABIJAH JUST PASSED AWAY ...
AFTER RULING OVER ISRAEL FOR TWENTY-TWO YEARS, JEROBOAM PASSED AWAY, AND HIS SON NADAB TOOK THE THRONE.

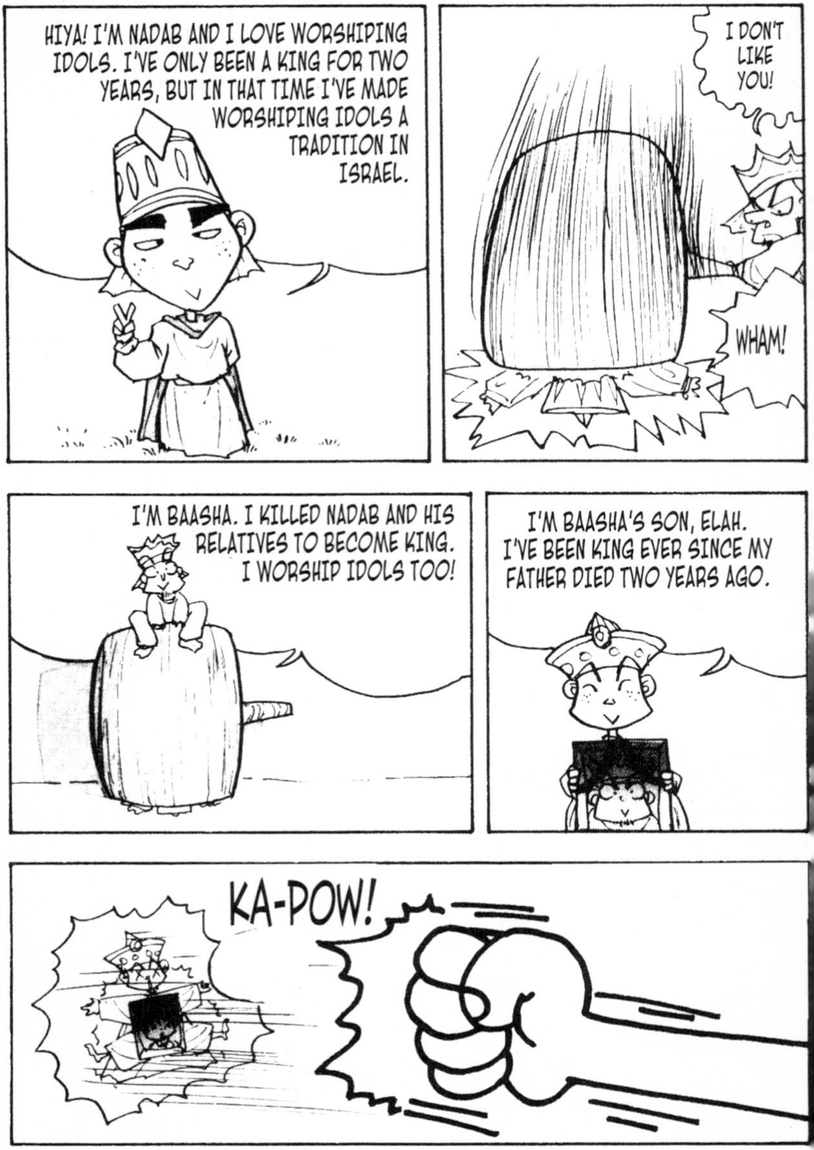
HIYA! I'M NADAB AND I LOVE WORSHIPING IDOLS. I'VE ONLY BEEN A KING FOR TWO YEARS, BUT IN THAT TIME I'VE MADE WORSHIPING IDOLS A TRADITION IN ISRAEL.
I DON'T LIKE YOU!
WHAM!
I'M BAASHA. I KILLED NADAB AND HIS RELATIVES TO BECOME KING. I WORSHIP IDOLS TOO!
I'M BAASHA'S SON, ELAH. I'VE BEEN KING EVER SINCE MY FATHER DIED TWO YEARS AGO.
KA-POW!

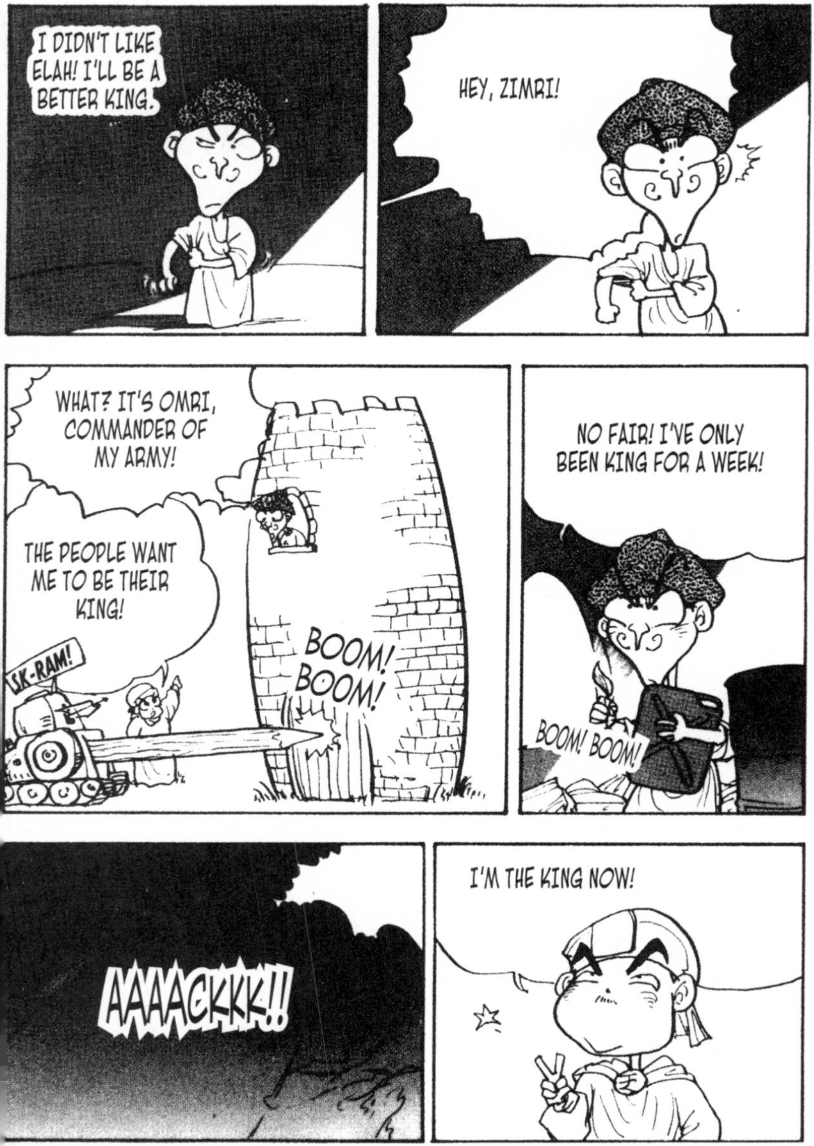
I DIDN'T LIKE ELAH! I'LL BE A BETTER KING.
HEY, ZIMRI!
WHAT? IT'S OMRI, COMMANDER OF MY ARMY!
THE PEOPLE WANT ME TO BE THEIR KING!
SK-RAM!
BOOM! BOOM!
NO FAIR! I'VE ONLY BEEN KING FOR A WEEK!
BOOM! BOOM!
AAAACKKK!!
I'M THE KING NOW!

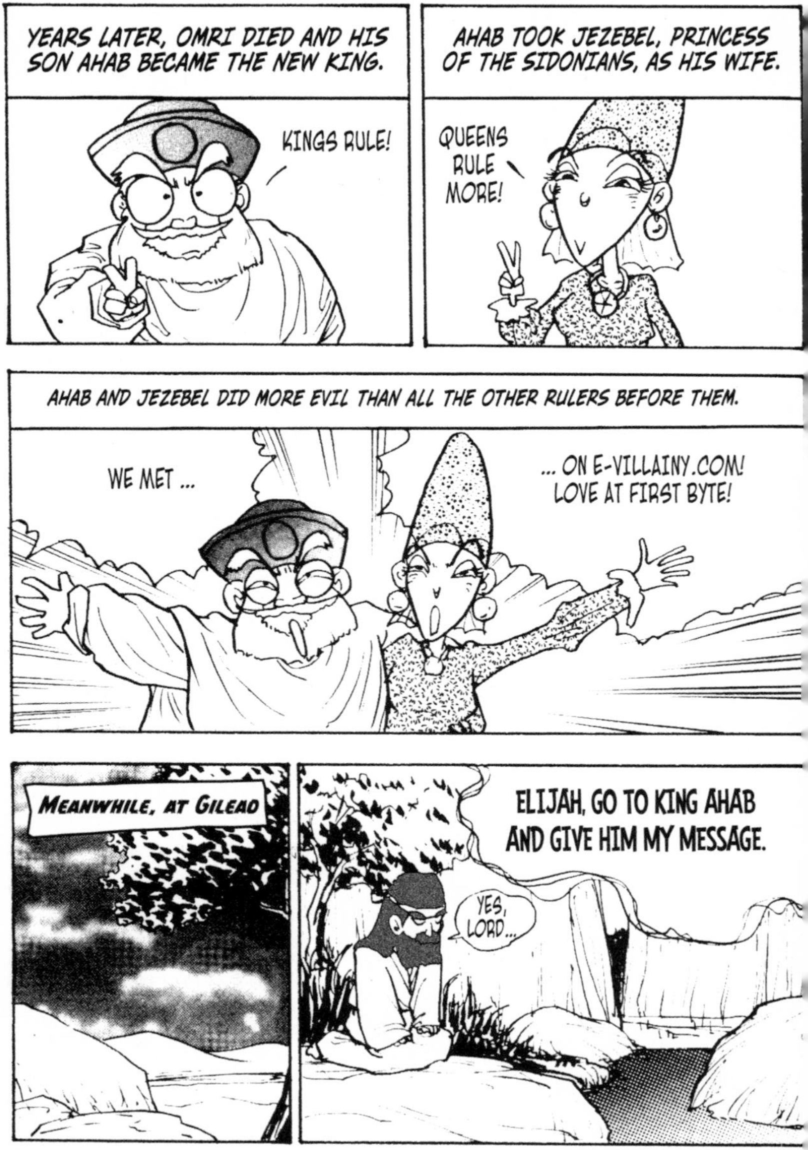
YEARS LATER, OMRI DIED AND HIS SON AHAB BECAME THE NEW KING.
KINGS RULE!
AHAB TOOK JEZEBEL, PRINCESS OF THE SIDONIANS, AS HIS WIFE.
QUEENS RULE MORE!
AHAB AND JEZEBEL DID MORE EVIL THAN ALL THE OTHER RULERS BEFORE THEM.
WE MET ...
... ON E-VILLAINY.COM! LOVE AT FIRST BYTE!
MEANWHILE, AT GILEAD
ELIJAH, GO TO KING AHAB AND GIVE HIM MY MESSAGE.
YES, LORD...

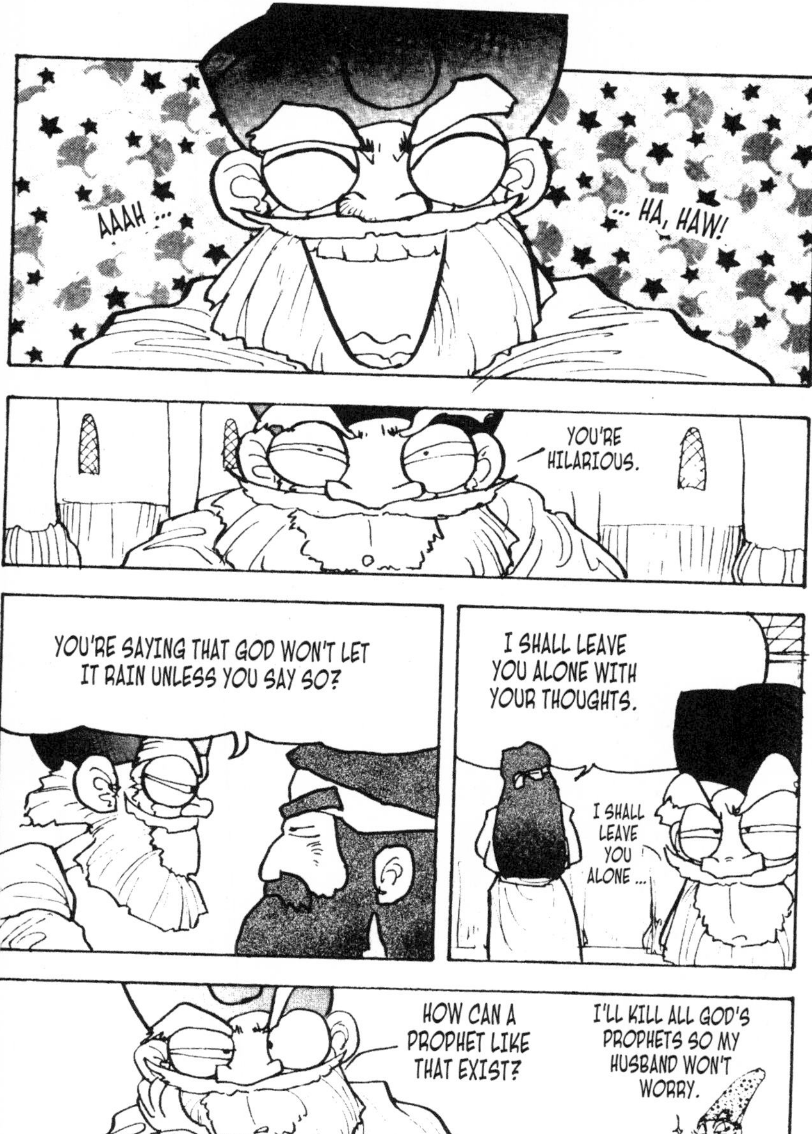

AAAH ...
... HA, HAW!
YOU'RE HILARIOUS.
YOU'RE SAYING THAT GOD WON'T LET IT RAIN UNLESS YOU SAY SO?
I SHALL LEAVE YOU ALONE WITH YOUR THOUGHTS.
I SHALL LEAVE YOU ALONE ...
HOW CAN A PROPHET LIKE THAT EXIST?
I'LL KILL ALL GOD'S PROPHETS SO MY HUSBAND WON'T WORRY.

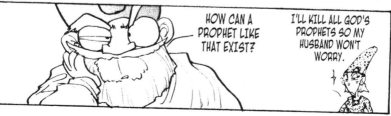

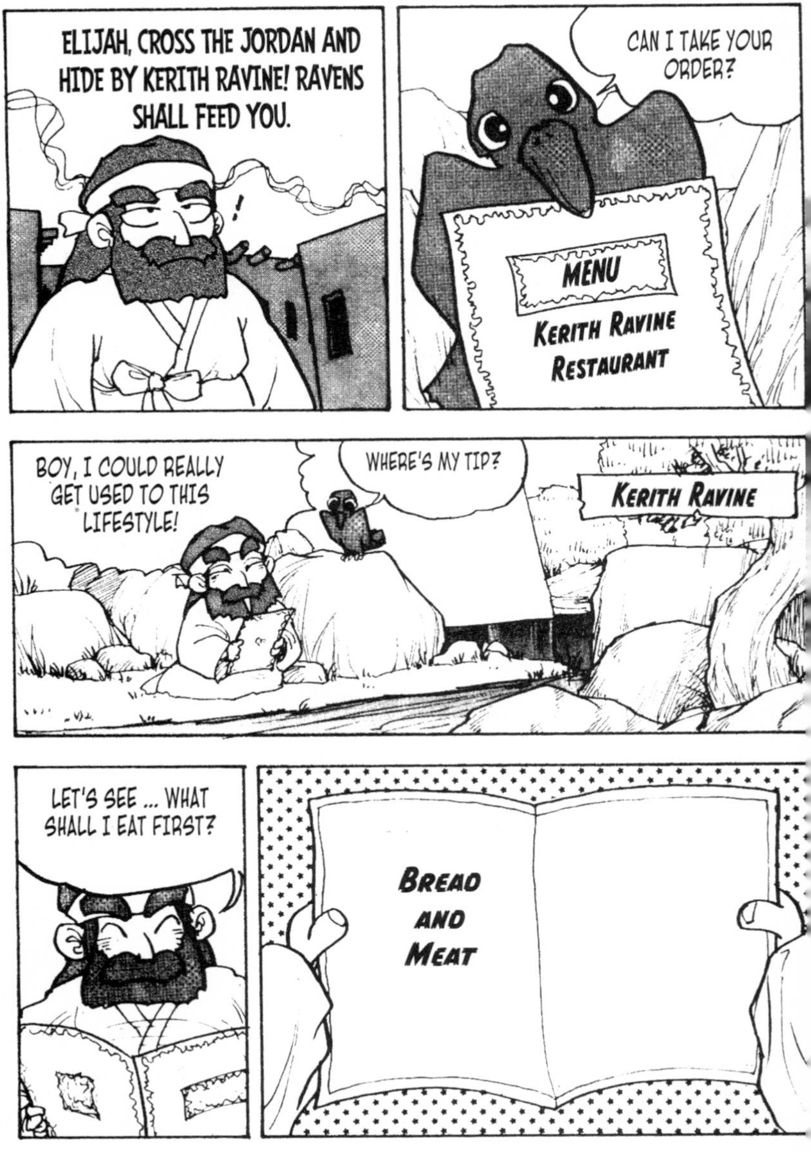
ELIJAH, CROSS THE JORDAN AND HIDE BY KERITH RAVINE! RAVENS SHALL FEED YOU.
!
CAN I TAKE YOUR ORDER?
MENU
KERITH RAVINE RESTAURANT
BOY, I COULD REALLY GET USED TO THIS LIFESTYLE!
WHERE'S MY TIP?
KERITH RAVINE
LET'S SEE ... WHAT SHALL I EAT FIRST?
BREAD AND MEAT

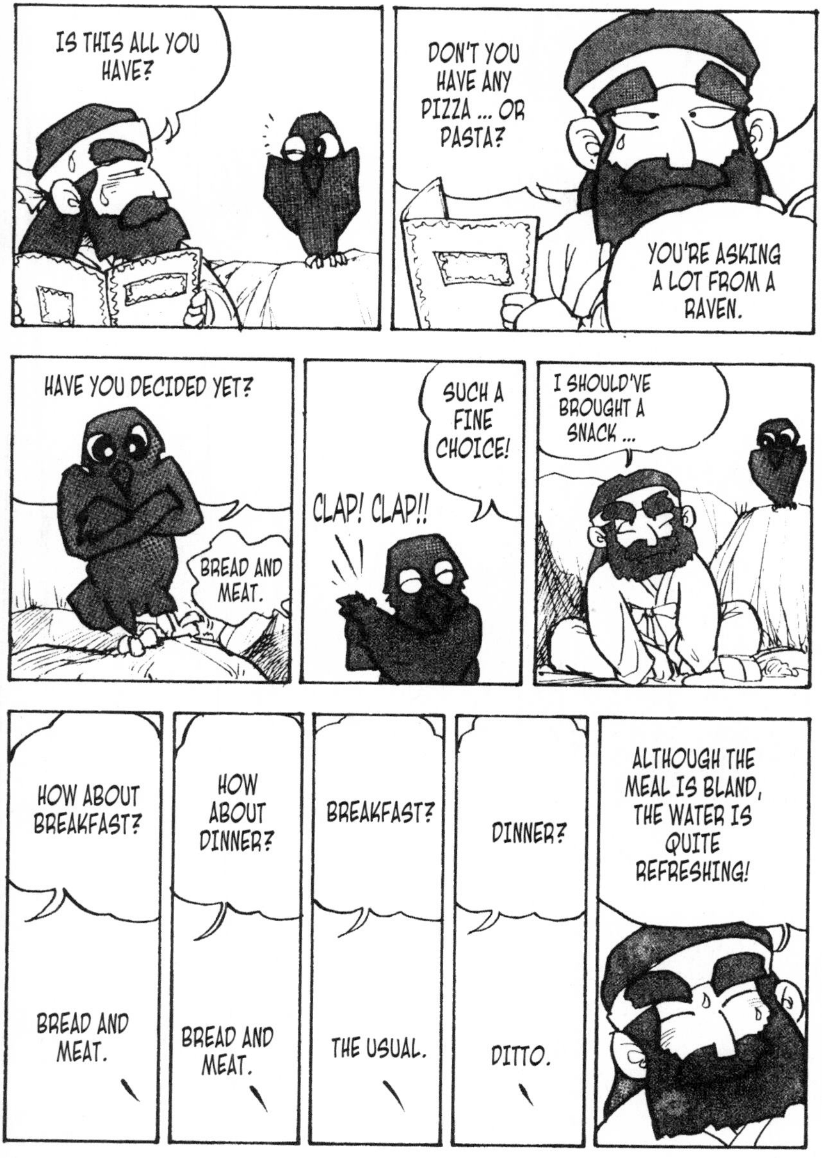
IS THIS ALL YOU HAVE?
DON'T YOU HAVE ANY PIZZA ... OR PASTA?
YOU'RE ASKING A LOT FROM A RAVEN.
HAVE YOU DECIDED YET?
BREAD AND MEAT.
CLAP! CLAP!!
SUCH A FINE CHOICE!
I SHOULD'VE BROUGHT A SNACK ...
HOW ABOUT BREAKFAST?
BREAD AND MEAT.
HOW ABOUT DINNER?
BREAD AND MEAT.
BREAKFAST?
THE USUAL.
DINNER?
DITTO.
ALTHOUGH THE MEAL IS BLAND, THE WATER IS QUITE REFRESHING!

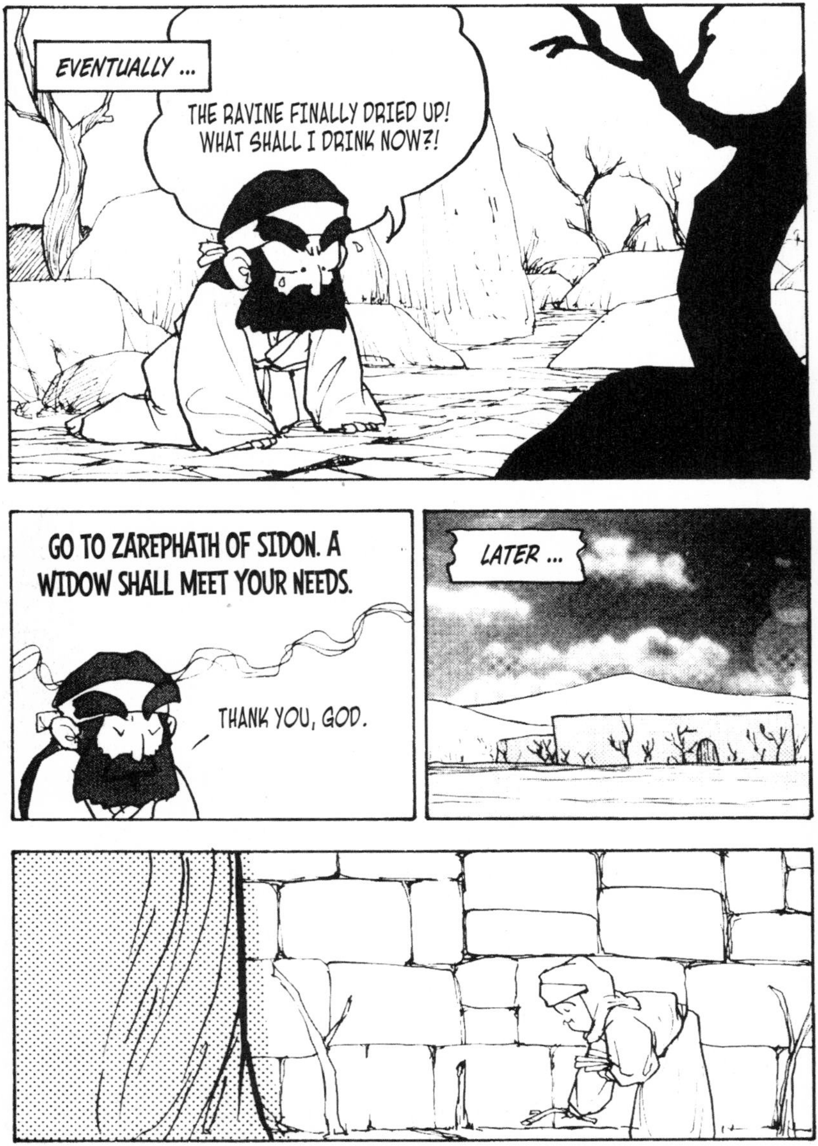
EVENTUALLY ...
THE RAVINE FINALLY DRIED UP! WHAT SHALL I DRINK NOW?!
GO TO ZAREPHATH OF SIDON. A WIDOW SHALL MEET YOUR NEEDS.
THANK YOU, GOD.
LATER ...

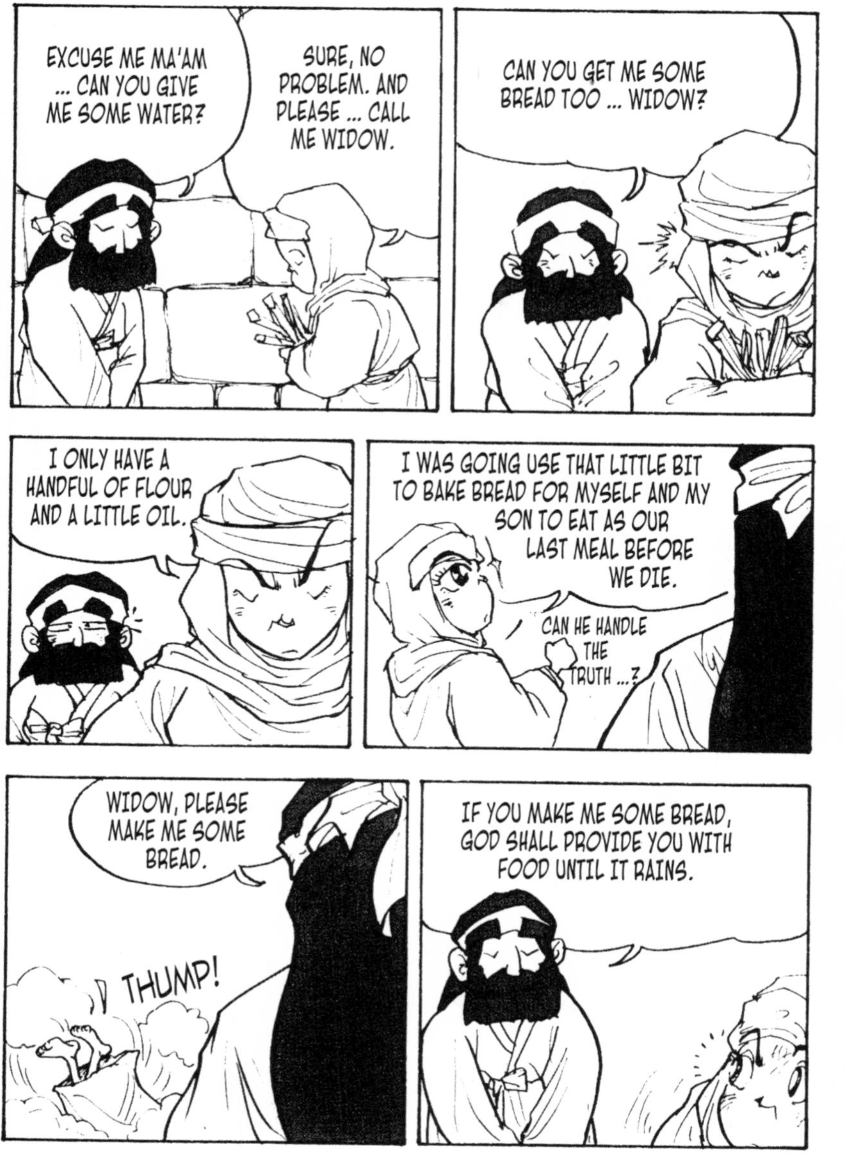
EXCUSE ME MA'AM ... CAN YOU GIVE ME SOME WATER?
SURE, NO PROBLEM. AND PLEASE ... CALL ME WIDOW.
CAN YOU GET ME SOME BREAD TOO ... WIDOW?
I ONLY HAVE A HANDFUL OF FLOUR AND A LITTLE OIL.
I WAS GOING USE THAT LITTLE BIT TO BAKE BREAD FOR MYSELF AND MY SON TO EAT AS OUR LAST MEAL BEFORE WE DIE.
CAN HE HANDLE THE TRUTH ...?
WIDOW, PLEASE MAKE ME SOME BREAD.
THUMP!
IF YOU MAKE ME SOME BREAD, GOD SHALL PROVIDE YOU WITH FOOD UNTIL IT RAINS.

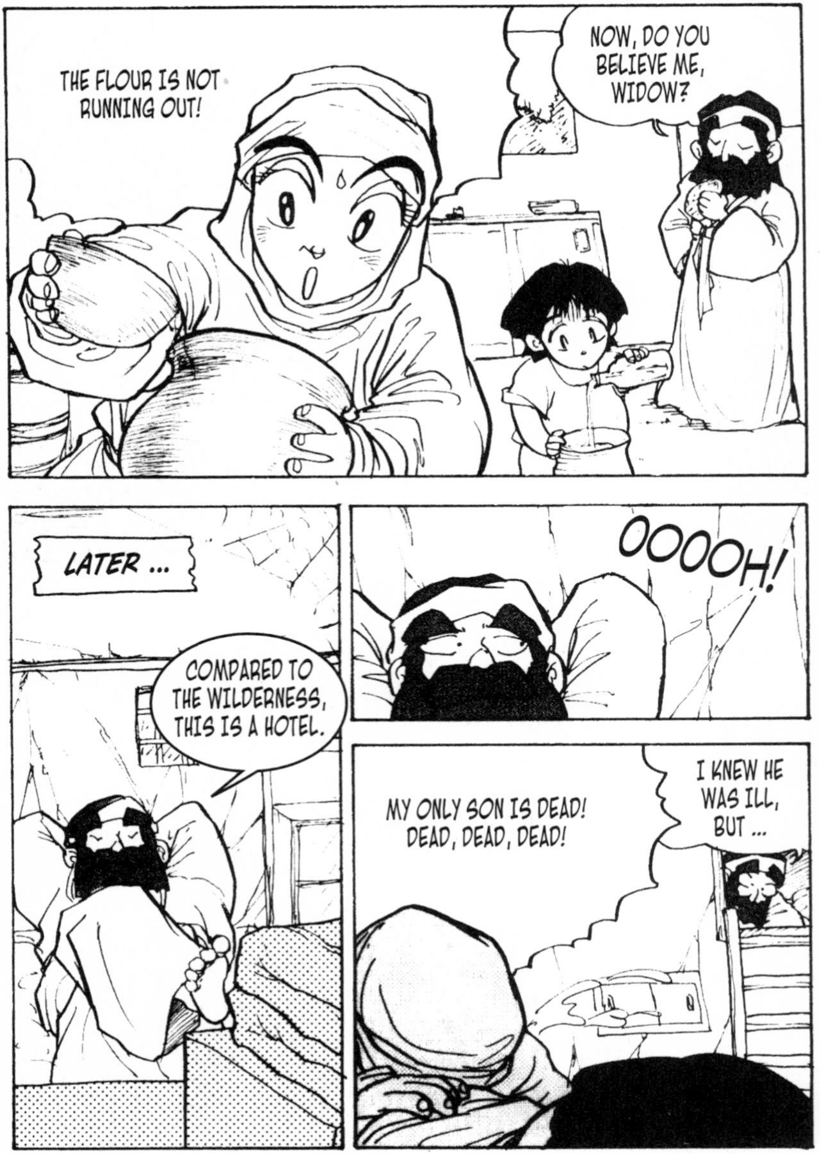
THE FLOUR IS NOT RUNNING OUT!
NOW, DO YOU BELIEVE ME, WIDOW?
LATER ...
COMPARED TO THE WILDERNESS, THIS IS A HOTEL.
OOOOH!
MY ONLY SON IS DEAD! DEAD, DEAD, DEAD!
I KNEW HE WAS ILL, BUT ...

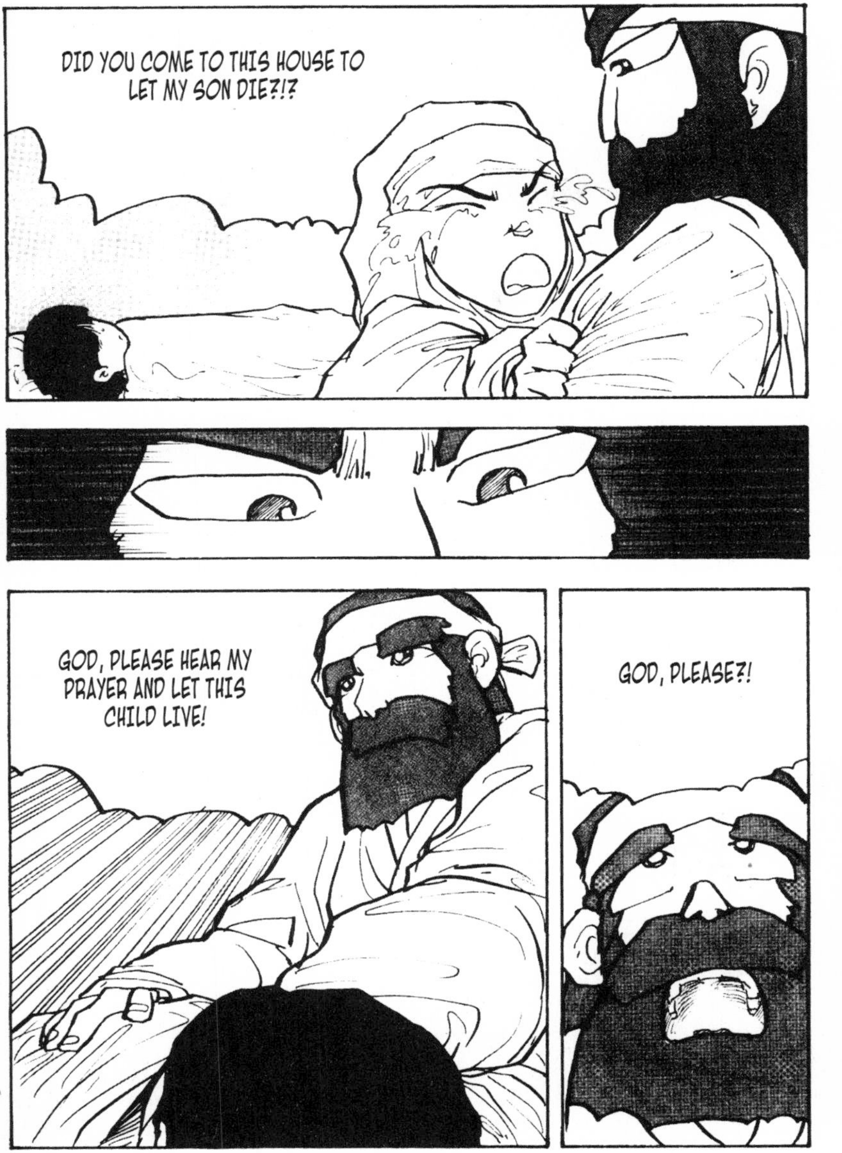
DID YOU COME TO THIS HOUSE TO LET MY SON DIE?!?
GOD, PLEASE HEAR MY PRAYER AND LET THIS CHILD LIVE!
GOD, PLEASE?!

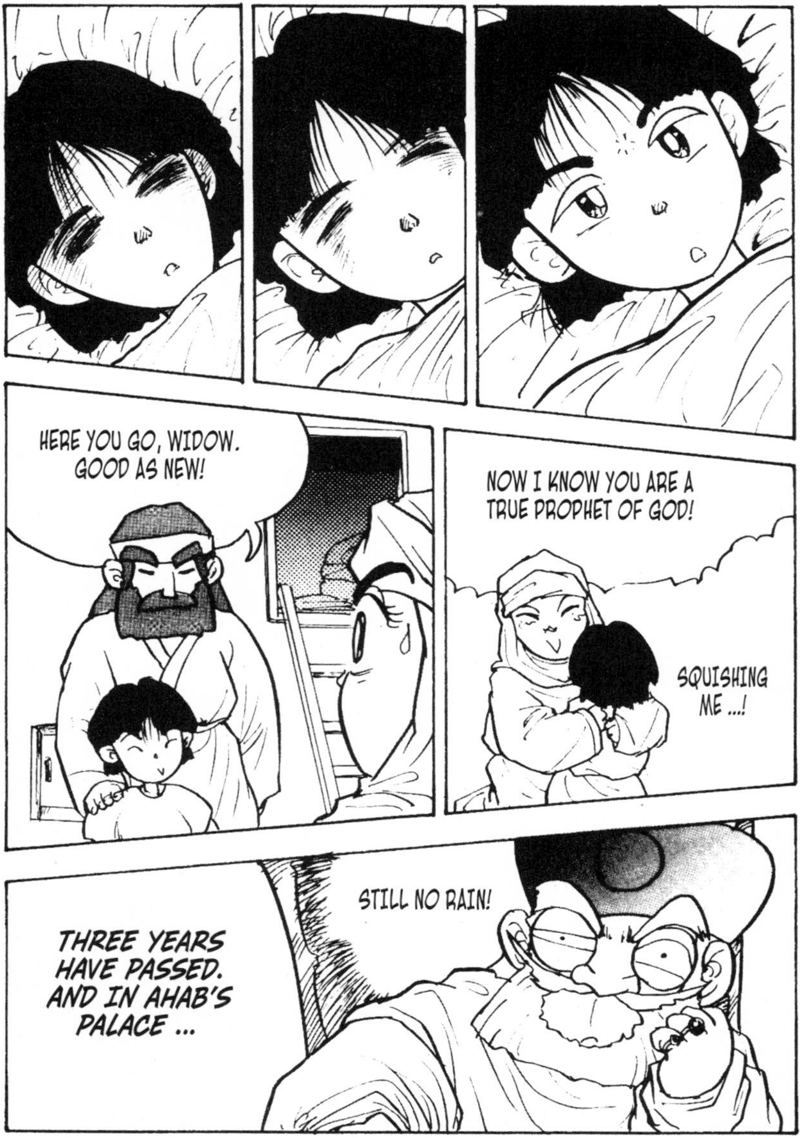
HERE YOU GO, WIDOW.
GOOD AS NEW!
NOW I KNOW YOU ARE A
TRUE PROPHET OF GOD!
SQUISHING
ME ...!
THREE YEARS
HAVE PASSED.
AND IN AHAB'S
PALACE ...
STILL NO RAIN!

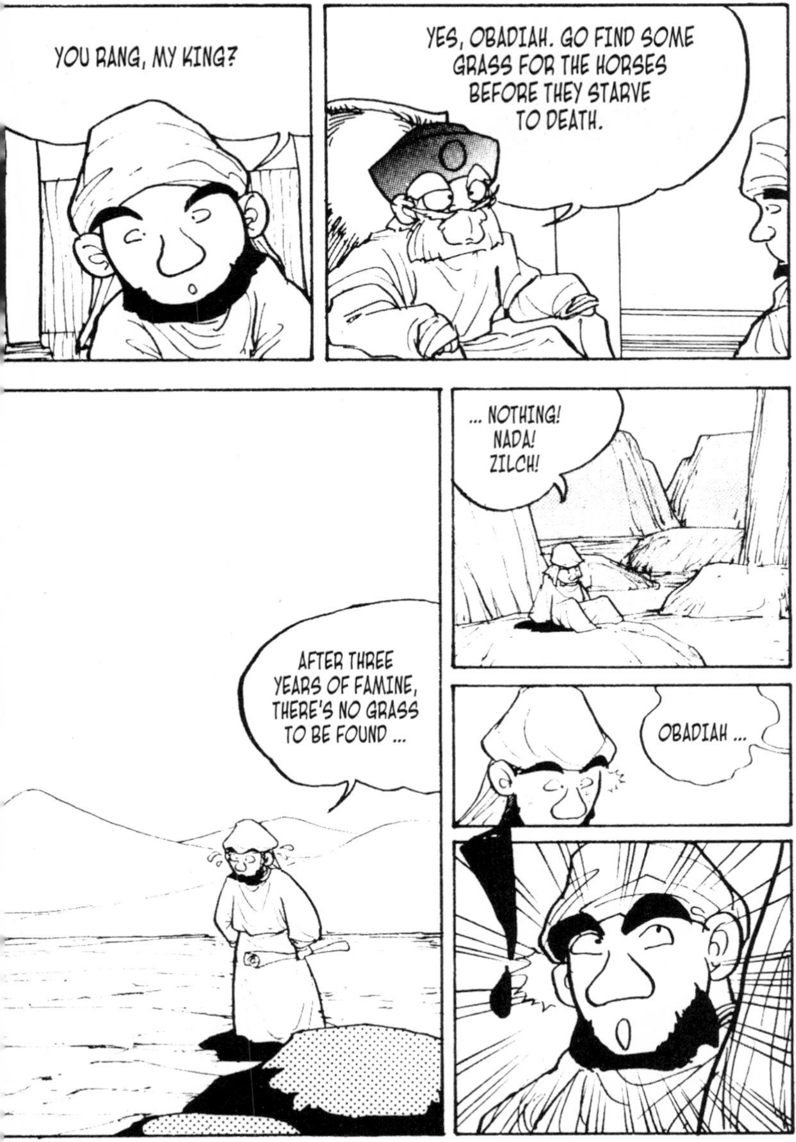
YOU RANG, MY KING?
YES, OBADIAH. GO FIND SOME GRASS FOR THE HORSES BEFORE THEY STARVE TO DEATH.
AFTER THREE YEARS OF FAMINE, THERE'S NO GRASS TO BE FOUND ...
... NOTHING! NADA! ZILCH!
OBADIAH ...

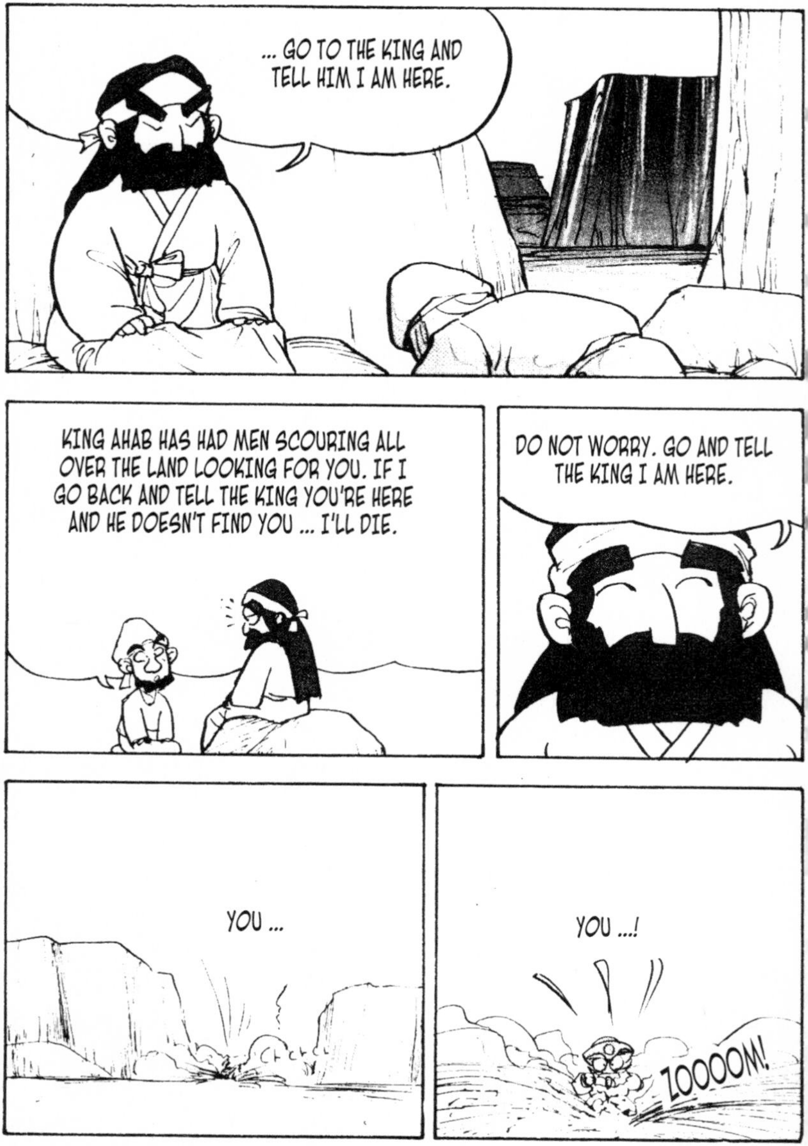
... GO TO THE KING AND TELL HIM I AM HERE.
KING AHAB HAS HAD MEN SCOURING ALL OVER THE LAND LOOKING FOR YOU. IF I GO BACK AND TELL THE KING YOU'RE HERE AND HE DOESN'T FIND YOU ... I'LL DIE.
DO NOT WORRY. GO AND TELL THE KING I AM HERE.
YOU ...
YOU ...!
ZOOOOM!

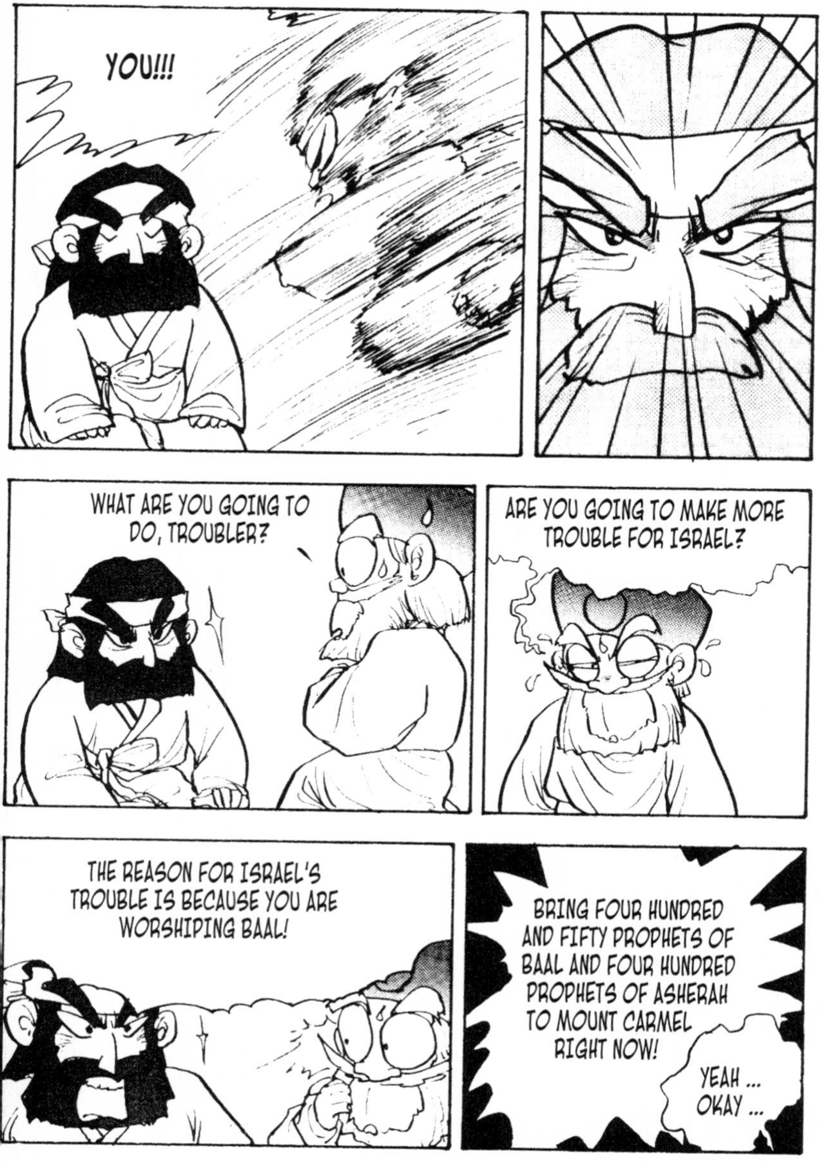
YOU!!!
WHAT ARE YOU GOING TO DO, TROUBLER?
ARE YOU GOING TO MAKE MORE TROUBLE FOR ISRAEL?
THE REASON FOR ISRAEL'S TROUBLE IS BECAUSE YOU ARE WORSHIPING BAAL!
BRING FOUR HUNDRED AND FIFTY PROPHETS OF BAAL AND FOUR HUNDRED PROPHETS OF ASHERAH TO MOUNT CARMEL RIGHT NOW!
YEAH ... OKAY ...

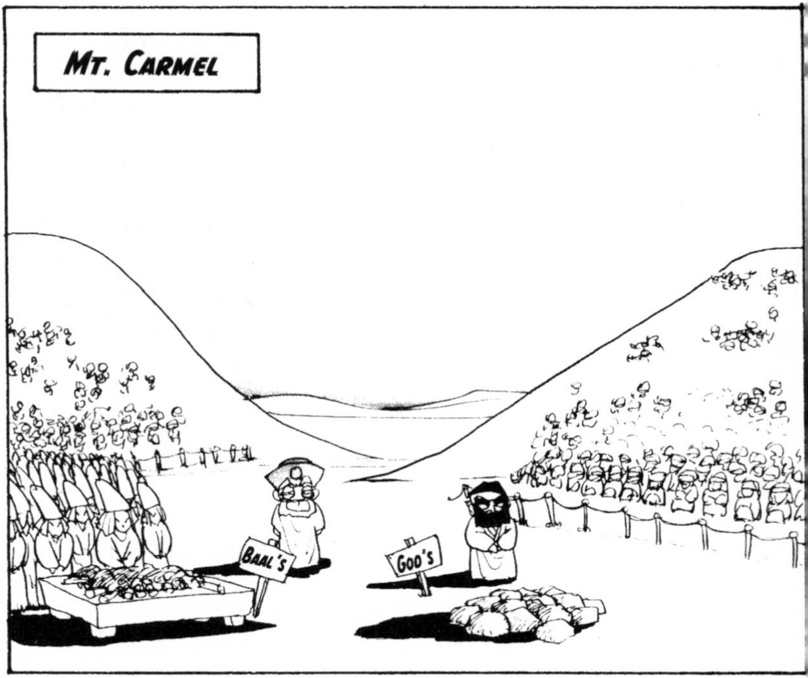
MT. CARMEL
BAAL'S
GOD'S

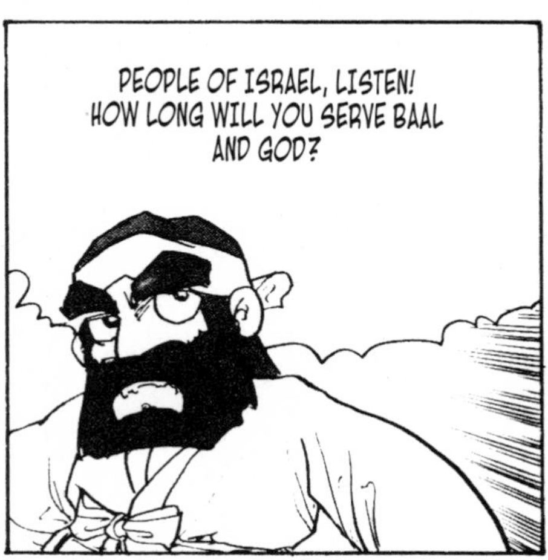
PEOPLE OF ISRAEL, LISTEN! HOW LONG WILL YOU SERVE BAAL AND GOD?

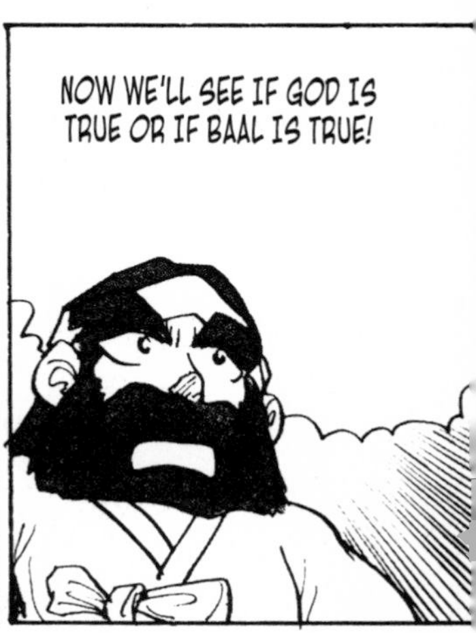
NOW WE'LL SEE IF GOD IS TRUE OR IF BAAL IS TRUE!

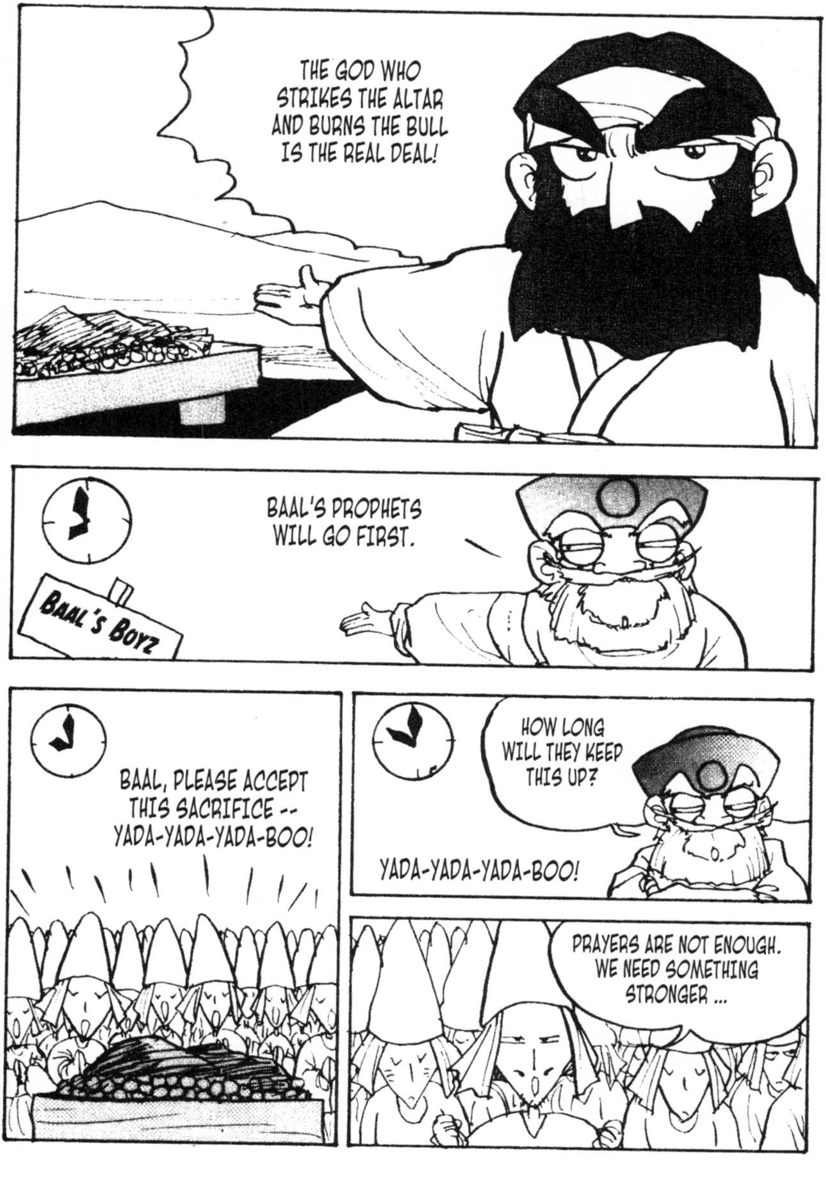
THE GOD WHO STRIKES THE ALTAR AND BURNS THE BULL IS THE REAL DEAL!
BAAL'S PROPHETS WILL GO FIRST.
BAAL'S BOYZ
BAAL, PLEASE ACCEPT THIS SACRIFICE -- YADA-YADA-YADA-BOO!
HOW LONG WILL THEY KEEP THIS UP?
YADA-YADA-YADA-BOO!
PRAYERS ARE NOT ENOUGH. WE NEED SOMETHING STRONGER ...

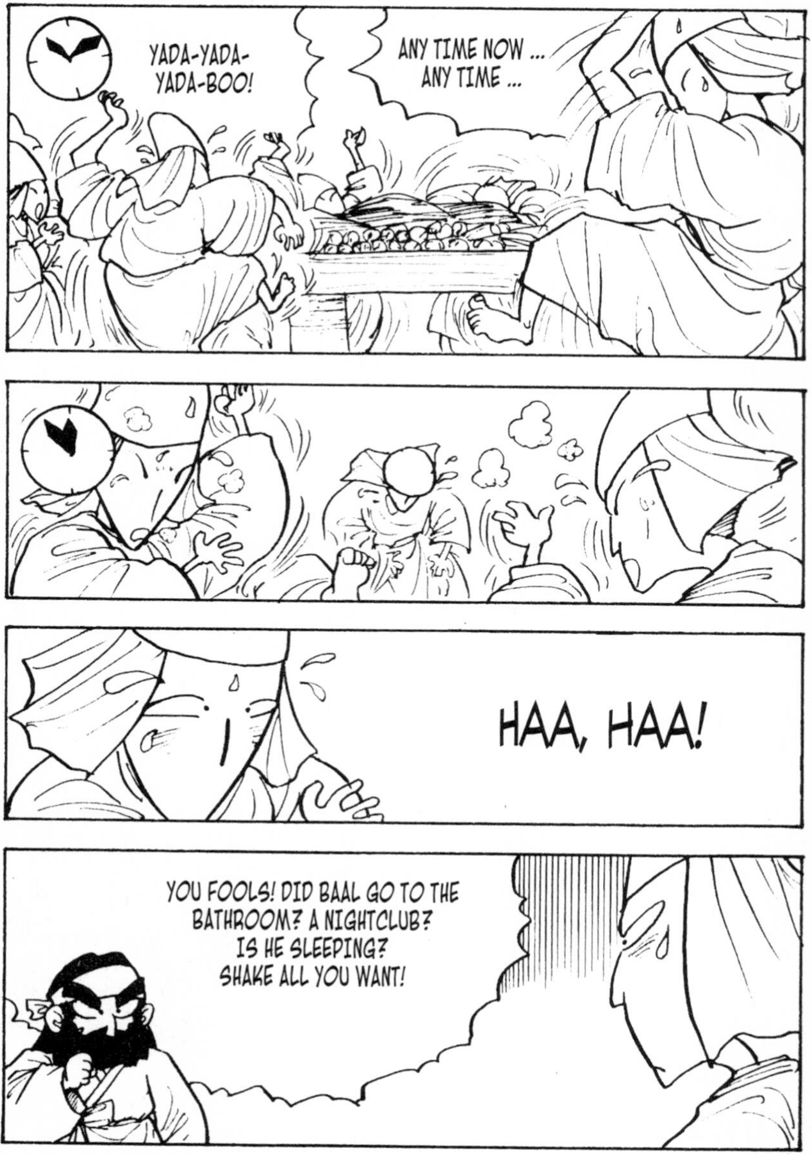
YADA-YADA-YADA-BOO!
ANY TIME NOW ... ANY TIME ...
HAA, HAA!
YOU FOOLS! DID BAAL GO TO THE BATHROOM? A NIGHTCLUB? IS HE SLEEPING? SHAKE ALL YOU WANT!

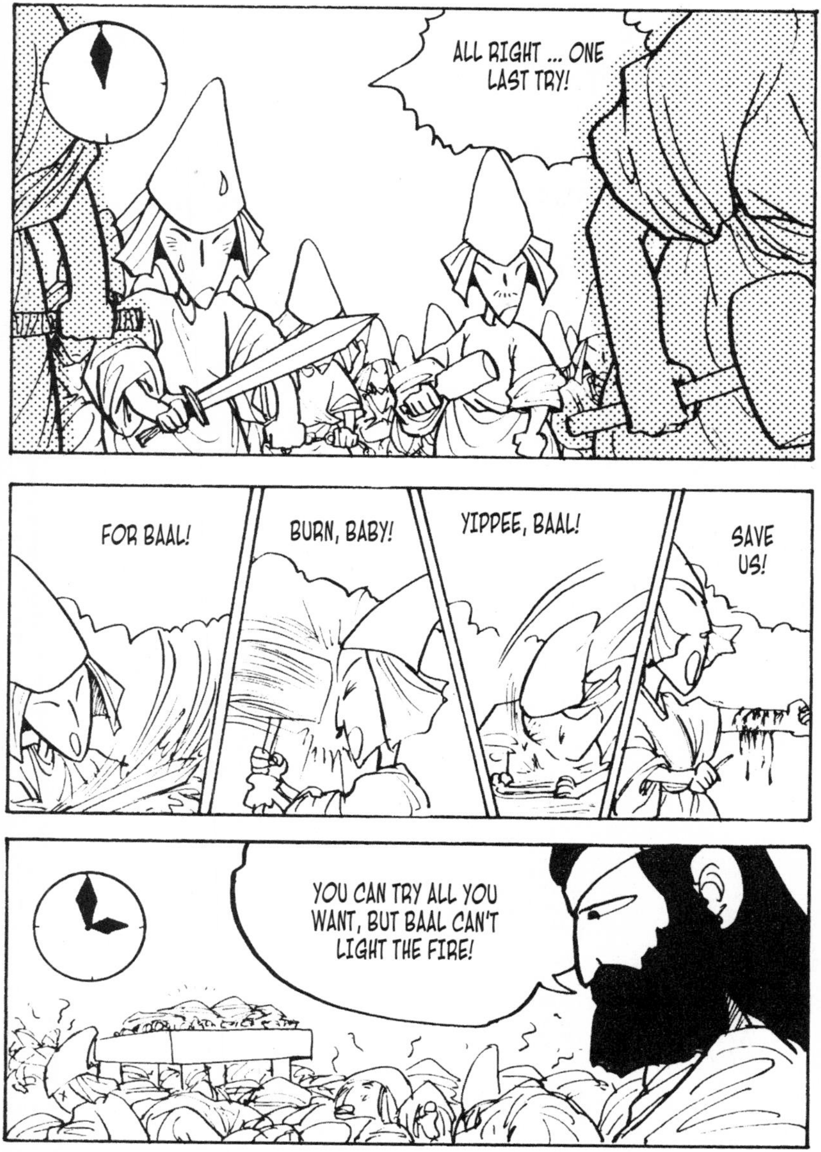
ALL RIGHT ... ONE LAST TRY!
FOR BAAL!
BURN, BABY!
YIPPEE, BAAL!
SAVE US!
YOU CAN TRY ALL YOU WANT, BUT BAAL CAN'T LIGHT THE FIRE!

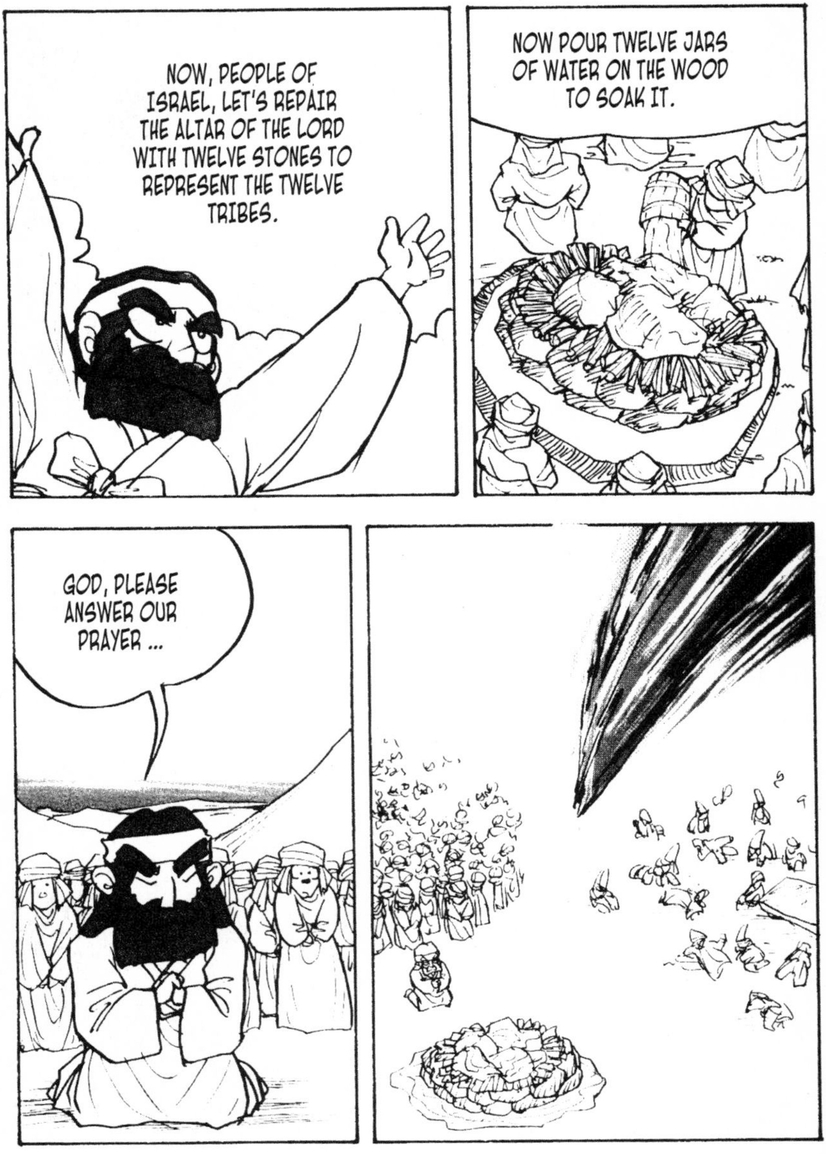
NOW, PEOPLE OF ISRAEL, LET'S REPAIR THE ALTAR OF THE LORD WITH TWELVE STONES TO REPRESENT THE TWELVE TRIBES.
NOW POUR TWELVE JARS OF WATER ON THE WOOD TO SOAK IT.
GOD, PLEASE ANSWER OUR PRAYER ...

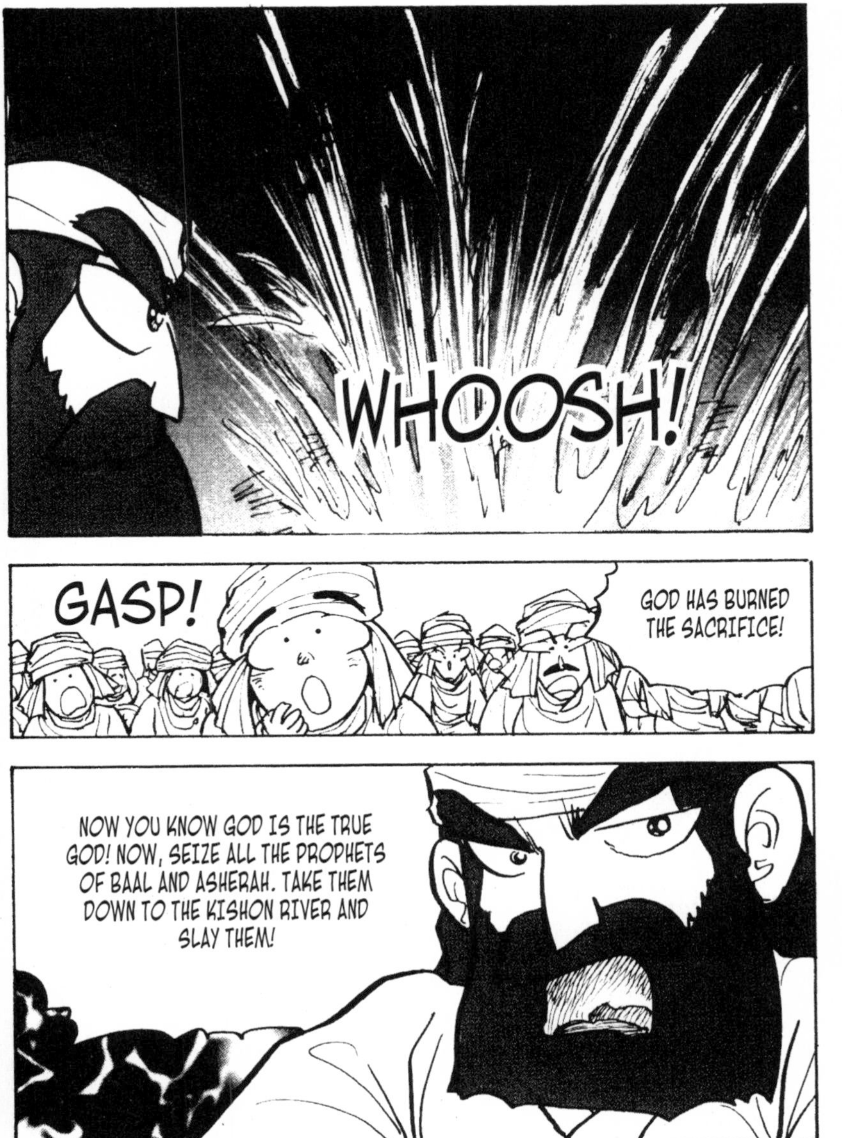
WHOOSH!
GASP!
GOD HAS BURNED THE SACRIFICE!
NOW YOU KNOW GOD IS THE TRUE GOD! NOW, SEIZE ALL THE PROPHETS OF BAAL AND ASHERAH. TAKE THEM DOWN TO THE KISHON RIVER AND SLAY THEM!

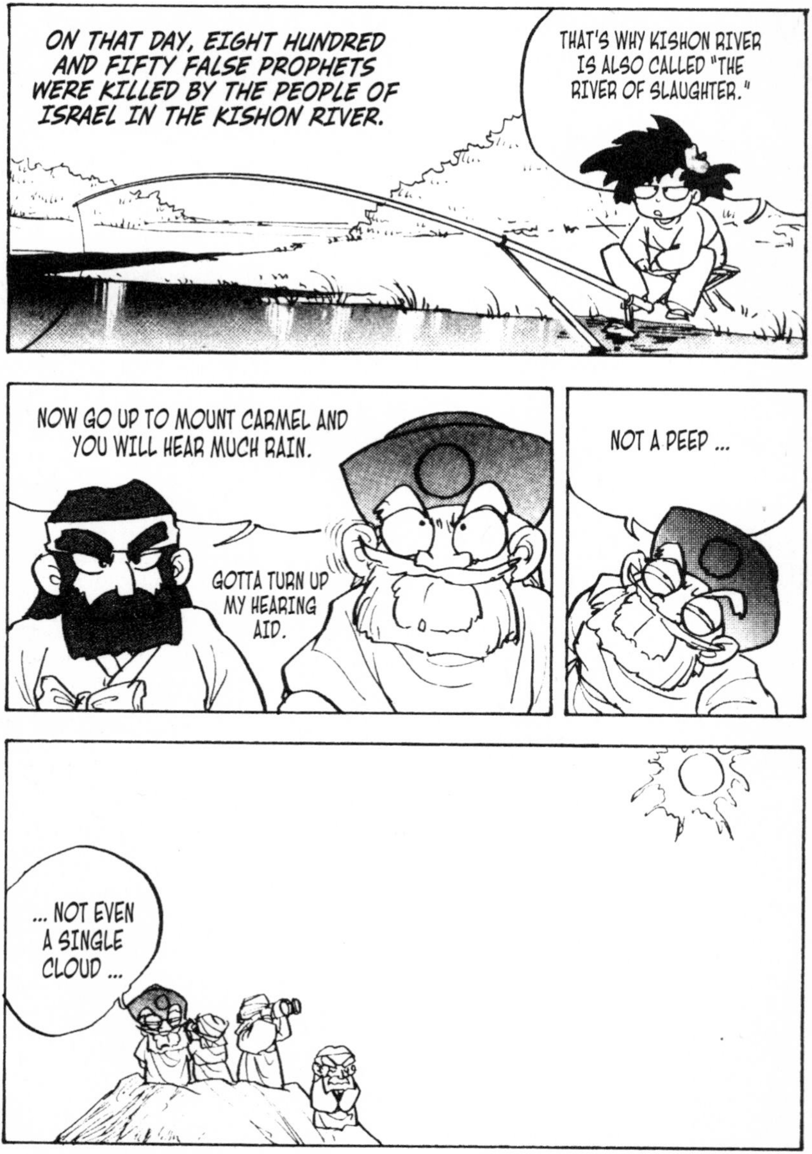
ON THAT DAY, EIGHT HUNDRED AND FIFTY FALSE PROPHETS WERE KILLED BY THE PEOPLE OF ISRAEL IN THE KISHON RIVER.
THAT'S WHY KISHON RIVER IS ALSO CALLED "THE RIVER OF SLAUGHTER."
NOW GO UP TO MOUNT CARMEL AND YOU WILL HEAR MUCH RAIN.
GOTTA TURN UP MY HEARING AID.
NOT A PEEP ...
... NOT EVEN A SINGLE CLOUD ...

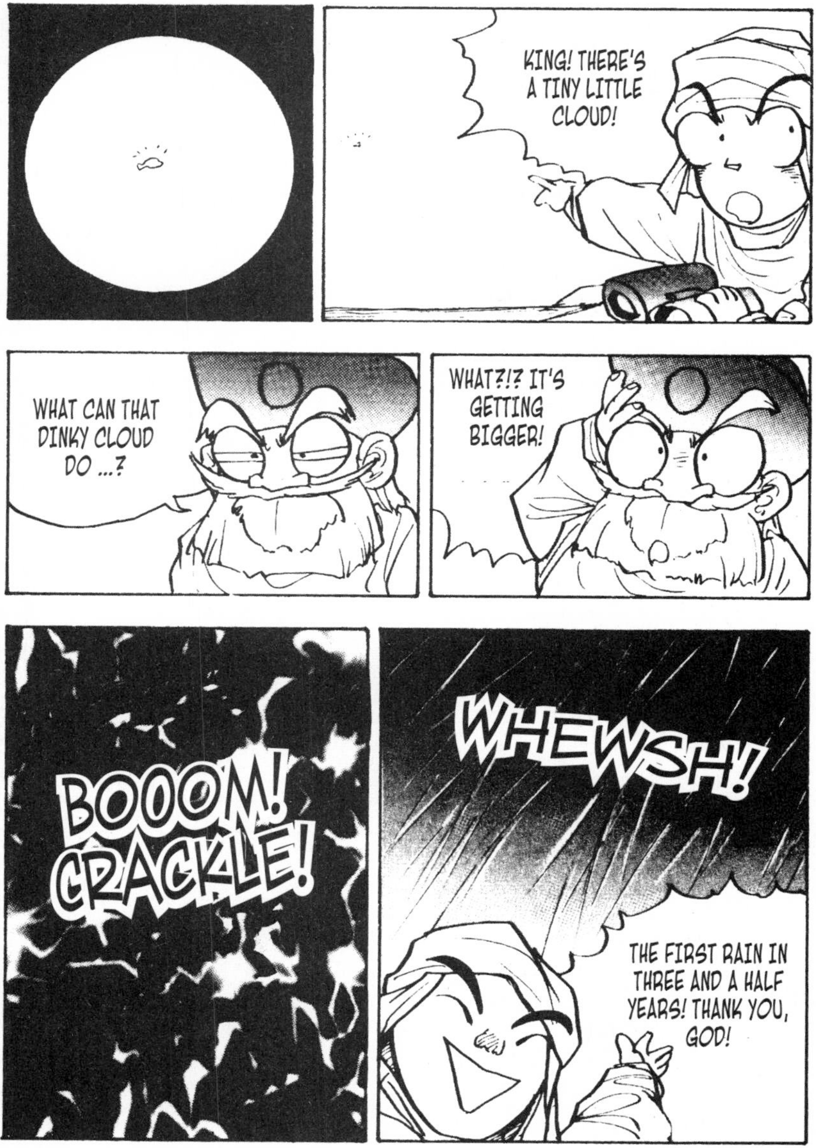
KING! THERE'S A TINY LITTLE CLOUD!
WHAT CAN THAT DINKY CLOUD DO ...?
WHAT?!? IT'S GETTING BIGGER!
BOOOM! CRACKLE!
WHEWSH!
THE FIRST RAIN IN THREE AND A HALF YEARS! THANK YOU, GOD!

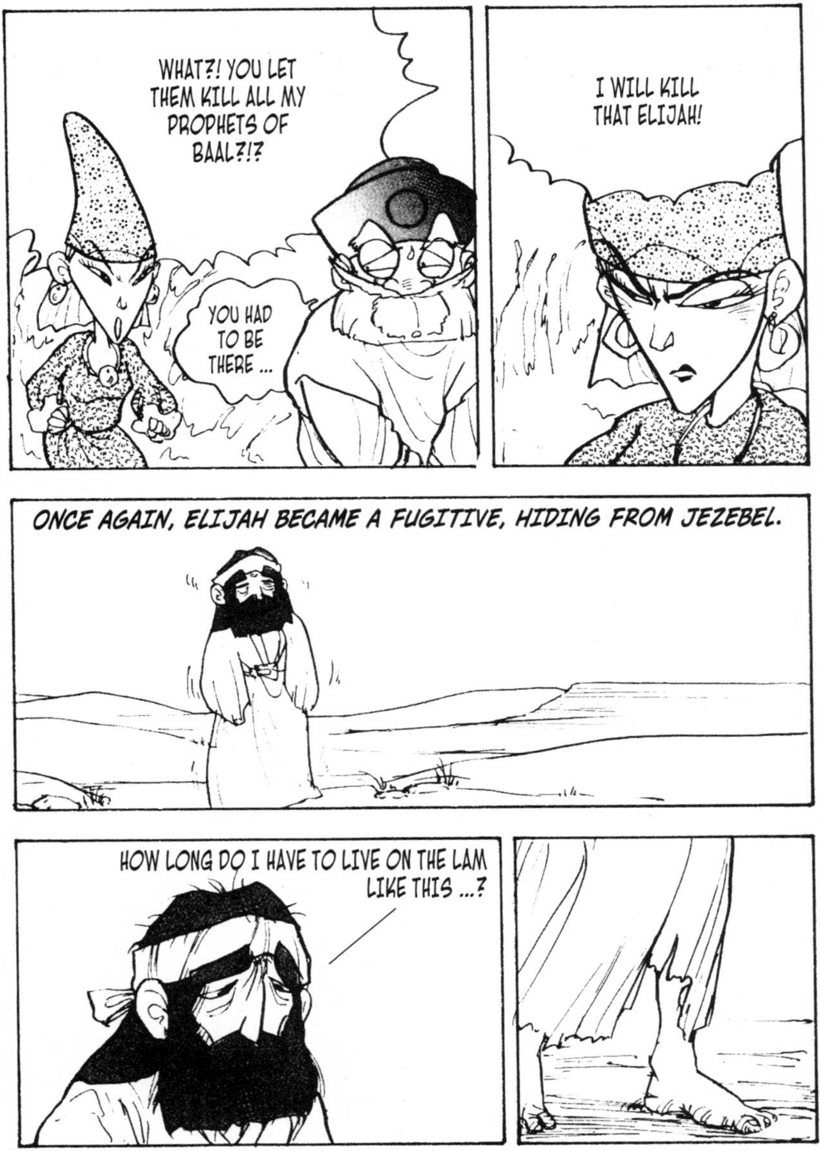
WHAT?! YOU LET THEM KILL ALL MY PROPHETS OF BAAL?!?
YOU HAD TO BE THERE ...
I WILL KILL THAT ELIJAH!
ONCE AGAIN, ELIJAH BECAME A FUGITIVE, HIDING FROM JEZEBEL.
HOW LONG DO I HAVE TO LIVE ON THE LAM LIKE THIS ...?

LORD, JUST LET ME DIE IN THIS PLACE.

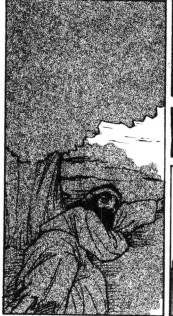

AN ANGEL ...

HERE IS BREAD AND WATER. GET UP!

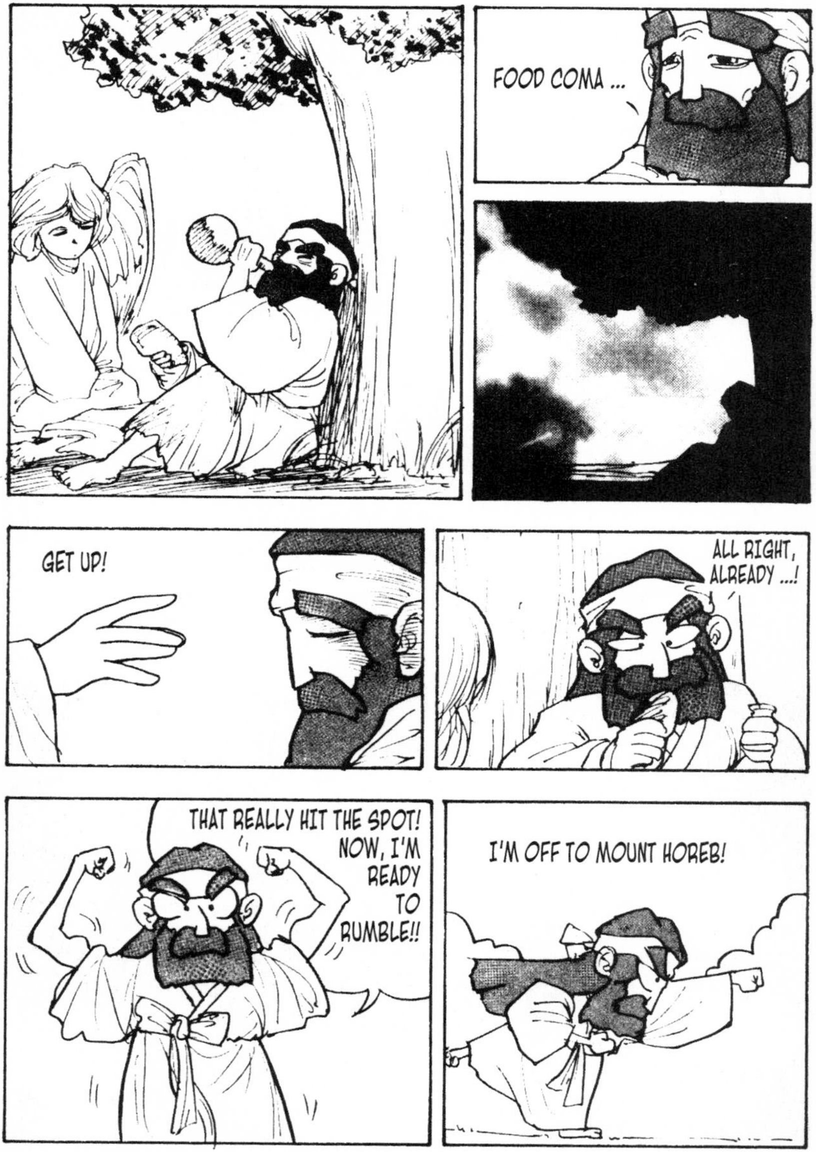
FOOD COMA ...
GET UP!
ALL RIGHT, ALREADY ...!
THAT REALLY HIT THE SPOT! NOW, I'M READY TO RUMBLE!!
I'M OFF TO MOUNT HOREB!

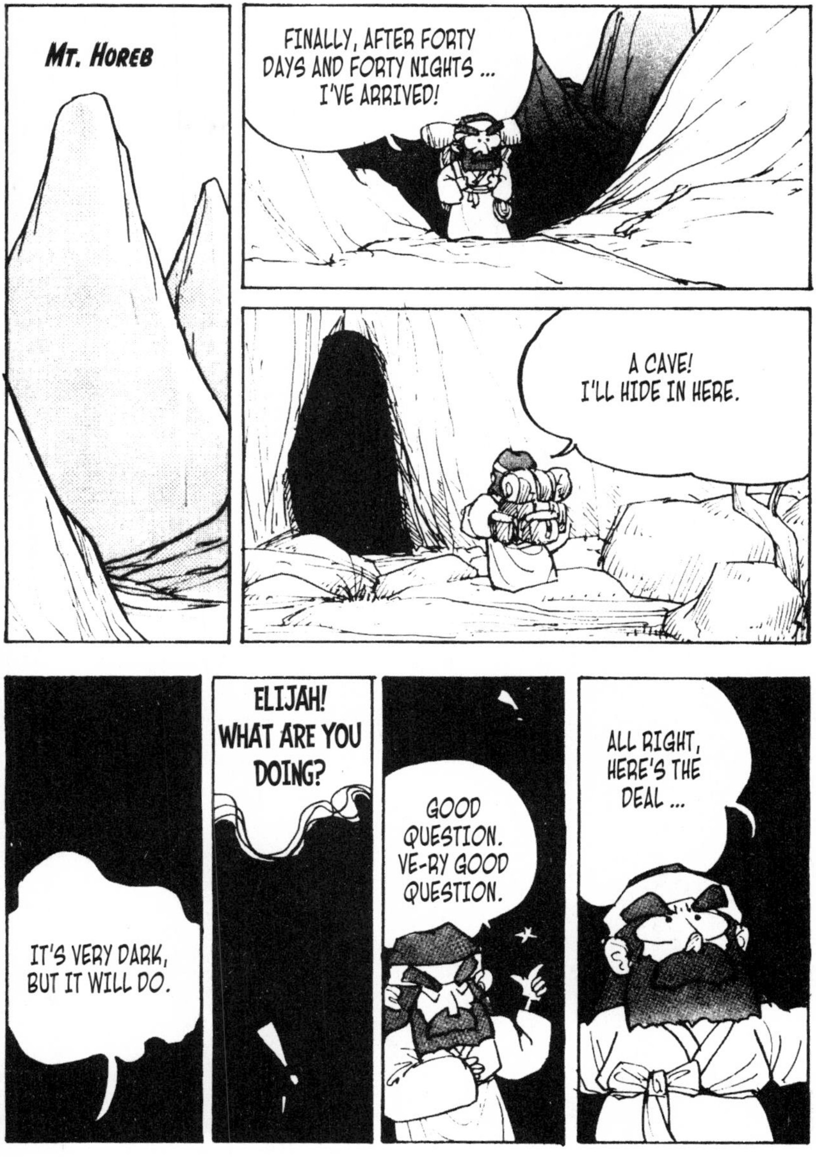
MT. HOREB
FINALLY, AFTER FORTY DAYS AND FORTY NIGHTS ... I'VE ARRIVED!
A CAVE! I'LL HIDE IN HERE.
IT'S VERY DARK, BUT IT WILL DO.
ELIJAH! WHAT ARE YOU DOING?
GOOD QUESTION. VE-RY GOOD QUESTION.
ALL RIGHT, HERE'S THE DEAL ...

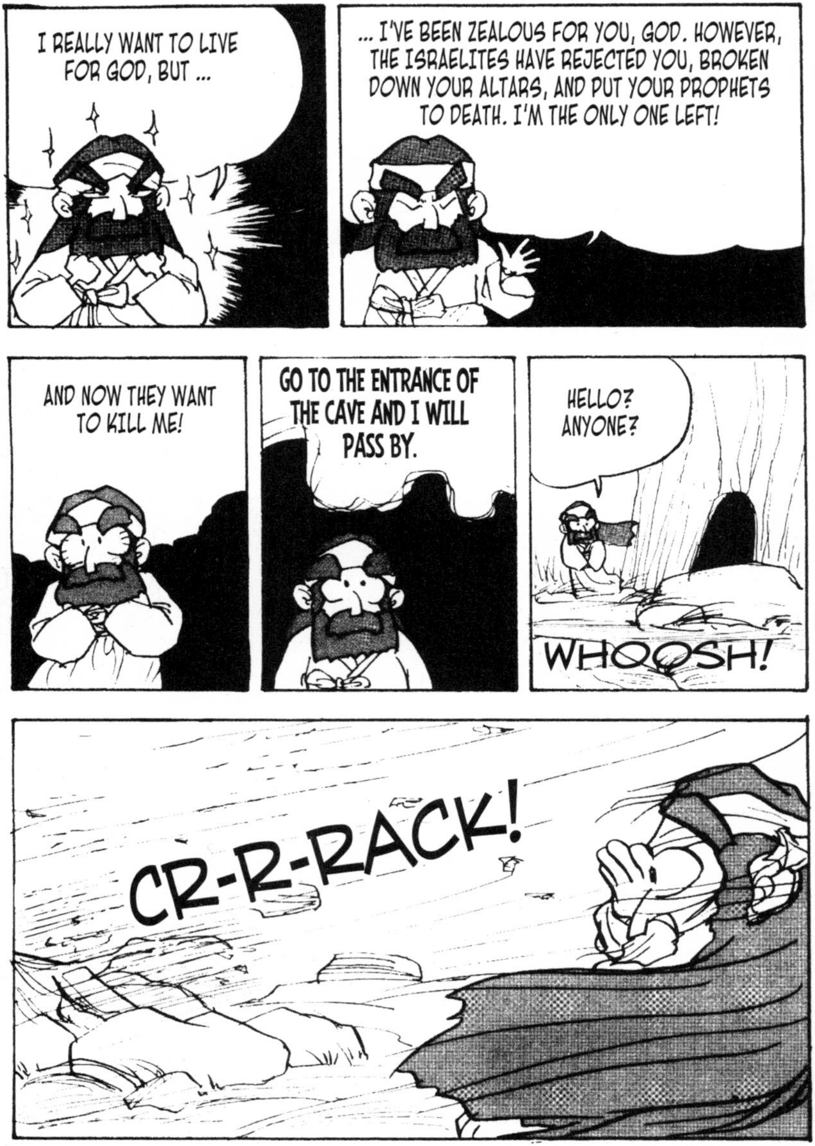
I REALLY WANT TO LIVE FOR GOD, BUT ...
... I'VE BEEN ZEALOUS FOR YOU, GOD. HOWEVER, THE ISRAELITES HAVE REJECTED YOU, BROKEN DOWN YOUR ALTARS, AND PUT YOUR PROPHETS TO DEATH. I'M THE ONLY ONE LEFT!
AND NOW THEY WANT TO KILL ME!
GO TO THE ENTRANCE OF THE CAVE AND I WILL PASS BY.
HELLO? ANYONE?
WHOOSH!
CR-R-RACK!

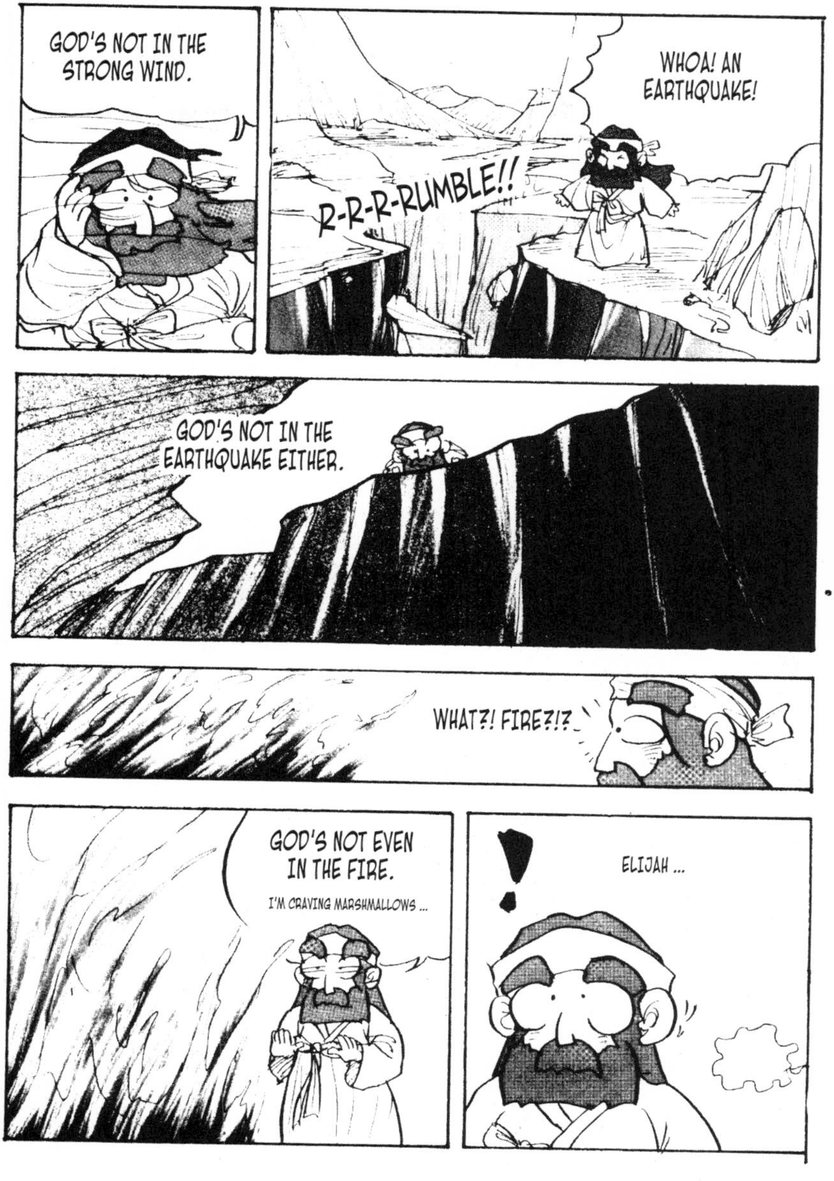
GOD'S NOT IN THE STRONG WIND.
WHOA! AN EARTHQUAKE!
R-R-R-RUMBLE!!
GOD'S NOT IN THE EARTHQUAKE EITHER.
WHAT?! FIRE?!?
GOD'S NOT EVEN IN THE FIRE.
I'M CRAVING MARSHMALLOWS ...
!
ELIJAH ...

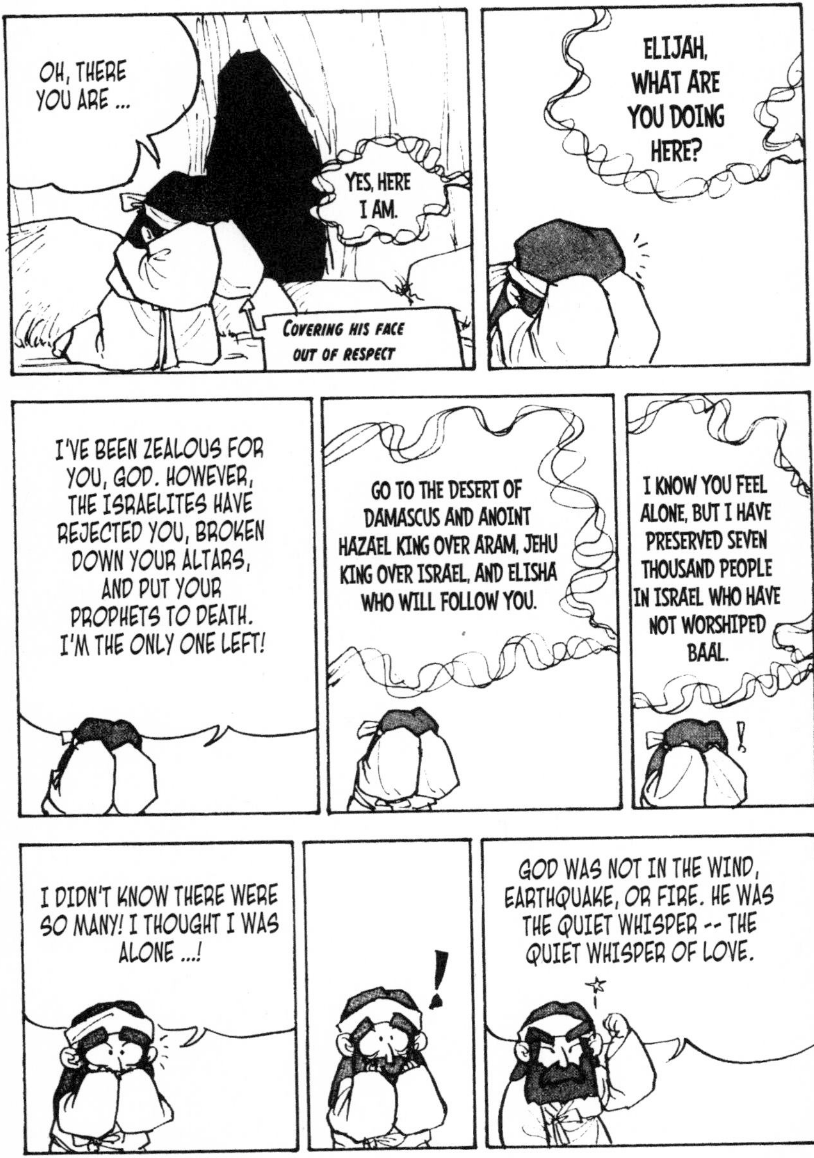
OH, THERE YOU ARE ...
YES, HERE I AM.
COVERING HIS FACE OUT OF RESPECT
ELIJAH, WHAT ARE YOU DOING HERE?
I'VE BEEN ZEALOUS FOR YOU, GOD. HOWEVER, THE ISRAELITES HAVE REJECTED YOU, BROKEN DOWN YOUR ALTARS, AND PUT YOUR PROPHETS TO DEATH. I'M THE ONLY ONE LEFT!
GO TO THE DESERT OF DAMASCUS AND ANOINT HAZAEL KING OVER ARAM, JEHU KING OVER ISRAEL, AND ELISHA WHO WILL FOLLOW YOU.
I KNOW YOU FEEL ALONE, BUT I HAVE PRESERVED SEVEN THOUSAND PEOPLE IN ISRAEL WHO HAVE NOT WORSHIPED BAAL.
!
I DIDN'T KNOW THERE WERE SO MANY! I THOUGHT I WAS ALONE ...!
!
GOD WAS NOT IN THE WIND, EARTHQUAKE, OR FIRE. HE WAS THE QUIET WHISPER -- THE QUIET WHISPER OF LOVE.

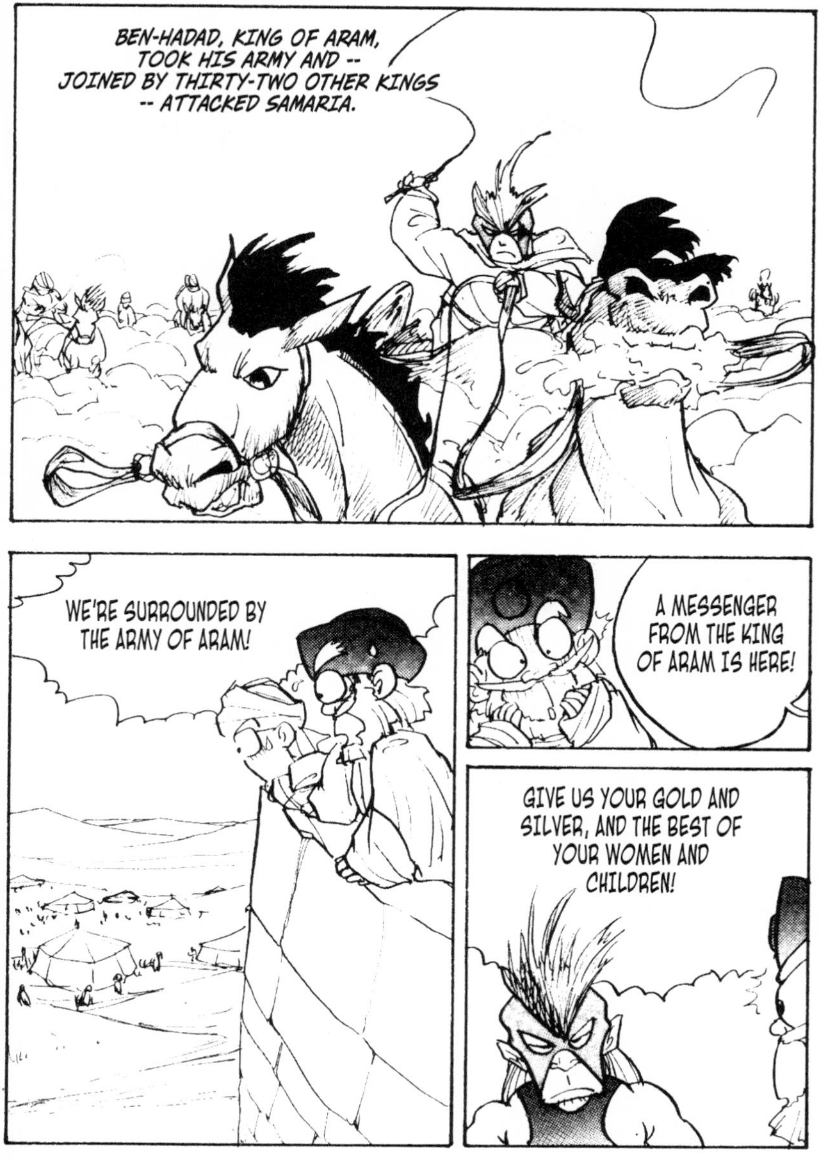
BEN-HADAD, KING OF ARAM, TOOK HIS ARMY AND -- JOINED BY THIRTY-TWO OTHER KINGS -- ATTACKED SAMARIA.
WE'RE SURROUNDED BY THE ARMY OF ARAM!
A MESSENGER FROM THE KING OF ARAM IS HERE!
GIVE US YOUR GOLD AND SILVER, AND THE BEST OF YOUR WOMEN AND CHILDREN!

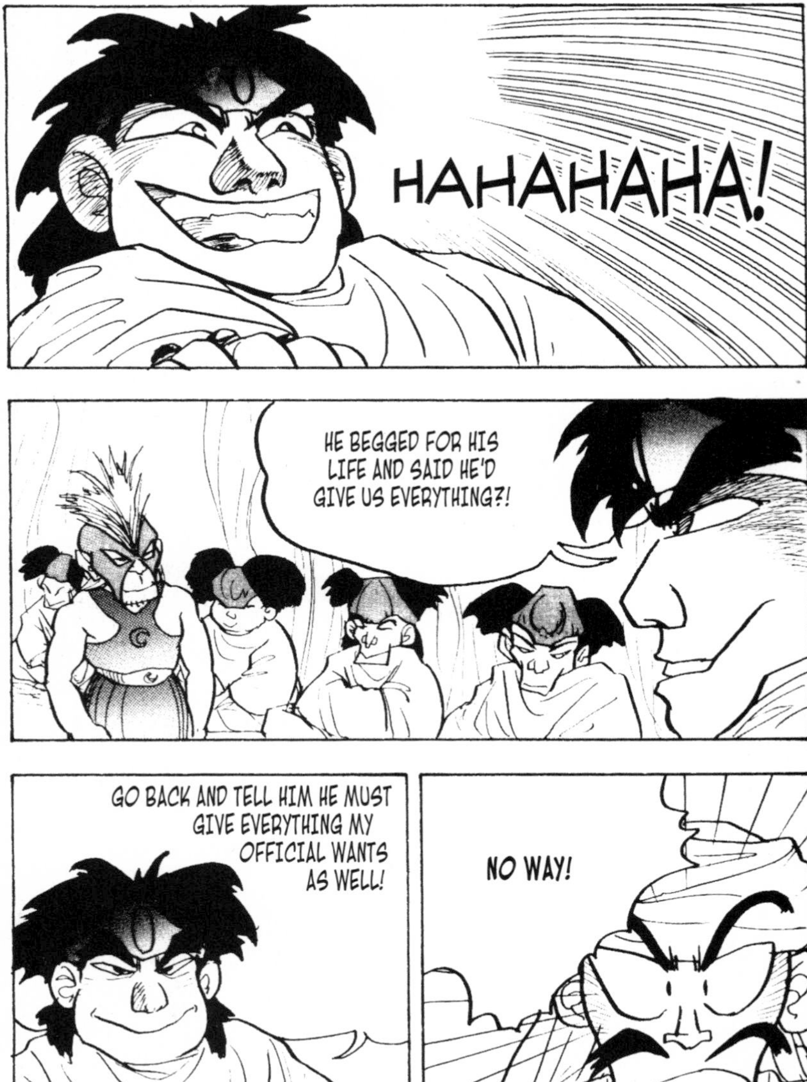
HAHAHAHA!
HE BEGGED FOR HIS LIFE AND SAID HE'D GIVE US EVERYTHING?!
GO BACK AND TELL HIM HE MUST GIVE EVERYTHING MY OFFICIAL WANTS AS WELL!
NO WAY!

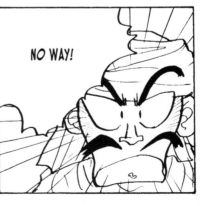

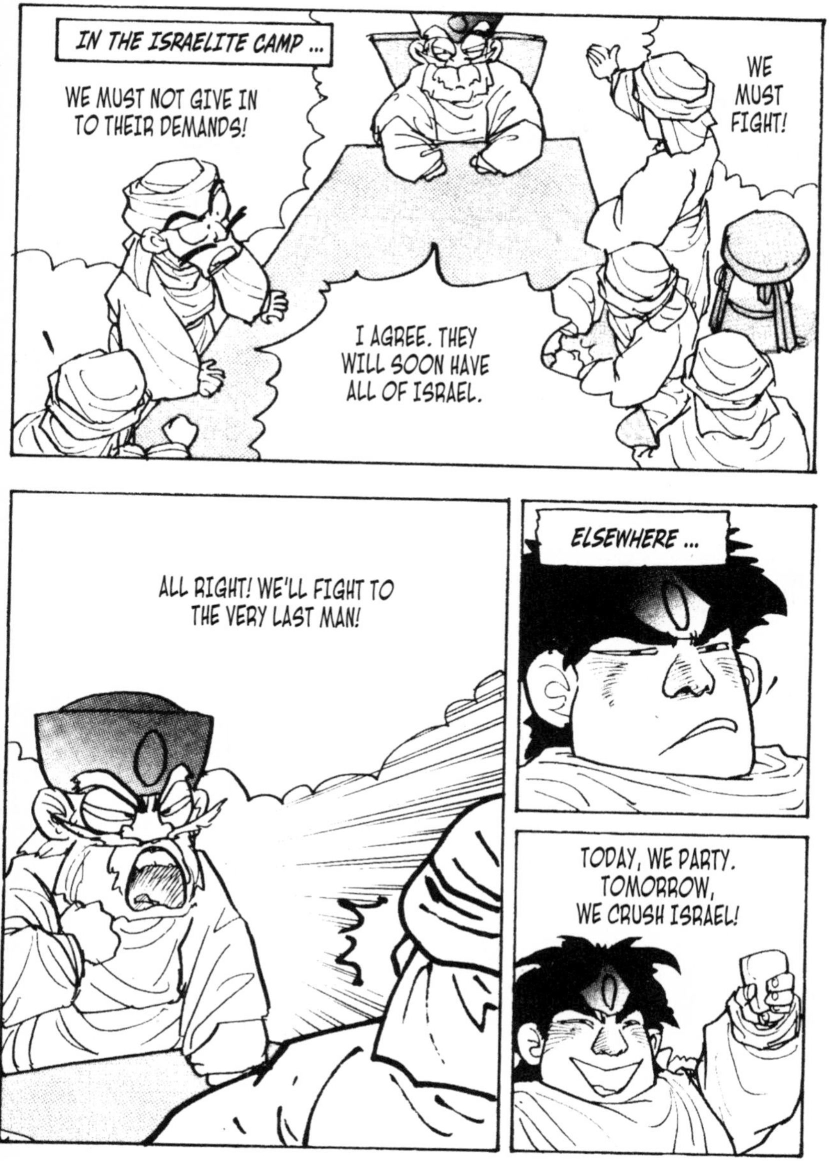
IN THE ISRAELITE CAMP ...
WE MUST NOT GIVE IN TO THEIR DEMANDS!
WE MUST FIGHT!
I AGREE. THEY WILL SOON HAVE ALL OF ISRAEL.
ALL RIGHT! WE'LL FIGHT TO THE VERY LAST MAN!
ELSEWHERE ...
TODAY, WE PARTY. TOMORROW, WE CRUSH ISRAEL!

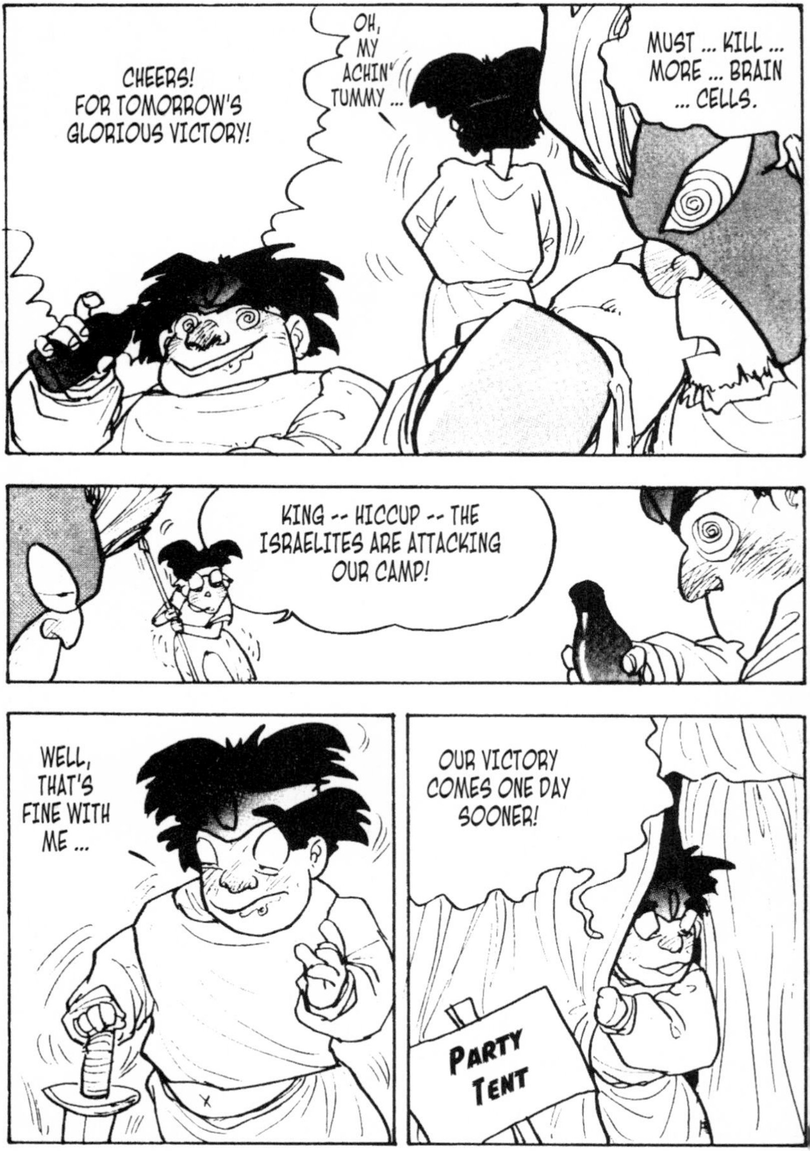

CHEERS! FOR TOMORROW'S GLORIOUS VICTORY!
OH, MY ACHIN' TUMMY ...
MUST ... KILL ... MORE ... BRAIN ... CELLS.
KING -- HICCUP -- THE ISRAELITES ARE ATTACKING OUR CAMP!
WELL, THAT'S FINE WITH ME ...
OUR VICTORY COMES ONE DAY SOONER!
PARTY TENT

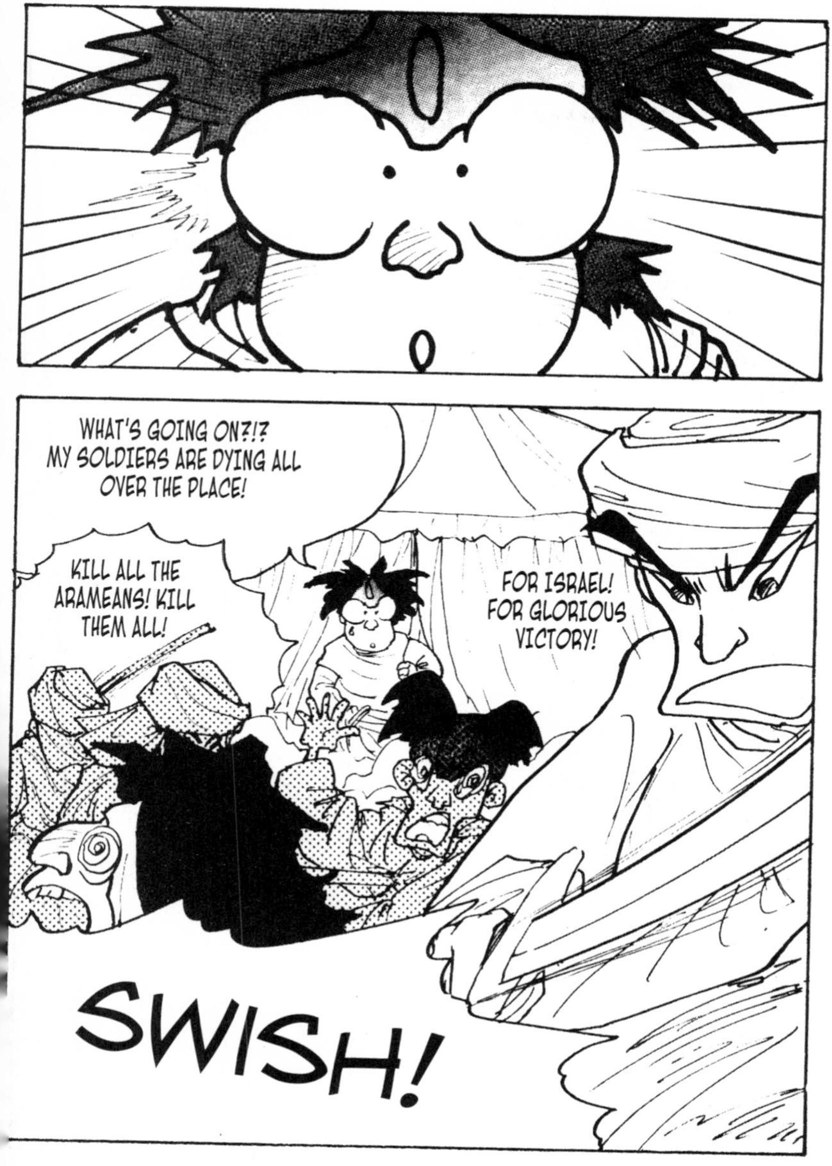
WHAT'S GOING ON?!?
MY SOLDIERS ARE DYING ALL OVER THE PLACE!
KILL ALL THE ARAMEANS! KILL THEM ALL!
FOR ISRAEL! FOR GLORIOUS VICTORY!
SWISH!

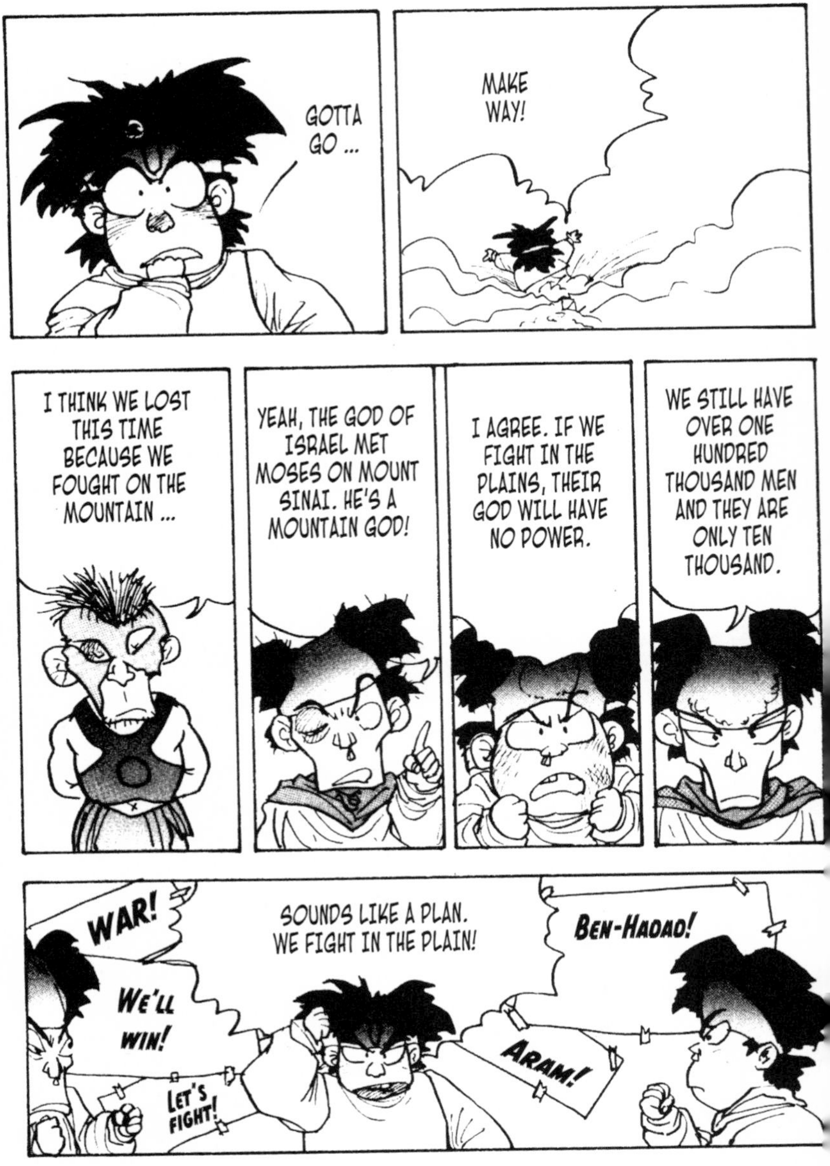
GOTTA GO ...
MAKE WAY!
I THINK WE LOST THIS TIME BECAUSE WE FOUGHT ON THE MOUNTAIN ...
YEAH, THE GOD OF ISRAEL MET MOSES ON MOUNT SINAI. HE'S A MOUNTAIN GOD!
I AGREE. IF WE FIGHT IN THE PLAINS, THEIR GOD WILL HAVE NO POWER.
WE STILL HAVE OVER ONE HUNDRED THOUSAND MEN AND THEY ARE ONLY TEN THOUSAND.
WAR!
WE'LL WIN!
LET'S FIGHT!
SOUNDS LIKE A PLAN. WE FIGHT IN THE PLAIN!
ARAM!
BEN-HADAD!

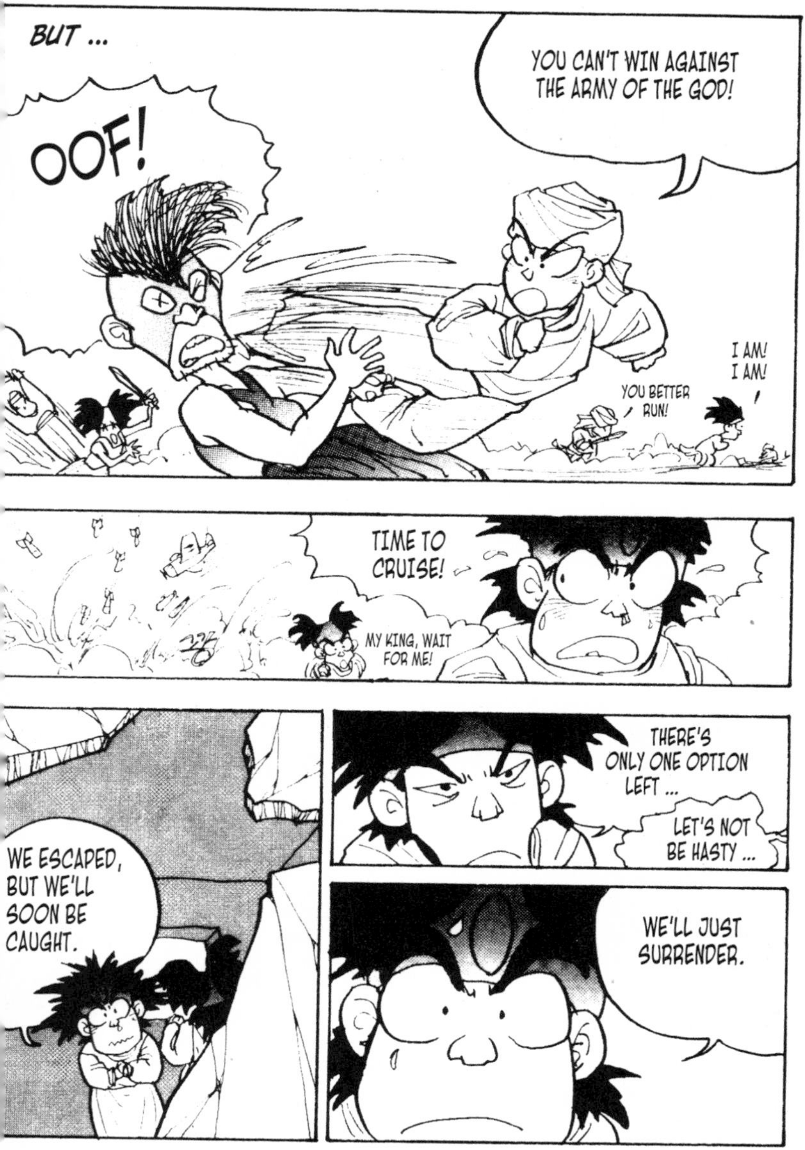
BUT ...
OOF!
YOU CAN'T WIN AGAINST THE ARMY OF THE GOD!
YOU BETTER RUN!
I AM! I AM!
TIME TO CRUISE!
MY KING, WAIT FOR ME!
WE ESCAPED, BUT WE'LL SOON BE CAUGHT.
THERE'S ONLY ONE OPTION LEFT ...
LET'S NOT BE HASTY ...
WE'LL JUST SURRENDER.

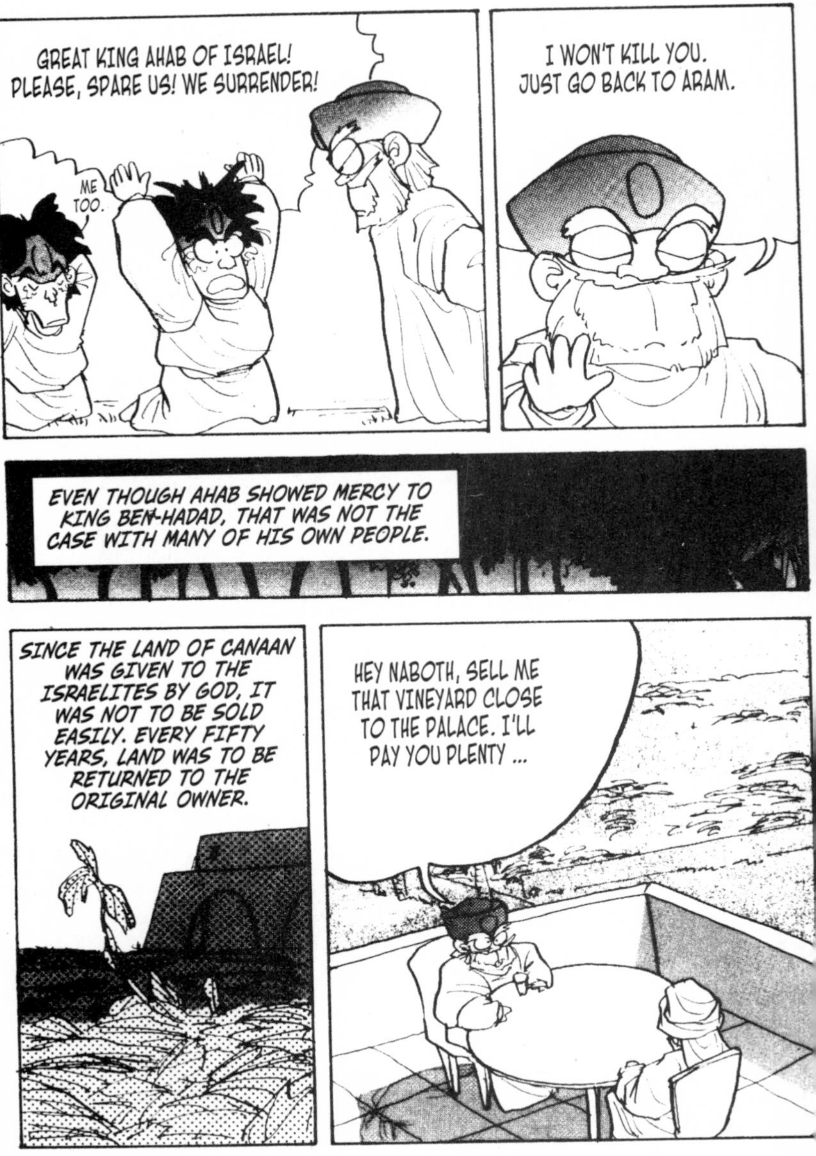
GREAT KING AHAB OF ISRAEL! PLEASE, SPARE US! WE SURRENDER!
ME TOO.
I WON'T KILL YOU. JUST GO BACK TO ARAM.
EVEN THOUGH AHAB SHOWED MERCY TO KING BEN-HADAD, THAT WAS NOT THE CASE WITH MANY OF HIS OWN PEOPLE.
SINCE THE LAND OF CANAAN WAS GIVEN TO THE ISRAELITES BY GOD, IT WAS NOT TO BE SOLD EASILY. EVERY FIFTY YEARS, LAND WAS TO BE RETURNED TO THE ORIGINAL OWNER.
HEY NABOTH, SELL ME THAT VINEYARD CLOSE TO THE PALACE. I'LL PAY YOU PLENTY ...

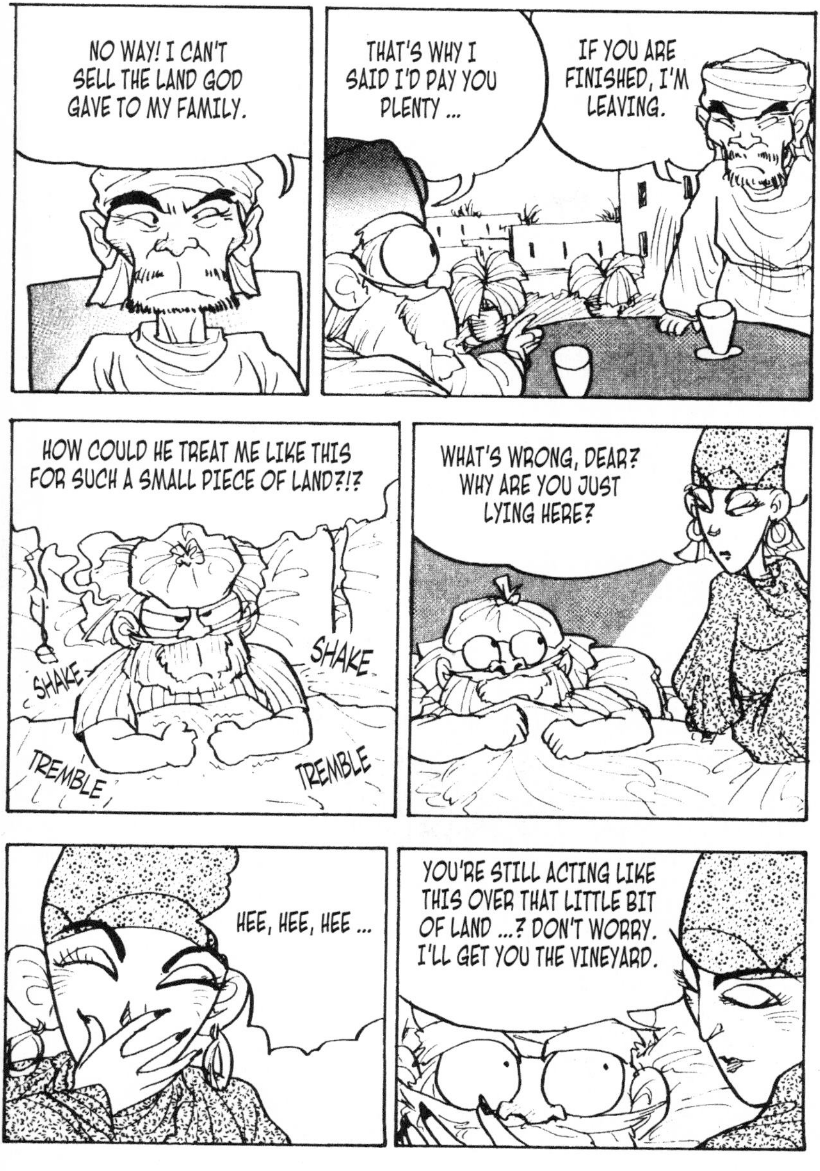
NO WAY! I CAN'T SELL THE LAND GOD GAVE TO MY FAMILY.
THAT'S WHY I SAID I'D PAY YOU PLENTY ...
IF YOU ARE FINISHED, I'M LEAVING.
HOW COULD HE TREAT ME LIKE THIS FOR SUCH A SMALL PIECE OF LAND?!?
SHAKE
SHAKE
TREMBLE
TREMBLE
WHAT'S WRONG, DEAR? WHY ARE YOU JUST LYING HERE?
HEE, HEE, HEE ...
YOU'RE STILL ACTING LIKE THIS OVER THAT LITTLE BIT OF LAND ...? DON'T WORRY. I'LL GET YOU THE VINEYARD.

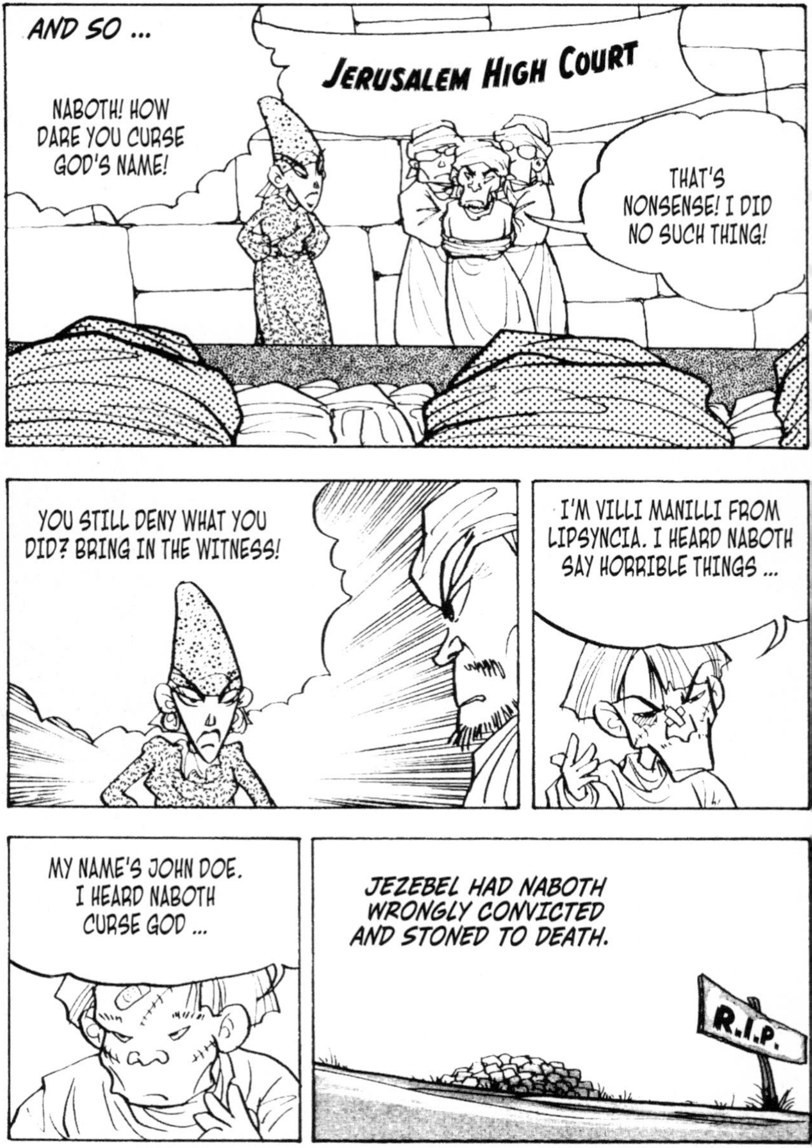
AND SO ...
JERUSALEM HIGH COURT
NABOTH! HOW DARE YOU CURSE GOD'S NAME!
THAT'S NONSENSE! I DID NO SUCH THING!
YOU STILL DENY WHAT YOU DID? BRING IN THE WITNESS!
I'M VILLI MANILLI FROM LIPSYNCIA. I HEARD NABOTH SAY HORRIBLE THINGS ...
MY NAME'S JOHN DOE. I HEARD NABOTH CURSE GOD ...
JEZEBEL HAD NABOTH WRONGLY CONVICTED AND STONED TO DEATH.
R.I.P.

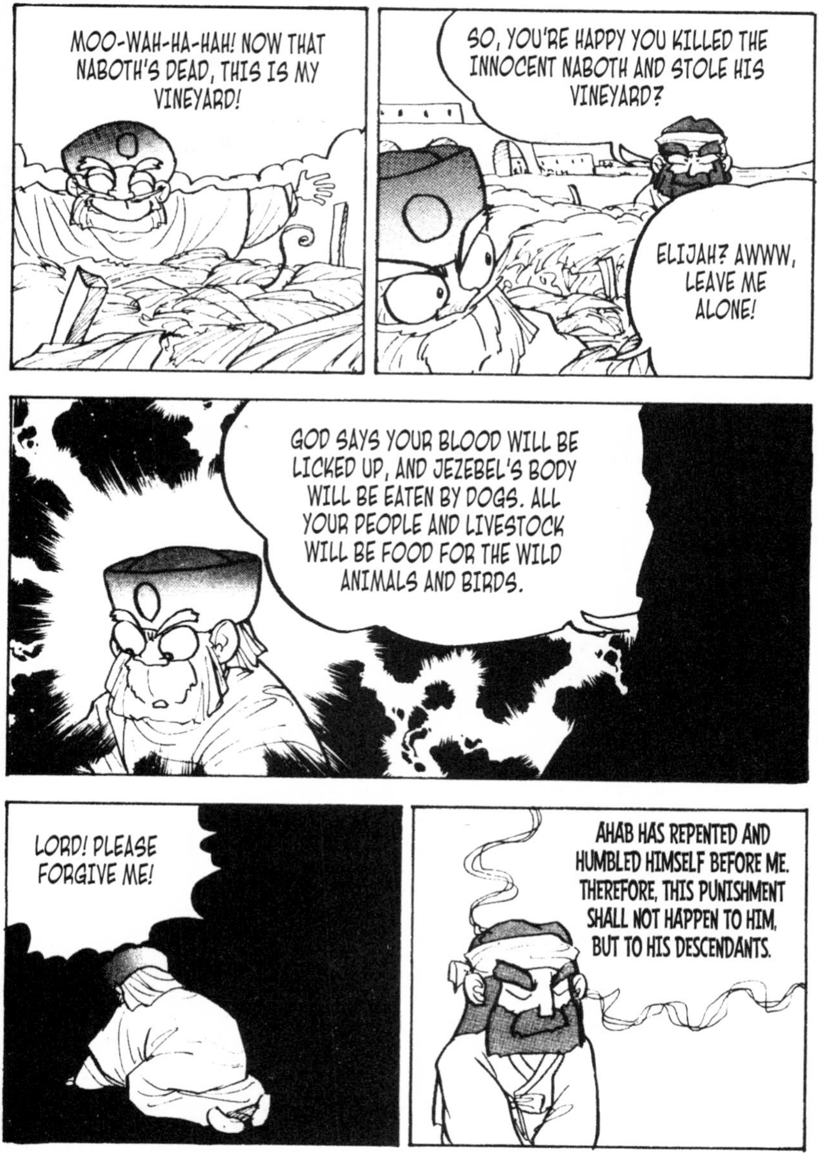
MOO-WAH-HA-HAH! NOW THAT NABOTH'S DEAD, THIS IS MY VINEYARD!
SO, YOU'RE HAPPY YOU KILLED THE INNOCENT NABOTH AND STOLE HIS VINEYARD?
ELIJAH? AWWW, LEAVE ME ALONE!
GOD SAYS YOUR BLOOD WILL BE LICKED UP, AND JEZEBEL'S BODY WILL BE EATEN BY DOGS. ALL YOUR PEOPLE AND LIVESTOCK WILL BE FOOD FOR THE WILD ANIMALS AND BIRDS.
LORD! PLEASE FORGIVE ME!
AHAB HAS REPENTED AND HUMBLED HIMSELF BEFORE ME. THEREFORE, THIS PUNISHMENT SHALL NOT HAPPEN TO HIM, BUT TO HIS DESCENDANTS.

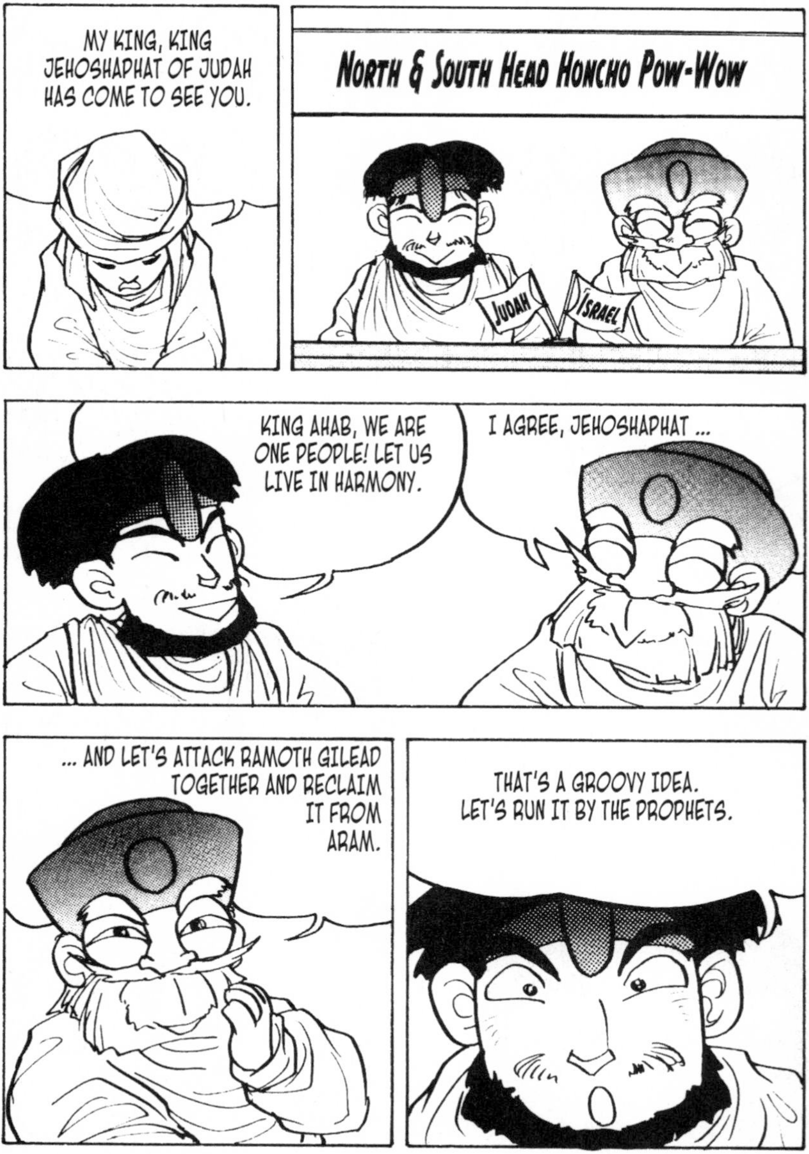
MY KING, KING JEHOSHAPHAT OF JUDAH HAS COME TO SEE YOU.
NORTH & SOUTH HEAD HONCHO POW-WOW
JUDAH
ISRAEL
KING AHAB, WE ARE ONE PEOPLE! LET US LIVE IN HARMONY.
I AGREE, JEHOSHAPHAT ...
... AND LET'S ATTACK RAMOTH GILEAD TOGETHER AND RECLAIM IT FROM ARAM.
THAT'S A GROOVY IDEA. LET'S RUN IT BY THE PROPHETS.

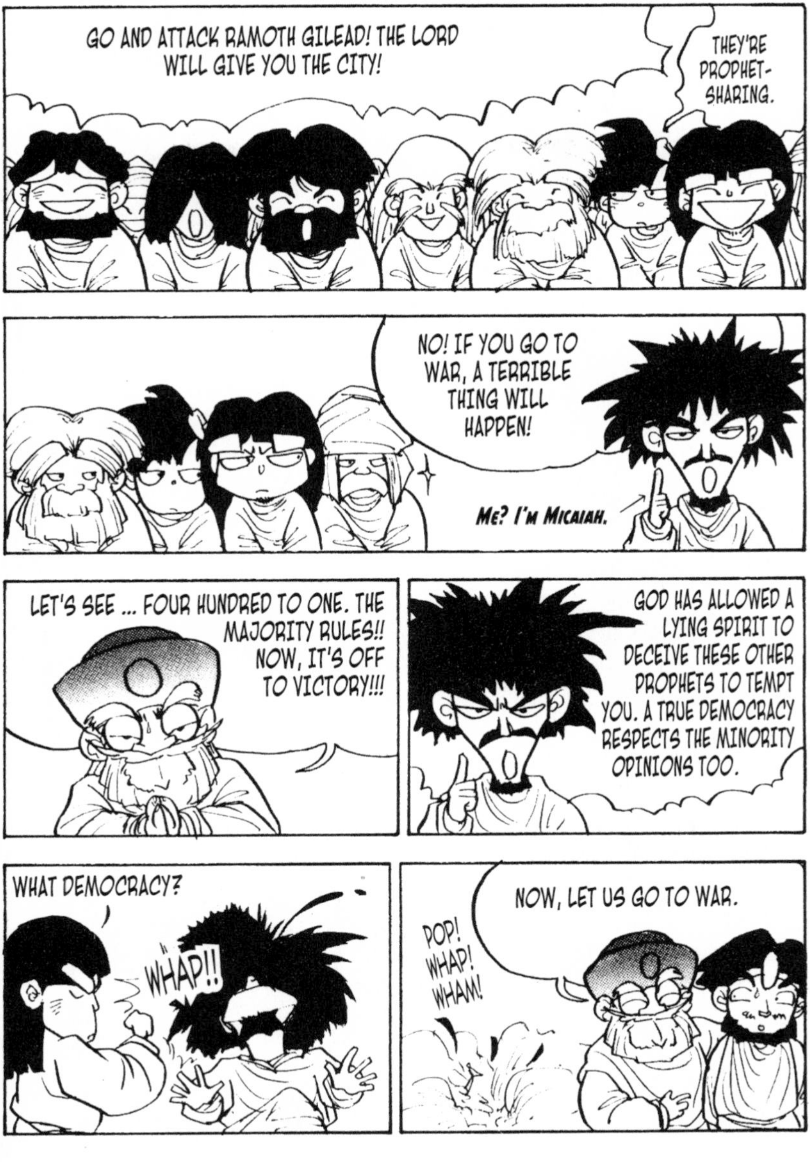
GO AND ATTACK RAMOTH GILEAD! THE LORD WILL GIVE YOU THE CITY!
THEY'RE PROPHET-SHARING.
NO! IF YOU GO TO WAR, A TERRIBLE THING WILL HAPPEN!
ME? I'M MICAIAH.
LET'S SEE ... FOUR HUNDRED TO ONE. THE MAJORITY RULES!! NOW, IT'S OFF TO VICTORY!!!
GOD HAS ALLOWED A LYING SPIRIT TO DECEIVE THESE OTHER PROPHETS TO TEMPT YOU. A TRUE DEMOCRACY RESPECTS THE MINORITY OPINIONS TOO.
WHAT DEMOCRACY?
WHAP!!
NOW, LET US GO TO WAR.
POP! WHAP! WHAM!

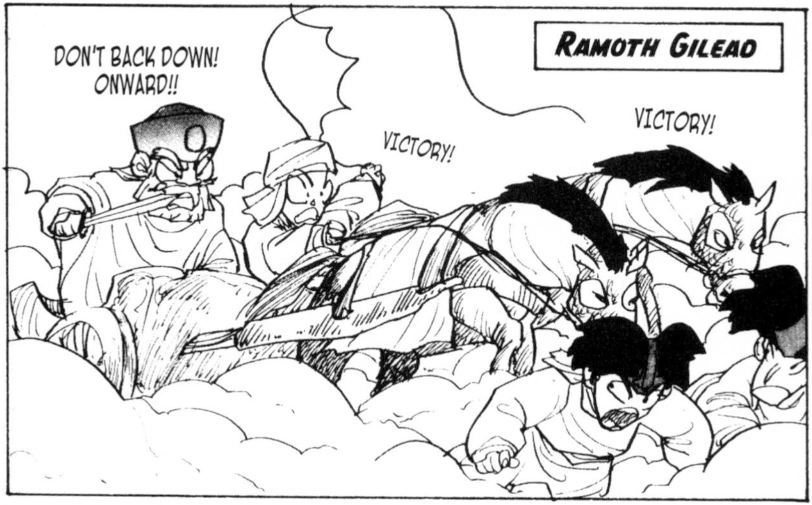
RAMOTH GILEAD
DON'T BACK DOWN! ONWARD!!
VICTORY!
VICTORY!

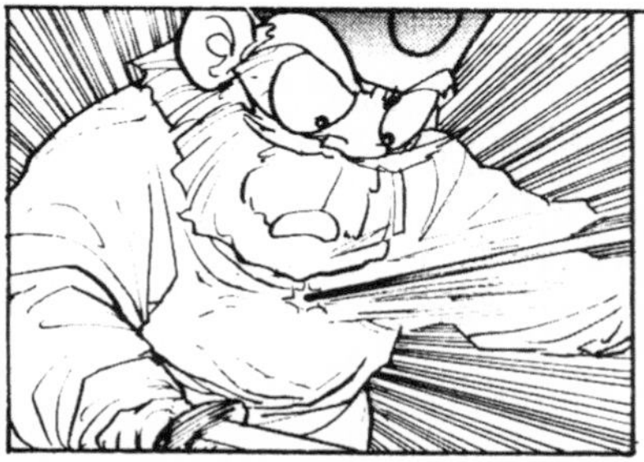

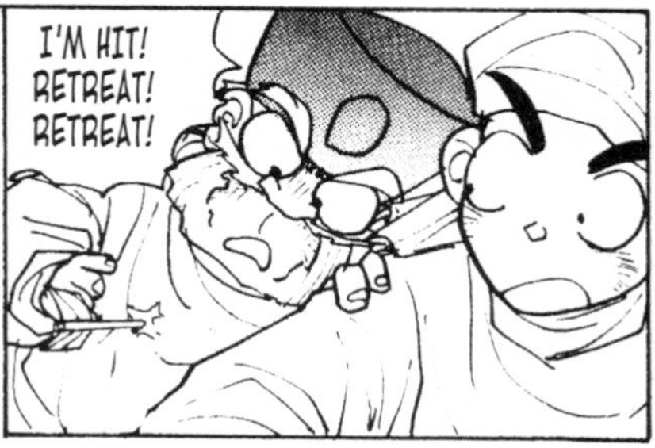
I'M HIT! RETREAT! RETREAT!

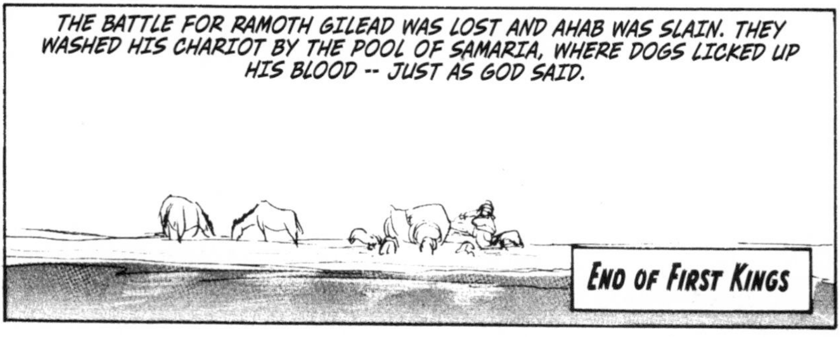
THE BATTLE FOR RAMOTH GILEAD WAS LOST AND AHAB WAS SLAIN. THEY WASHED HIS CHARIOT BY THE POOL OF SAMARIA, WHERE DOGS LICKED UP HIS BLOOD -- JUST AS GOD SAID.
END OF FIRST KINGS

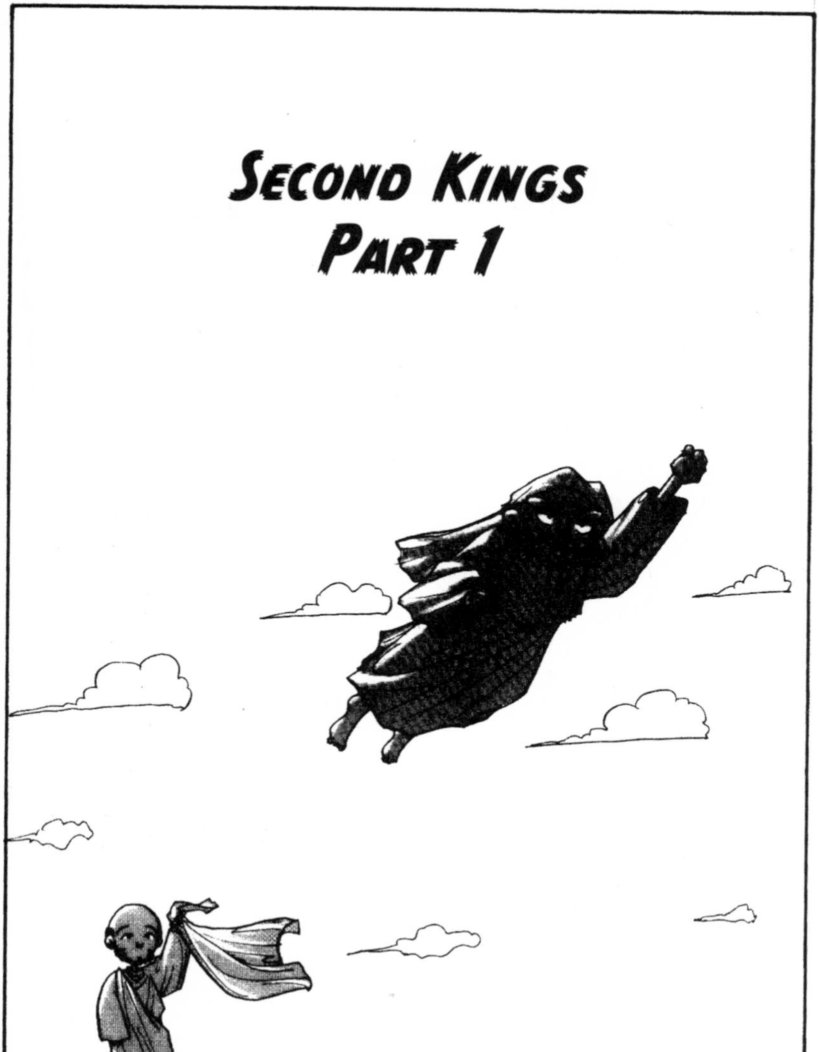
SECOND KINGS
PART 1

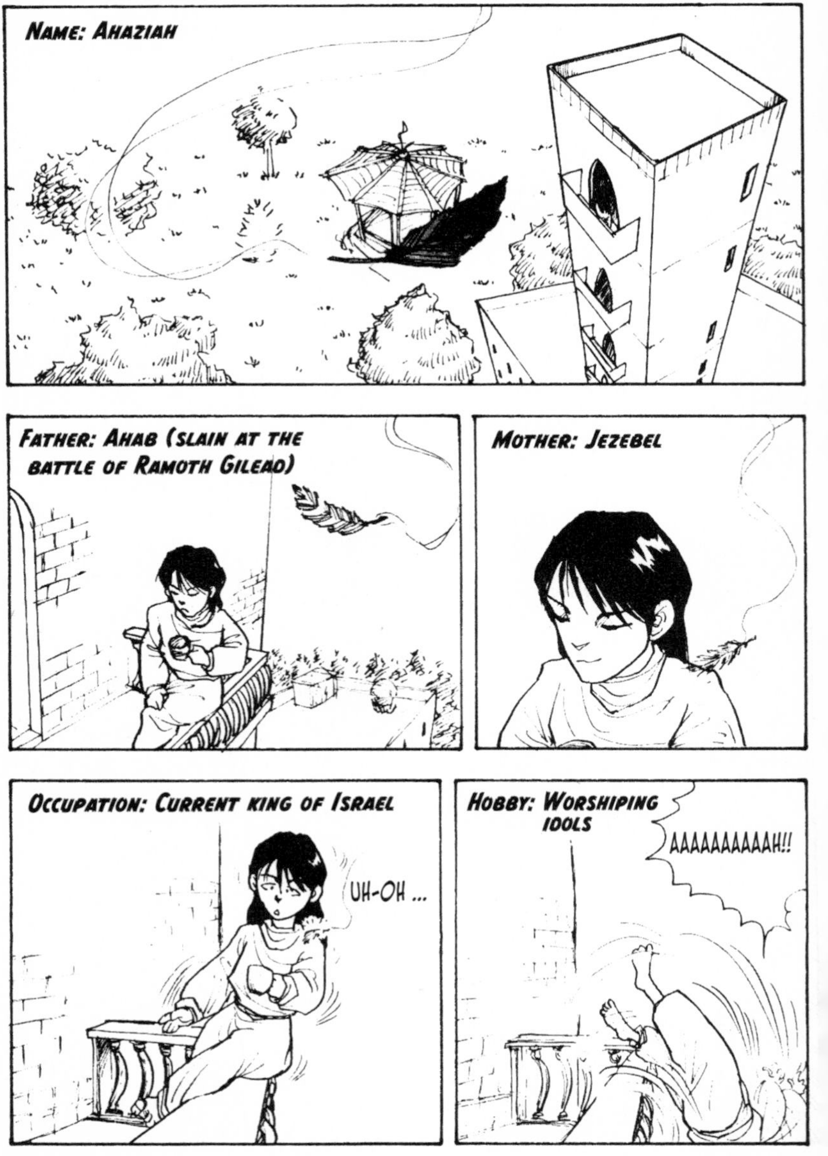
NAME: AHAZIAH
FATHER: AHAB (SLAIN AT THE BATTLE OF RAMOTH GILEAD)
MOTHER: JEZEBEL
OCCUPATION: CURRENT KING OF ISRAEL
UH-OH ...
HOBBY: WORSHIPING IDOLS
AAAAAAAAAAH!!

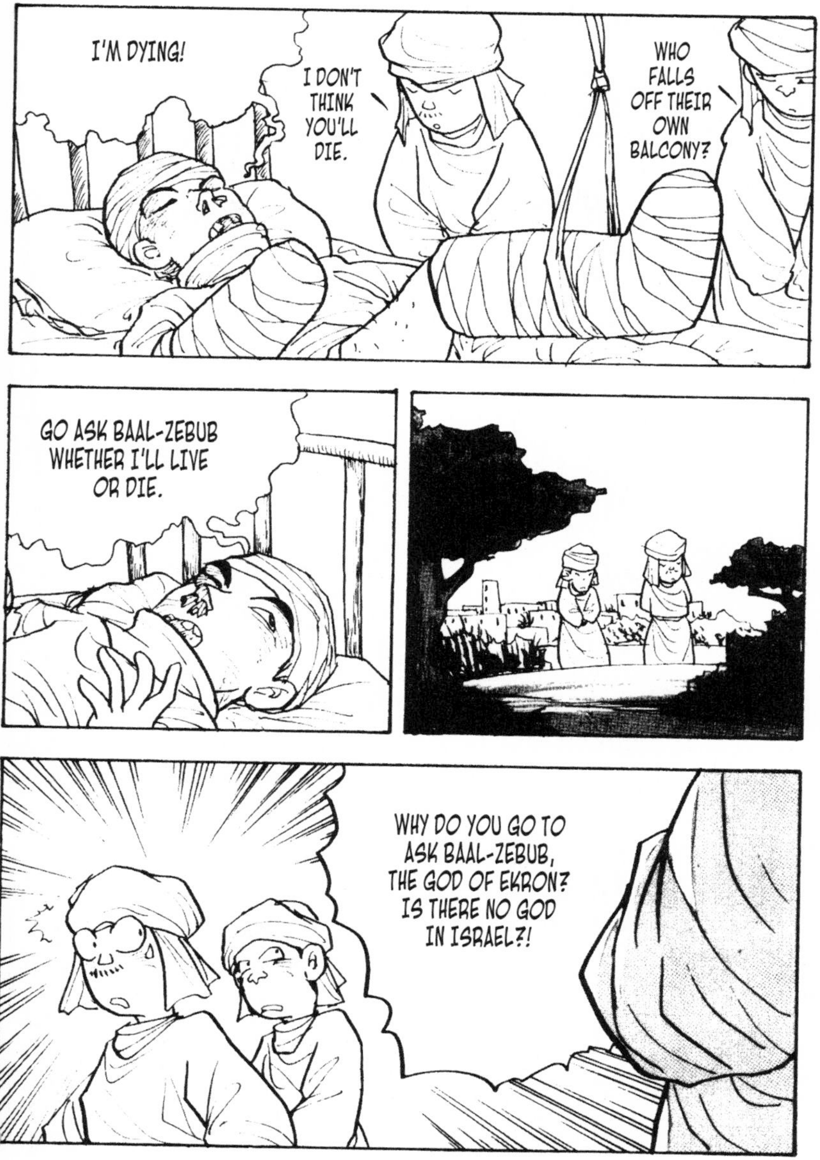
I'M DYING!
I DON'T THINK YOU'LL DIE.
WHO FALLS OFF THEIR OWN BALCONY?
GO ASK BAAL-ZEBUB WHETHER I'LL LIVE OR DIE.
WHY DO YOU GO TO ASK BAAL-ZEBUB, THE GOD OF EKRON? IS THERE NO GOD IN ISRAEL?!

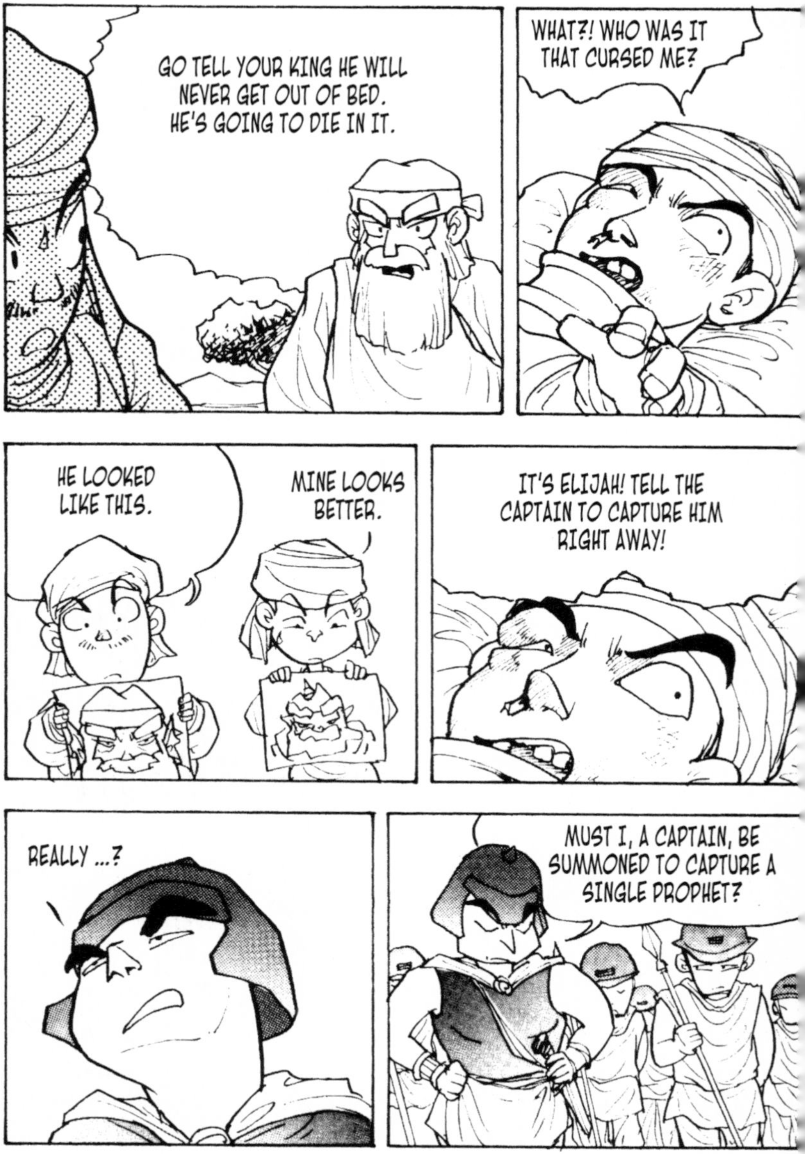
GO TELL YOUR KING HE WILL NEVER GET OUT OF BED. HE'S GOING TO DIE IN IT.
WHAT?! WHO WAS IT THAT CURSED ME?
HE LOOKED LIKE THIS.
MINE LOOKS BETTER.
IT'S ELIJAH! TELL THE CAPTAIN TO CAPTURE HIM RIGHT AWAY!
REALLY ...?
MUST I, A CAPTAIN, BE SUMMONED TO CAPTURE A SINGLE PROPHET?

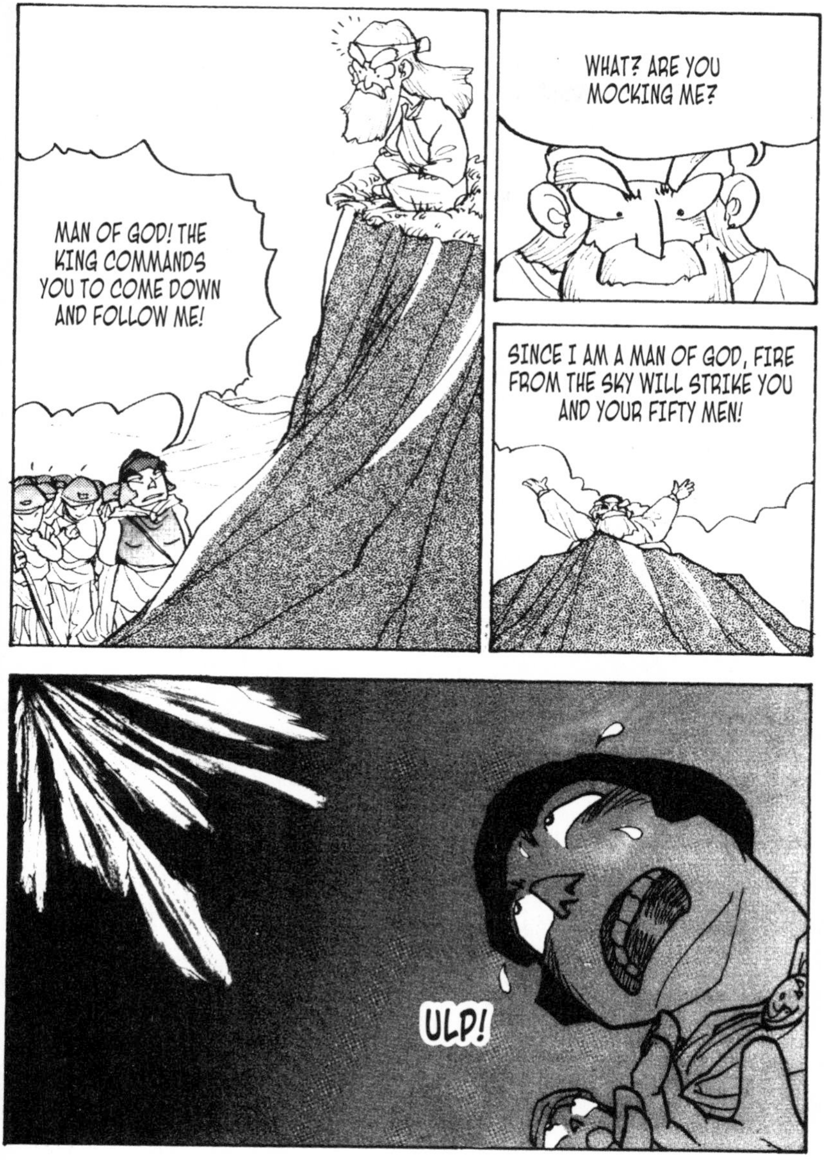
MAN OF GOD! THE KING COMMANDS YOU TO COME DOWN AND FOLLOW ME!
WHAT? ARE YOU MOCKING ME?
SINCE I AM A MAN OF GOD, FIRE FROM THE SKY WILL STRIKE YOU AND YOUR FIFTY MEN!
ULP!

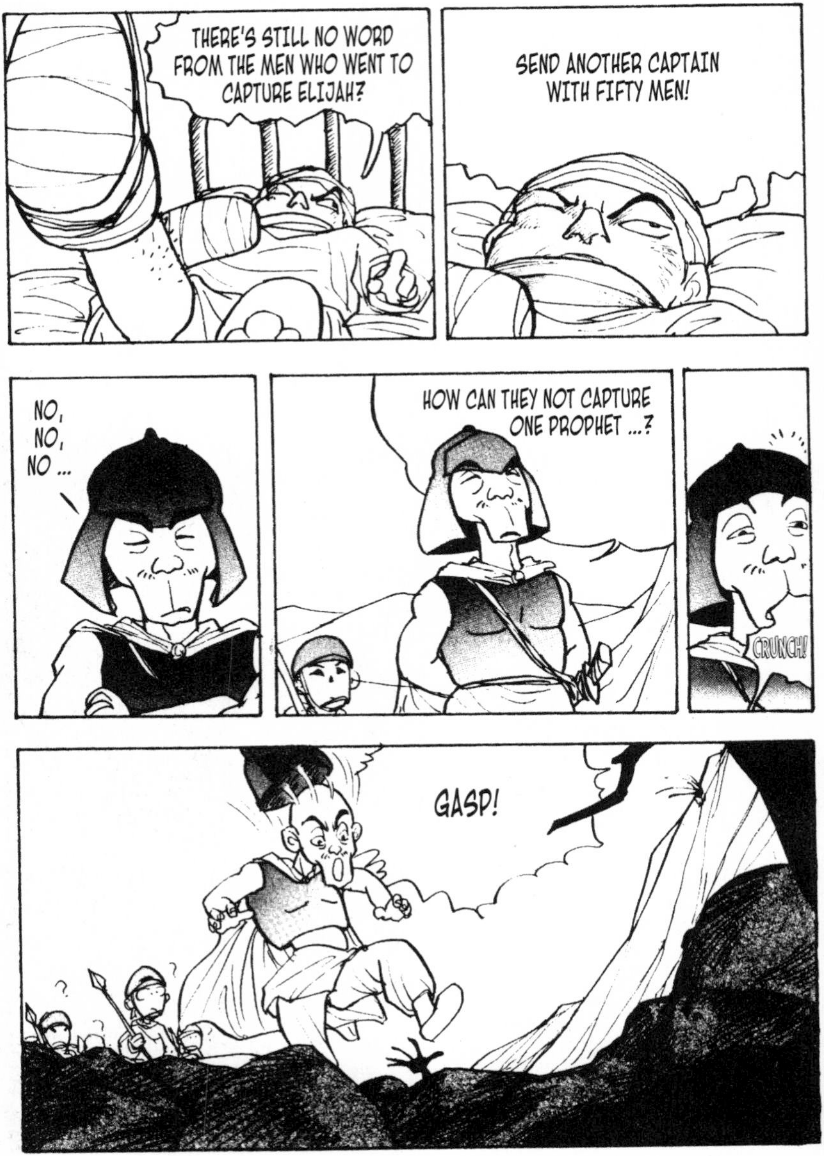
THERE'S STILL NO WORD FROM THE MEN WHO WENT TO CAPTURE ELIJAH?
SEND ANOTHER CAPTAIN WITH FIFTY MEN!
NO, NO, NO ...
HOW CAN THEY NOT CAPTURE ONE PROPHET ...?
CRUNCH!
GASP!

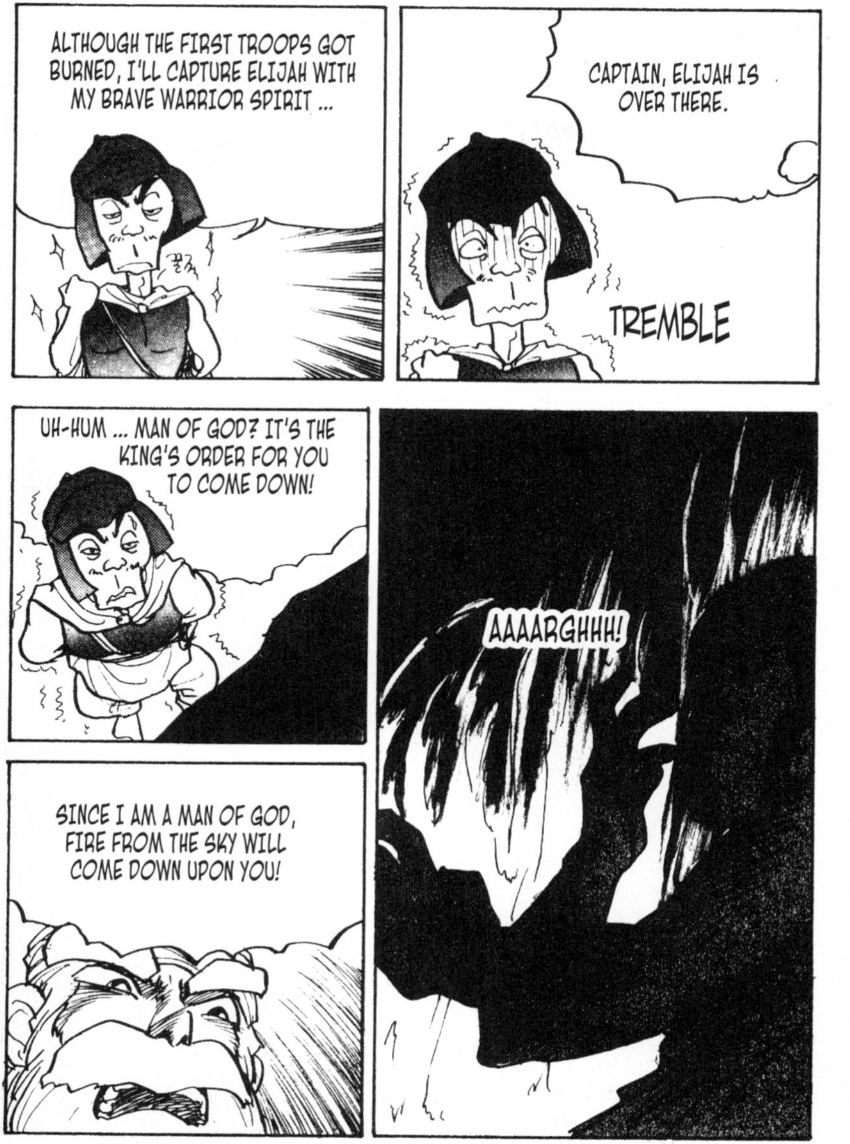
ALTHOUGH THE FIRST TROOPS GOT BURNED, I'LL CAPTURE ELIJAH WITH MY BRAVE WARRIOR SPIRIT ...
CAPTAIN, ELIJAH IS OVER THERE.
TREMBLE
UH-HUM ... MAN OF GOD? IT'S THE KING'S ORDER FOR YOU TO COME DOWN!
AAAARGHHH!
SINCE I AM A MAN OF GOD, FIRE FROM THE SKY WILL COME DOWN UPON YOU!

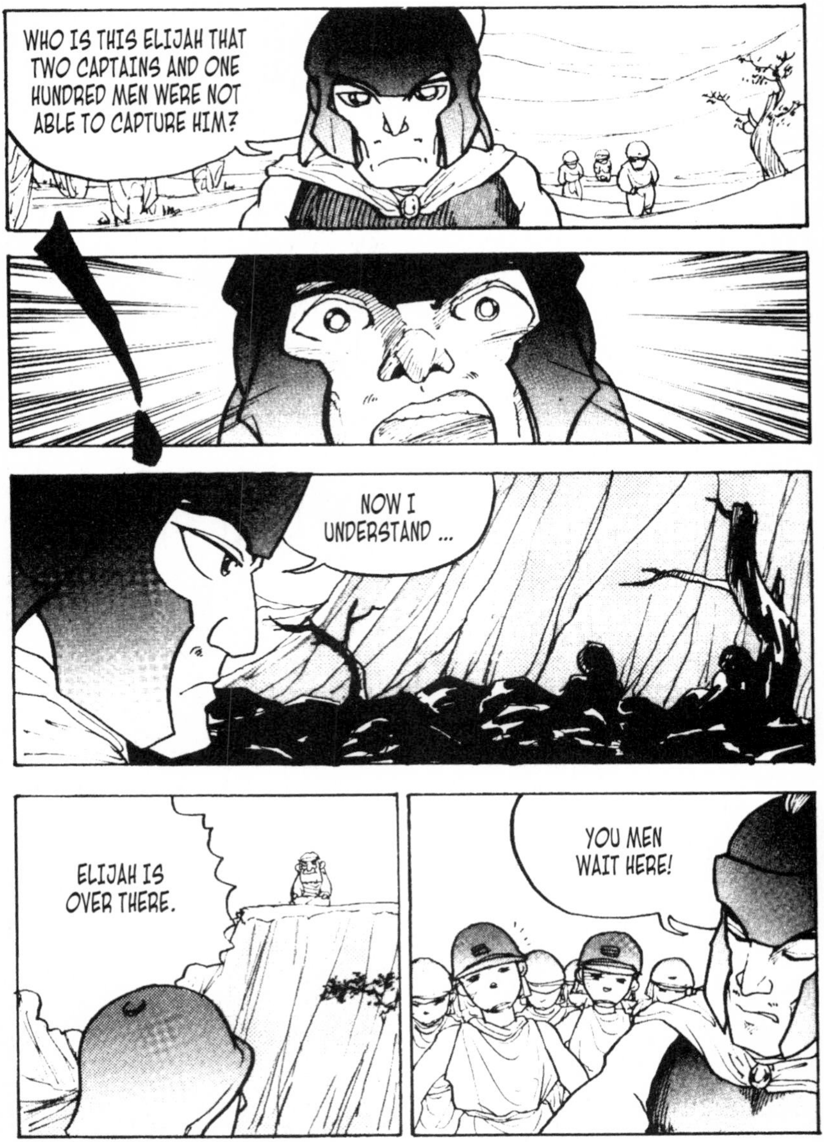
WHO IS THIS ELIJAH THAT TWO CAPTAINS AND ONE HUNDRED MEN WERE NOT ABLE TO CAPTURE HIM?
!
NOW I UNDERSTAND ...
ELIJAH IS OVER THERE.
YOU MEN WAIT HERE!

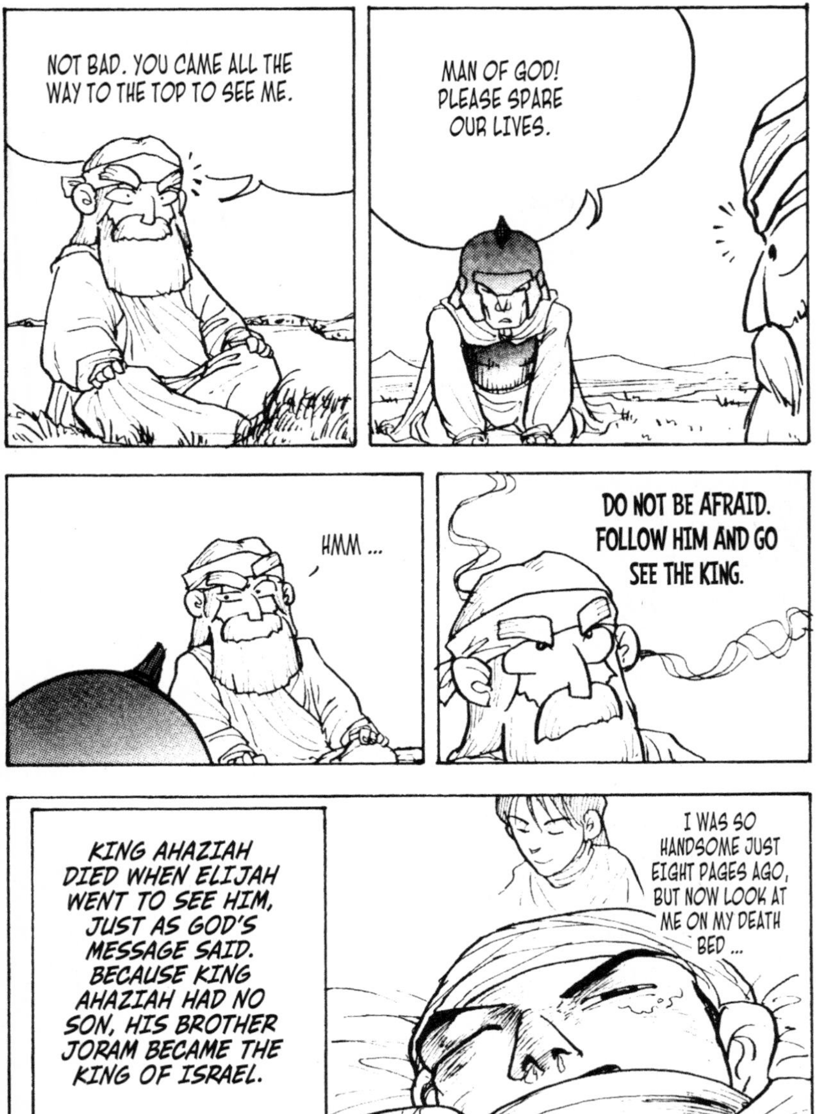
NOT BAD. YOU CAME ALL THE WAY TO THE TOP TO SEE ME.
MAN OF GOD! PLEASE SPARE OUR LIVES.
HMM ...
DO NOT BE AFRAID. FOLLOW HIM AND GO SEE THE KING.
KING AHAZIAH DIED WHEN ELIJAH WENT TO SEE HIM, JUST AS GOD'S MESSAGE SAID. BECAUSE KING AHAZIAH HAD NO SON, HIS BROTHER JORAM BECAME THE KING OF ISRAEL.
I WAS SO HANDSOME JUST EIGHT PAGES AGO, BUT NOW LOOK AT ME ON MY DEATH BED ...

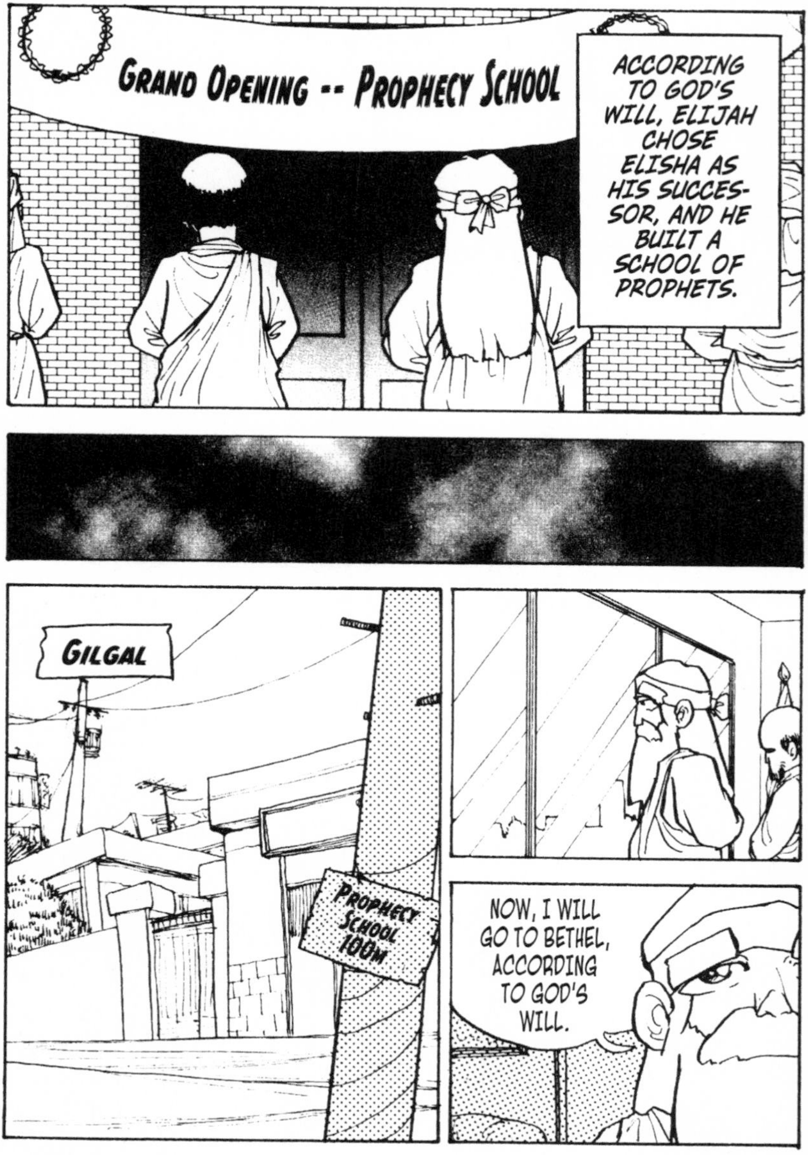
GRAND OPENING -- PROPHECY SCHOOL
ACCORDING TO GOD'S WILL, ELIJAH CHOSE ELISHA AS HIS SUCCES-SOR, AND HE BUILT A SCHOOL OF PROPHETS.
GILGAL
PROPHECY SCHOOL 100M
NOW, I WILL GO TO BETHEL, ACCORDING TO GOD'S WILL.

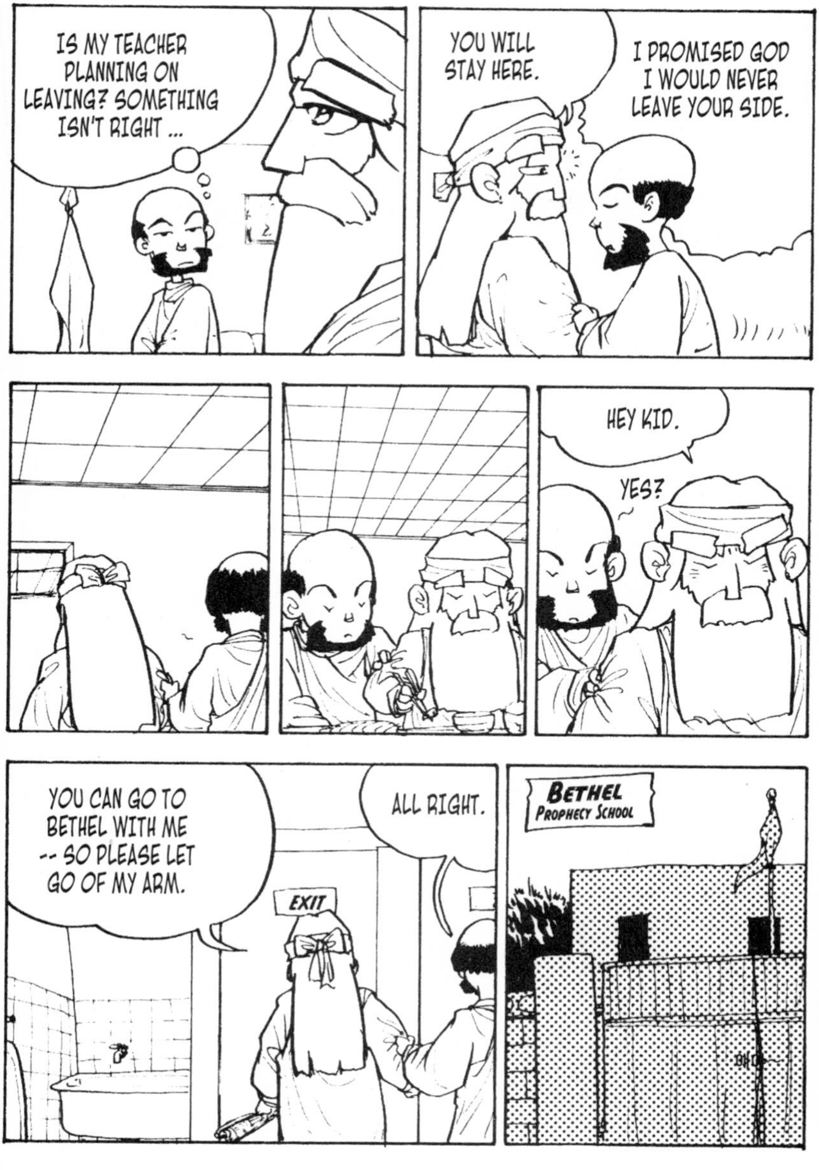
IS MY TEACHER PLANNING ON LEAVING? SOMETHING ISN'T RIGHT ...
YOU WILL STAY HERE.
I PROMISED GOD I WOULD NEVER LEAVE YOUR SIDE.
HEY KID.
YES?
YOU CAN GO TO BETHEL WITH ME -- SO PLEASE LET GO OF MY ARM.
EXIT
ALL RIGHT.
BETHEL
PROPHECY SCHOOL

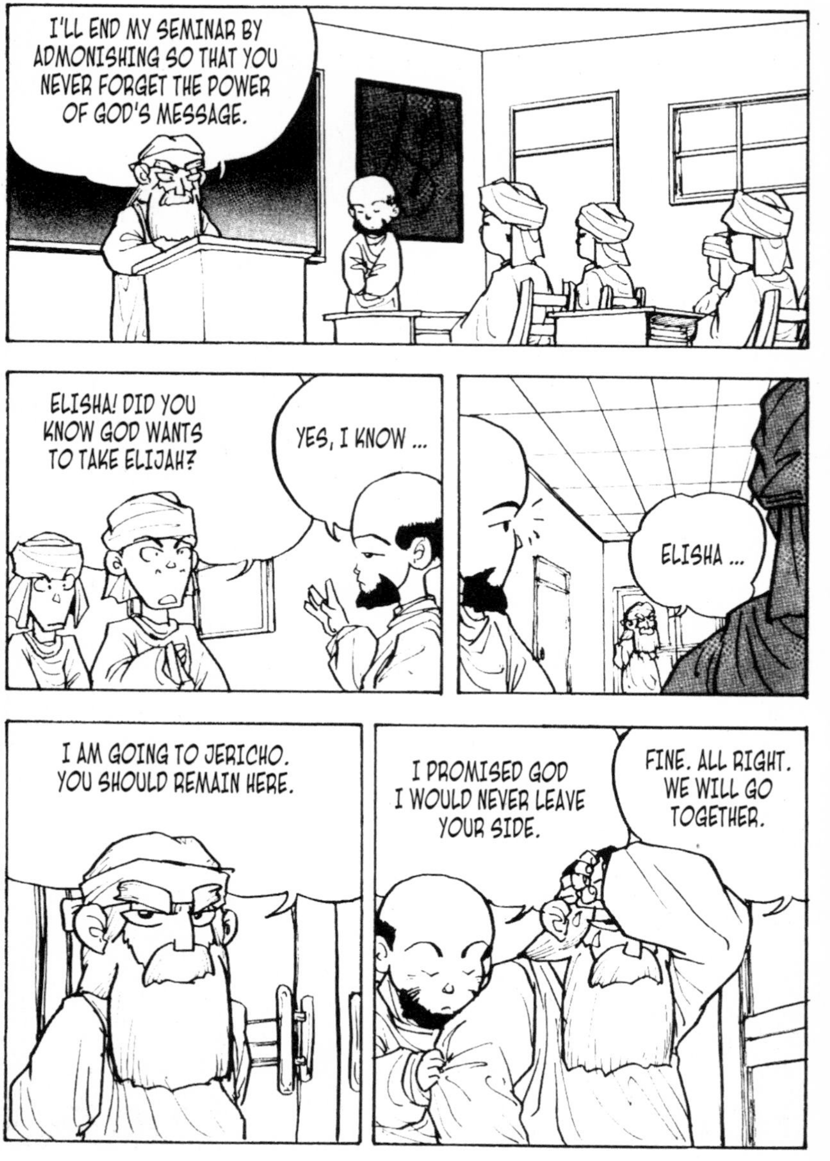
I'LL END MY SEMINAR BY ADMONISHING SO THAT YOU NEVER FORGET THE POWER OF GOD'S MESSAGE.
ELISHA! DID YOU KNOW GOD WANTS TO TAKE ELIJAH?
YES, I KNOW ...
ELISHA ...
I AM GOING TO JERICHO. YOU SHOULD REMAIN HERE.
I PROMISED GOD I WOULD NEVER LEAVE YOUR SIDE.
FINE. ALL RIGHT. WE WILL GO TOGETHER.

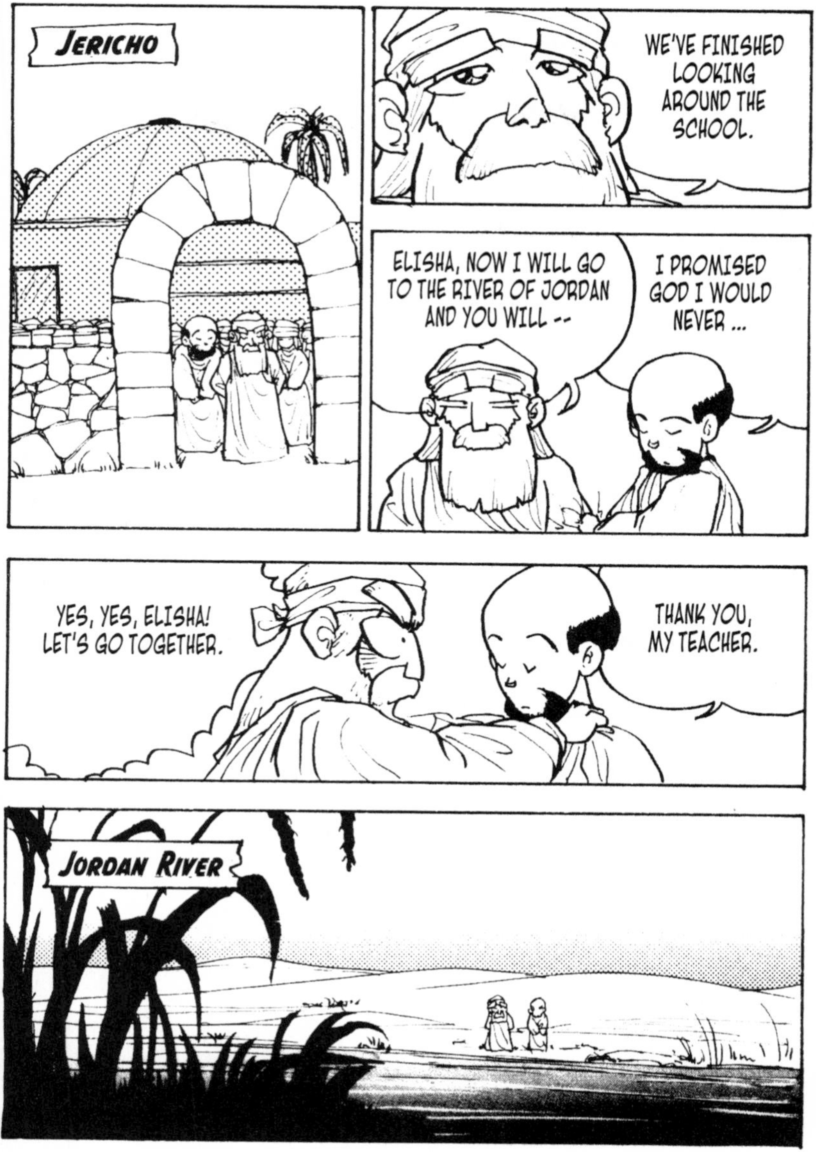
JERICHO
WE'VE FINISHED LOOKING AROUND THE SCHOOL.
ELISHA, NOW I WILL GO TO THE RIVER OF JORDAN AND YOU WILL --
I PROMISED GOD I WOULD NEVER ...
YES, YES, ELISHA! LET'S GO TOGETHER.
THANK YOU, MY TEACHER.
JORDAN RIVER

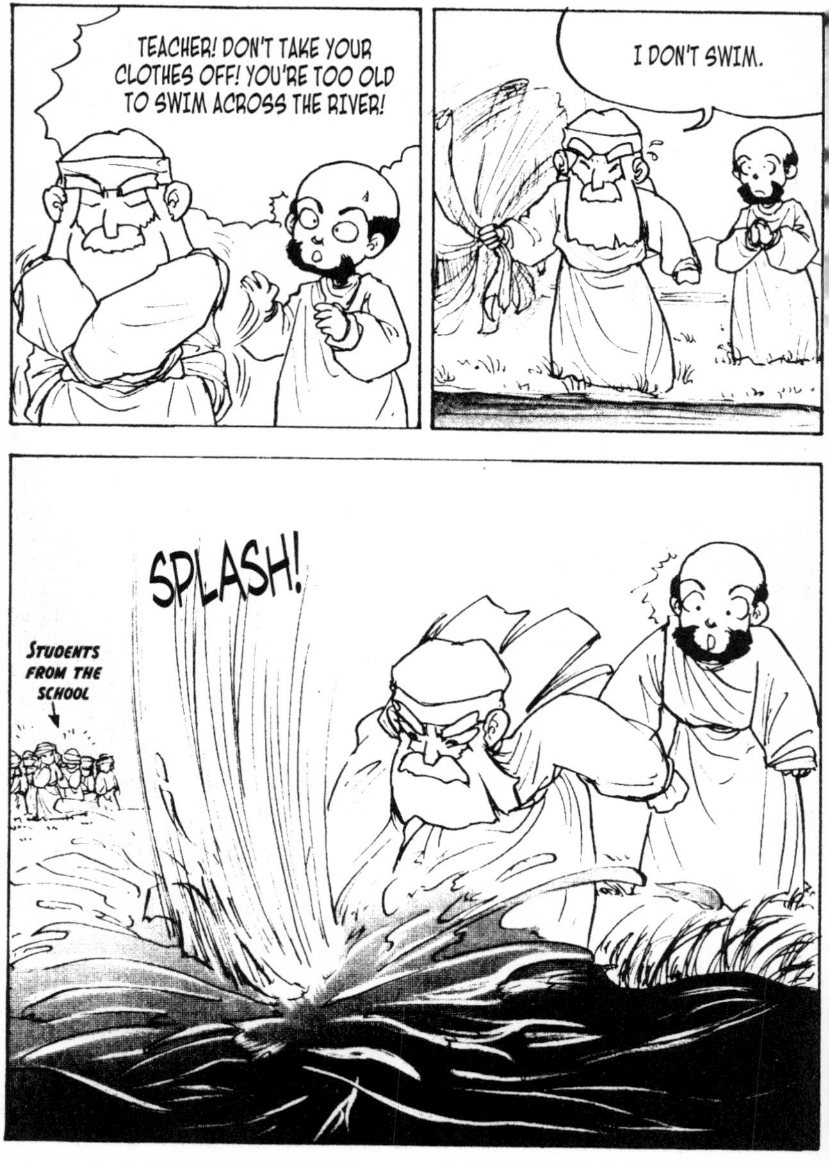
TEACHER! DON'T TAKE YOUR CLOTHES OFF! YOU'RE TOO OLD TO SWIM ACROSS THE RIVER!
I DON'T SWIM.
SPLASH!
STUDENTS FROM THE SCHOOL

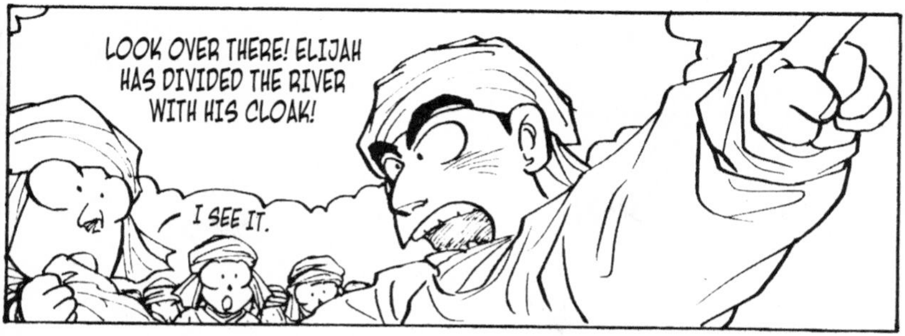
LOOK OVER THERE! ELIJAH HAS DIVIDED THE RIVER WITH HIS CLOAK!
I SEE IT.
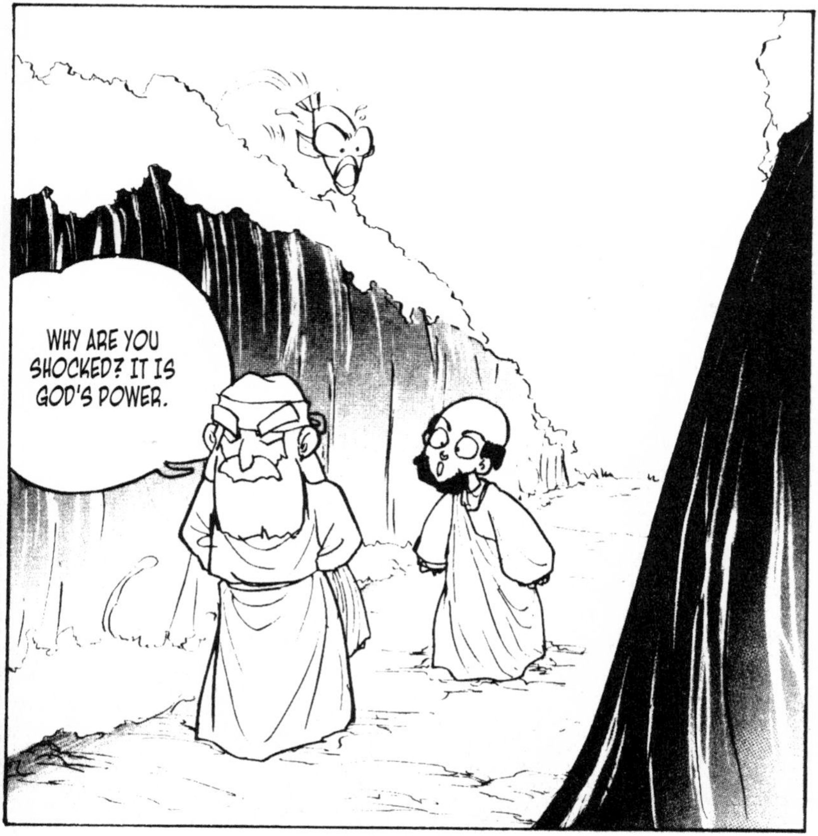
WHY ARE YOU SHOCKED? IT IS GOD'S POWER.

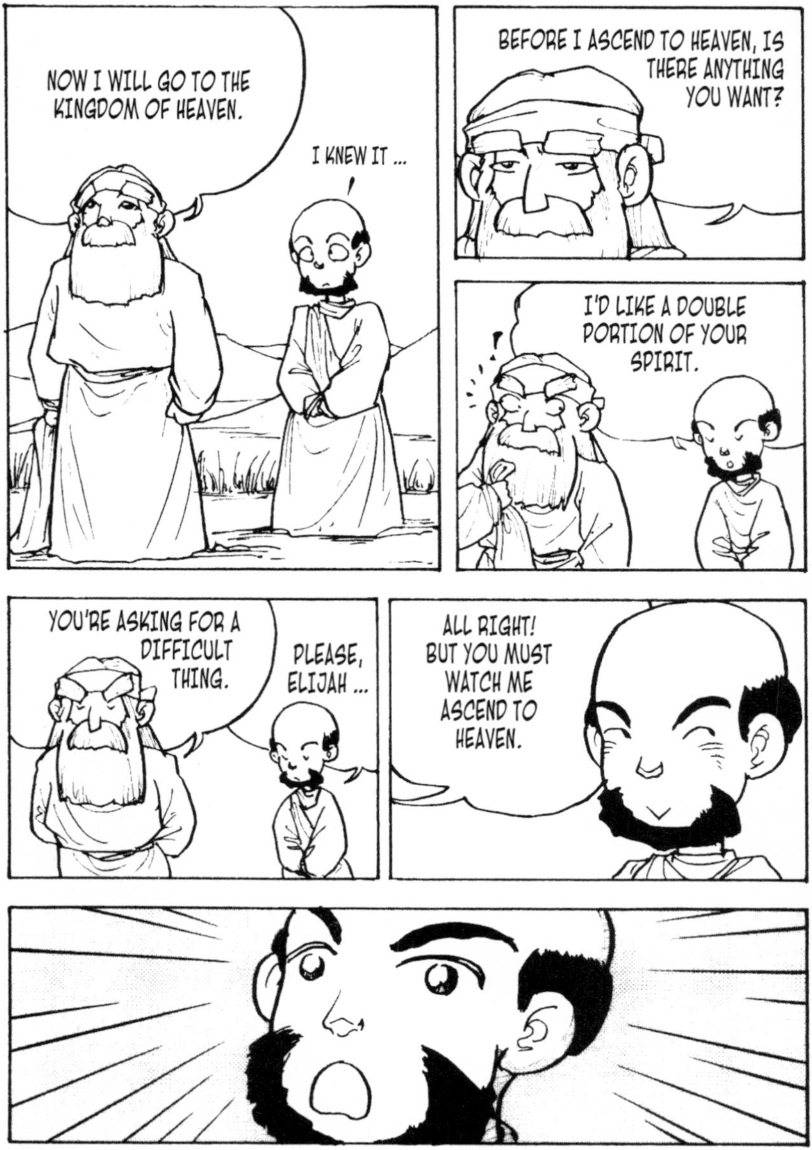
NOW I WILL GO TO THE KINGDOM OF HEAVEN.
I KNEW IT ...
BEFORE I ASCEND TO HEAVEN, IS THERE ANYTHING YOU WANT?
I'D LIKE A DOUBLE PORTION OF YOUR SPIRIT.
YOU'RE ASKING FOR A DIFFICULT THING.
PLEASE, ELIJAH ...
ALL RIGHT! BUT YOU MUST WATCH ME ASCEND TO HEAVEN.

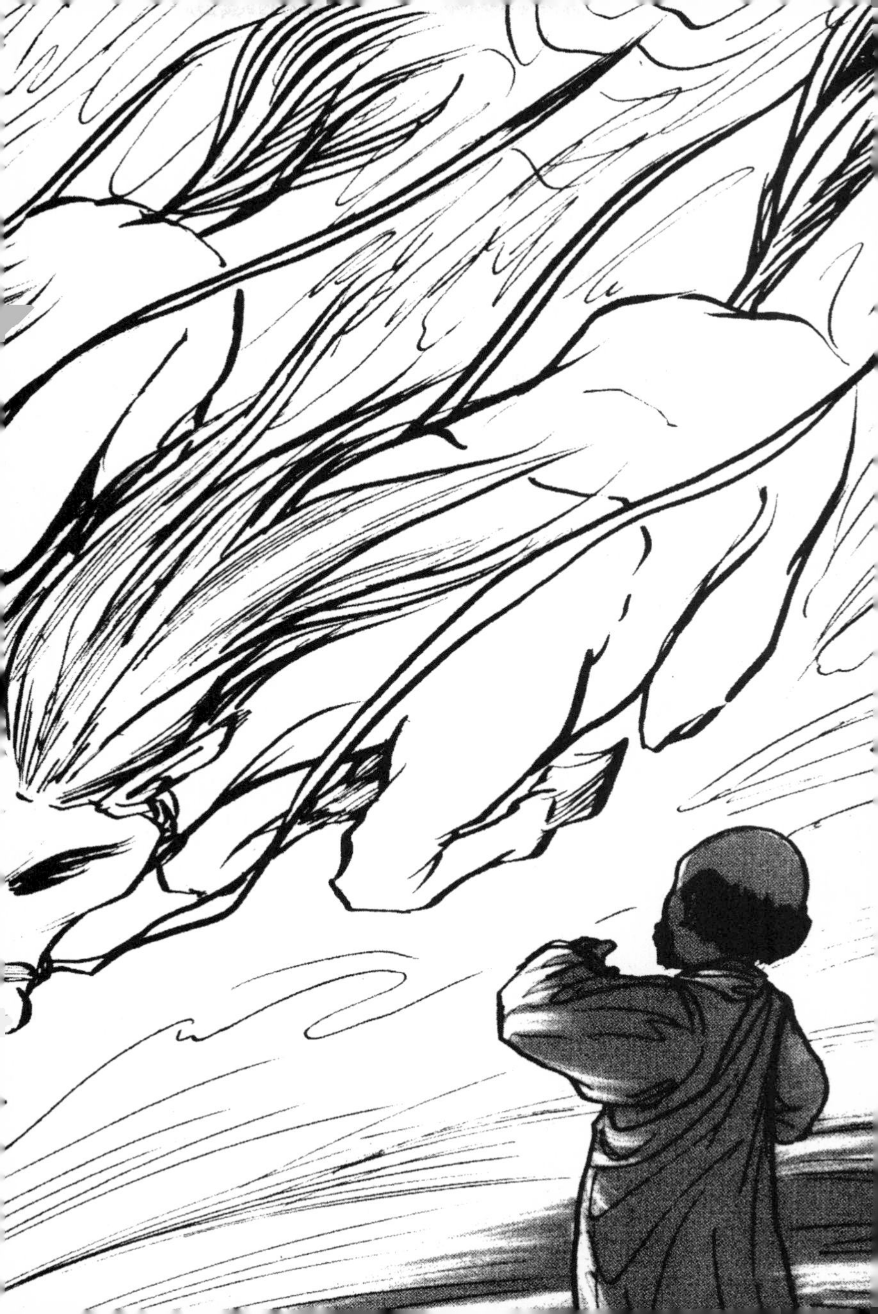

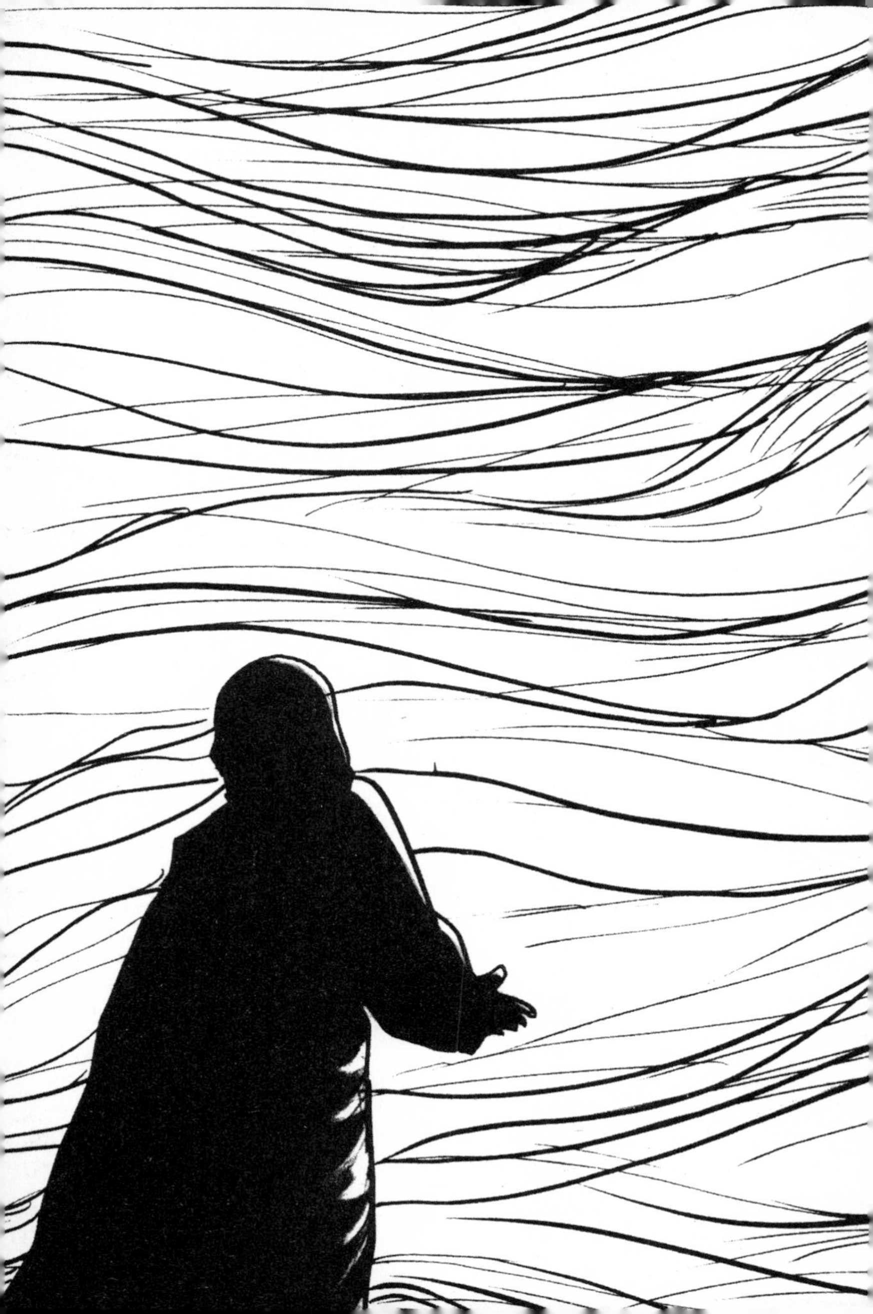

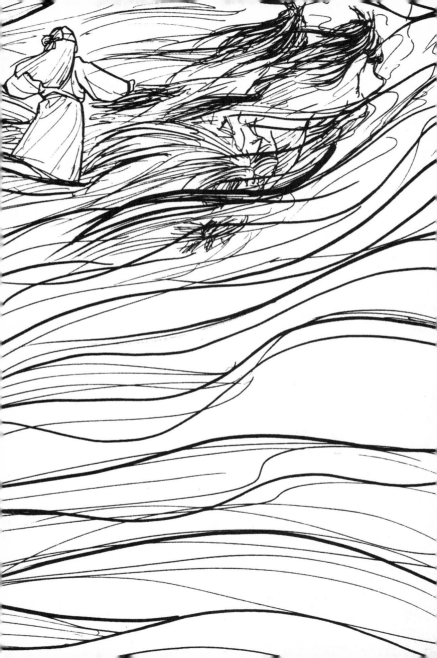

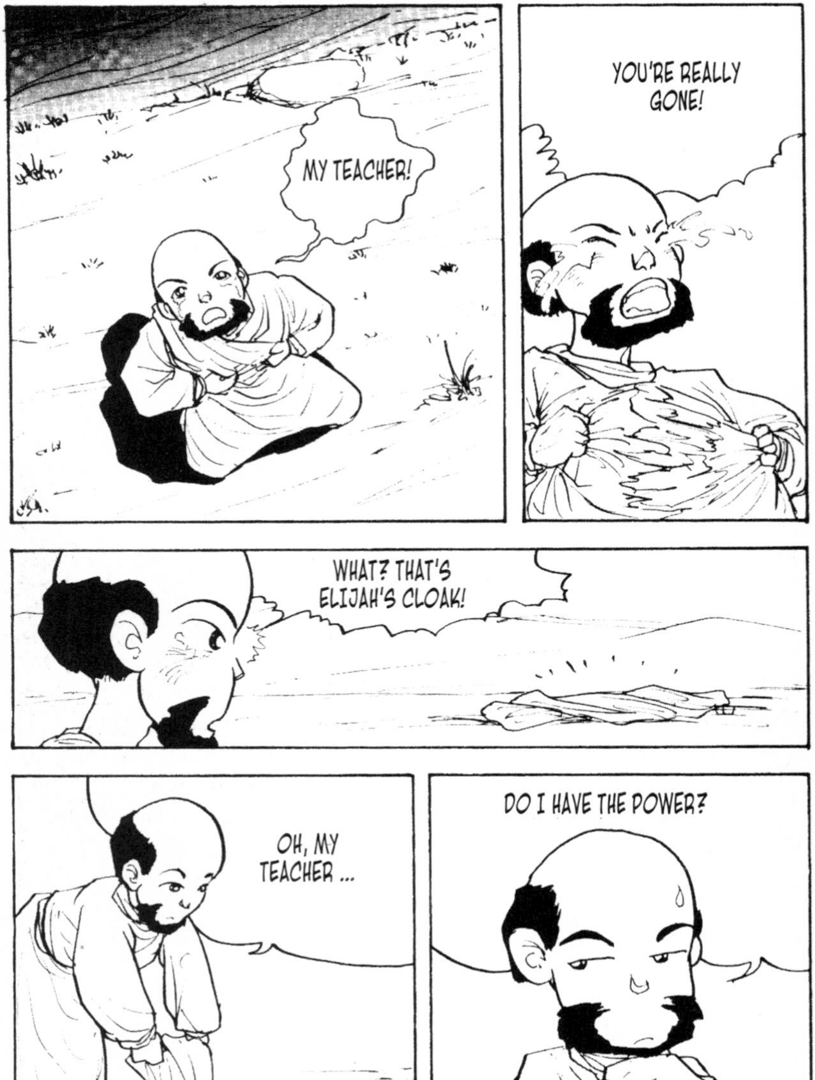
MY TEACHER!
YOU'RE REALLY GONE!
WHAT? THAT'S ELIJAH'S CLOAK!
OH, MY TEACHER ...
DO I HAVE THE POWER?

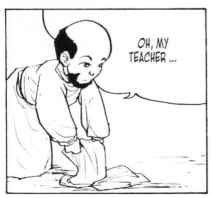

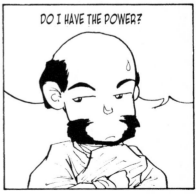

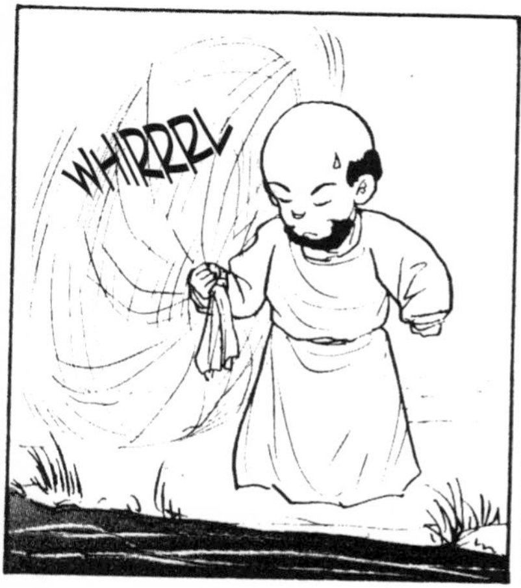
WHIRRRL

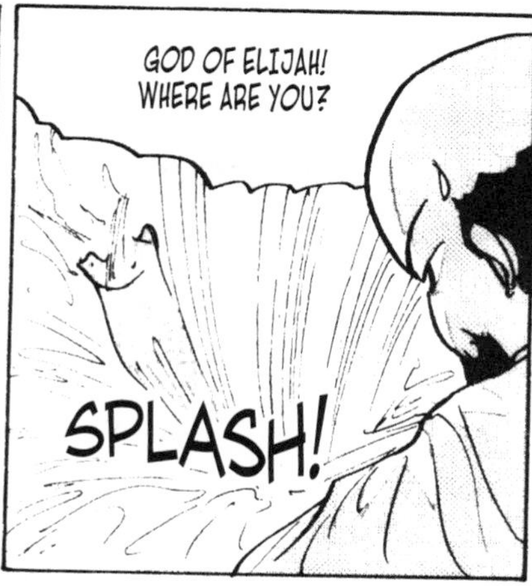
GOD OF ELIJAH! WHERE ARE YOU?
SPLASH!

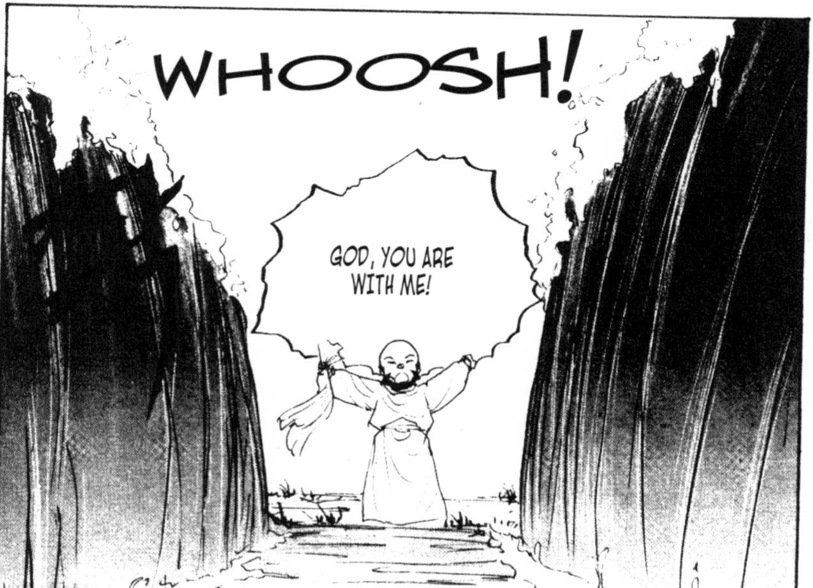
WHOOSH!
GOD, YOU ARE WITH ME!

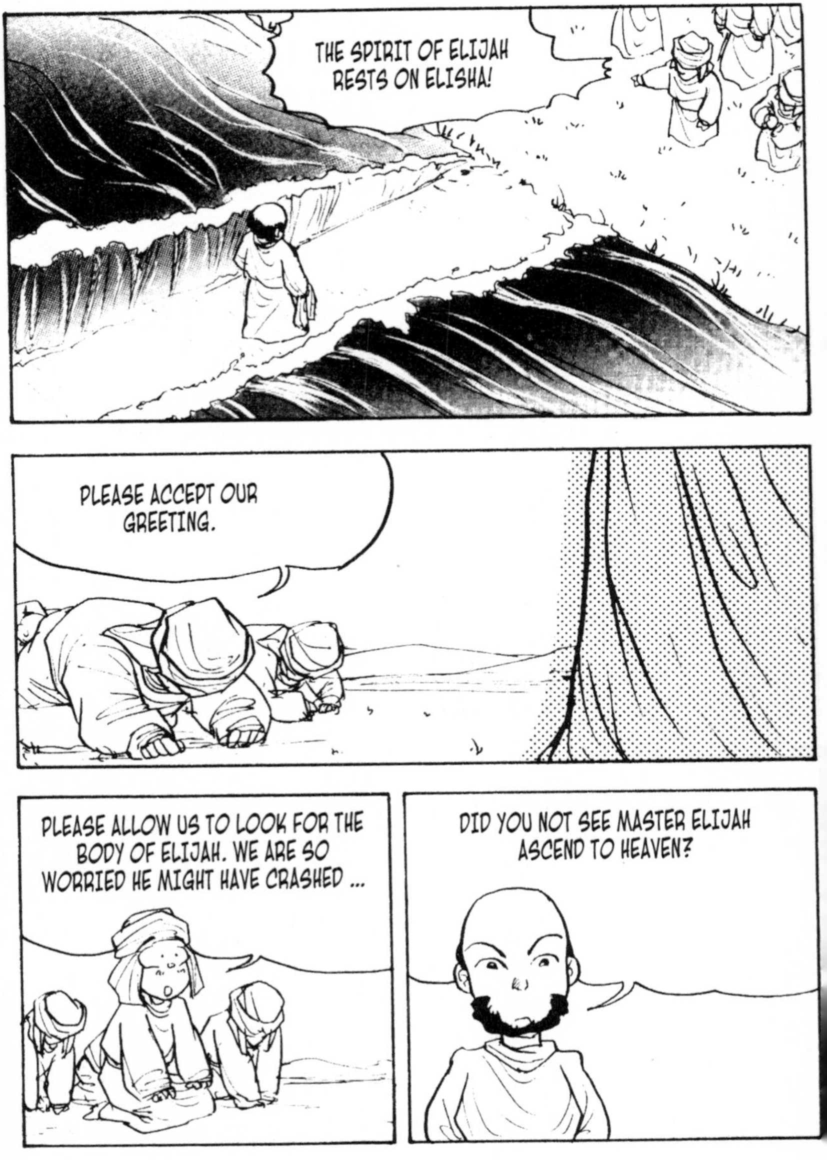
THE SPIRIT OF ELIJAH RESTS ON ELISHA!
PLEASE ACCEPT OUR GREETING.
PLEASE ALLOW US TO LOOK FOR THE BODY OF ELIJAH. WE ARE SO WORRIED HE MIGHT HAVE CRASHED ...
DID YOU NOT SEE MASTER ELIJAH ASCEND TO HEAVEN?

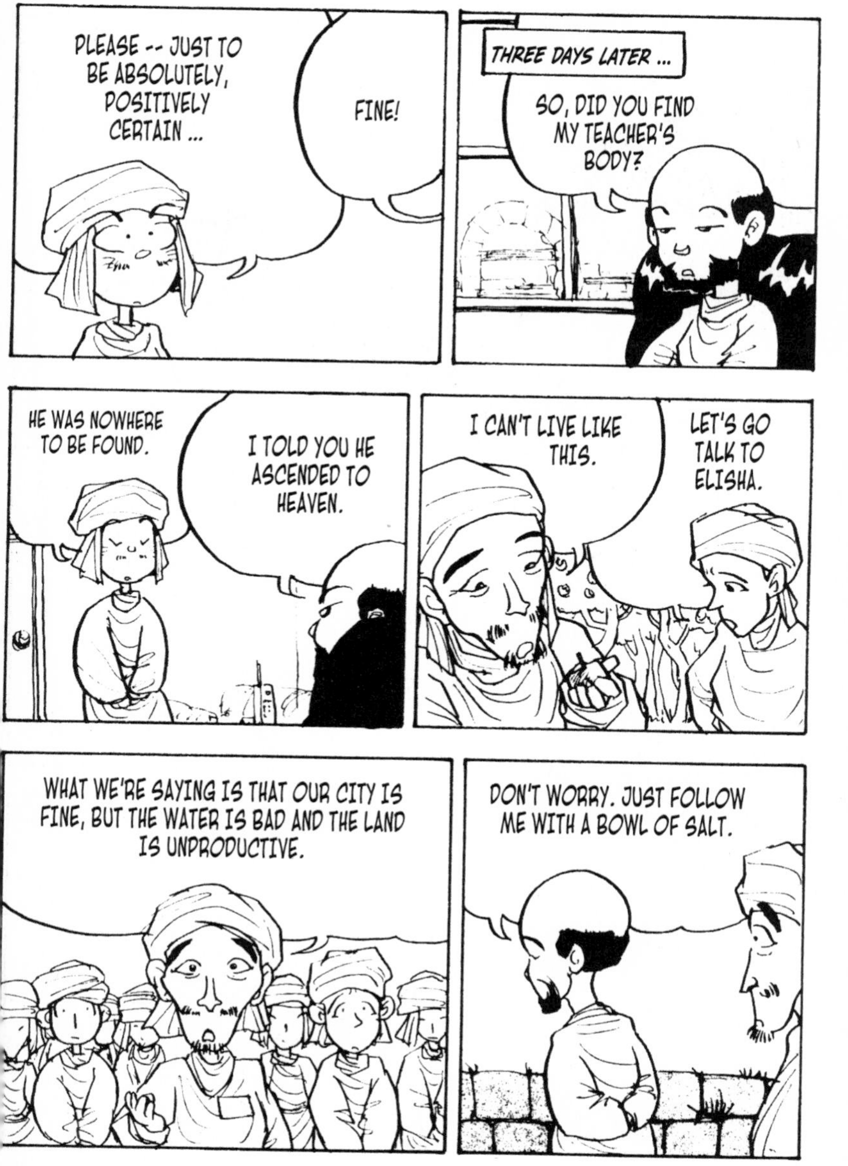
PLEASE -- JUST TO BE ABSOLUTELY, POSITIVELY CERTAIN ...
FINE!
THREE DAYS LATER ...
SO, DID YOU FIND MY TEACHER'S BODY?
HE WAS NOWHERE TO BE FOUND.
I TOLD YOU HE ASCENDED TO HEAVEN.
I CAN'T LIVE LIKE THIS.
LET'S GO TALK TO ELISHA.
WHAT WE'RE SAYING IS THAT OUR CITY IS FINE, BUT THE WATER IS BAD AND THE LAND IS UNPRODUCTIVE.
DON'T WORRY. JUST FOLLOW ME WITH A BOWL OF SALT.

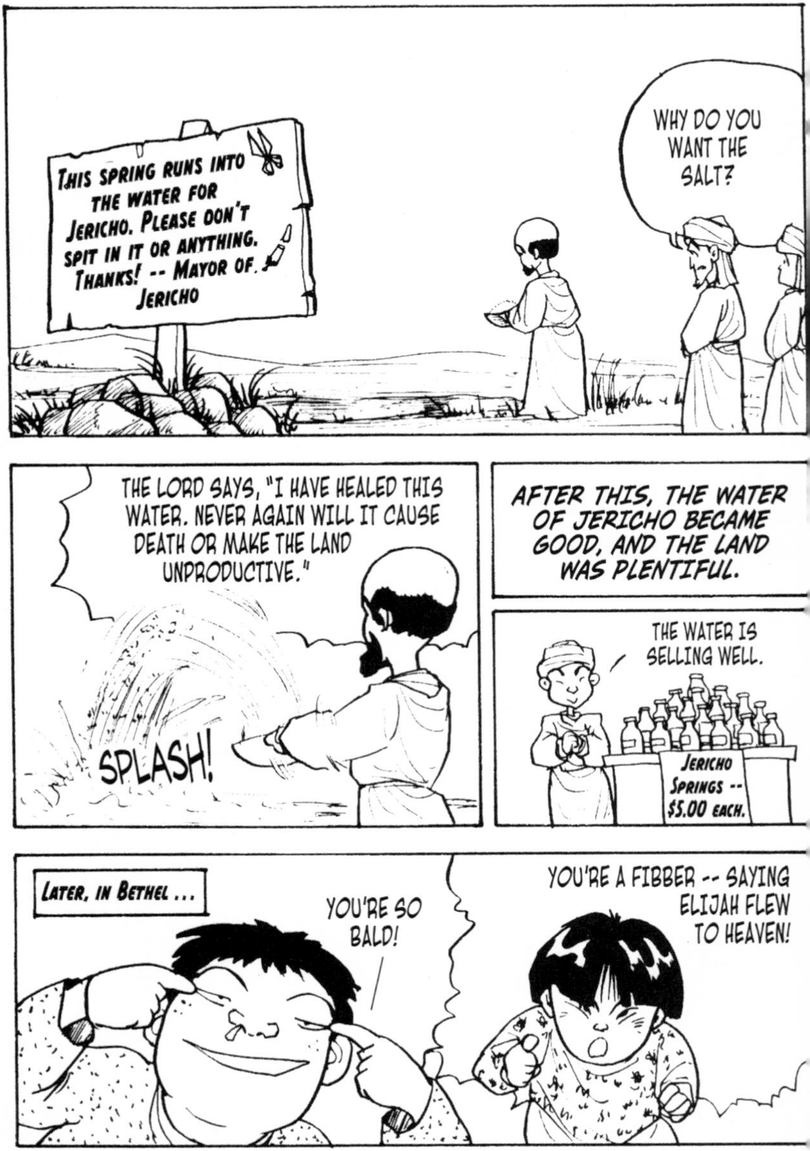
THIS SPRING RUNS INTO THE WATER FOR JERICHO. PLEASE DON'T SPIT IN IT OR ANYTHING. THANKS! -- MAYOR OF JERICHO
WHY DO YOU WANT THE SALT?
THE LORD SAYS, "I HAVE HEALED THIS WATER. NEVER AGAIN WILL IT CAUSE DEATH OR MAKE THE LAND UNPRODUCTIVE."
SPLASH!
AFTER THIS, THE WATER OF JERICHO BECAME GOOD, AND THE LAND WAS PLENTIFUL.
THE WATER IS SELLING WELL.
JERICHO SPRINGS -- $5.00 EACH.
LATER, IN BETHEL ...
YOU'RE SO BALD!
YOU'RE A FIBBER -- SAYING ELIJAH FLEW TO HEAVEN!

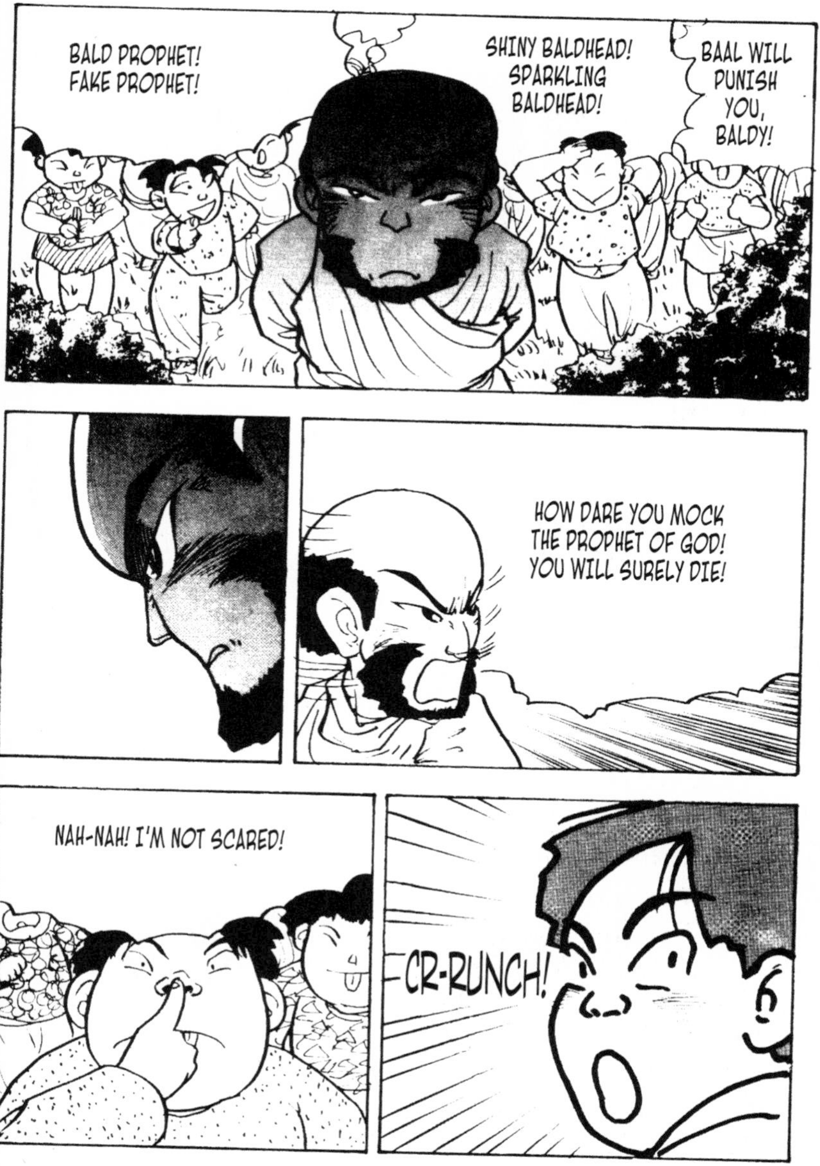
BALD PROPHET! FAKE PROPHET!
SHINY BALDHEAD! SPARKLING BALDHEAD!
BAAL WILL PUNISH YOU, BALDY!
HOW DARE YOU MOCK THE PROPHET OF GOD! YOU WILL SURELY DIE!
NAH-NAH! I'M NOT SCARED!
CR-RUNCH!

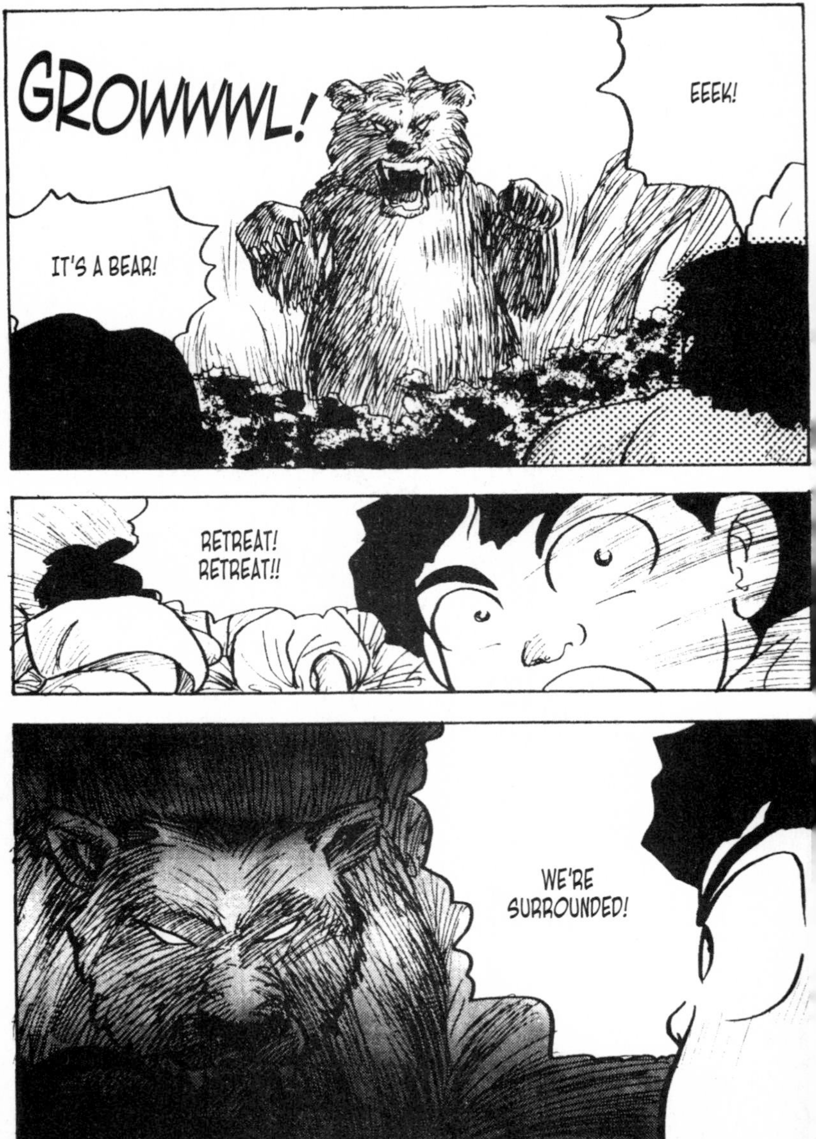
GROWWWL!
EEEK!
IT'S A BEAR!
RETREAT!
RETREAT!!
WE'RE
SURROUNDED!

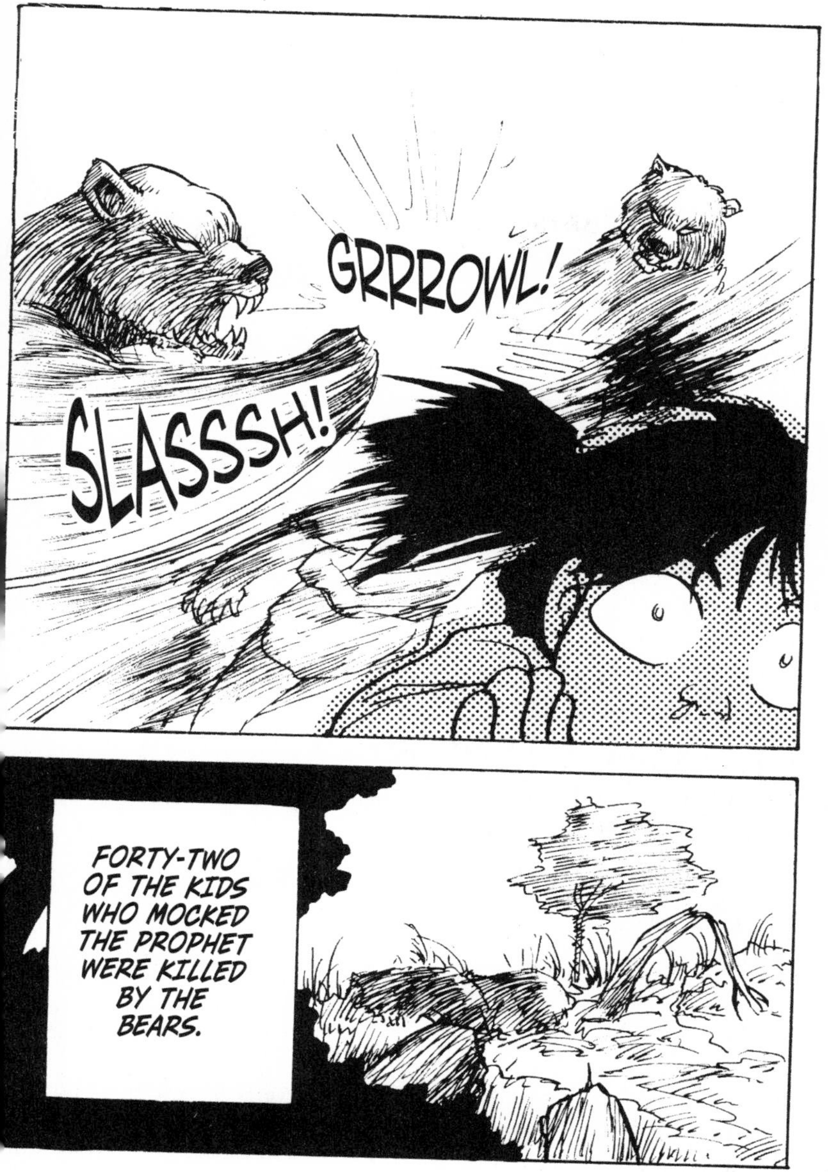
GRRROWL!
SLASSSH!
FORTY-TWO OF THE KIDS WHO MOCKED THE PROPHET WERE KILLED BY THE BEARS.

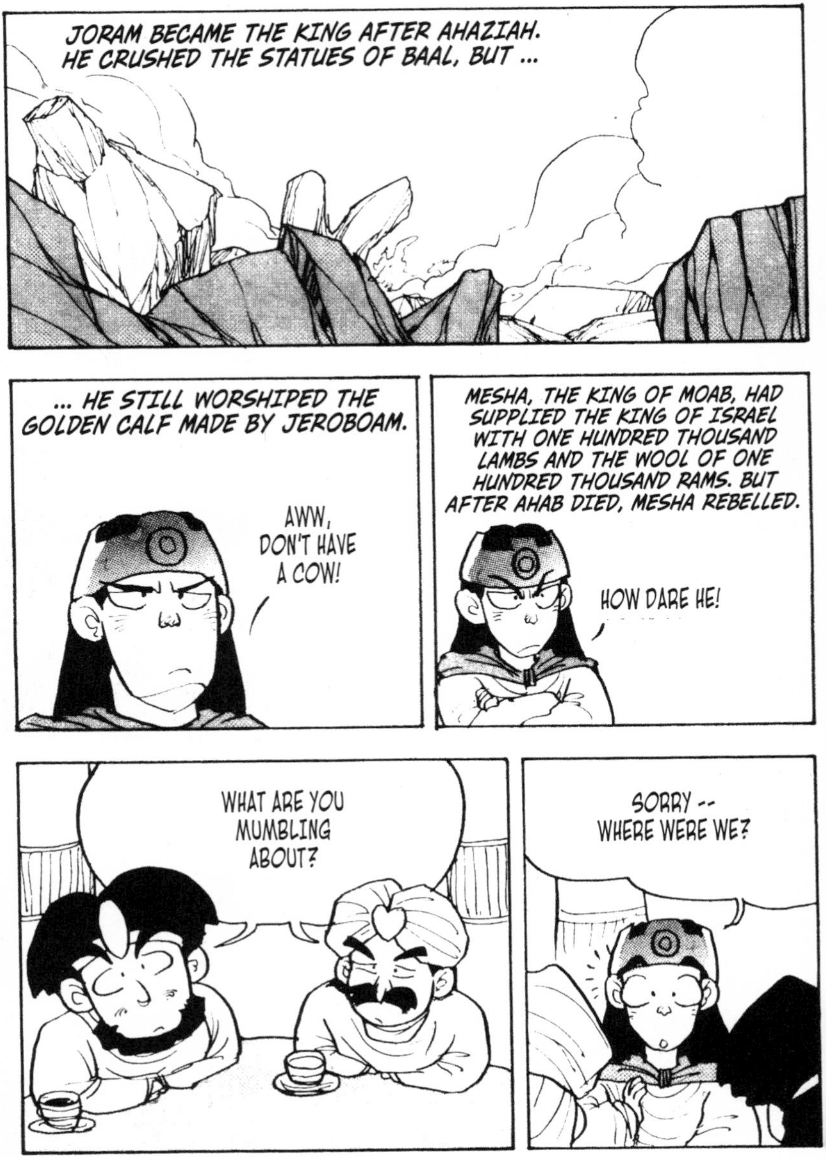
JORAM BECAME THE KING AFTER AHAZIAH. HE CRUSHED THE STATUES OF BAAL, BUT ...
... HE STILL WORSHIPED THE GOLDEN CALF MADE BY JEROBOAM.
AWW, DON'T HAVE A COW!
MESHA, THE KING OF MOAB, HAD SUPPLIED THE KING OF ISRAEL WITH ONE HUNDRED THOUSAND LAMBS AND THE WOOL OF ONE HUNDRED THOUSAND RAMS. BUT AFTER AHAB DIED, MESHA REBELLED.
HOW DARE HE!
WHAT ARE YOU MUMBLING ABOUT?
SORRY -- WHERE WERE WE?

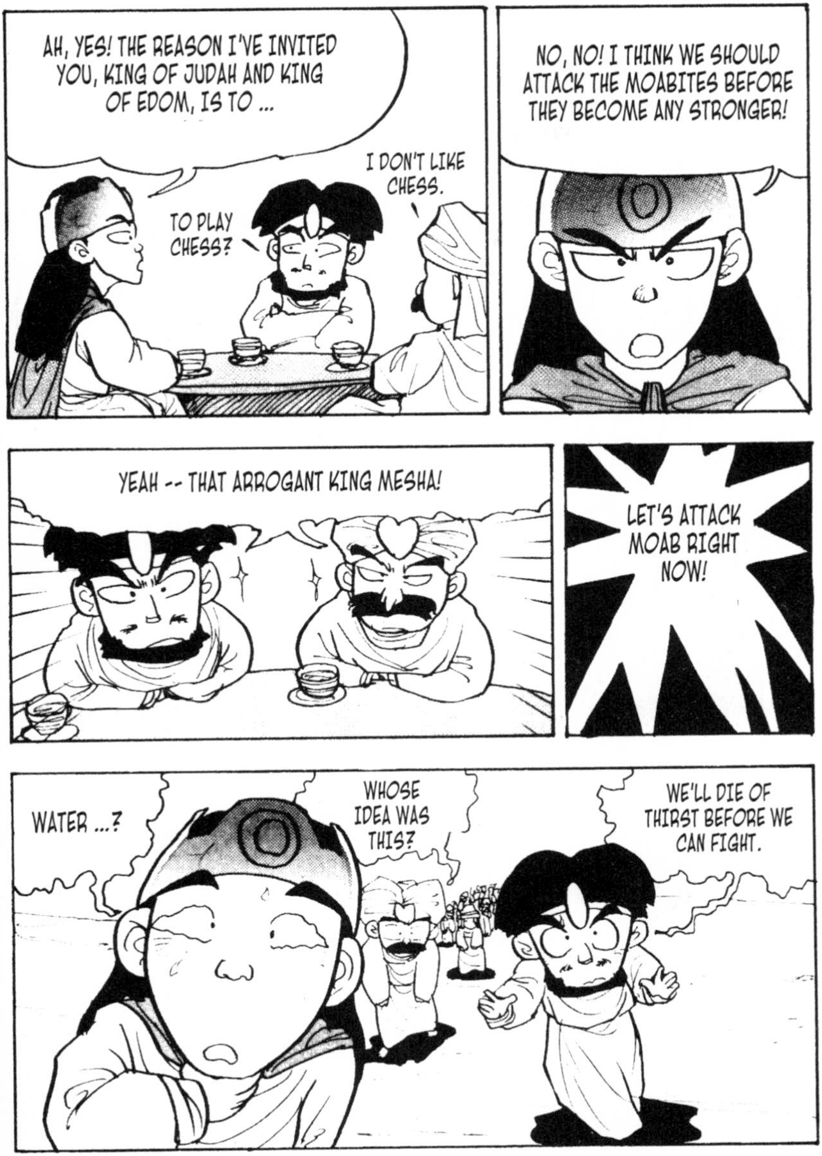
AH, YES! THE REASON I'VE INVITED YOU, KING OF JUDAH AND KING OF EDOM, IS TO ...
TO PLAY CHESS?
I DON'T LIKE CHESS.
NO, NO! I THINK WE SHOULD ATTACK THE MOABITES BEFORE THEY BECOME ANY STRONGER!
YEAH -- THAT ARROGANT KING MESHA!
LET'S ATTACK MOAB RIGHT NOW!
WATER ...?
WHOSE IDEA WAS THIS?
WE'LL DIE OF THIRST BEFORE WE CAN FIGHT.

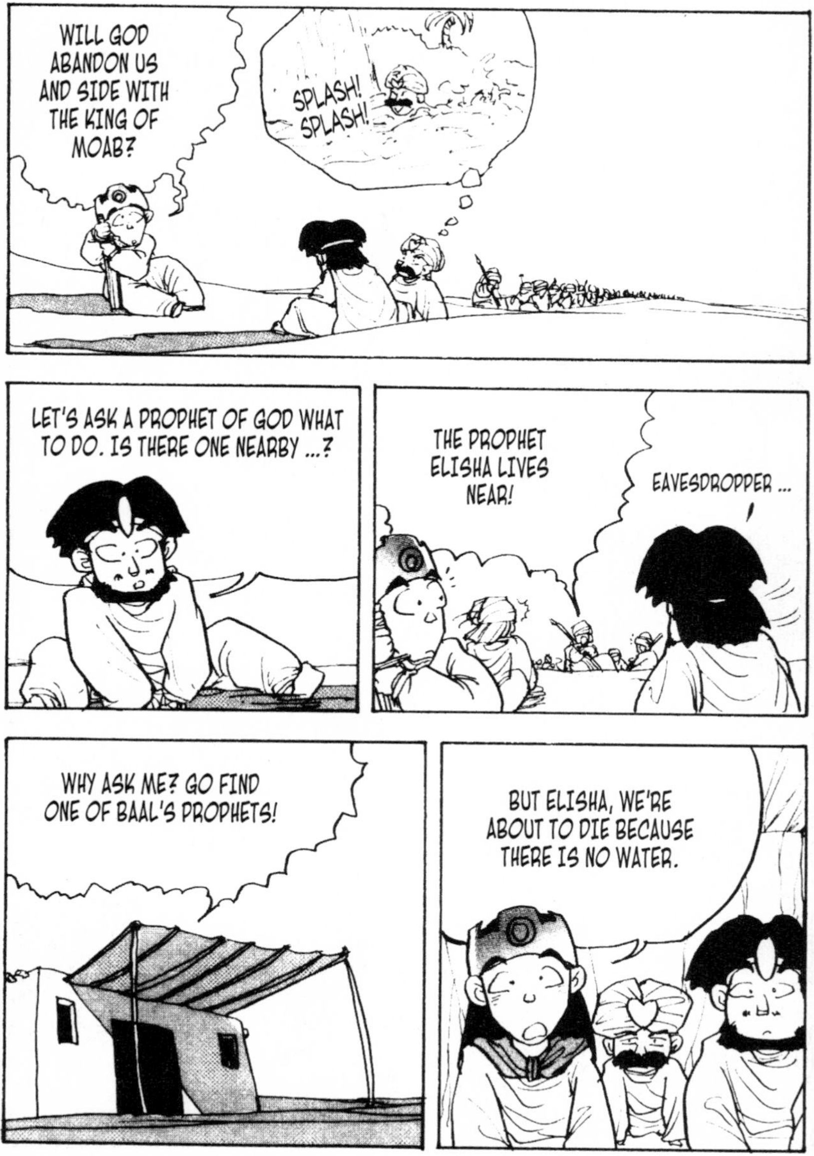
WILL GOD ABANDON US AND SIDE WITH THE KING OF MOAB?
SPLASH! SPLASH!
LET'S ASK A PROPHET OF GOD WHAT TO DO. IS THERE ONE NEARBY ...?
THE PROPHET ELISHA LIVES NEAR!
EAVESDROPPER ...
WHY ASK ME? GO FIND ONE OF BAAL'S PROPHETS!
BUT ELISHA, WE'RE ABOUT TO DIE BECAUSE THERE IS NO WATER.

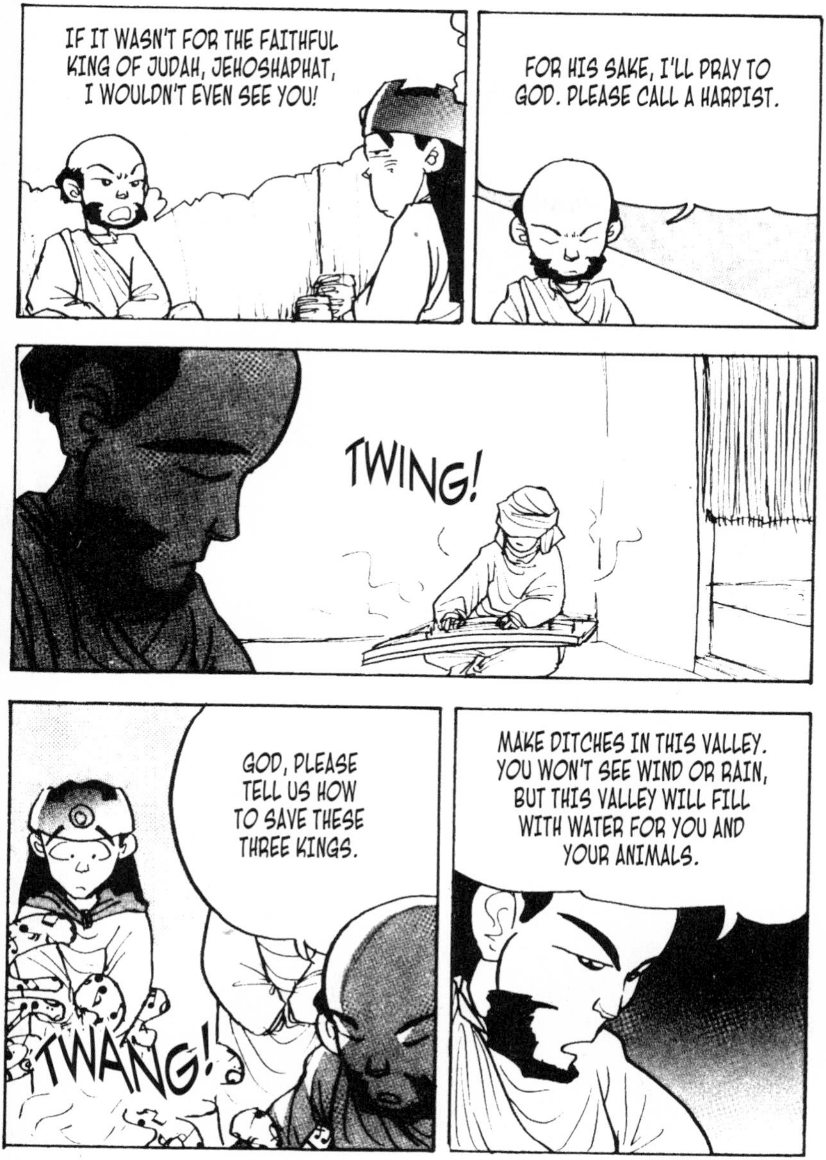
IF IT WASN'T FOR THE FAITHFUL KING OF JUDAH, JEHOSHAPHAT, I WOULDN'T EVEN SEE YOU!
FOR HIS SAKE, I'LL PRAY TO GOD. PLEASE CALL A HARPIST.
TWING!
GOD, PLEASE TELL US HOW TO SAVE THESE THREE KINGS.
TWANG!
MAKE DITCHES IN THIS VALLEY. YOU WON'T SEE WIND OR RAIN, BUT THIS VALLEY WILL FILL WITH WATER FOR YOU AND YOUR ANIMALS.

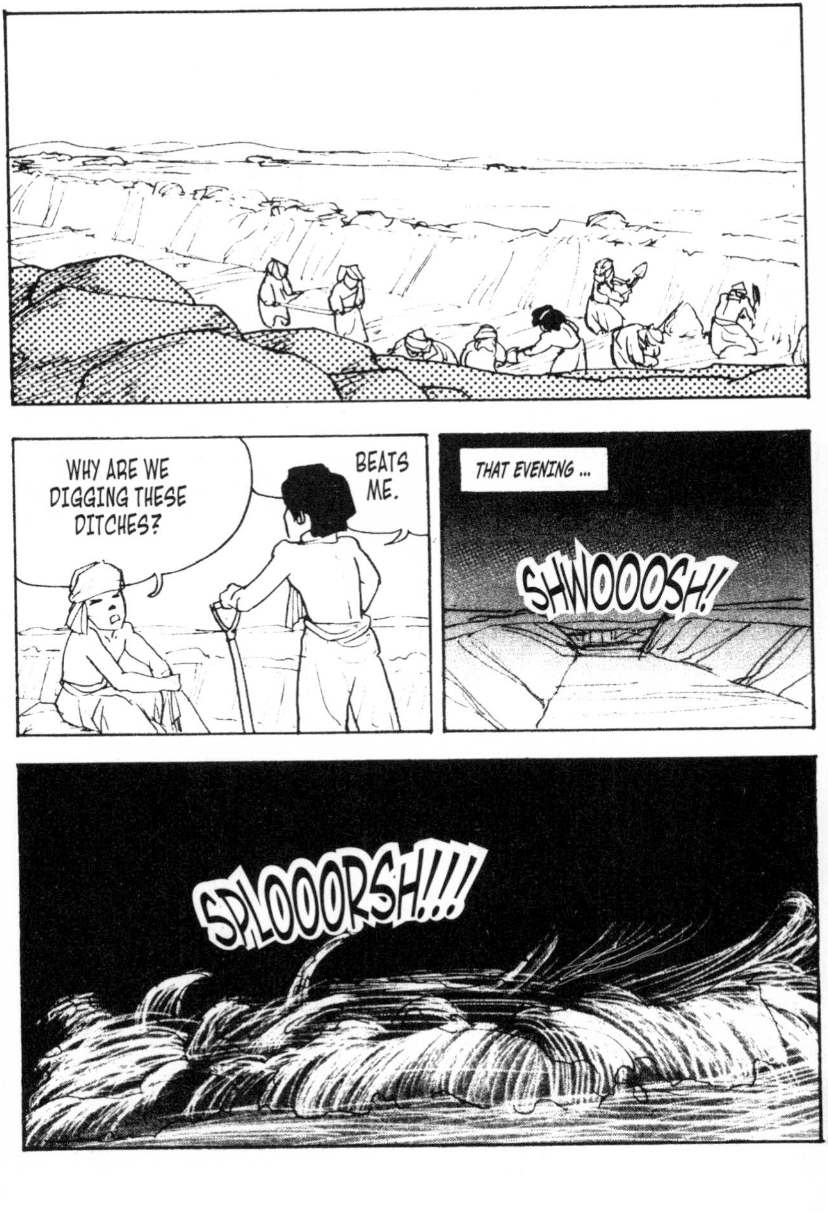
WHY ARE WE DIGGING THESE DITCHES?
BEATS ME.
THAT EVENING ...
SHWOOOSH!
SPLOOORSH!!!!

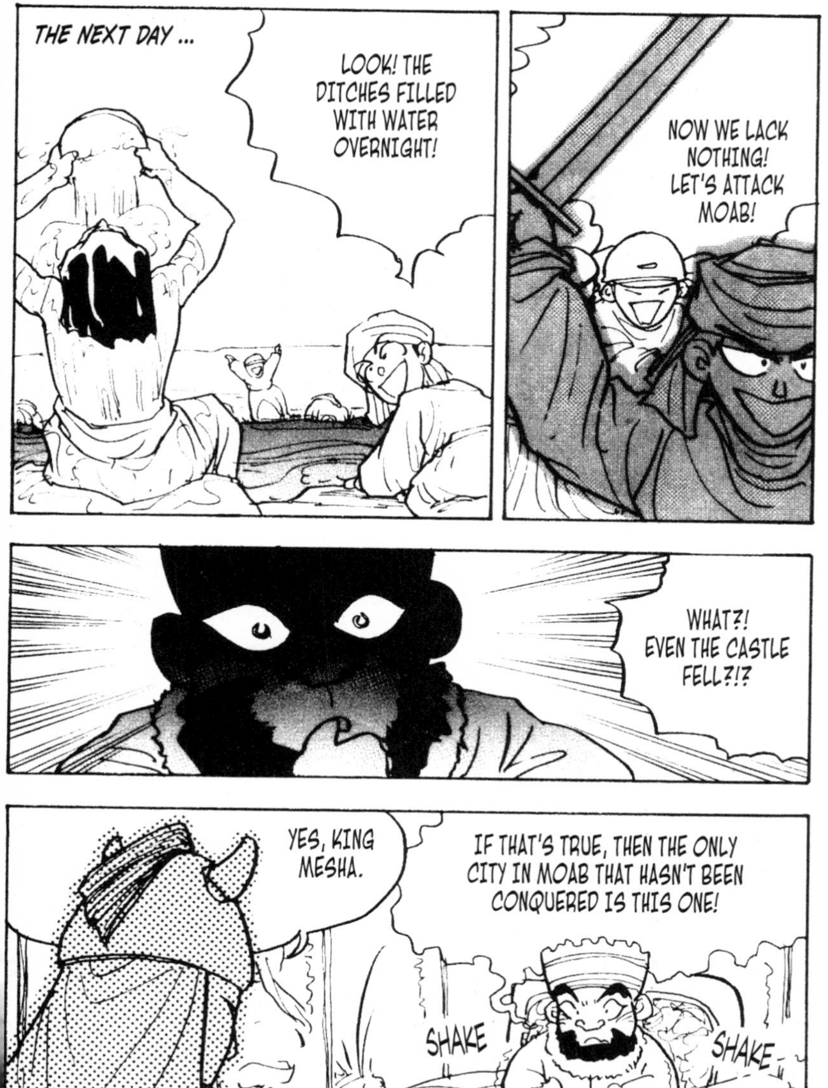
THE NEXT DAY ...
LOOK! THE DITCHES FILLED WITH WATER OVERNIGHT!
NOW WE LACK NOTHING! LET'S ATTACK MOAB!
WHAT?! EVEN THE CASTLE FELL?!?
YES, KING MESHA.
IF THAT'S TRUE, THEN THE ONLY CITY IN MOAB THAT HASN'T BEEN CONQUERED IS THIS ONE!
SHAKE
SHAKE

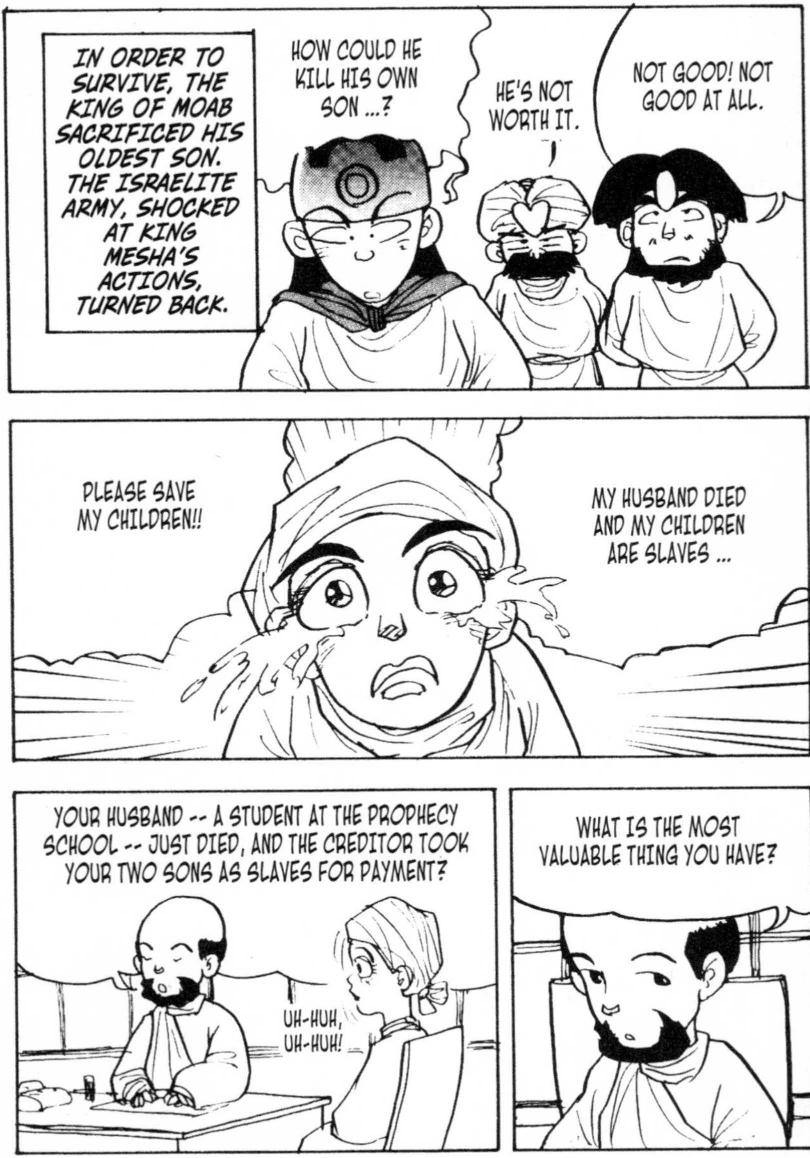
IN ORDER TO SURVIVE, THE KING OF MOAB SACRIFICED HIS OLDEST SON. THE ISRAELITE ARMY, SHOCKED AT KING MESHA'S ACTIONS, TURNED BACK.
HOW COULD HE KILL HIS OWN SON ...?
HE'S NOT WORTH IT.
NOT GOOD! NOT GOOD AT ALL.
PLEASE SAVE MY CHILDREN!!
MY HUSBAND DIED AND MY CHILDREN ARE SLAVES ...
YOUR HUSBAND -- A STUDENT AT THE PROPHECY SCHOOL -- JUST DIED, AND THE CREDITOR TOOK YOUR TWO SONS AS SLAVES FOR PAYMENT?
UH-HUH, UH-HUH!
WHAT IS THE MOST VALUABLE THING YOU HAVE?

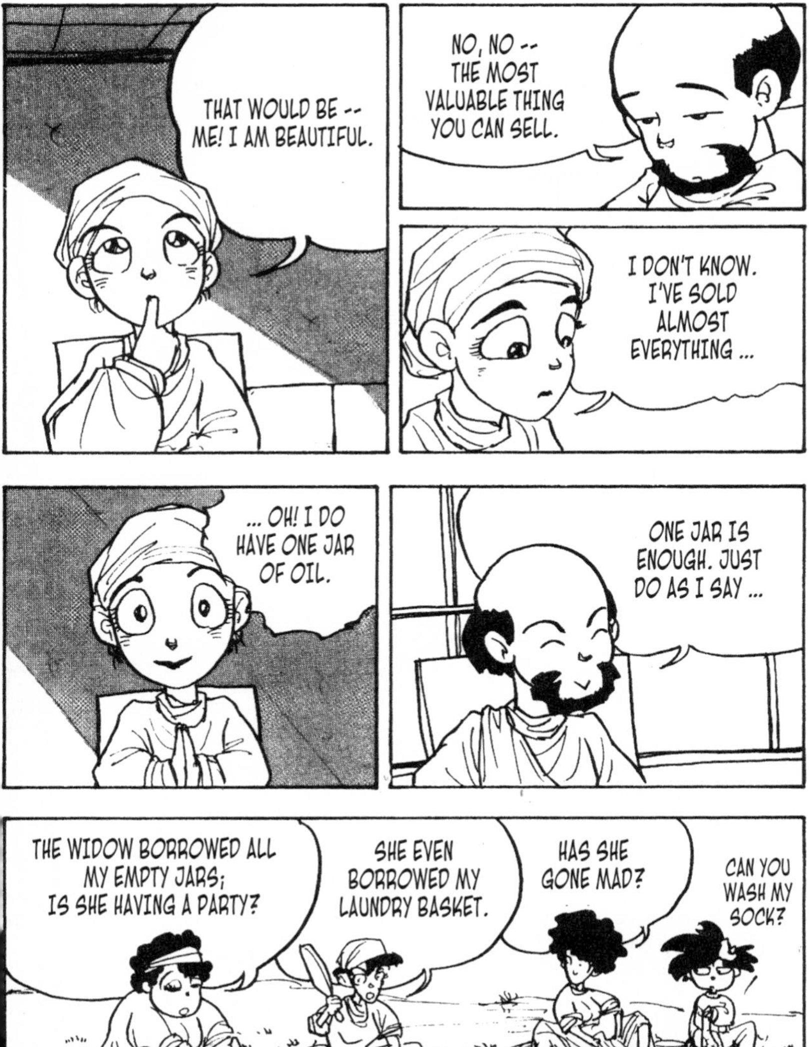
THAT WOULD BE --
ME! I AM BEAUTIFUL.
NO, NO --
THE MOST
VALUABLE THING
YOU CAN SELL.
I DON'T KNOW.
I'VE SOLD
ALMOST
EVERYTHING ...
... OH! I DO
HAVE ONE JAR
OF OIL.
ONE JAR IS
ENOUGH. JUST
DO AS I SAY ...
THE WIDOW BORROWED ALL
MY EMPTY JARS;
IS SHE HAVING A PARTY?
SHE EVEN
BORROWED MY
LAUNDRY BASKET.
HAS SHE
GONE MAD?
CAN YOU
WASH MY
SOCK?

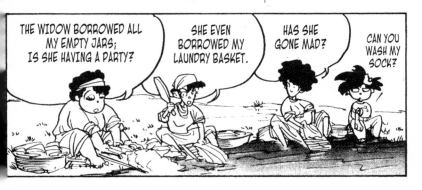

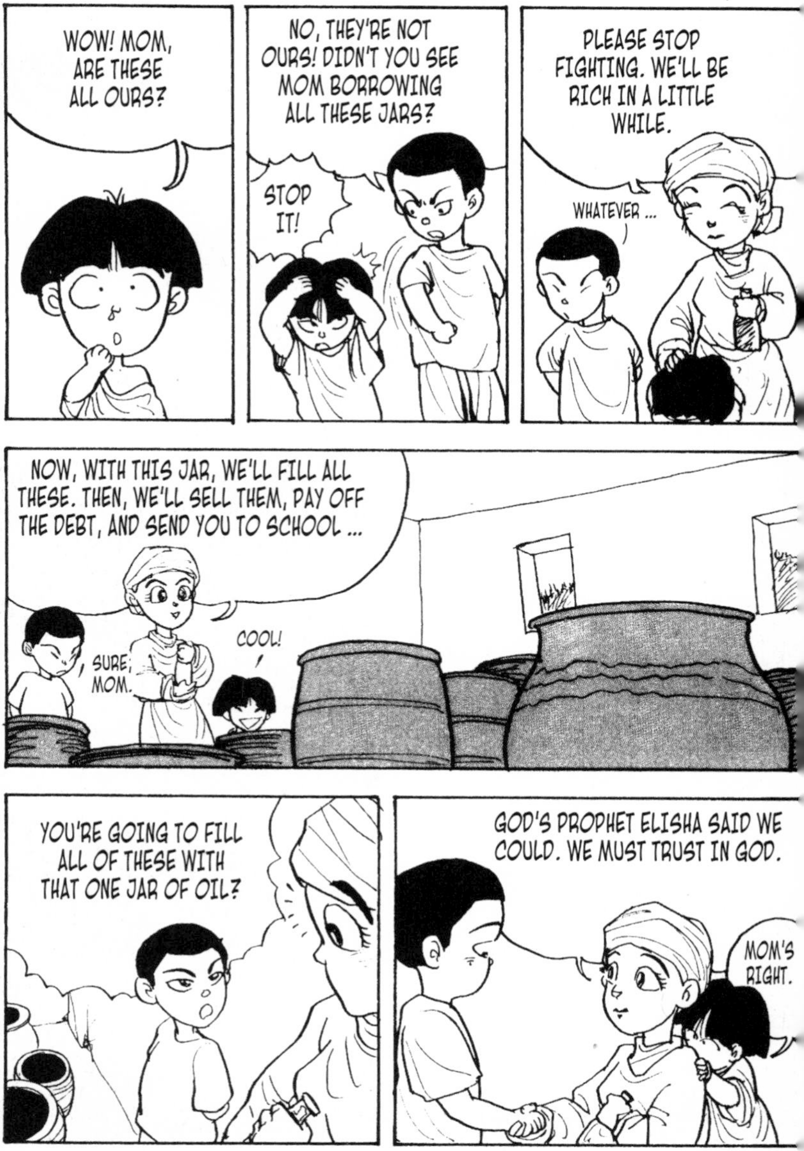

WOW! MOM, ARE THESE ALL OURS?
NO, THEY'RE NOT OURS! DIDN'T YOU SEE MOM BORROWING ALL THESE JARS?
STOP IT!
PLEASE STOP FIGHTING. WE'LL BE RICH IN A LITTLE WHILE.
WHATEVER ...
NOW, WITH THIS JAR, WE'LL FILL ALL THESE. THEN, WE'LL SELL THEM, PAY OFF THE DEBT, AND SEND YOU TO SCHOOL ...
SURE, MOM.
COOL!
YOU'RE GOING TO FILL ALL OF THESE WITH THAT ONE JAR OF OIL?
GOD'S PROPHET ELISHA SAID WE COULD. WE MUST TRUST IN GOD.
MOM'S RIGHT.

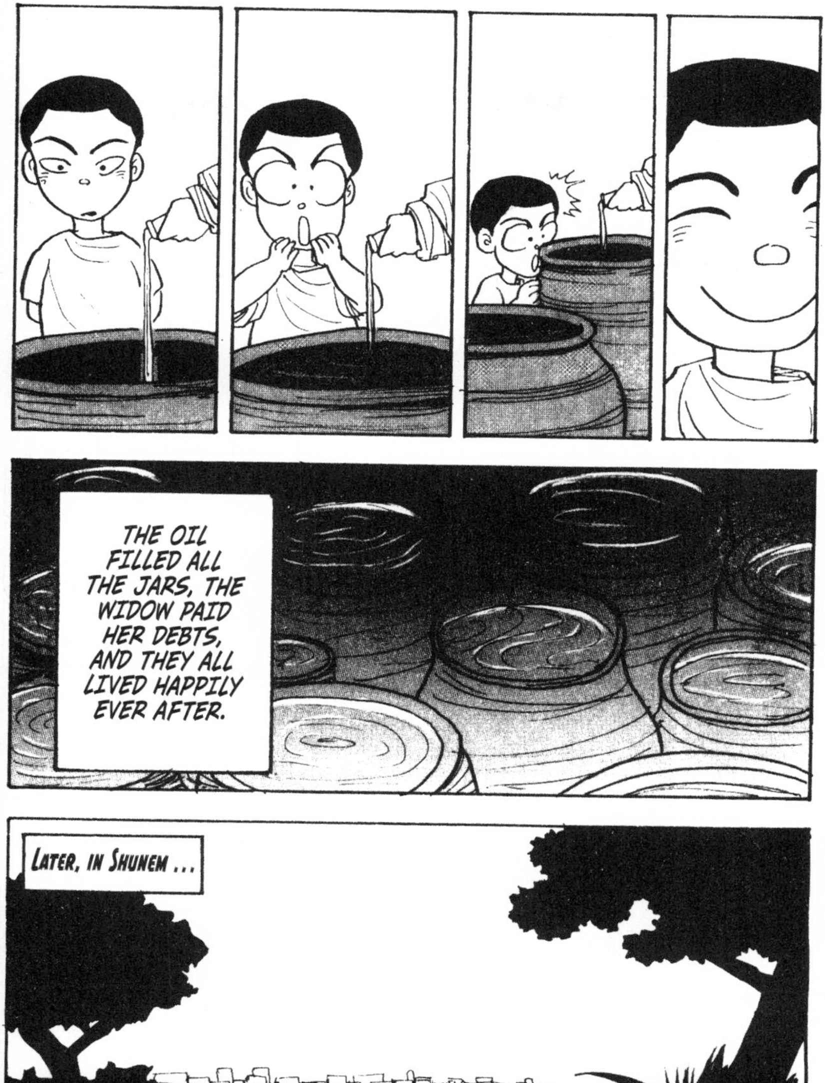
THE OIL FILLED ALL THE JARS, THE WIDOW PAID HER DEBTS, AND THEY ALL LIVED HAPPILY EVER AFTER.
LATER, IN SHUNEM ...

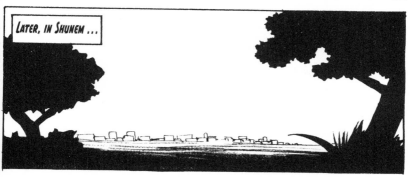

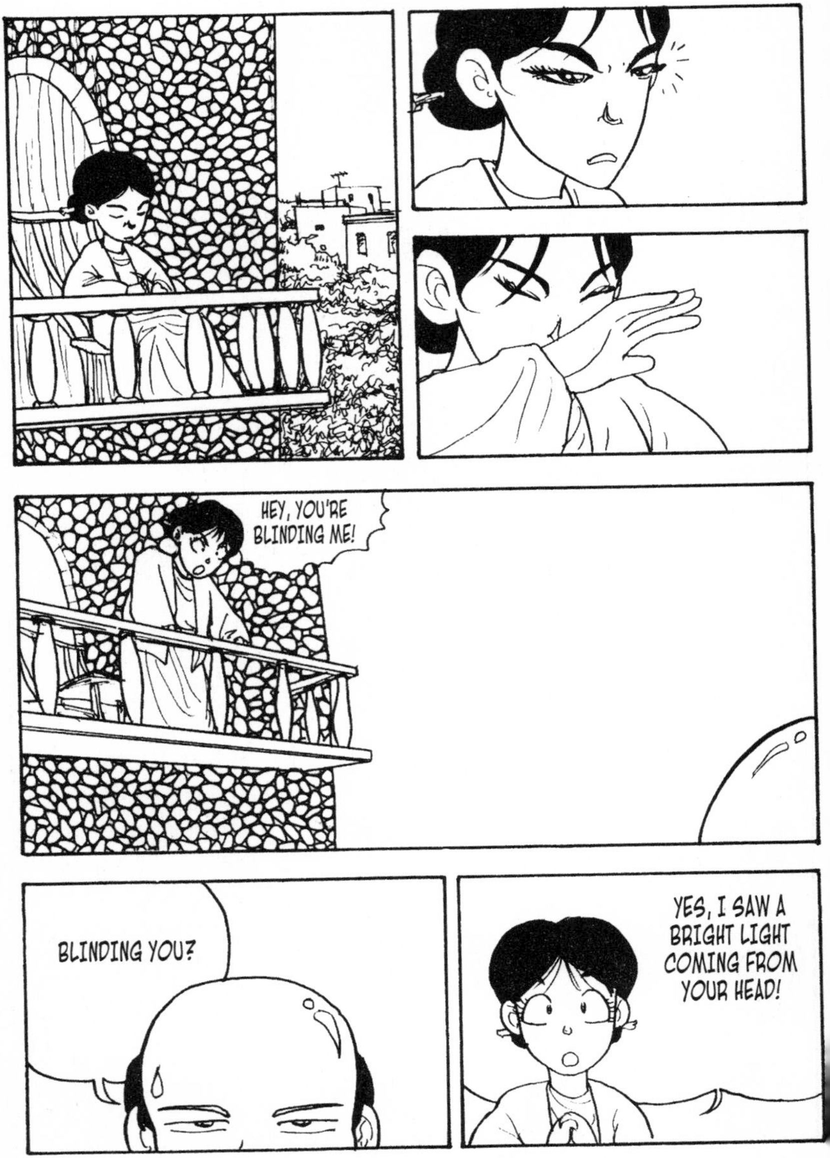
HEY, YOU'RE BLINDING ME!
BLINDING YOU?
YES, I SAW A BRIGHT LIGHT COMING FROM YOUR HEAD!

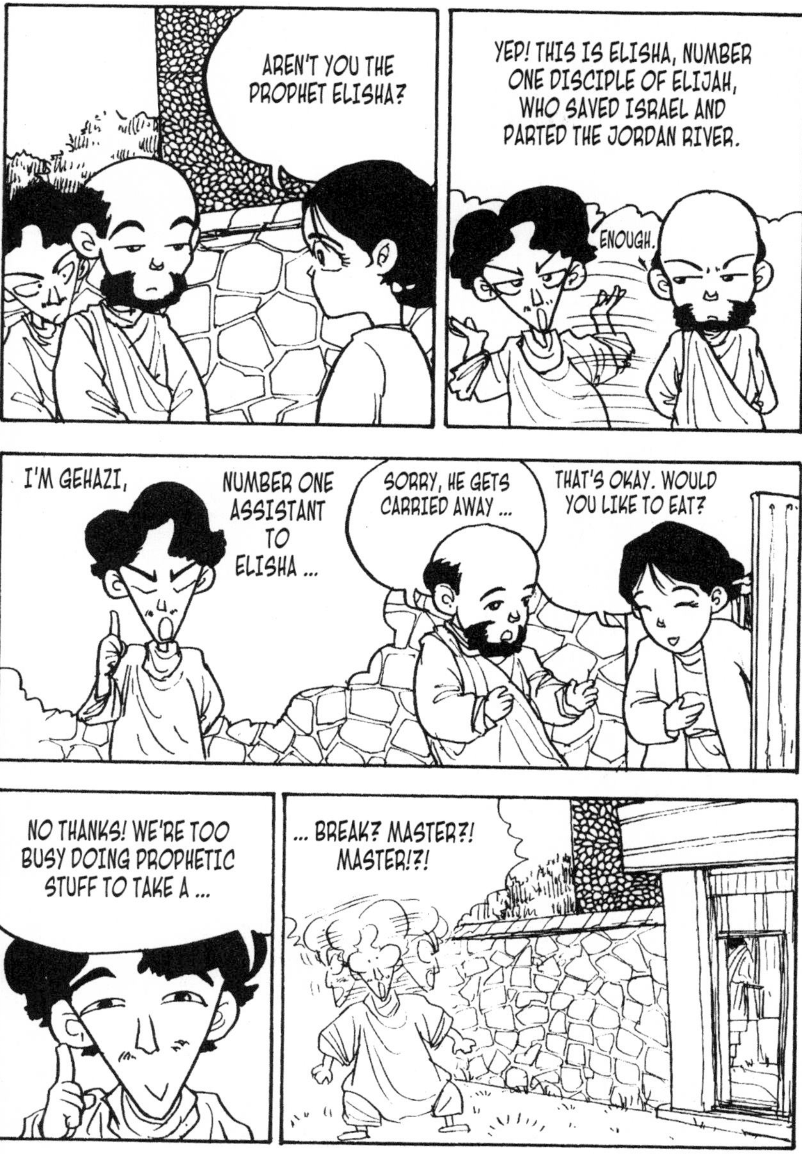
AREN'T YOU THE PROPHET ELISHA?
YEP! THIS IS ELISHA, NUMBER ONE DISCIPLE OF ELIJAH, WHO SAVED ISRAEL AND PARTED THE JORDAN RIVER.
ENOUGH.
I'M GEHAZI,
NUMBER ONE ASSISTANT TO ELISHA ...
SORRY, HE GETS CARRIED AWAY ...
THAT'S OKAY. WOULD YOU LIKE TO EAT?
NO THANKS! WE'RE TOO BUSY DOING PROPHETIC STUFF TO TAKE A ...
... BREAK? MASTER?!
MASTER!?!

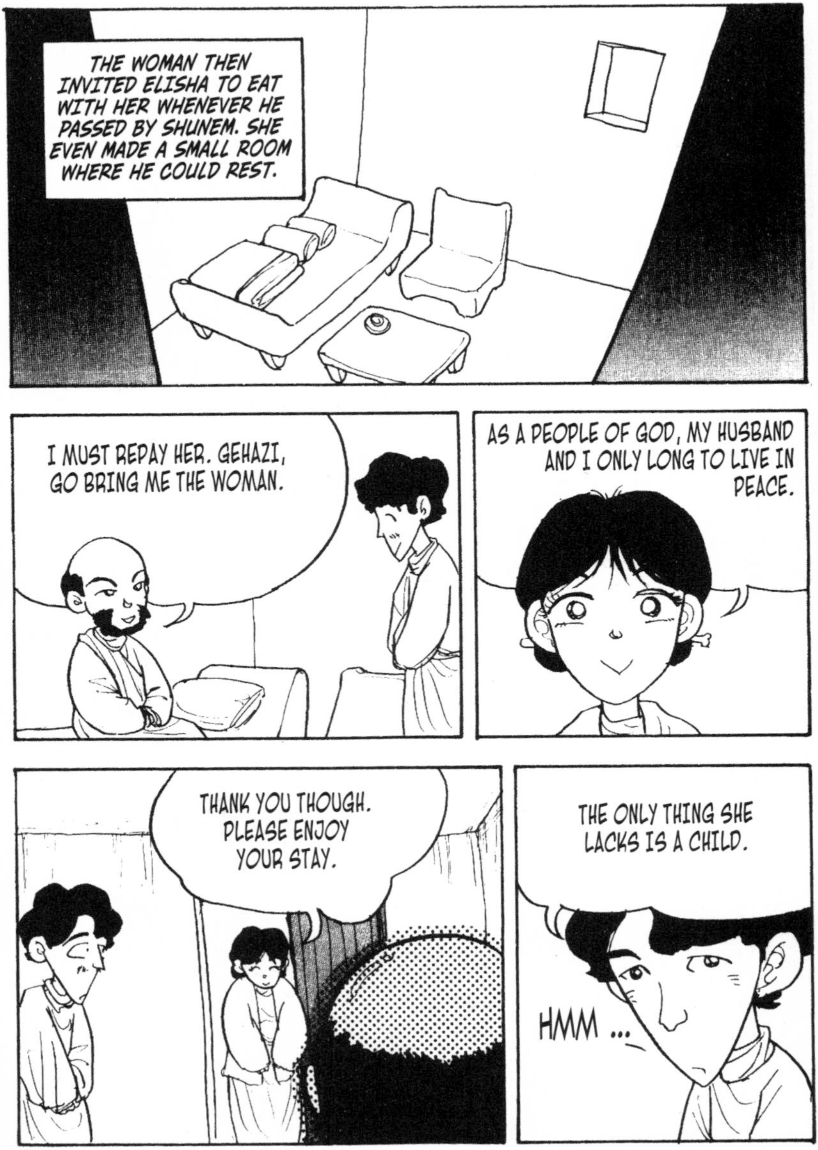
THE WOMAN THEN INVITED ELISHA TO EAT WITH HER WHENEVER HE PASSED BY SHUNEM. SHE EVEN MADE A SMALL ROOM WHERE HE COULD REST.
I MUST REPAY HER. GEHAZI, GO BRING ME THE WOMAN.
AS A PEOPLE OF GOD, MY HUSBAND AND I ONLY LONG TO LIVE IN PEACE.
THANK YOU THOUGH. PLEASE ENJOY YOUR STAY.
THE ONLY THING SHE LACKS IS A CHILD.
HMM ...

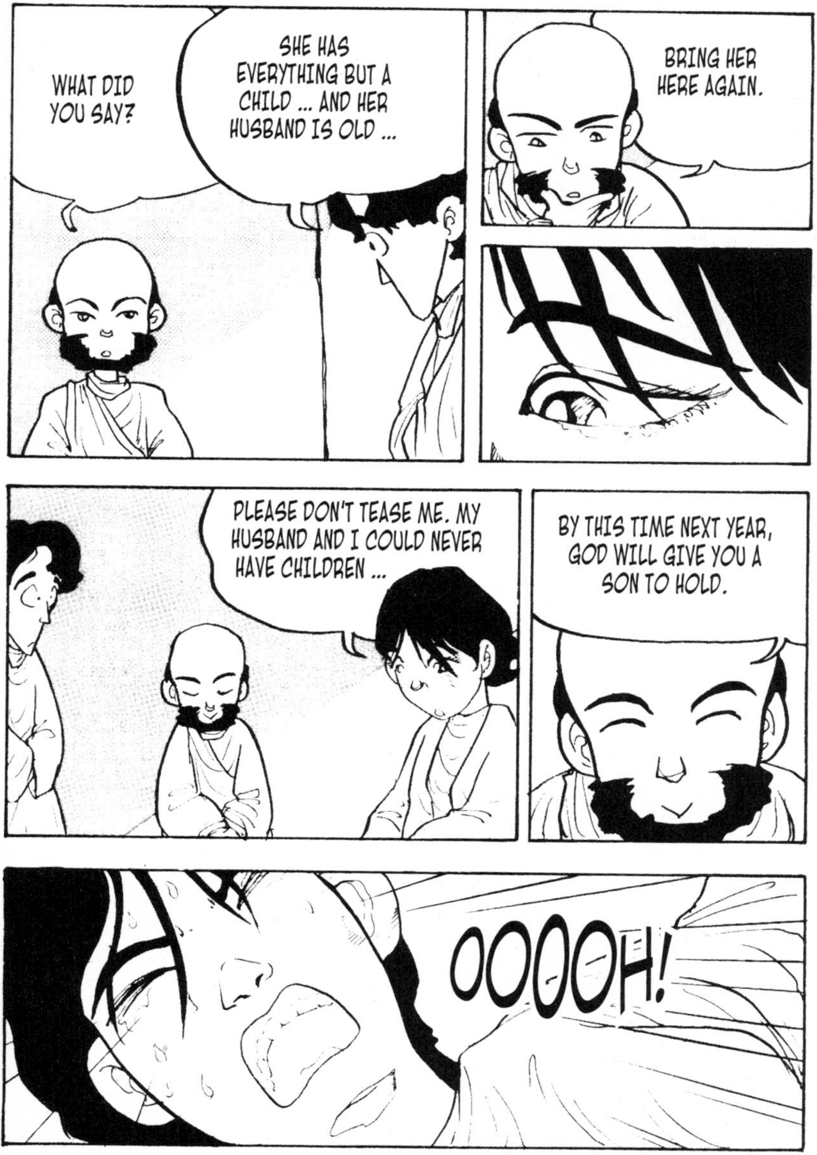
WHAT DID YOU SAY?
SHE HAS EVERYTHING BUT A CHILD ... AND HER HUSBAND IS OLD ...
BRING HER HERE AGAIN.
PLEASE DON'T TEASE ME. MY HUSBAND AND I COULD NEVER HAVE CHILDREN ...
BY THIS TIME NEXT YEAR, GOD WILL GIVE YOU A SON TO HOLD.
OOOOH!

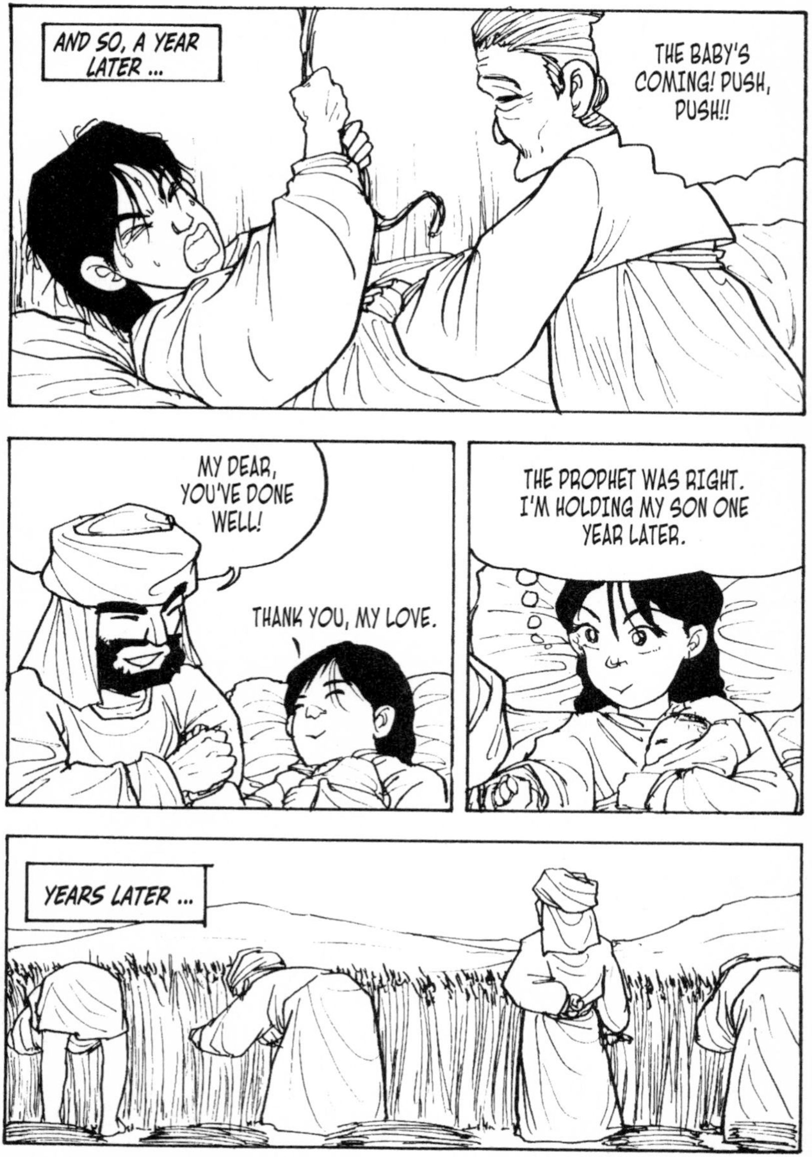
AND SO, A YEAR LATER ...
THE BABY'S COMING! PUSH, PUSH!!
MY DEAR, YOU'VE DONE WELL!
THANK YOU, MY LOVE.
THE PROPHET WAS RIGHT. I'M HOLDING MY SON ONE YEAR LATER.
YEARS LATER ...

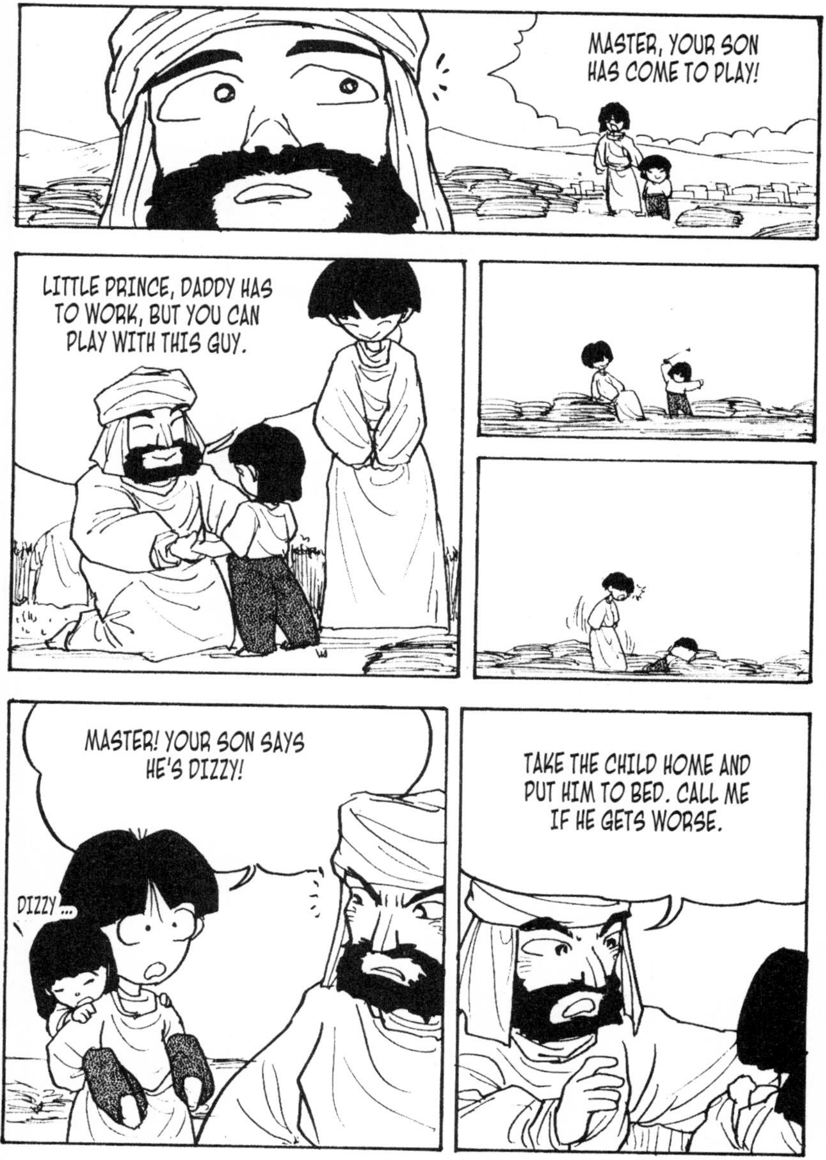
MASTER, YOUR SON HAS COME TO PLAY!
LITTLE PRINCE, DADDY HAS TO WORK, BUT YOU CAN PLAY WITH THIS GUY.
MASTER! YOUR SON SAYS HE'S DIZZY!
DIZZY...
TAKE THE CHILD HOME AND PUT HIM TO BED. CALL ME IF HE GETS WORSE.

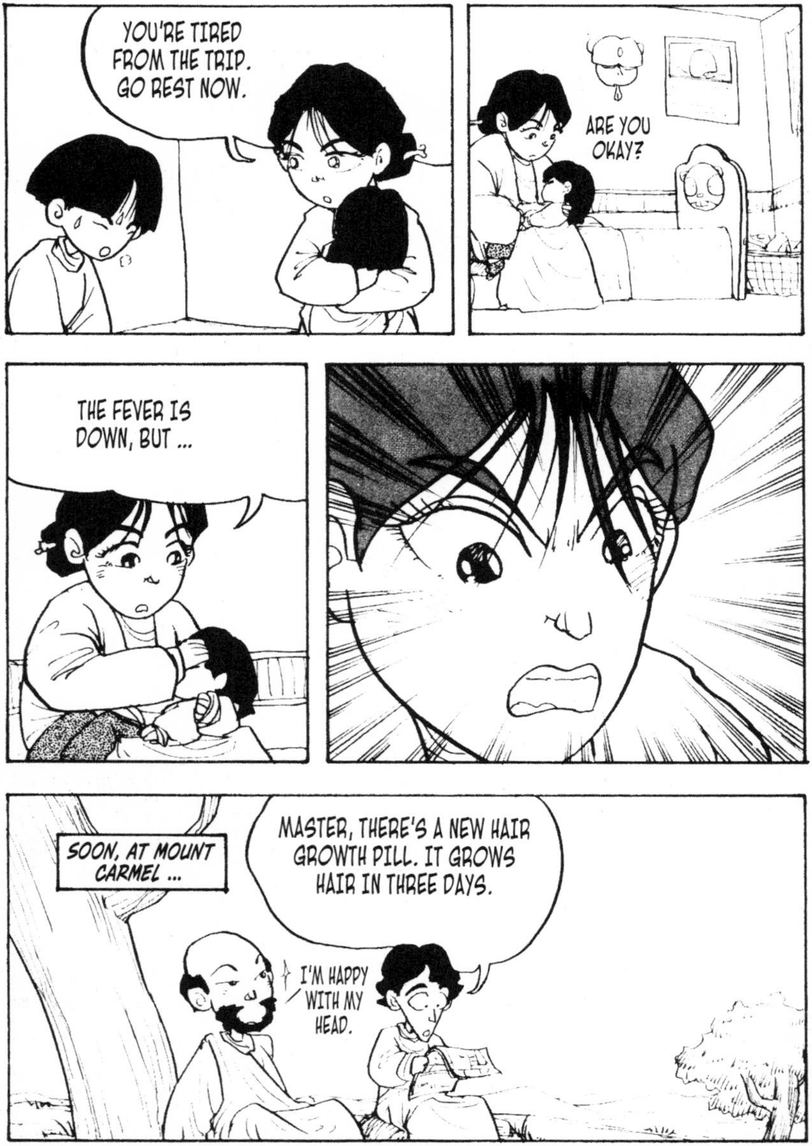
YOU'RE TIRED FROM THE TRIP. GO REST NOW.
ARE YOU OKAY?
THE FEVER IS DOWN, BUT ...
SOON, AT MOUNT CARMEL ...
MASTER, THERE'S A NEW HAIR GROWTH PILL. IT GROWS HAIR IN THREE DAYS.
I'M HAPPY WITH MY HEAD.

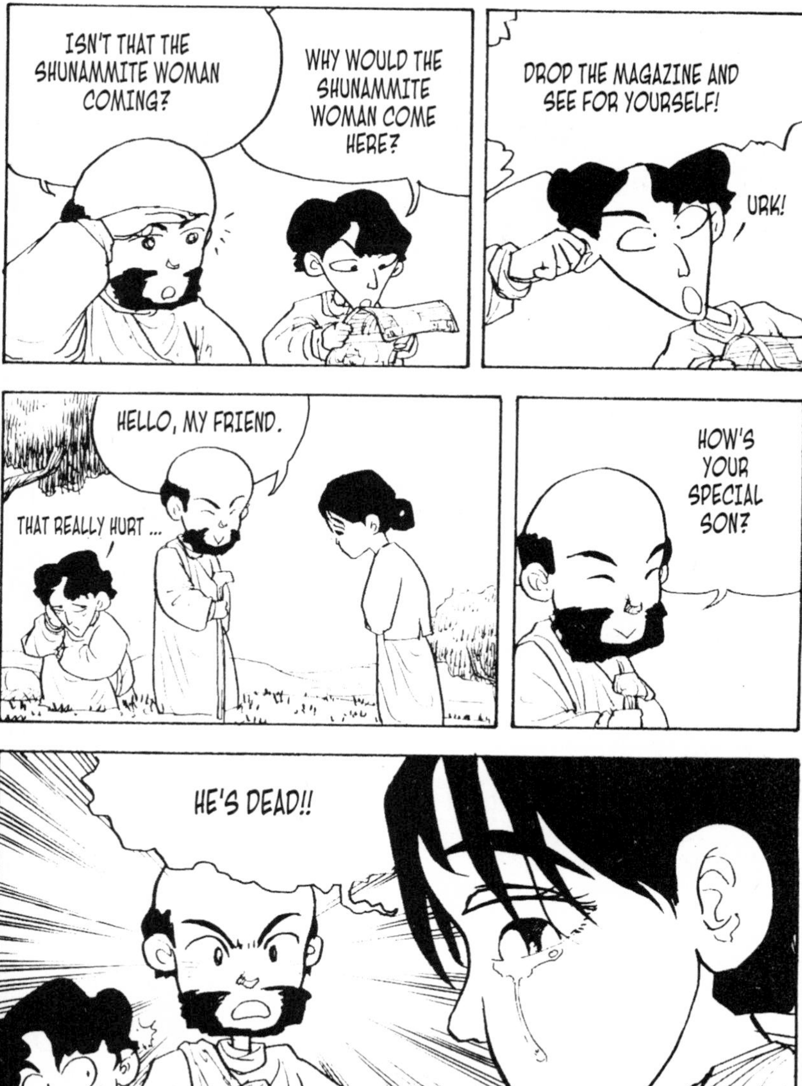
ISN'T THAT THE SHUNAMMITE WOMAN COMING?
WHY WOULD THE SHUNAMMITE WOMAN COME HERE?
DROP THE MAGAZINE AND SEE FOR YOURSELF!
URK!
HELLO, MY FRIEND.
THAT REALLY HURT ...
HOW'S YOUR SPECIAL SON?
HE'S DEAD!!

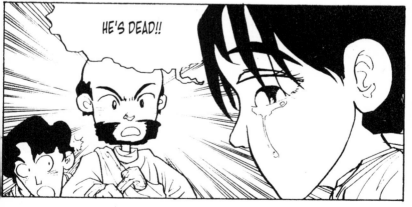

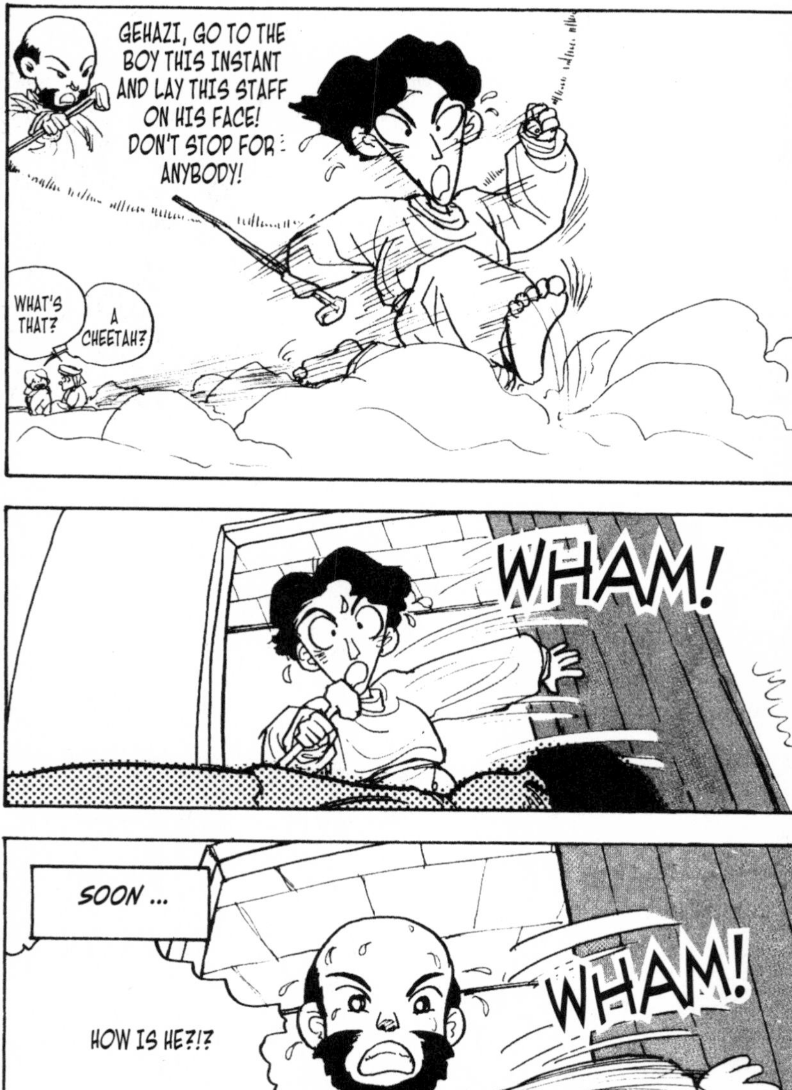
GEHAZI, GO TO THE BOY THIS INSTANT AND LAY THIS STAFF ON HIS FACE! DON'T STOP FOR ANYBODY!
WHAT'S THAT?
A CHEETAH?
WHAM!
SOON ...
HOW IS HE?!?
WHAM!

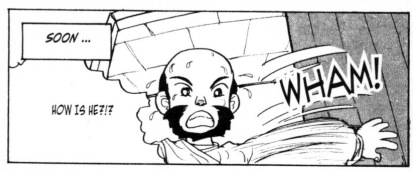

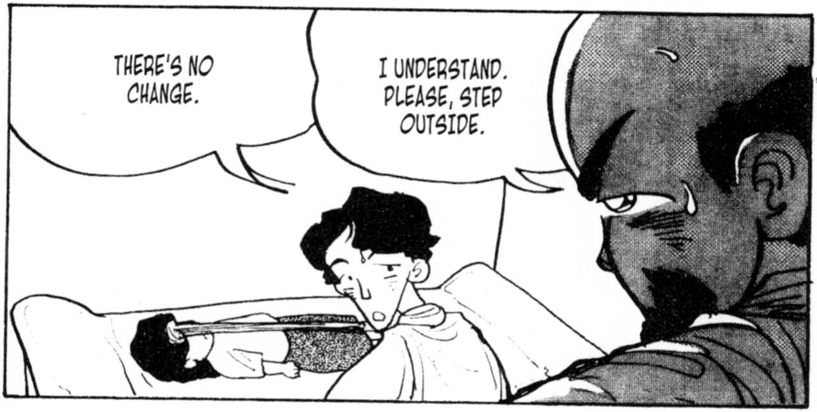
THERE'S NO CHANGE.
I UNDERSTAND. PLEASE, STEP OUTSIDE.
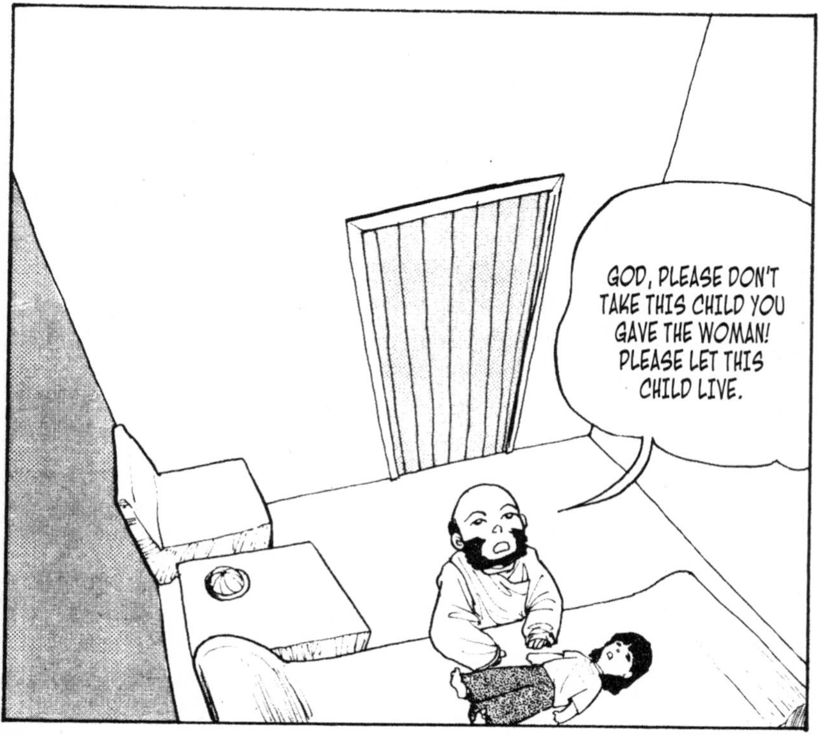
GOD, PLEASE DON'T TAKE THIS CHILD YOU GAVE THE WOMAN! PLEASE LET THIS CHILD LIVE.

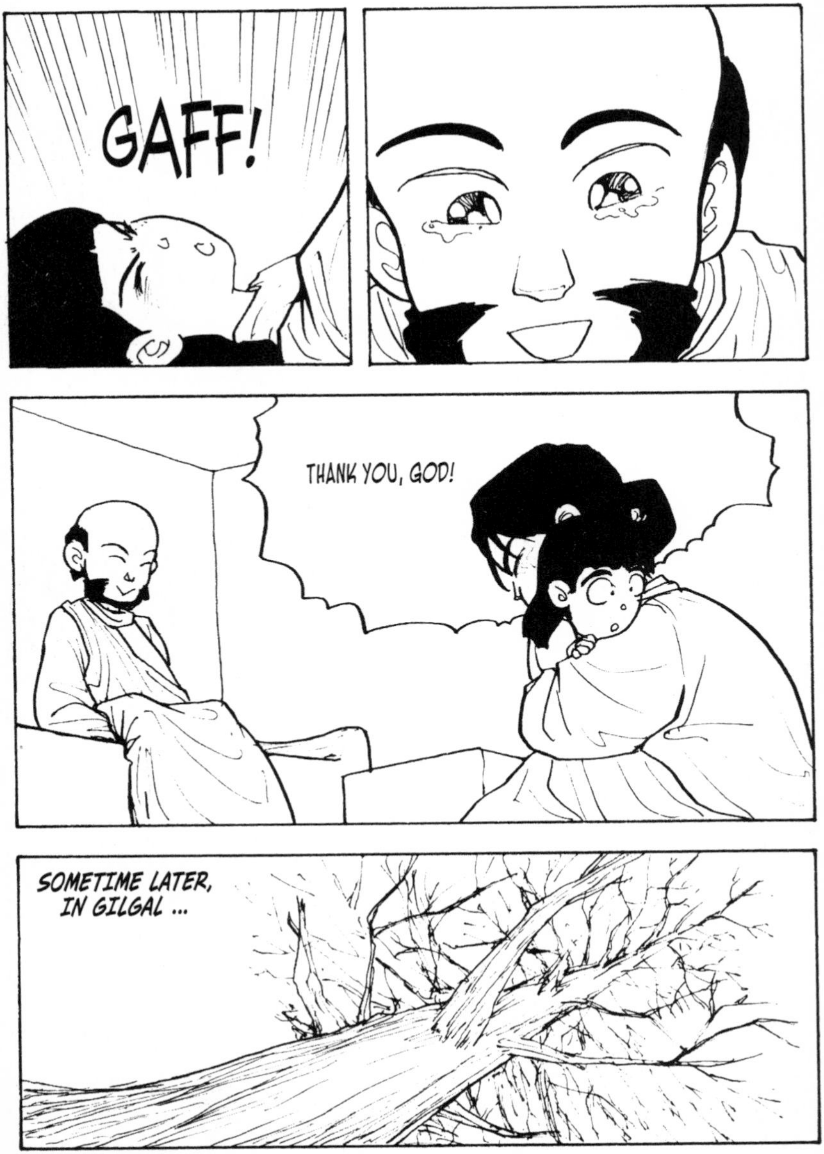
GAFF!
THANK YOU, GOD!
SOMETIME LATER, IN GILGAL ...

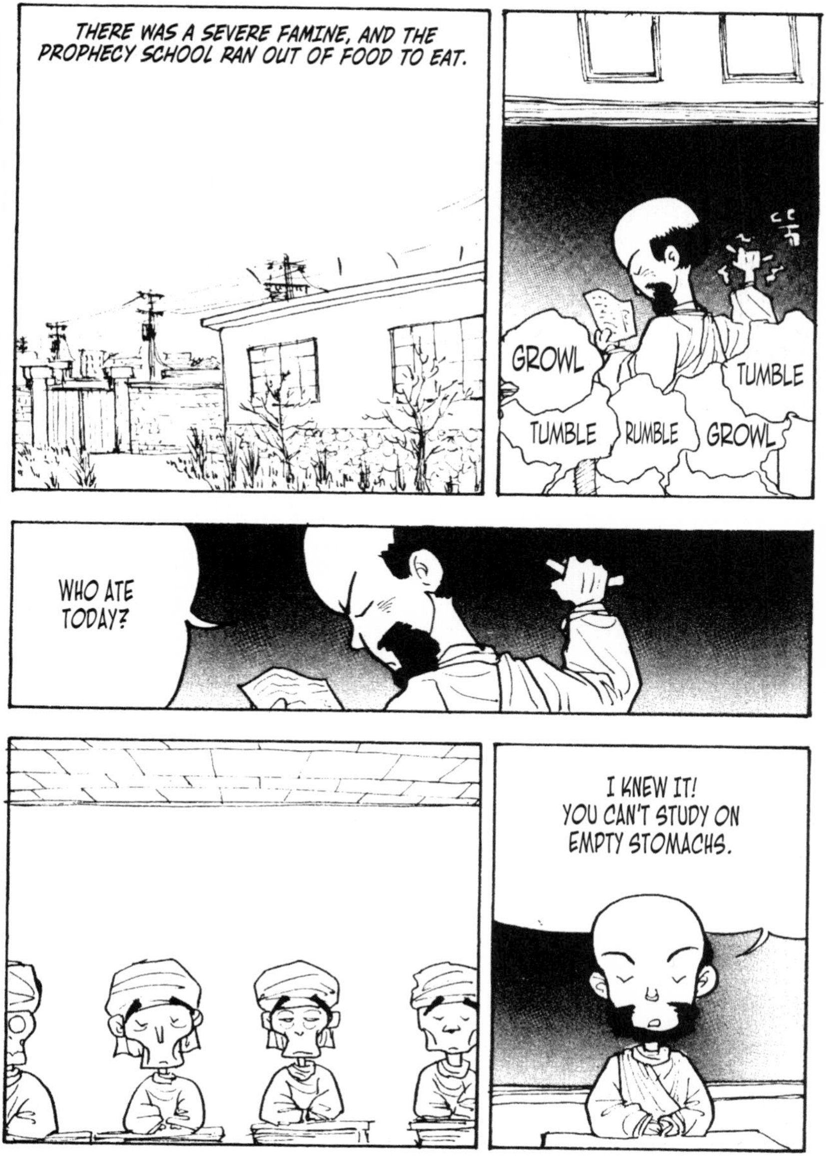
THERE WAS A SEVERE FAMINE, AND THE PROPHECY SCHOOL RAN OUT OF FOOD TO EAT.
GROWL
TUMBLE
TUMBLE
RUMBLE
GROWL
WHO ATE TODAY?
I KNEW IT! YOU CAN'T STUDY ON EMPTY STOMACHS.

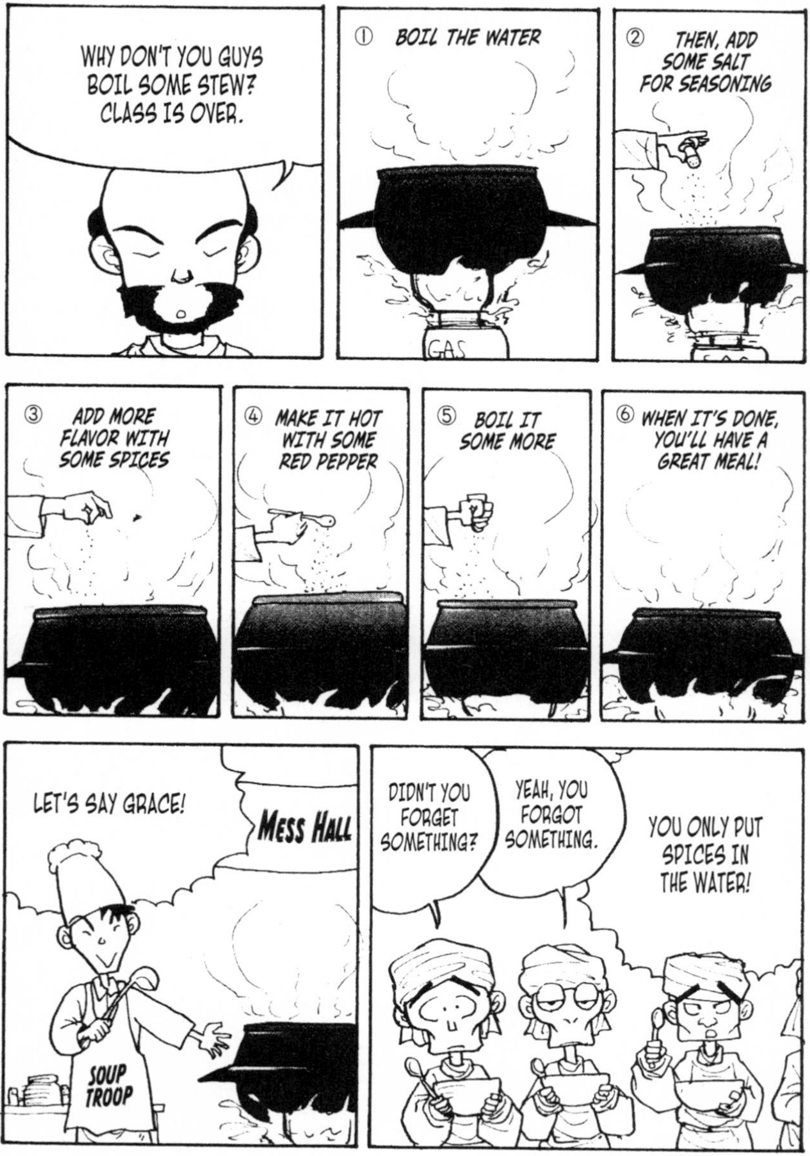
WHY DON'T YOU GUYS BOIL SOME STEW? CLASS IS OVER.
① BOIL THE WATER
GAS
② THEN, ADD SOME SALT FOR SEASONING
③ ADD MORE FLAVOR WITH SOME SPICES
④ MAKE IT HOT WITH SOME RED PEPPER
⑤ BOIL IT SOME MORE
⑥ WHEN IT'S DONE, YOU'LL HAVE A GREAT MEAL!
LET'S SAY GRACE!
MESS HALL
SOUP TROOP
DIDN'T YOU FORGET SOMETHING?
YEAH, YOU FORGOT SOMETHING.
YOU ONLY PUT SPICES IN THE WATER!

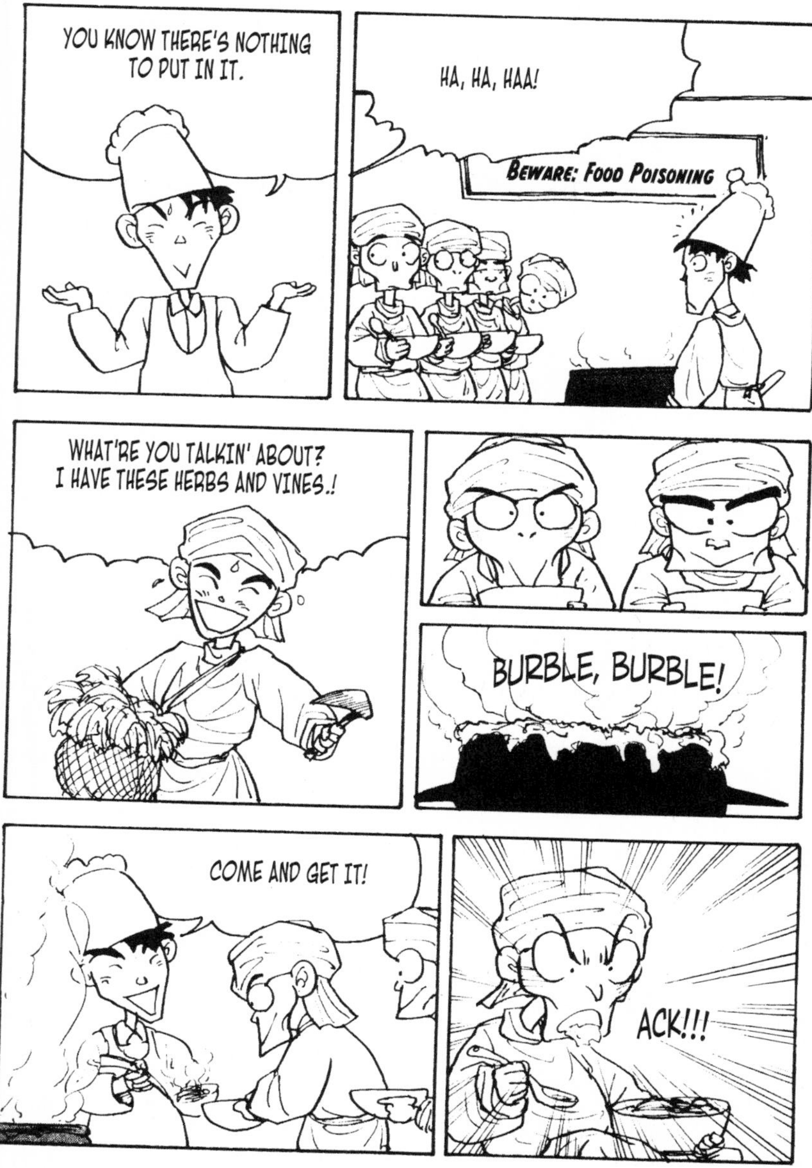
YOU KNOW THERE'S NOTHING TO PUT IN IT.
HA, HA, HAA!
BEWARE: FOOD POISONING
WHAT'RE YOU TALKIN' ABOUT? I HAVE THESE HERBS AND VINES.!
BURBLE, BURBLE!
COME AND GET IT!
ACK!!!

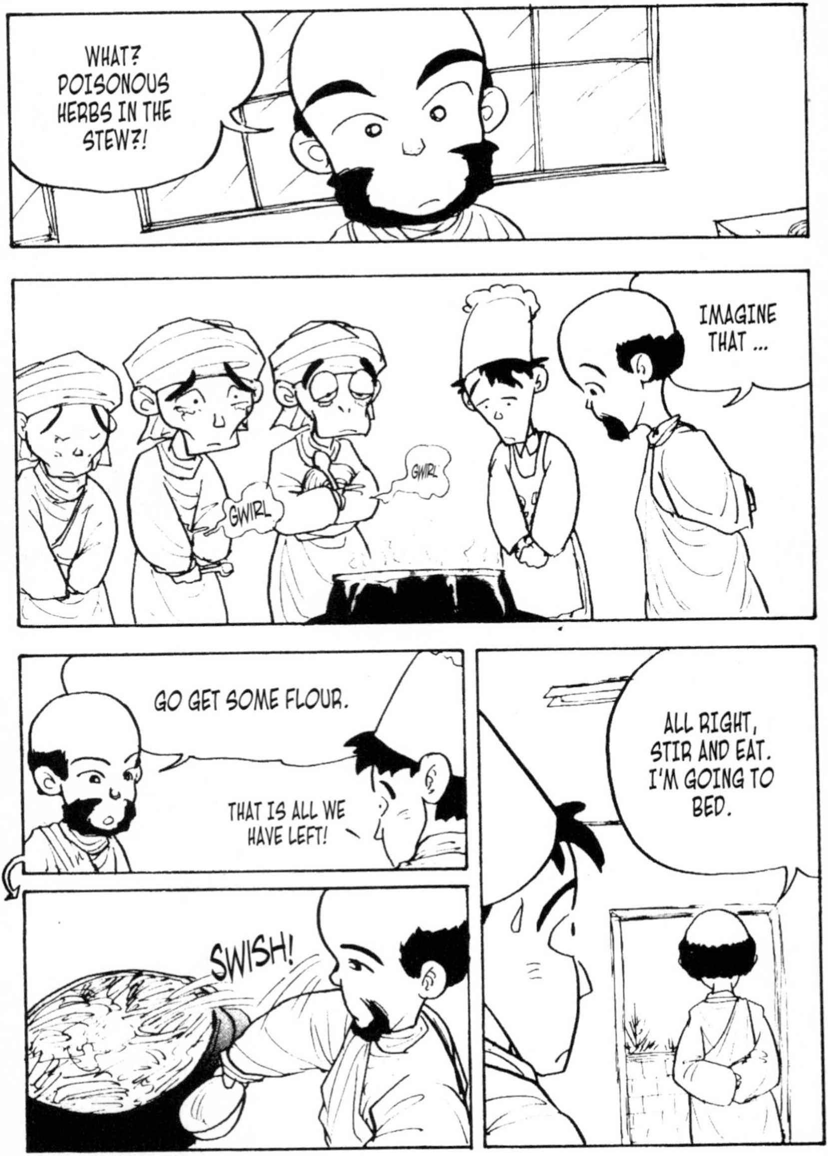
WHAT? POISONOUS HERBS IN THE STEW?!
IMAGINE THAT ...
GWIRL
GWIRL
GO GET SOME FLOUR.
THAT IS ALL WE HAVE LEFT!
SWISH!
ALL RIGHT, STIR AND EAT. I'M GOING TO BED.

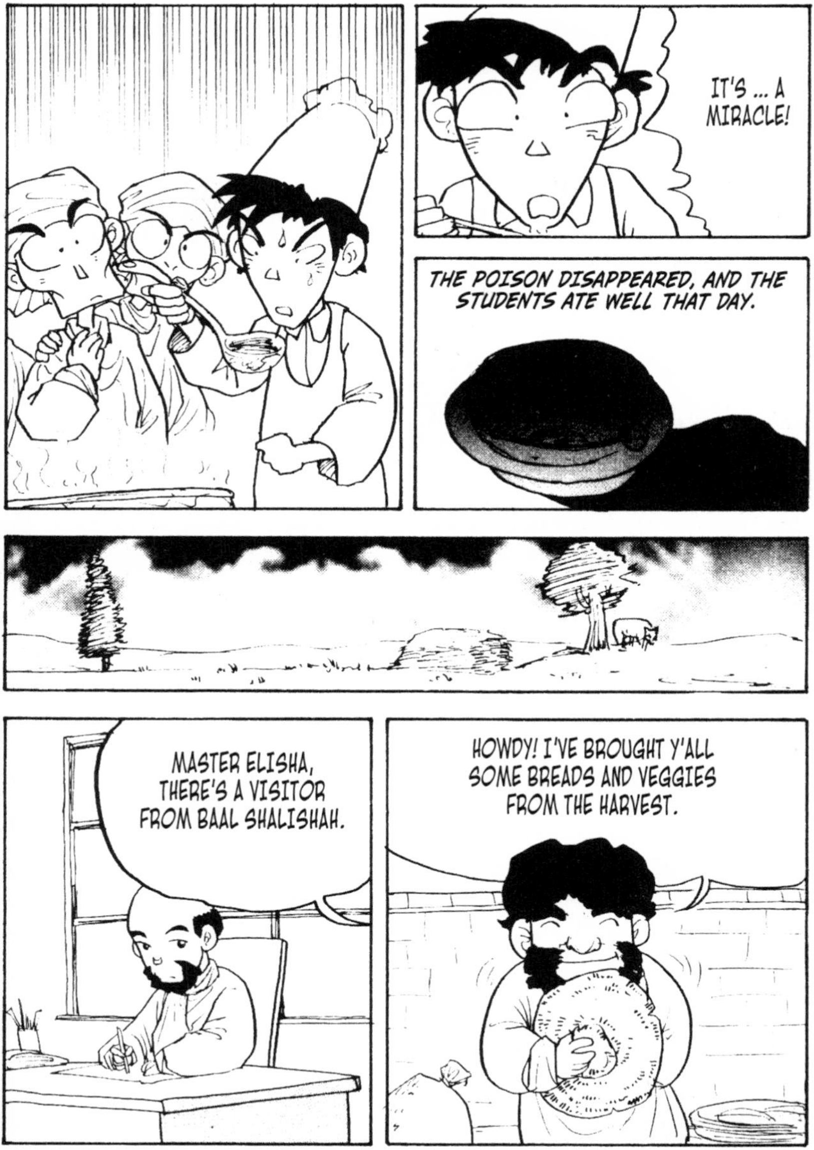
IT'S ... A MIRACLE!
THE POISON DISAPPEARED, AND THE STUDENTS ATE WELL THAT DAY.
MASTER ELISHA, THERE'S A VISITOR FROM BAAL SHALISHAH.
HOWDY! I'VE BROUGHT Y'ALL SOME BREADS AND VEGGIES FROM THE HARVEST.

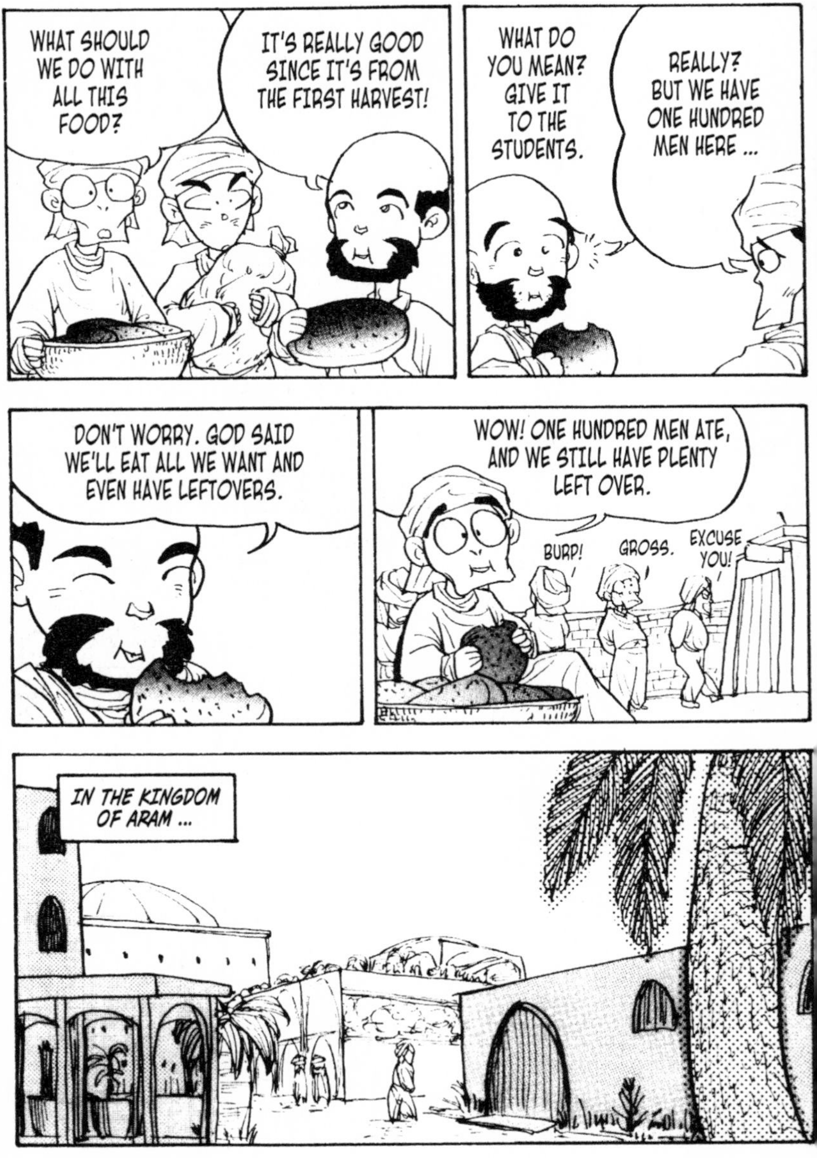
WHAT SHOULD WE DO WITH ALL THIS FOOD?
IT'S REALLY GOOD SINCE IT'S FROM THE FIRST HARVEST!
WHAT DO YOU MEAN? GIVE IT TO THE STUDENTS.
REALLY? BUT WE HAVE ONE HUNDRED MEN HERE ...
DON'T WORRY. GOD SAID WE'LL EAT ALL WE WANT AND EVEN HAVE LEFTOVERS.
WOW! ONE HUNDRED MEN ATE, AND WE STILL HAVE PLENTY LEFT OVER.
BURP!
GROSS.
EXCUSE YOU!
IN THE KINGDOM OF ARAM ...

HOW IS COMMANDER NAAMAN'S ILLNESS?

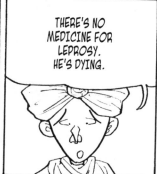

THERE'S NO MEDICINE FOR LEPROSY. HE'S DYING.

HOW SAD -- OUR MOST VALIANT COMMANDER HAS LEPROSY. WHAT CAN BE DONE?

NAAMAN ...

THIS IS AWFUL! DOESN'T ANYONE UNDERSTAND HOW I FEEL?

WHAT I WOULDN'T GIVE TO HAVE THE LEPROSY INSTEAD OF MY HUSBAND ...

IF ELISHA WERE HERE, THIS WOULDN'T BE A PROBLEM.

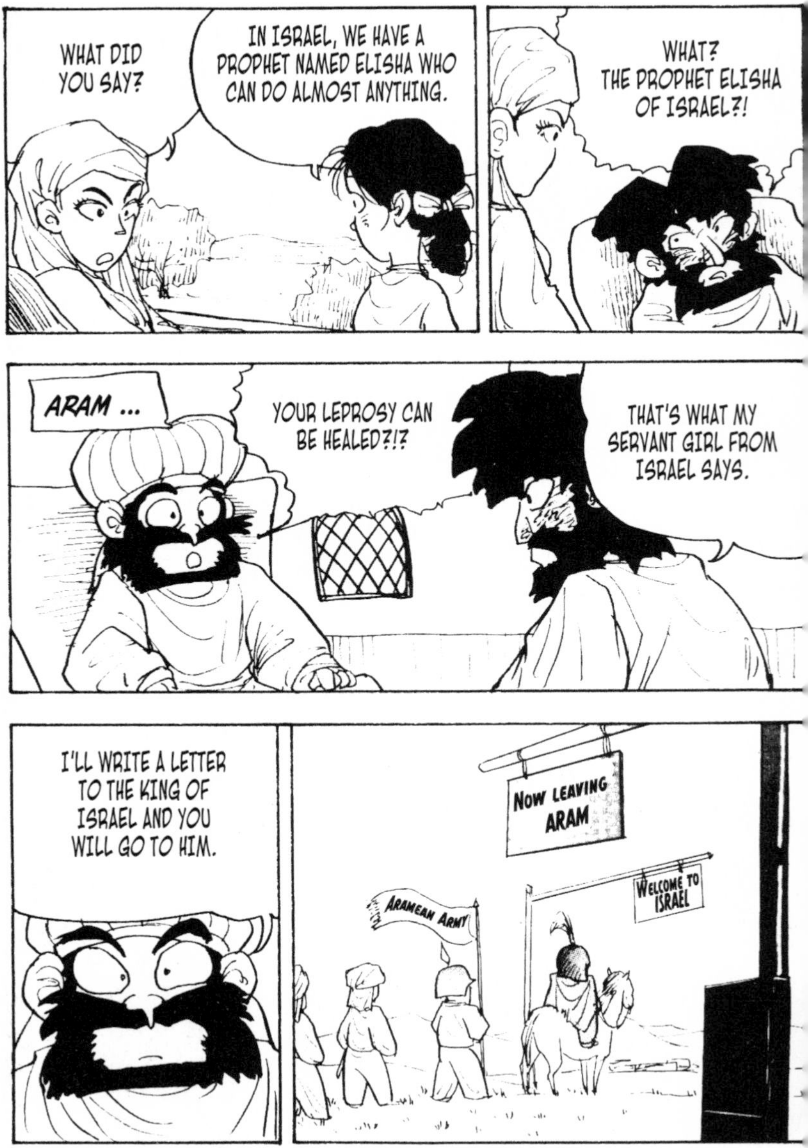
WHAT DID YOU SAY?
IN ISRAEL, WE HAVE A PROPHET NAMED ELISHA WHO CAN DO ALMOST ANYTHING.
WHAT? THE PROPHET ELISHA OF ISRAEL?!
ARAM ...
YOUR LEPROSY CAN BE HEALED?!?
THAT'S WHAT MY SERVANT GIRL FROM ISRAEL SAYS.
I'LL WRITE A LETTER TO THE KING OF ISRAEL AND YOU WILL GO TO HIM.
NOW LEAVING ARAM
ARAMEAN ARMY
WELCOME TO ISRAEL

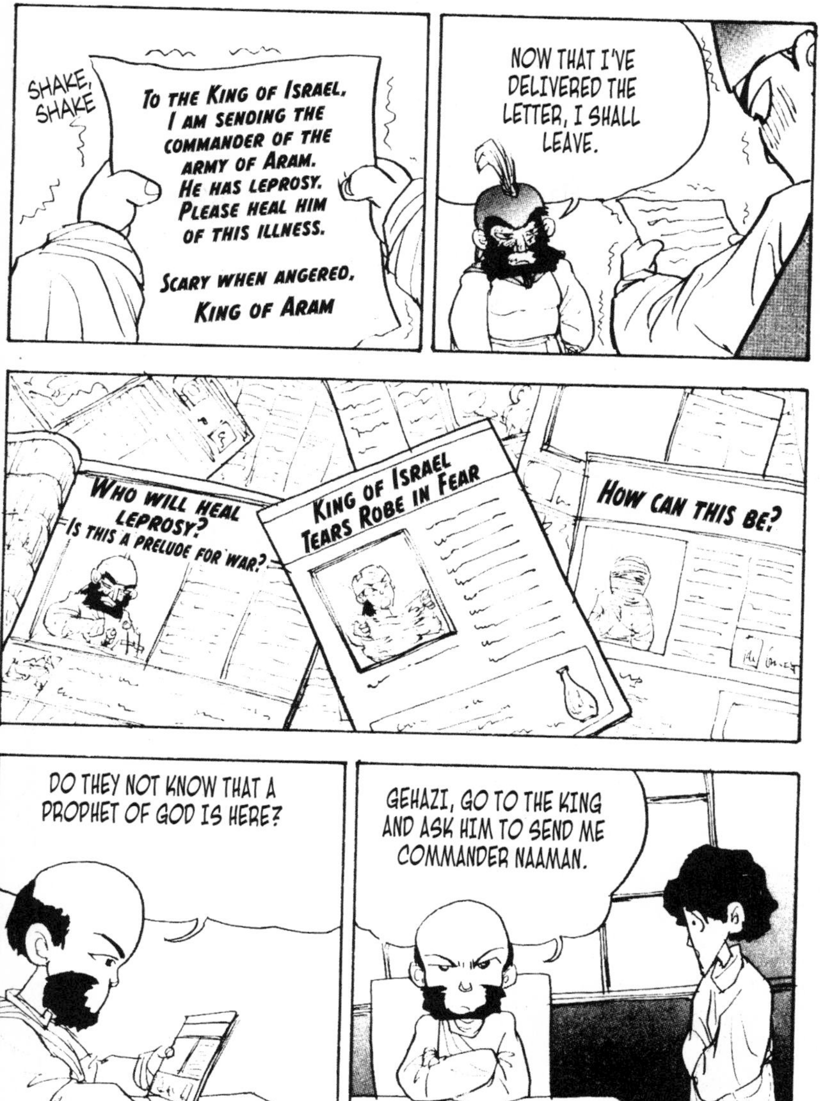
SHAKE, SHAKE
To the King of Israel, I am sending the commander of the army of Aram. He has leprosy. Please heal him of this illness.
Scary when angered, King of Aram
NOW THAT I'VE DELIVERED THE LETTER, I SHALL LEAVE.
Who will heal leprosy?
Is this a prelude for war?
King of Israel Tears Robe in Fear
How can this be?
DO THEY NOT KNOW THAT A PROPHET OF GOD IS HERE?
GEHAZI, GO TO THE KING AND ASK HIM TO SEND ME COMMANDER NAAMAN.

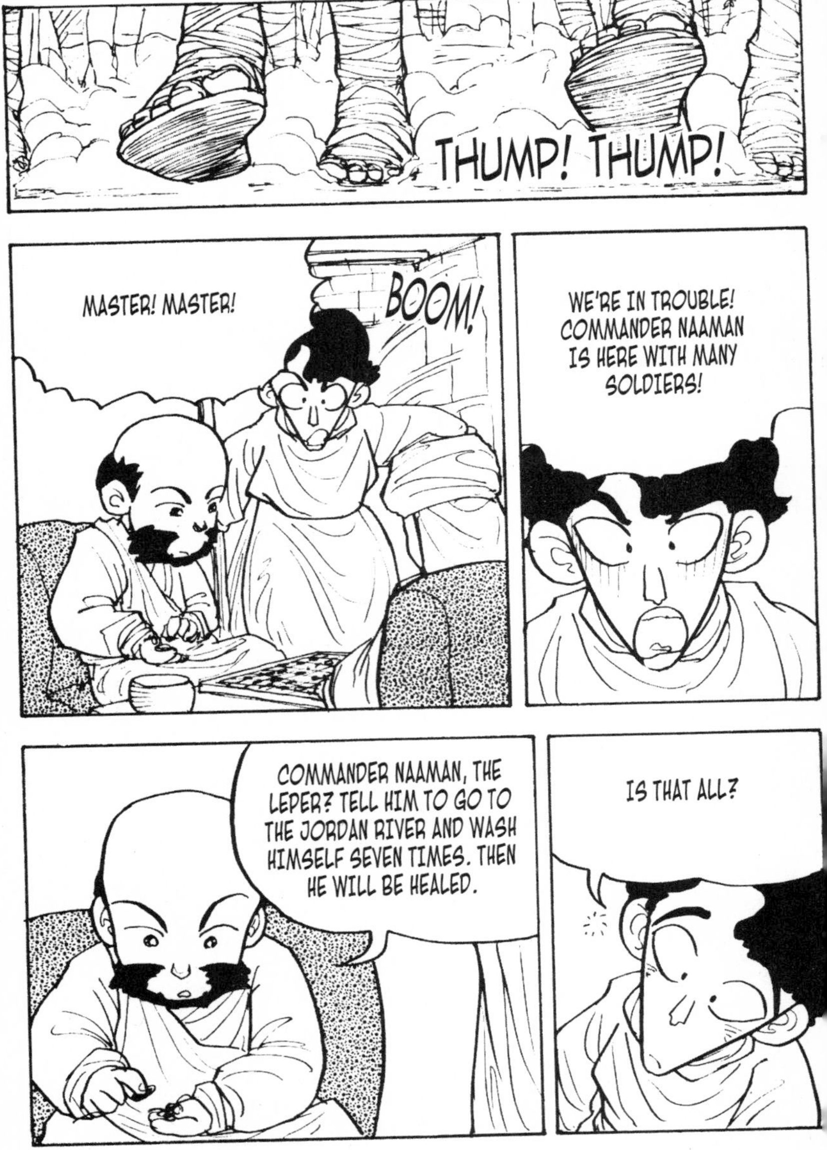
THUMP! THUMP!
MASTER! MASTER!
BOOM!
WE'RE IN TROUBLE! COMMANDER NAAMAN IS HERE WITH MANY SOLDIERS!
COMMANDER NAAMAN, THE LEPER? TELL HIM TO GO TO THE JORDAN RIVER AND WASH HIMSELF SEVEN TIMES. THEN HE WILL BE HEALED.
IS THAT ALL?

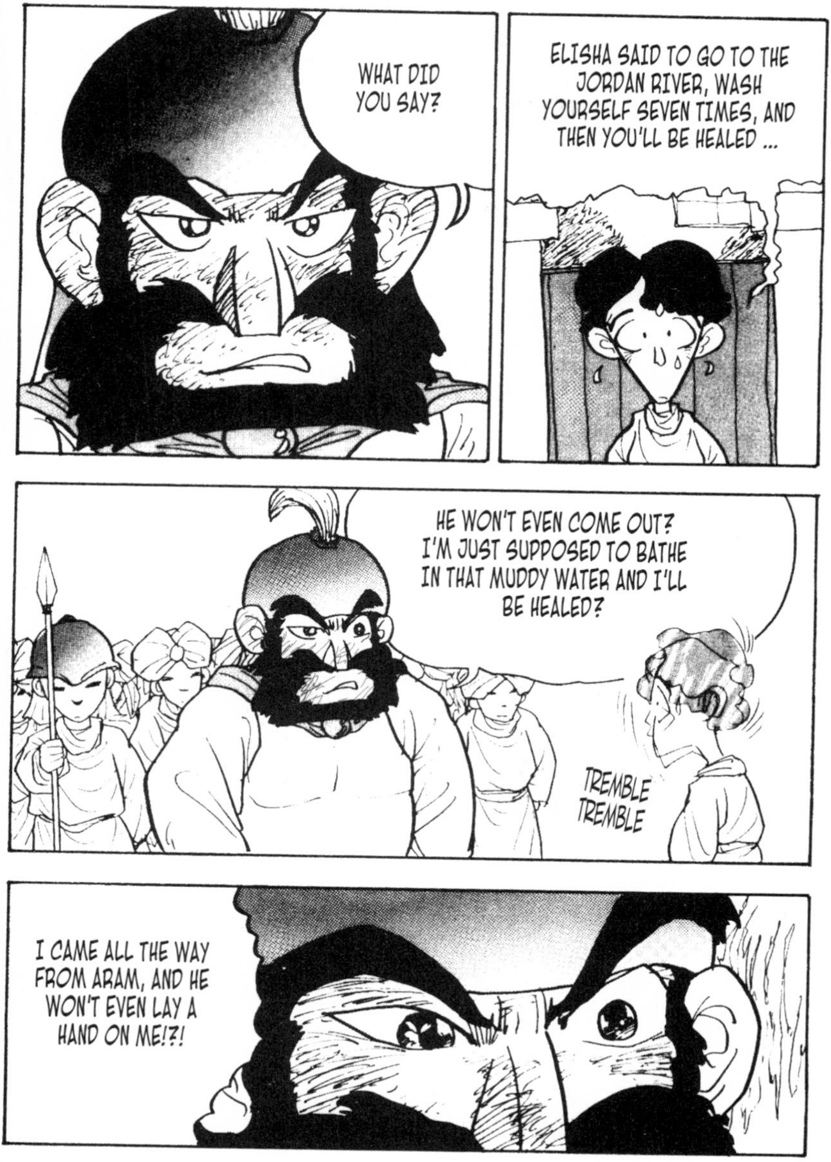
WHAT DID YOU SAY?
ELISHA SAID TO GO TO THE JORDAN RIVER, WASH YOURSELF SEVEN TIMES, AND THEN YOU'LL BE HEALED ...
HE WON'T EVEN COME OUT? I'M JUST SUPPOSED TO BATHE IN THAT MUDDY WATER AND I'LL BE HEALED?
TREMBLE TREMBLE
I CAME ALL THE WAY FROM ARAM, AND HE WON'T EVEN LAY A HAND ON ME!?!

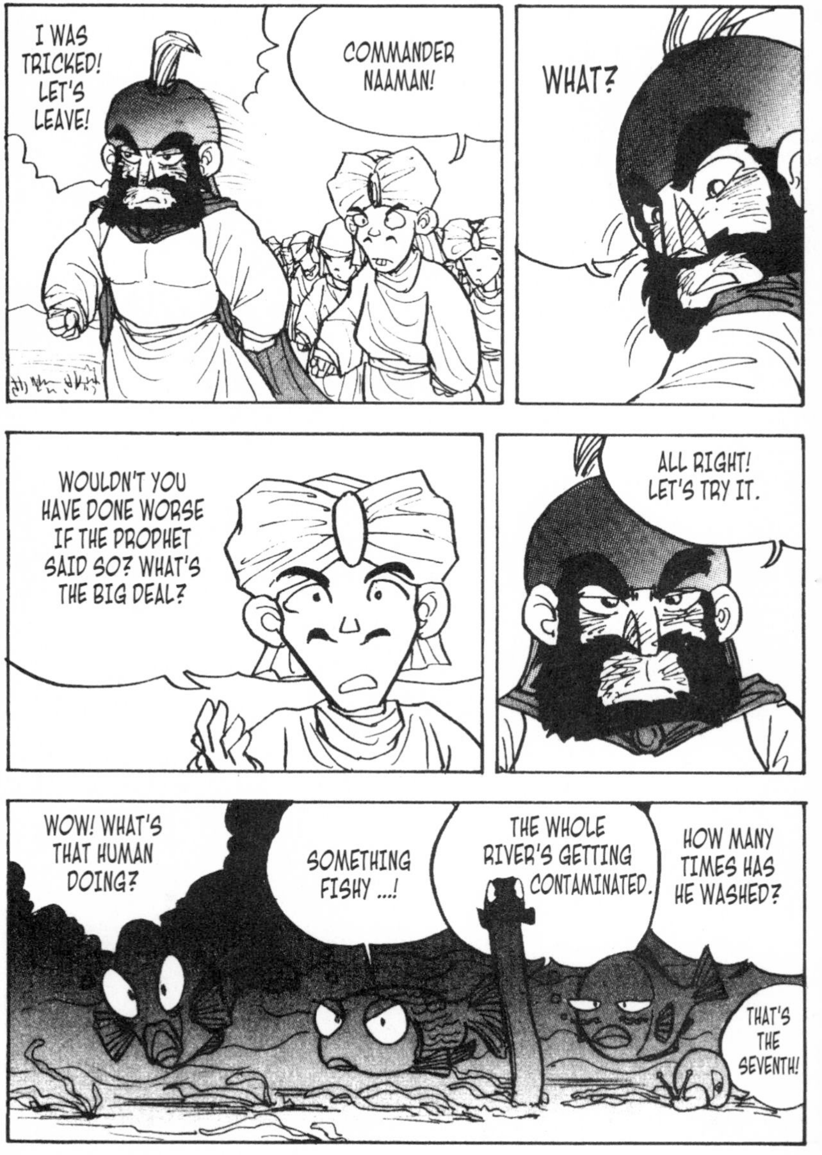
I WAS TRICKED! LET'S LEAVE!
COMMANDER NAAMAN!
WHAT?
WOULDN'T YOU HAVE DONE WORSE IF THE PROPHET SAID SO? WHAT'S THE BIG DEAL?
ALL RIGHT! LET'S TRY IT.
WOW! WHAT'S THAT HUMAN DOING?
SOMETHING FISHY ...!
THE WHOLE RIVER'S GETTING CONTAMINATED.
HOW MANY TIMES HAS HE WASHED?
THAT'S THE SEVENTH!

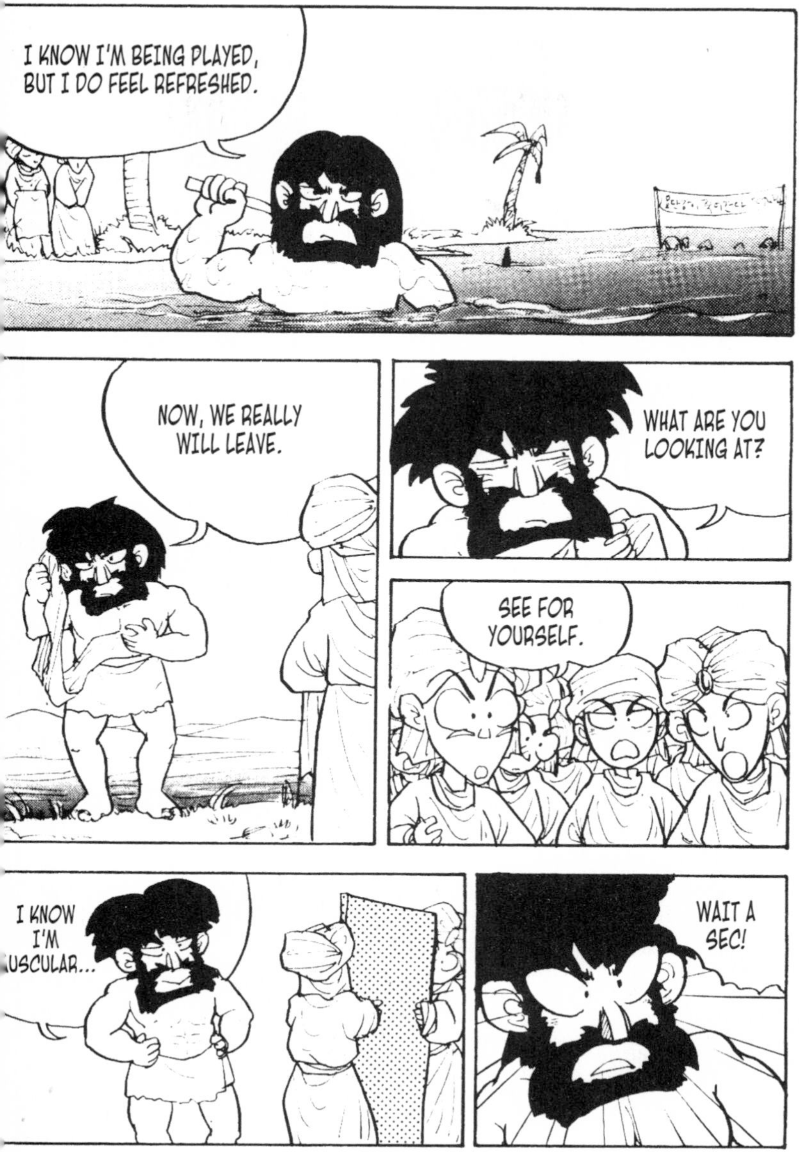
I KNOW I'M BEING PLAYED, BUT I DO FEEL REFRESHED.
NOW, WE REALLY WILL LEAVE.
WHAT ARE YOU LOOKING AT?
SEE FOR YOURSELF.
I KNOW I'M USCULAR...
WAIT A SEC!

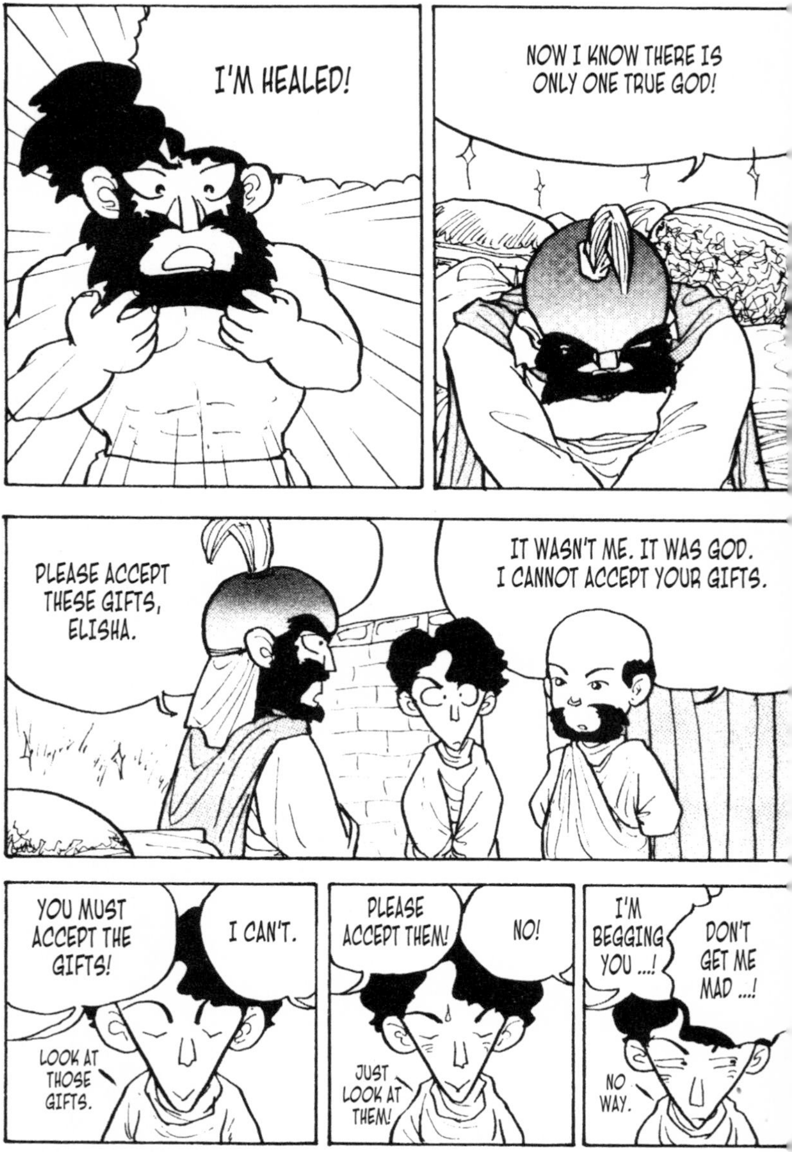
I'M HEALED!
NOW I KNOW THERE IS ONLY ONE TRUE GOD!
PLEASE ACCEPT THESE GIFTS, ELISHA.
IT WASN'T ME. IT WAS GOD. I CANNOT ACCEPT YOUR GIFTS.
YOU MUST ACCEPT THE GIFTS!
I CAN'T.
LOOK AT THOSE GIFTS.
PLEASE ACCEPT THEM!
NO!
JUST LOOK AT THEM!
I'M BEGGING YOU ...!
DON'T GET ME MAD ...!
NO WAY.

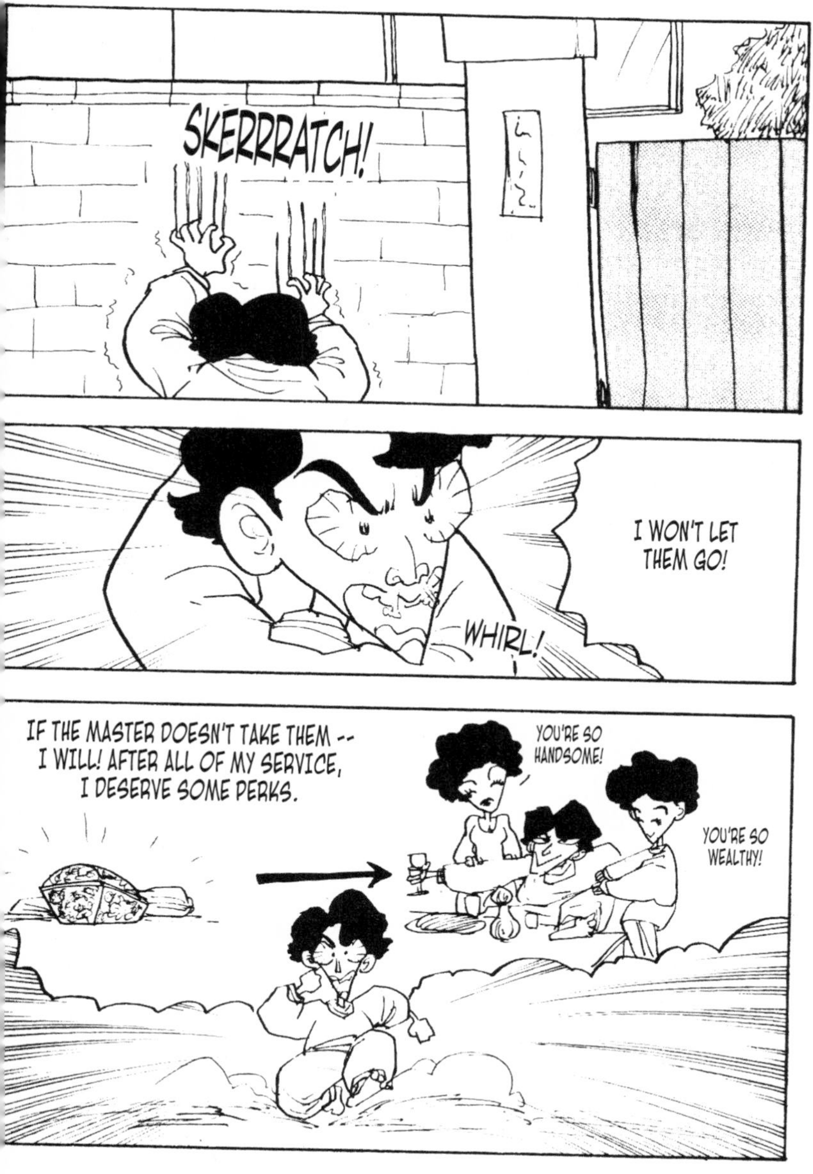
SKERRRATCH!
I WON'T LET THEM GO!
WHIRL!
IF THE MASTER DOESN'T TAKE THEM -- I WILL! AFTER ALL OF MY SERVICE, I DESERVE SOME PERKS.
YOU'RE SO HANDSOME!
YOU'RE SO WEALTHY!

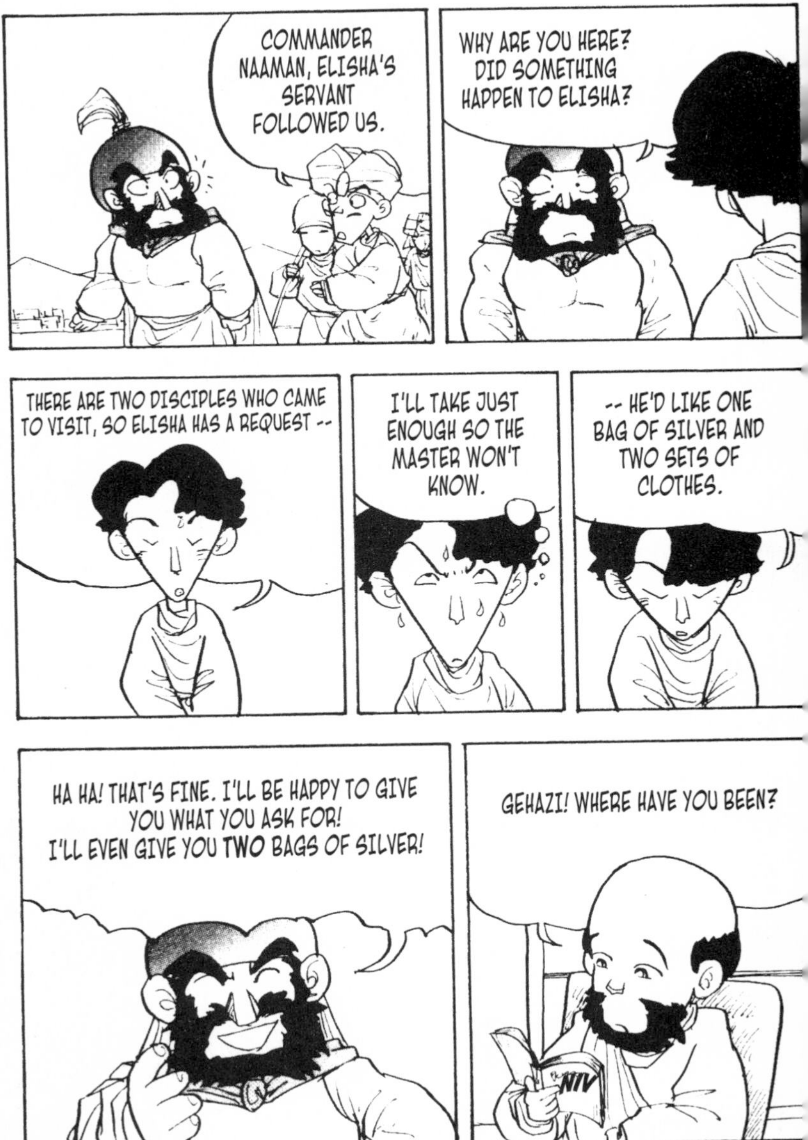
COMMANDER NAAMAN, ELISHA'S SERVANT FOLLOWED US.
WHY ARE YOU HERE? DID SOMETHING HAPPEN TO ELISHA?
THERE ARE TWO DISCIPLES WHO CAME TO VISIT, SO ELISHA HAS A REQUEST --
I'LL TAKE JUST ENOUGH SO THE MASTER WON'T KNOW.
-- HE'D LIKE ONE BAG OF SILVER AND TWO SETS OF CLOTHES.
HA HA! THAT'S FINE. I'LL BE HAPPY TO GIVE YOU WHAT YOU ASK FOR! I'LL EVEN GIVE YOU TWO BAGS OF SILVER!
GEHAZI! WHERE HAVE YOU BEEN?
NIV

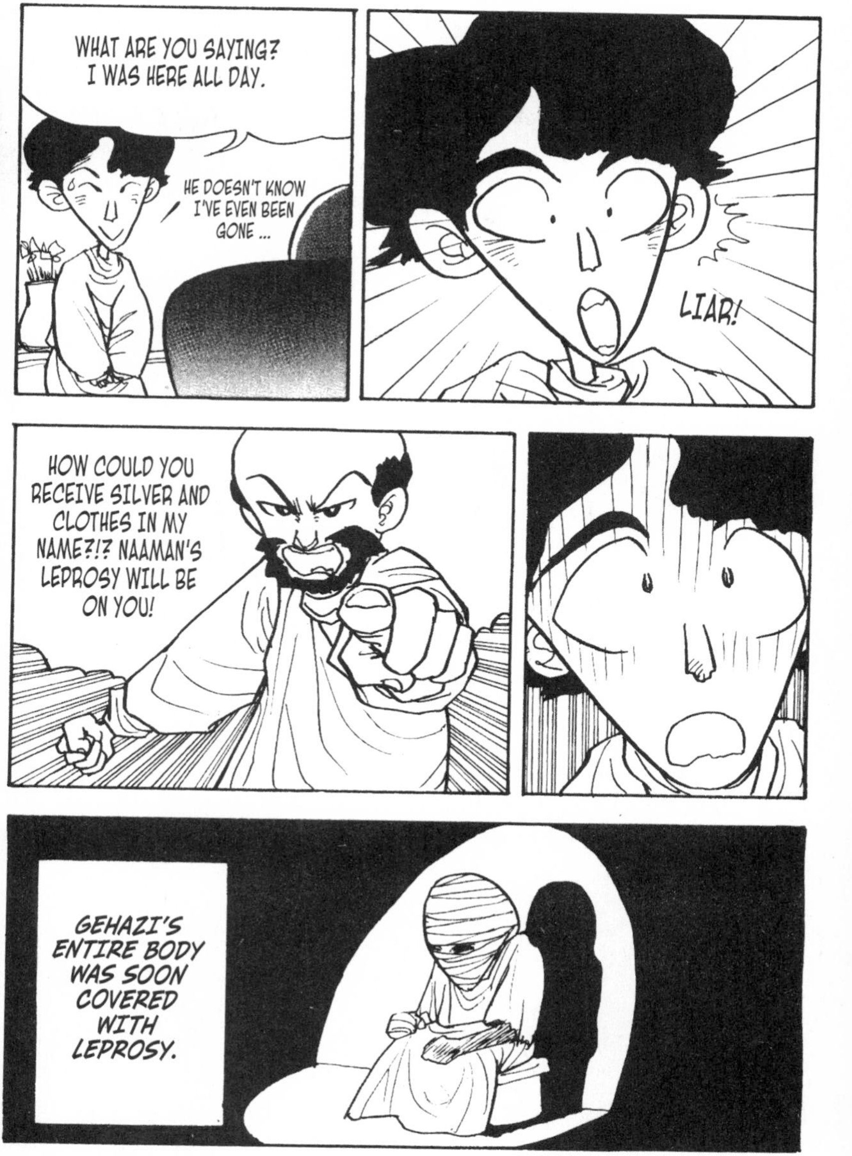
WHAT ARE YOU SAYING? I WAS HERE ALL DAY.
HE DOESN'T KNOW I'VE EVEN BEEN GONE ...
LIAR!
HOW COULD YOU RECEIVE SILVER AND CLOTHES IN MY NAME?!? NAAMAN'S LEPROSY WILL BE ON YOU!
GEHAZI'S ENTIRE BODY WAS SOON COVERED WITH LEPROSY.

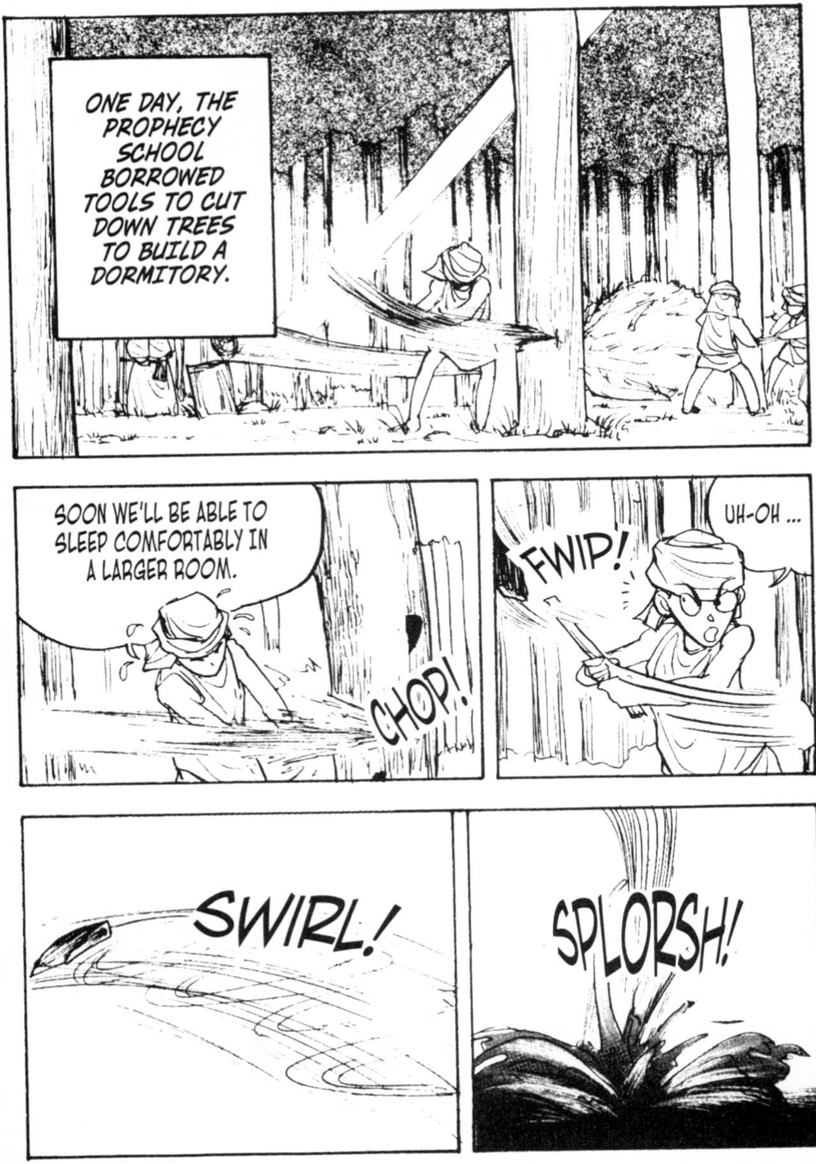
ONE DAY, THE PROPHECY SCHOOL BORROWED TOOLS TO CUT DOWN TREES TO BUILD A DORMITORY.
SOON WE'LL BE ABLE TO SLEEP COMFORTABLY IN A LARGER ROOM.
CHOP!
FWIP!
UH-OH ...
SWIRL!
SPLORSH!

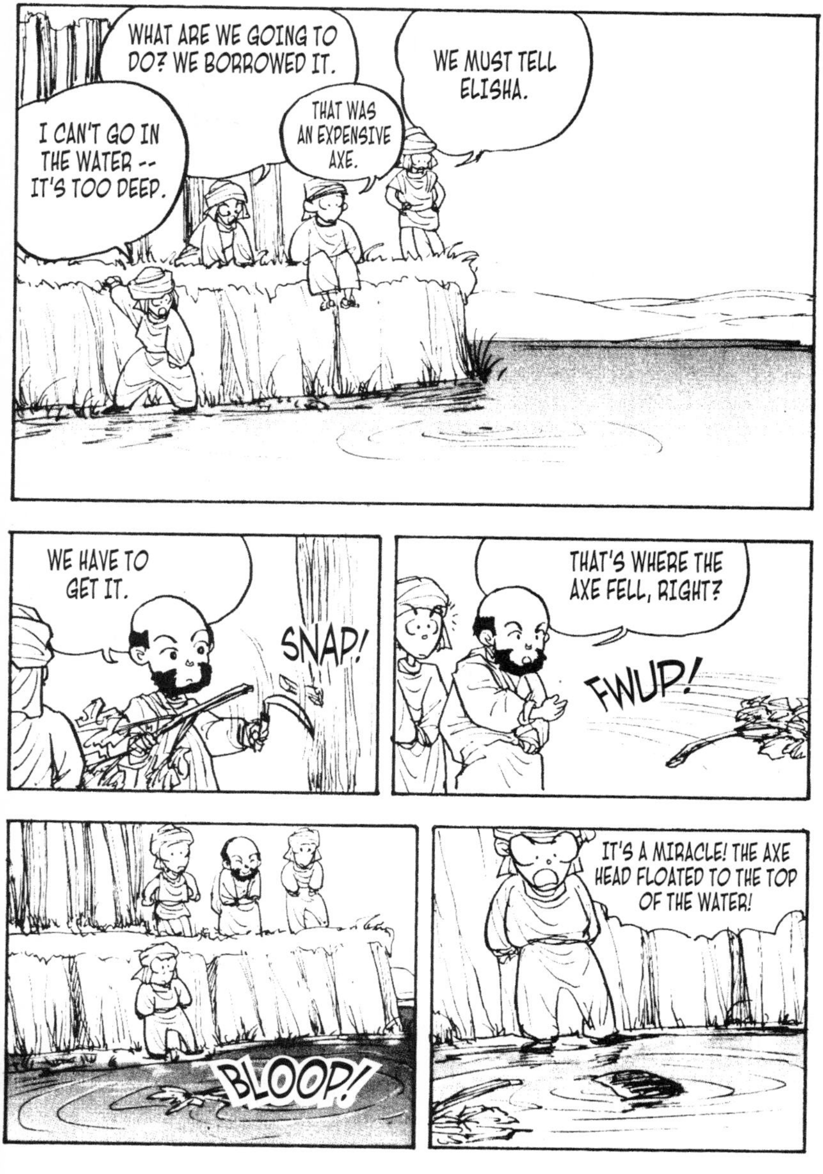
WHAT ARE WE GOING TO DO? WE BORROWED IT.
I CAN'T GO IN THE WATER -- IT'S TOO DEEP.
THAT WAS AN EXPENSIVE AXE.
WE MUST TELL ELISHA.
WE HAVE TO GET IT.
SNAP!
THAT'S WHERE THE AXE FELL, RIGHT?
FWUP!
BLOOP!
IT'S A MIRACLE! THE AXE HEAD FLOATED TO THE TOP OF THE WATER!

WHAT DID YOU SAY? THE ARMY OF ARAM CROSSED THE BORDER?!

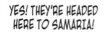

YES! THEY'RE HEADED HERE TO SAMARIA!

GO -- STOP THEM FROM REACHING SAMARIA!

BUT WE DON'T KNOW EXACTLY WHERE THEY'RE COMING FROM.

WHAT?! YOU'RE JUST GOING TO WAIT UNTIL THE ARAMEANS GET HERE?

OF COURSE.

HE'S A SMART ONE.

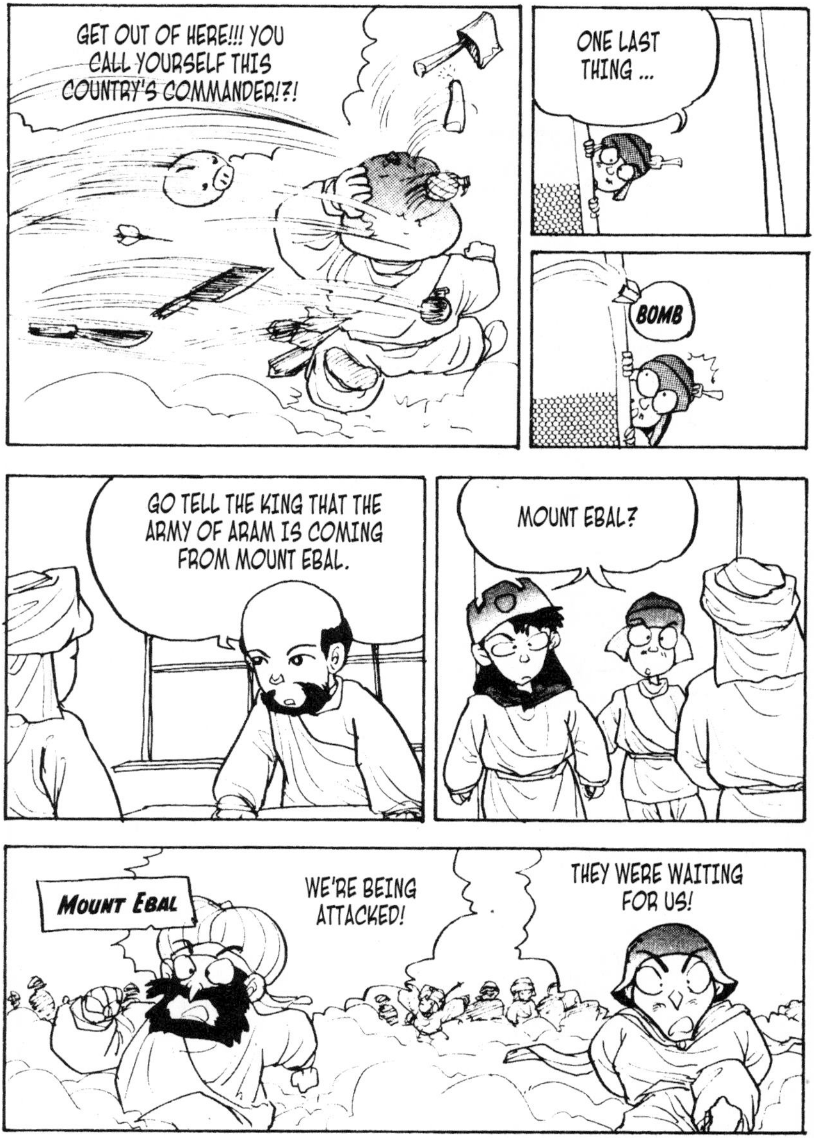
GET OUT OF HERE!!! YOU CALL YOURSELF THIS COUNTRY'S COMMANDER!?!
ONE LAST THING ...
BOMB
GO TELL THE KING THAT THE ARMY OF ARAM IS COMING FROM MOUNT EBAL.
MOUNT EBAL?
MOUNT EBAL
WE'RE BEING ATTACKED!
THEY WERE WAITING FOR US!

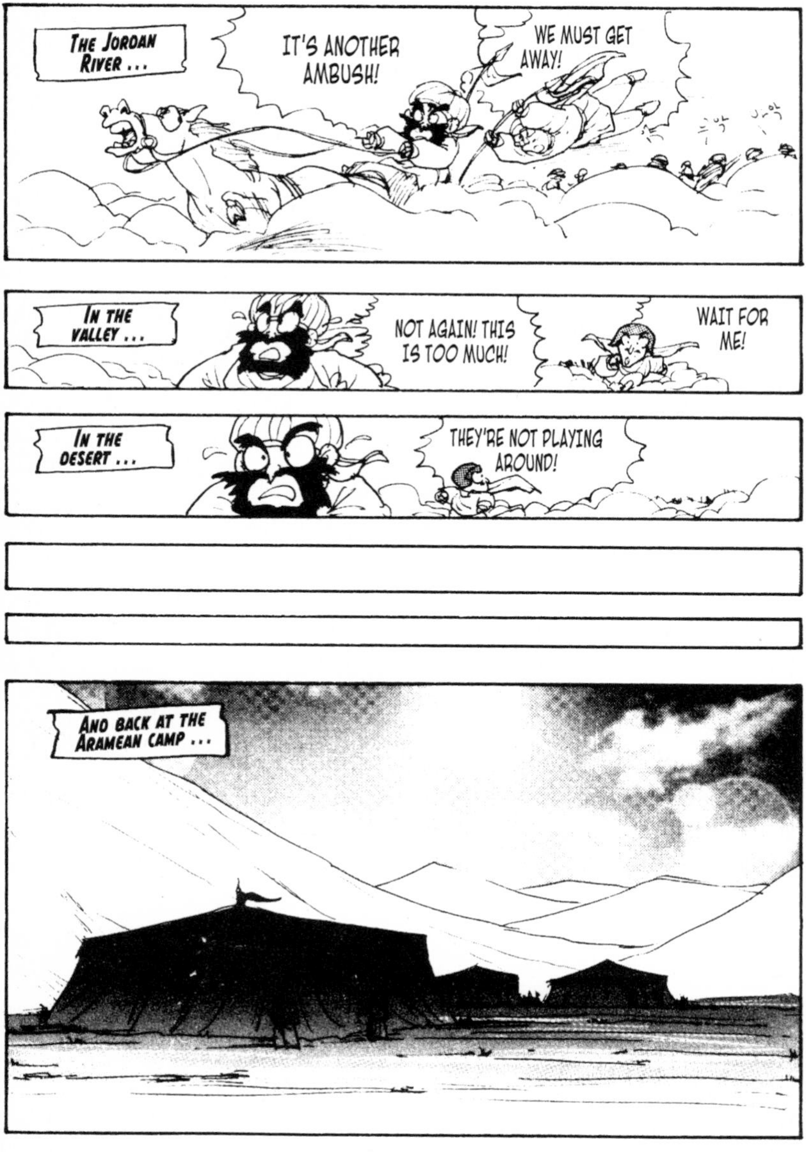
The Jordan River ...
IT'S ANOTHER AMBUSH!
WE MUST GET AWAY!
In the valley ...
NOT AGAIN! THIS IS TOO MUCH!
WAIT FOR ME!
In the desert ...
THEY'RE NOT PLAYING AROUND!
And back at the Aramean camp ...

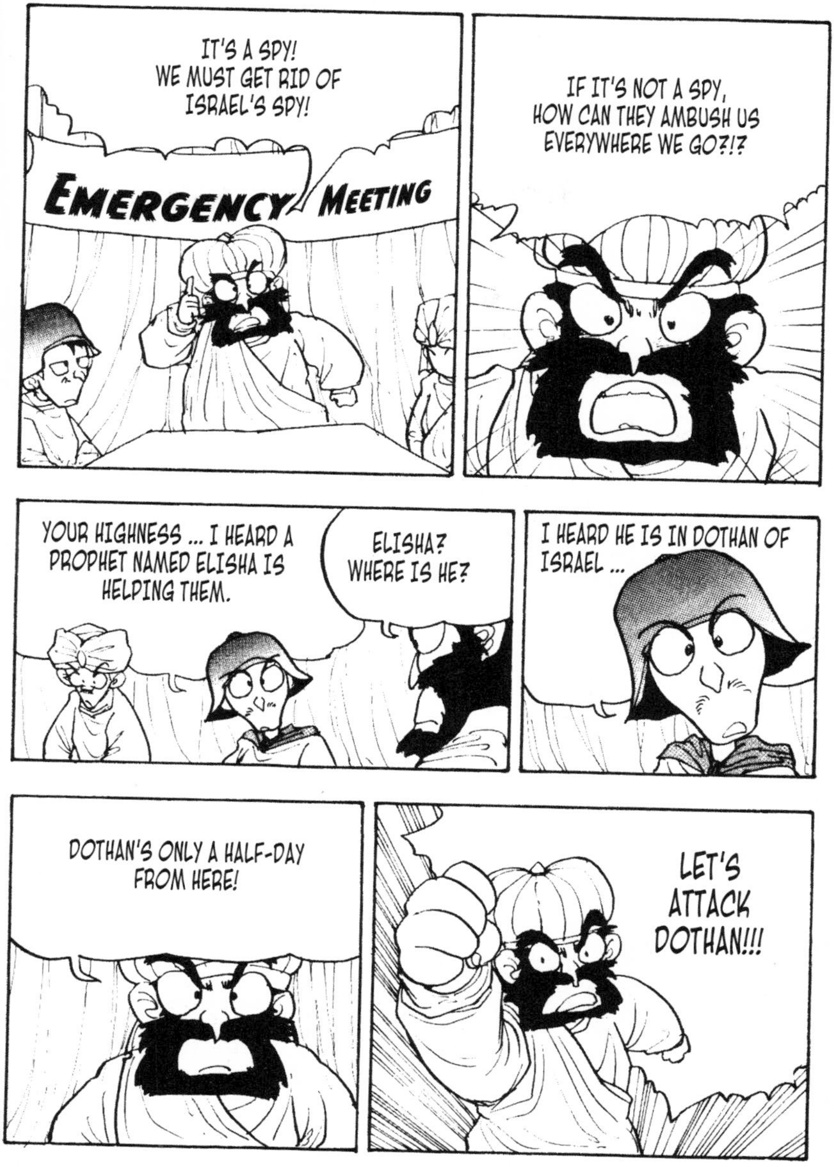
IT'S A SPY!
WE MUST GET RID OF ISRAEL'S SPY!
EMERGENCY MEETING
IF IT'S NOT A SPY, HOW CAN THEY AMBUSH US EVERYWHERE WE GO?!?
YOUR HIGHNESS ... I HEARD A PROPHET NAMED ELISHA IS HELPING THEM.
ELISHA? WHERE IS HE?
I HEARD HE IS IN DOTHAN OF ISRAEL ...
DOTHAN'S ONLY A HALF-DAY FROM HERE!
LET'S ATTACK DOTHAN!!!

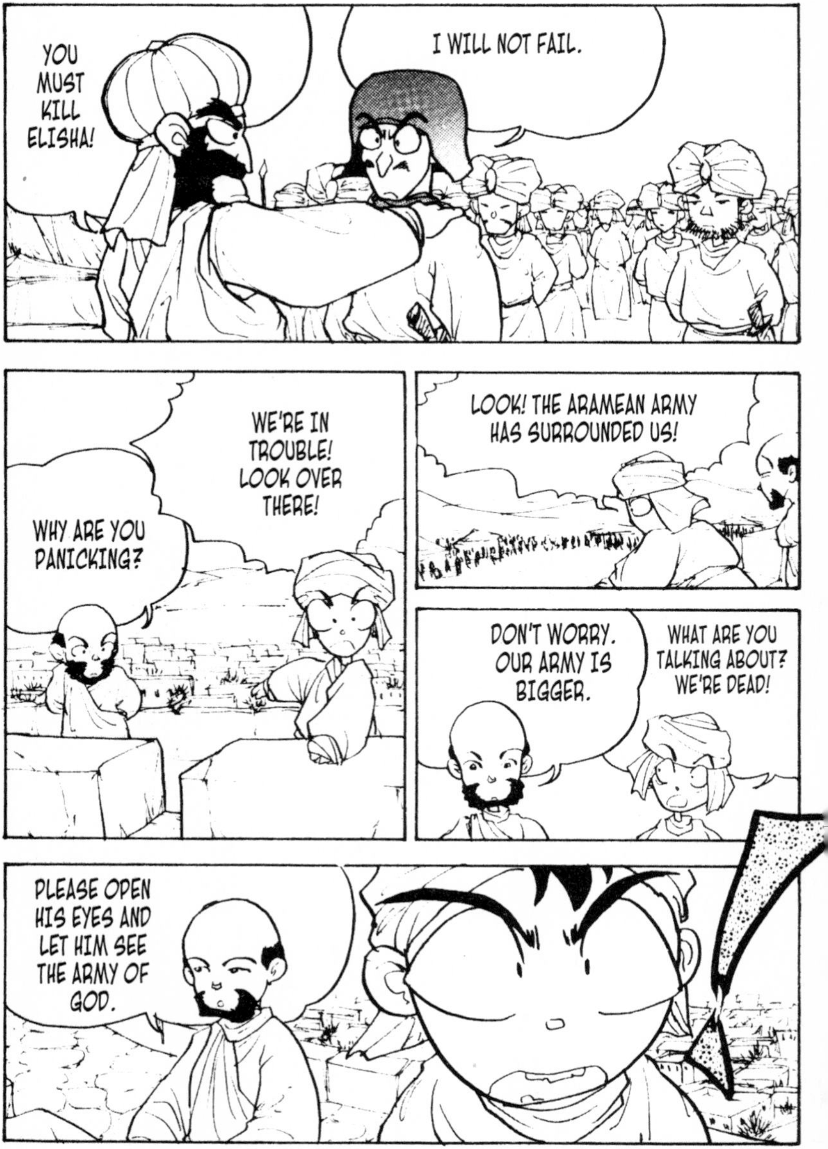
YOU MUST KILL ELISHA!
I WILL NOT FAIL.
WHY ARE YOU PANICKING?
WE'RE IN TROUBLE! LOOK OVER THERE!
LOOK! THE ARAMEAN ARMY HAS SURROUNDED US!
DON'T WORRY. OUR ARMY IS BIGGER.
WHAT ARE YOU TALKING ABOUT? WE'RE DEAD!
PLEASE OPEN HIS EYES AND LET HIM SEE THE ARMY OF GOD.

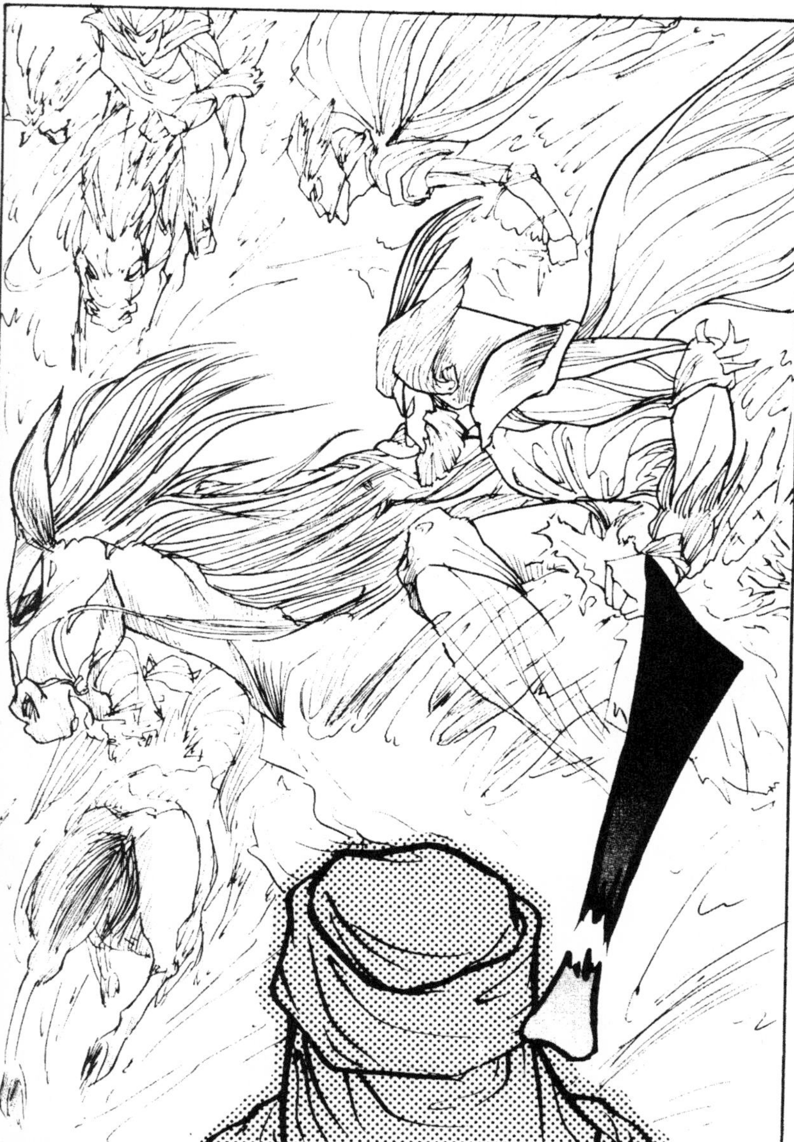

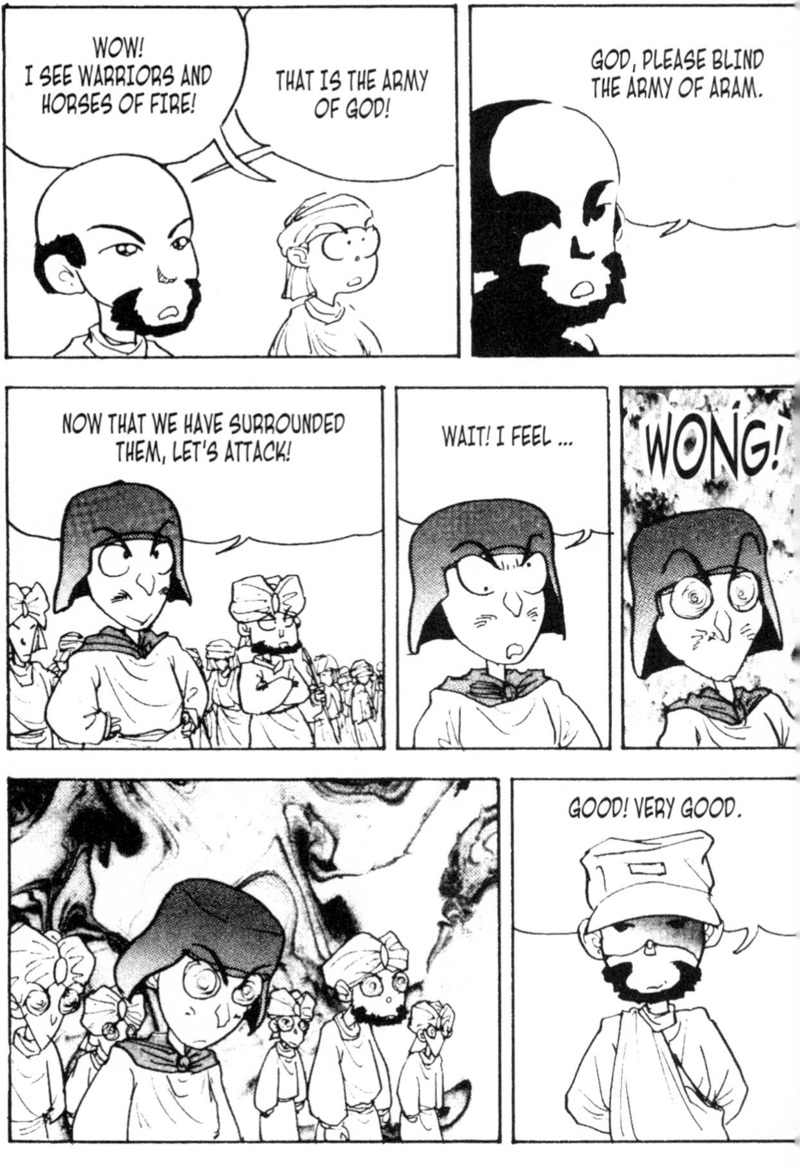
WOW!
I SEE WARRIORS AND HORSES OF FIRE!
THAT IS THE ARMY OF GOD!
GOD, PLEASE BLIND THE ARMY OF ARAM.
NOW THAT WE HAVE SURROUNDED THEM, LET'S ATTACK!
WAIT! I FEEL ...
WONG!
GOOD! VERY GOOD.

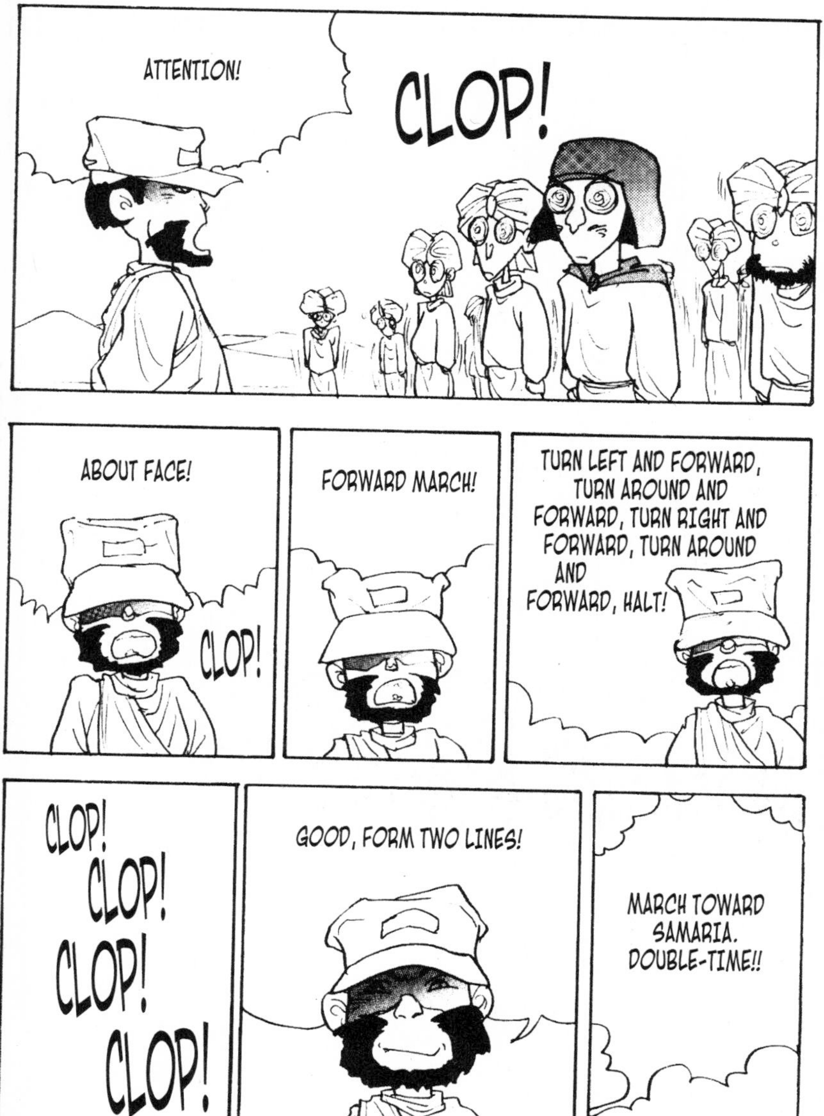
ATTENTION!
CLOP!
ABOUT FACE!
CLOP!
FORWARD MARCH!
TURN LEFT AND FORWARD, TURN AROUND AND FORWARD, TURN RIGHT AND FORWARD, TURN AROUND AND FORWARD, HALT!
CLOP! CLOP! CLOP! CLOP!
GOOD, FORM TWO LINES!
MARCH TOWARD SAMARIA. DOUBLE-TIME!!

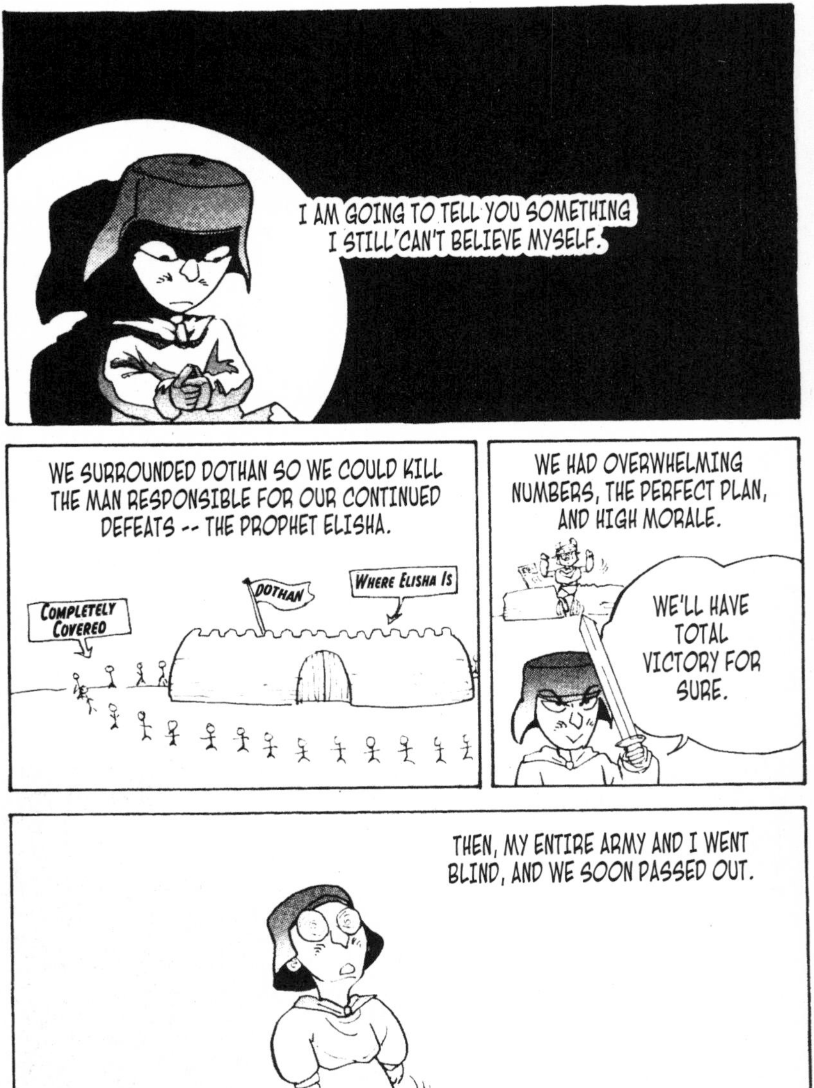
I AM GOING TO TELL YOU SOMETHING I STILL CAN'T BELIEVE MYSELF.
WE SURROUNDED DOTHAN SO WE COULD KILL THE MAN RESPONSIBLE FOR OUR CONTINUED DEFEATS -- THE PROPHET ELISHA.
COMPLETELY COVERED
DOTHAN
WHERE ELISHA IS
WE HAD OVERWHELMING NUMBERS, THE PERFECT PLAN, AND HIGH MORALE.
WE'LL HAVE TOTAL VICTORY FOR SURE.
THEN, MY ENTIRE ARMY AND I WENT BLIND, AND WE SOON PASSED OUT.

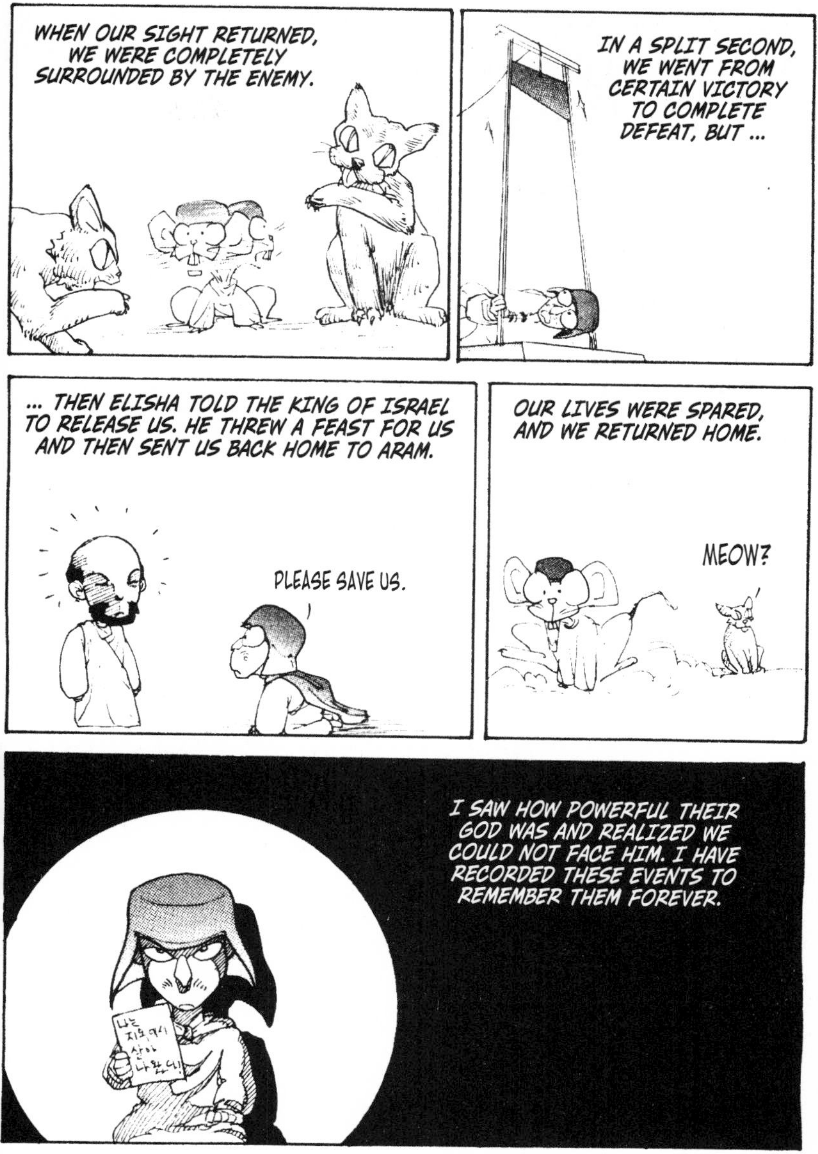
WHEN OUR SIGHT RETURNED, WE WERE COMPLETELY SURROUNDED BY THE ENEMY.
IN A SPLIT SECOND, WE WENT FROM CERTAIN VICTORY TO COMPLETE DEFEAT, BUT ...
... THEN ELISHA TOLD THE KING OF ISRAEL TO RELEASE US. HE THREW A FEAST FOR US AND THEN SENT US BACK HOME TO ARAM.
PLEASE SAVE US.
OUR LIVES WERE SPARED, AND WE RETURNED HOME.
MEOW?
I SAW HOW POWERFUL THEIR GOD WAS AND REALIZED WE COULD NOT FACE HIM. I HAVE RECORDED THESE EVENTS TO REMEMBER THEM FOREVER.

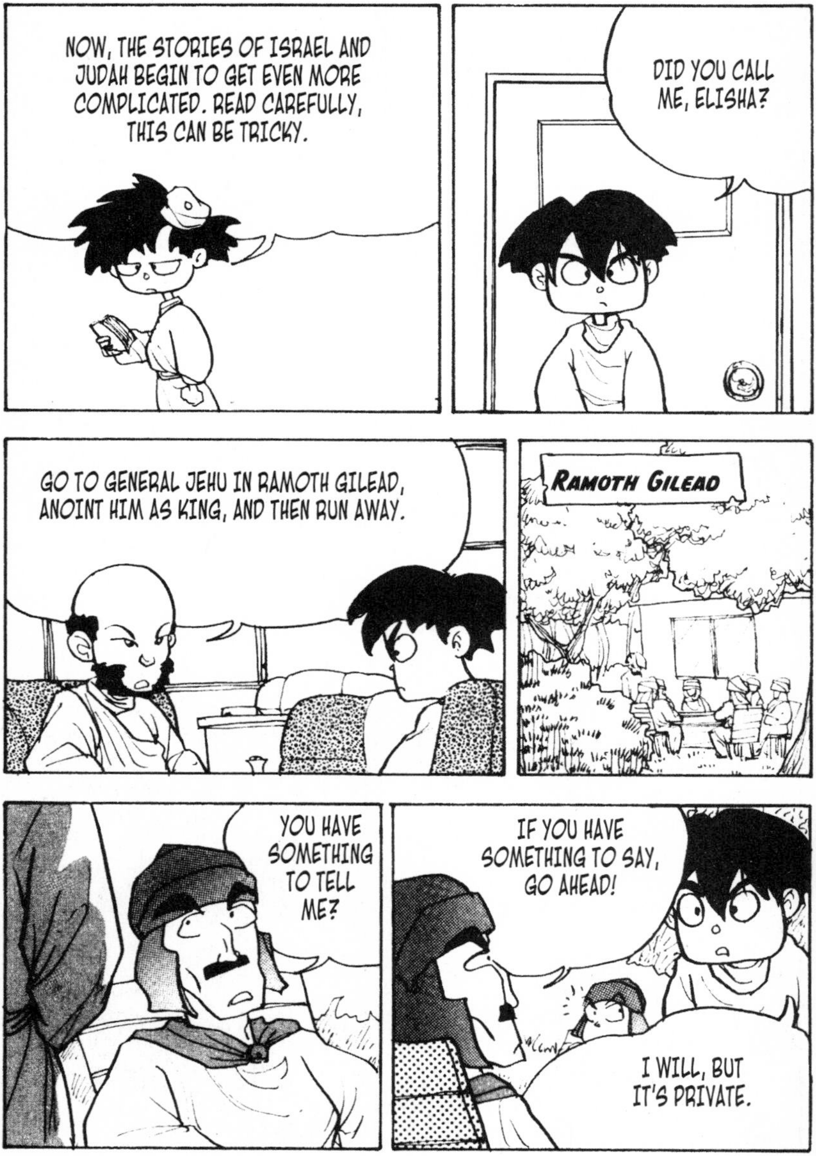
NOW, THE STORIES OF ISRAEL AND JUDAH BEGIN TO GET EVEN MORE COMPLICATED. READ CAREFULLY, THIS CAN BE TRICKY.
DID YOU CALL ME, ELISHA?
GO TO GENERAL JEHU IN RAMOTH GILEAD, ANOINT HIM AS KING, AND THEN RUN AWAY.
RAMOTH GILEAD
YOU HAVE SOMETHING TO TELL ME?
IF YOU HAVE SOMETHING TO SAY, GO AHEAD!
I WILL, BUT IT'S PRIVATE.

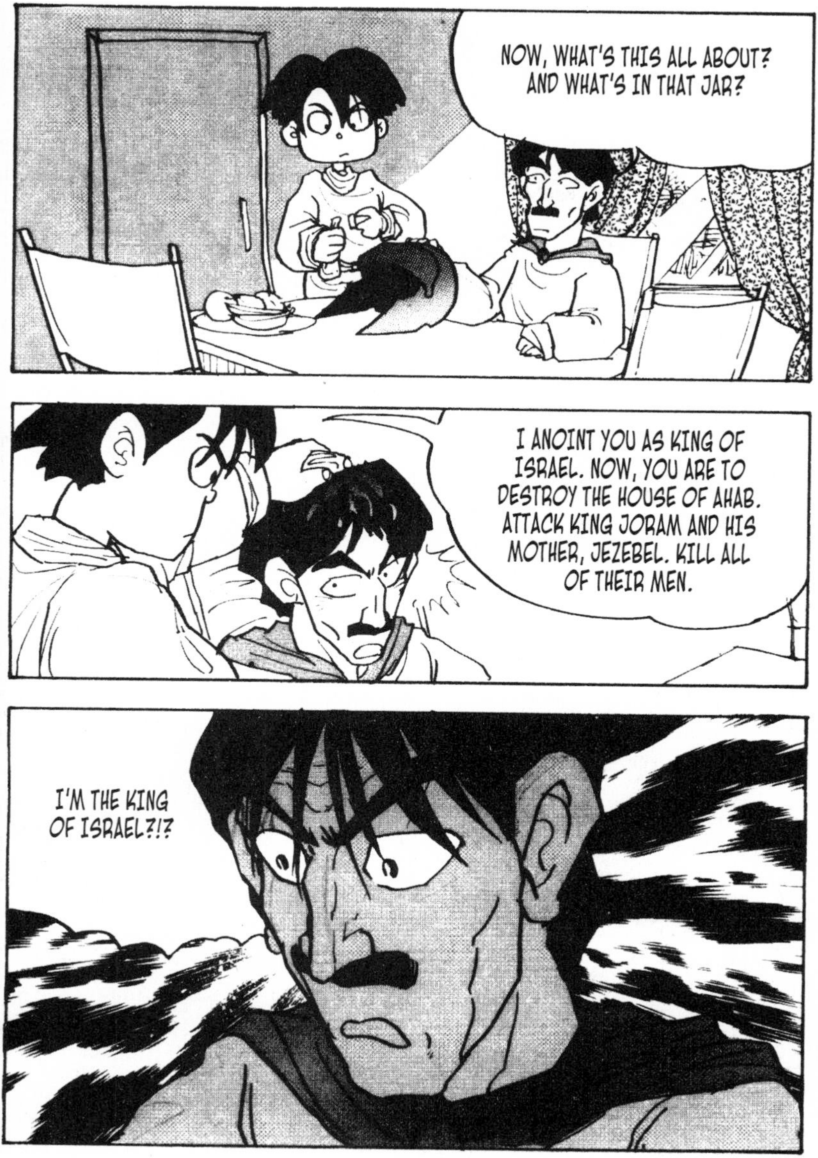
NOW, WHAT'S THIS ALL ABOUT? AND WHAT'S IN THAT JAR?
I ANOINT YOU AS KING OF ISRAEL. NOW, YOU ARE TO DESTROY THE HOUSE OF AHAB. ATTACK KING JORAM AND HIS MOTHER, JEZEBEL. KILL ALL OF THEIR MEN.
I'M THE KING OF ISRAEL?!?

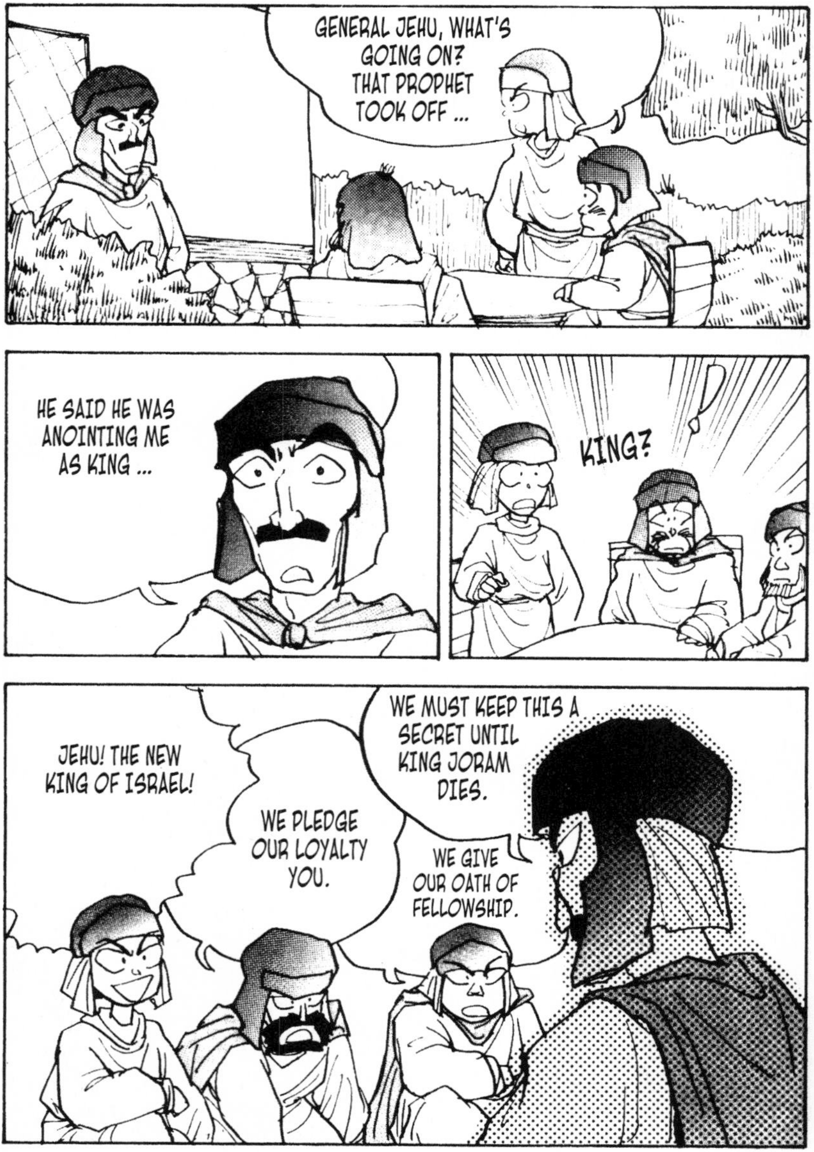
GENERAL JEHU, WHAT'S GOING ON? THAT PROPHET TOOK OFF ...
HE SAID HE WAS ANOINTING ME AS KING ...
KING?
JEHU! THE NEW KING OF ISRAEL!
WE PLEDGE OUR LOYALTY YOU.
WE MUST KEEP THIS A SECRET UNTIL KING JORAM DIES.
WE GIVE OUR OATH OF FELLOWSHIP.

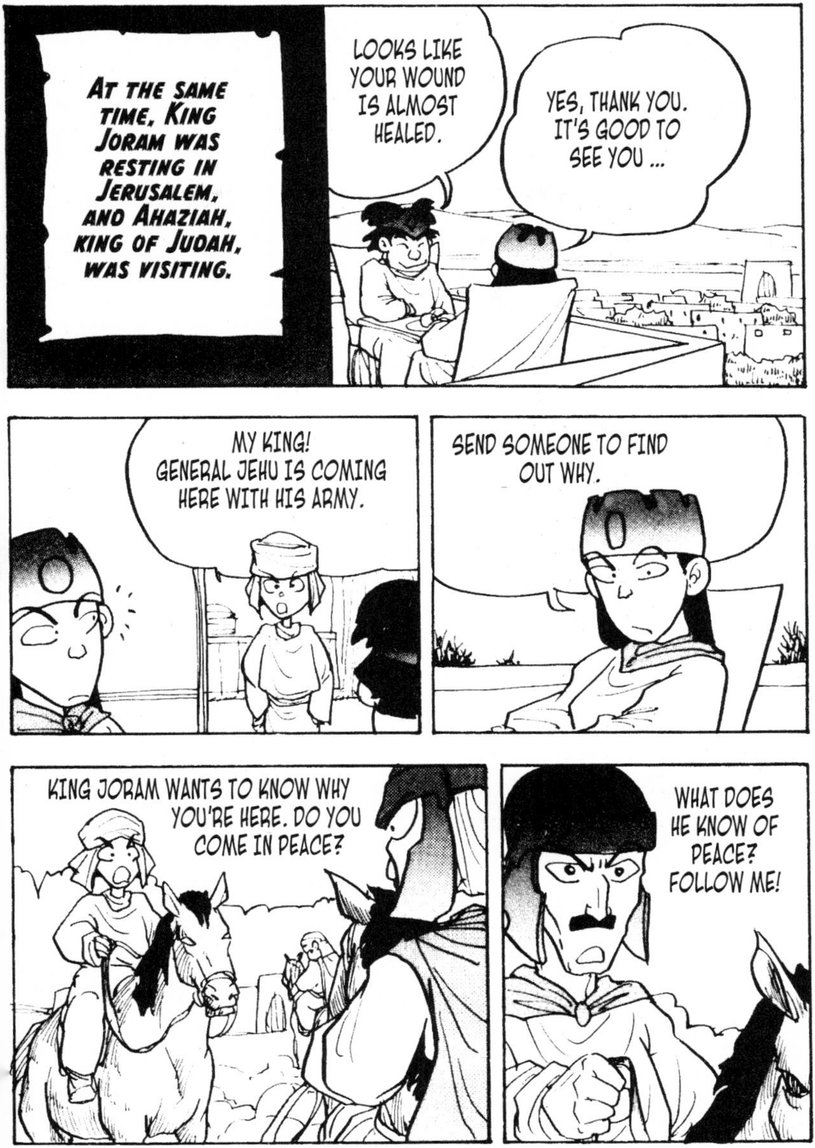

At the same time, King Joram was resting in Jerusalem, and Ahaziah, king of Judah, was visiting.
LOOKS LIKE YOUR WOUND IS ALMOST HEALED.
YES, THANK YOU. IT'S GOOD TO SEE YOU ...
MY KING! GENERAL JEHU IS COMING HERE WITH HIS ARMY.
SEND SOMEONE TO FIND OUT WHY.
KING JORAM WANTS TO KNOW WHY YOU'RE HERE. DO YOU COME IN PEACE?
WHAT DOES HE KNOW OF PEACE? FOLLOW ME!

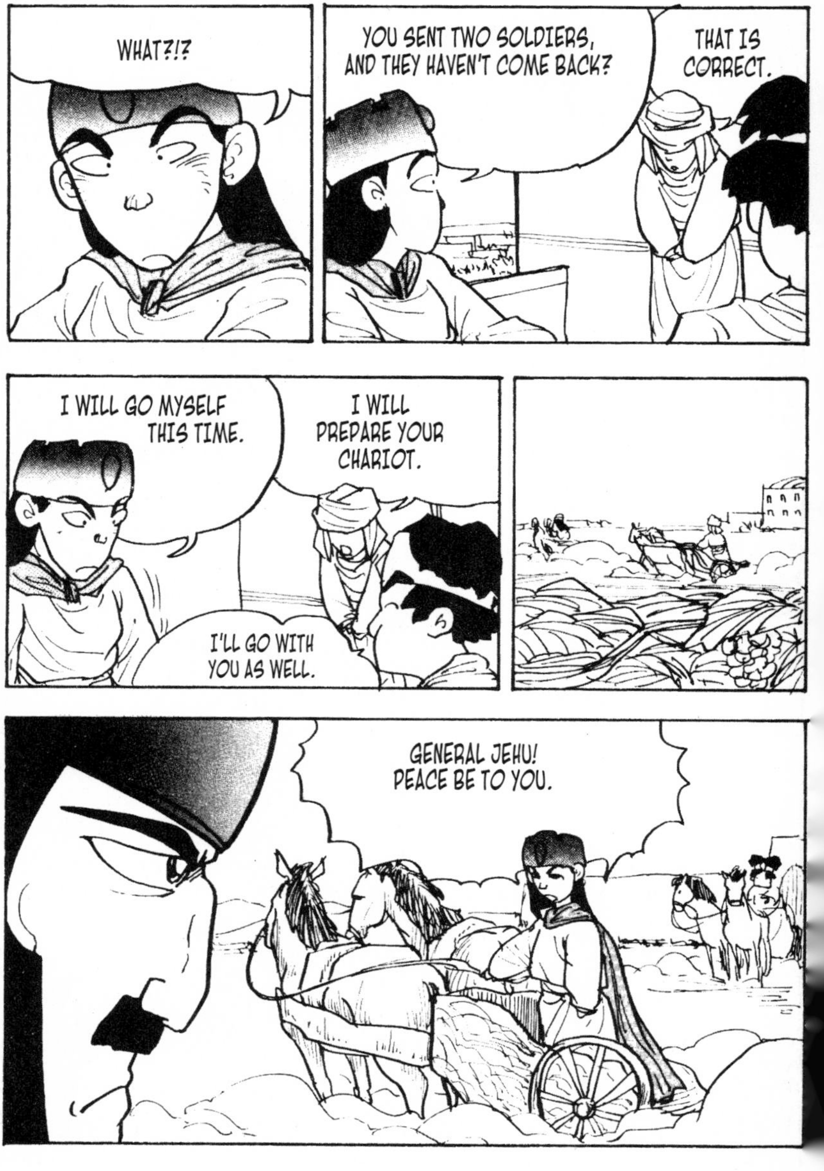
WHAT?!?
YOU SENT TWO SOLDIERS, AND THEY HAVEN'T COME BACK?
THAT IS CORRECT.
I WILL GO MYSELF THIS TIME.
I WILL PREPARE YOUR CHARIOT.
I'LL GO WITH YOU AS WELL.
GENERAL JEHU! PEACE BE TO YOU.

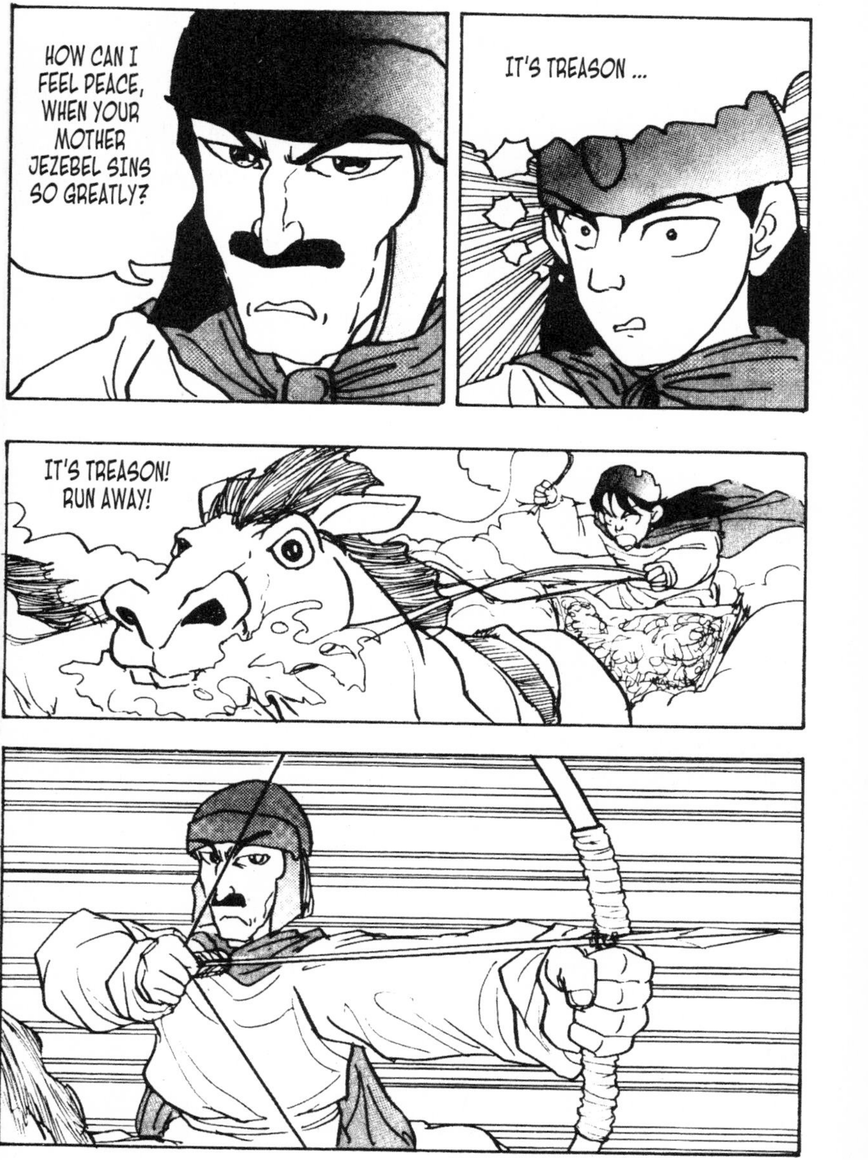
HOW CAN I FEEL PEACE, WHEN YOUR MOTHER JEZEBEL SINS SO GREATLY?
IT'S TREASON ...
IT'S TREASON! RUN AWAY!

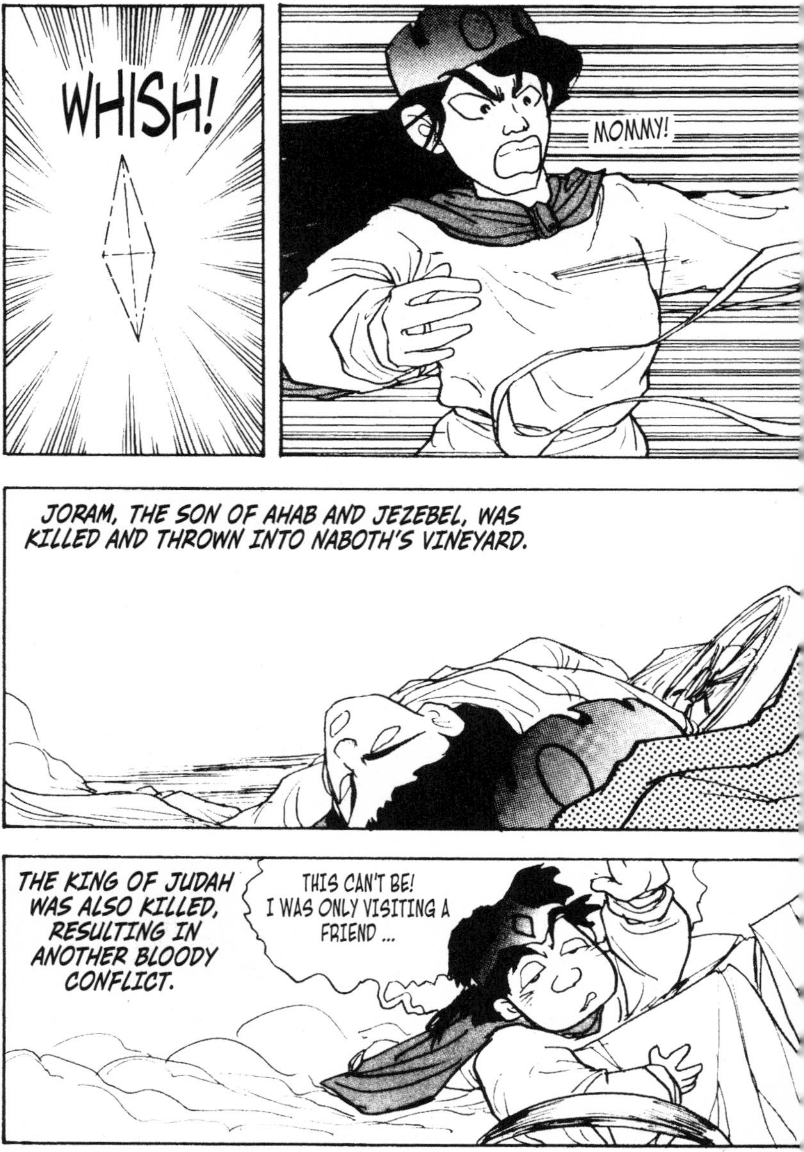
WHISH!
MOMMY!
JORAM, THE SON OF AHAB AND JEZEBEL, WAS KILLED AND THROWN INTO NABOTH'S VINEYARD.
THE KING OF JUDAH WAS ALSO KILLED, RESULTING IN ANOTHER BLOODY CONFLICT.
THIS CAN'T BE! I WAS ONLY VISITING A FRIEND ...

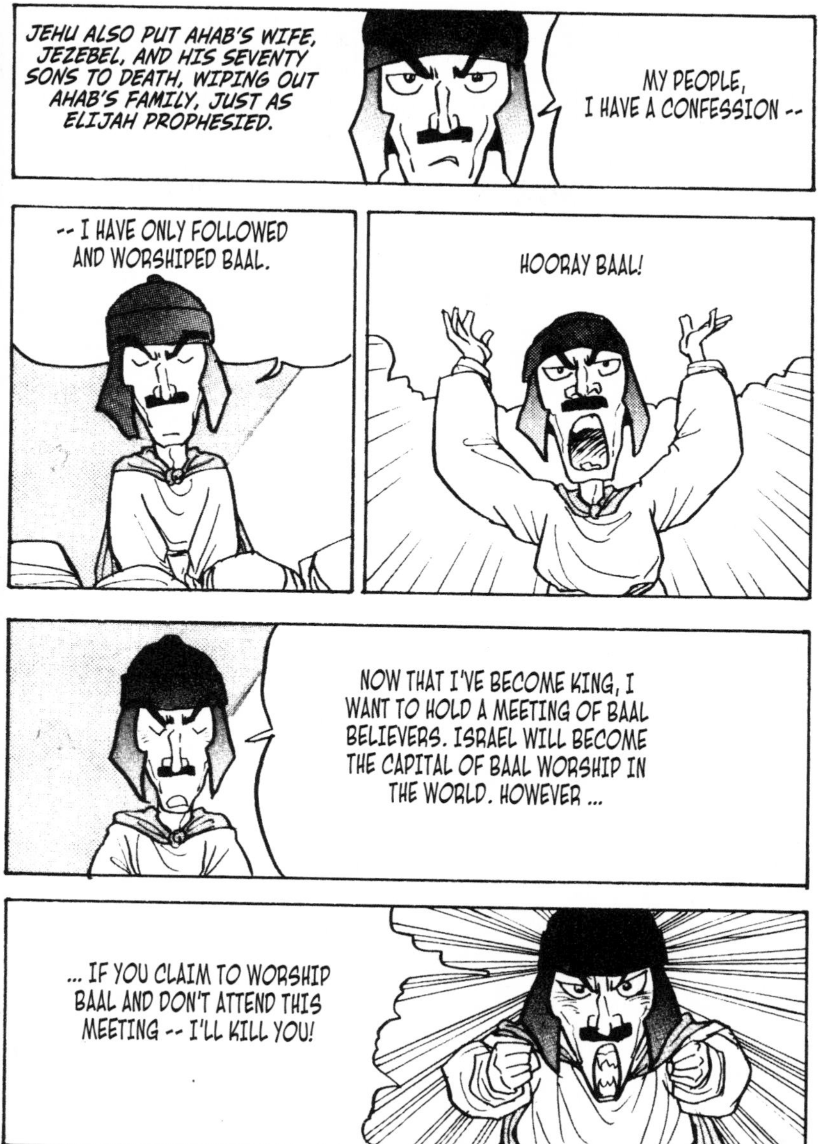
JEHU ALSO PUT AHAB'S WIFE, JEZEBEL, AND HIS SEVENTY SONS TO DEATH, WIPING OUT AHAB'S FAMILY, JUST AS ELIJAH PROPHESIED.
MY PEOPLE, I HAVE A CONFESSION --
-- I HAVE ONLY FOLLOWED AND WORSHIPED BAAL.
HOORAY BAAL!
NOW THAT I'VE BECOME KING, I WANT TO HOLD A MEETING OF BAAL BELIEVERS. ISRAEL WILL BECOME THE CAPITAL OF BAAL WORSHIP IN THE WORLD. HOWEVER ...
... IF YOU CLAIM TO WORSHIP BAAL AND DON'T ATTEND THIS MEETING -- I'LL KILL YOU!

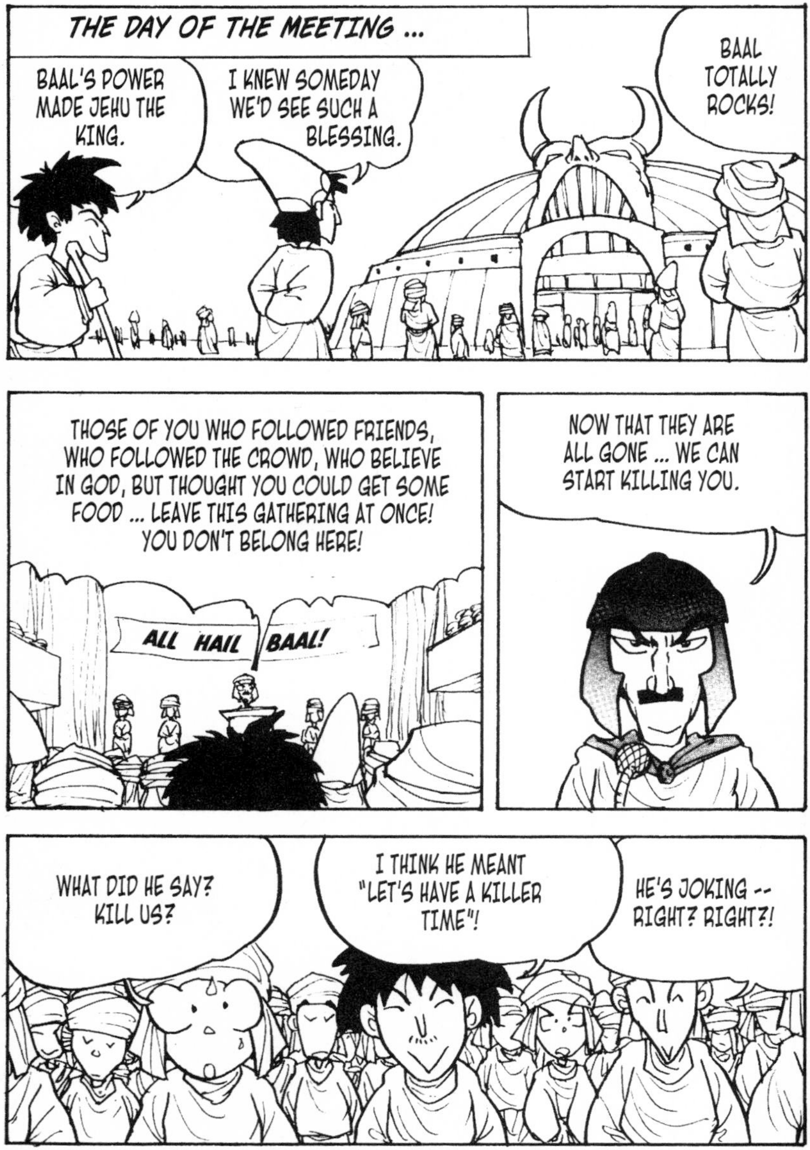
THE DAY OF THE MEETING ...
BAAL'S POWER MADE JEHU THE KING.
I KNEW SOMEDAY WE'D SEE SUCH A BLESSING.
BAAL TOTALLY ROCKS!
THOSE OF YOU WHO FOLLOWED FRIENDS, WHO FOLLOWED THE CROWD, WHO BELIEVE IN GOD, BUT THOUGHT YOU COULD GET SOME FOOD ... LEAVE THIS GATHERING AT ONCE! YOU DON'T BELONG HERE!
ALL HAIL BAAL!
NOW THAT THEY ARE ALL GONE ... WE CAN START KILLING YOU.
WHAT DID HE SAY? KILL US?
I THINK HE MEANT "LET'S HAVE A KILLER TIME"!
HE'S JOKING -- RIGHT? RIGHT?!

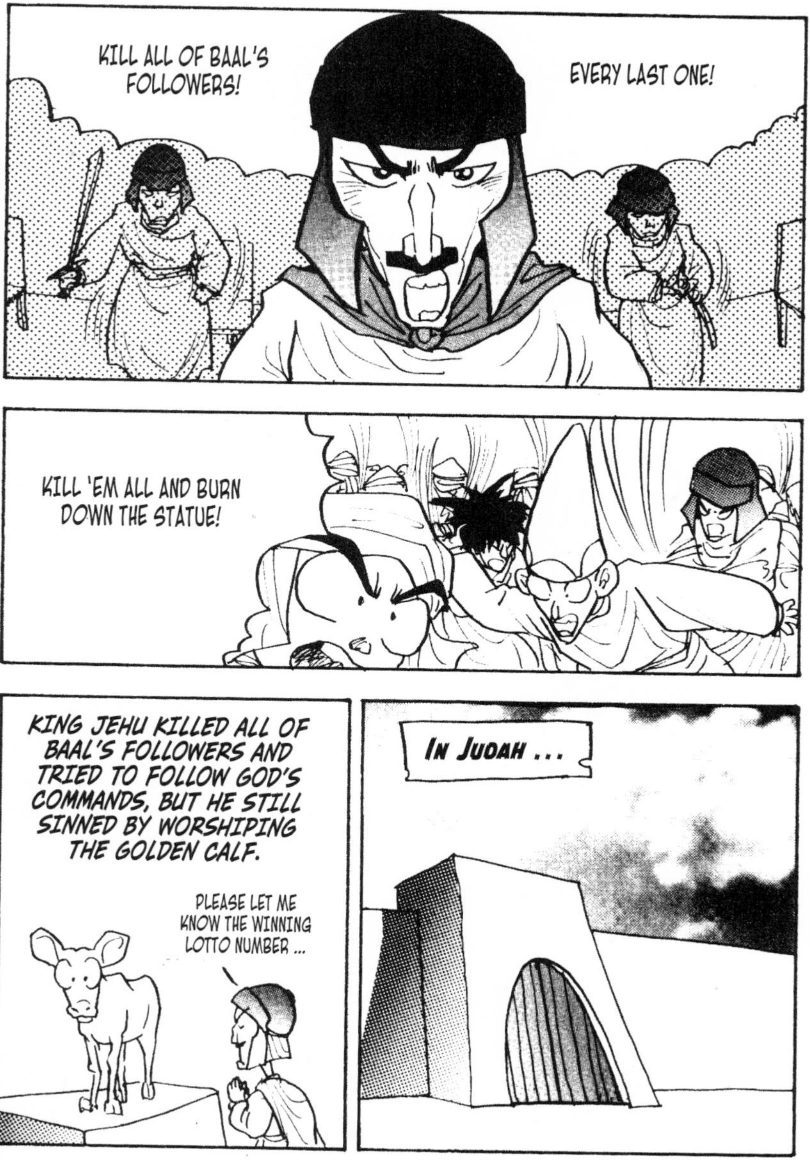
KILL ALL OF BAAL'S FOLLOWERS!
EVERY LAST ONE!
KILL 'EM ALL AND BURN DOWN THE STATUE!
KING JEHU KILLED ALL OF BAAL'S FOLLOWERS AND TRIED TO FOLLOW GOD'S COMMANDS, BUT HE STILL SINNED BY WORSHIPING THE GOLDEN CALF.
PLEASE LET ME KNOW THE WINNING LOTTO NUMBER ...
IN JUDAH ...

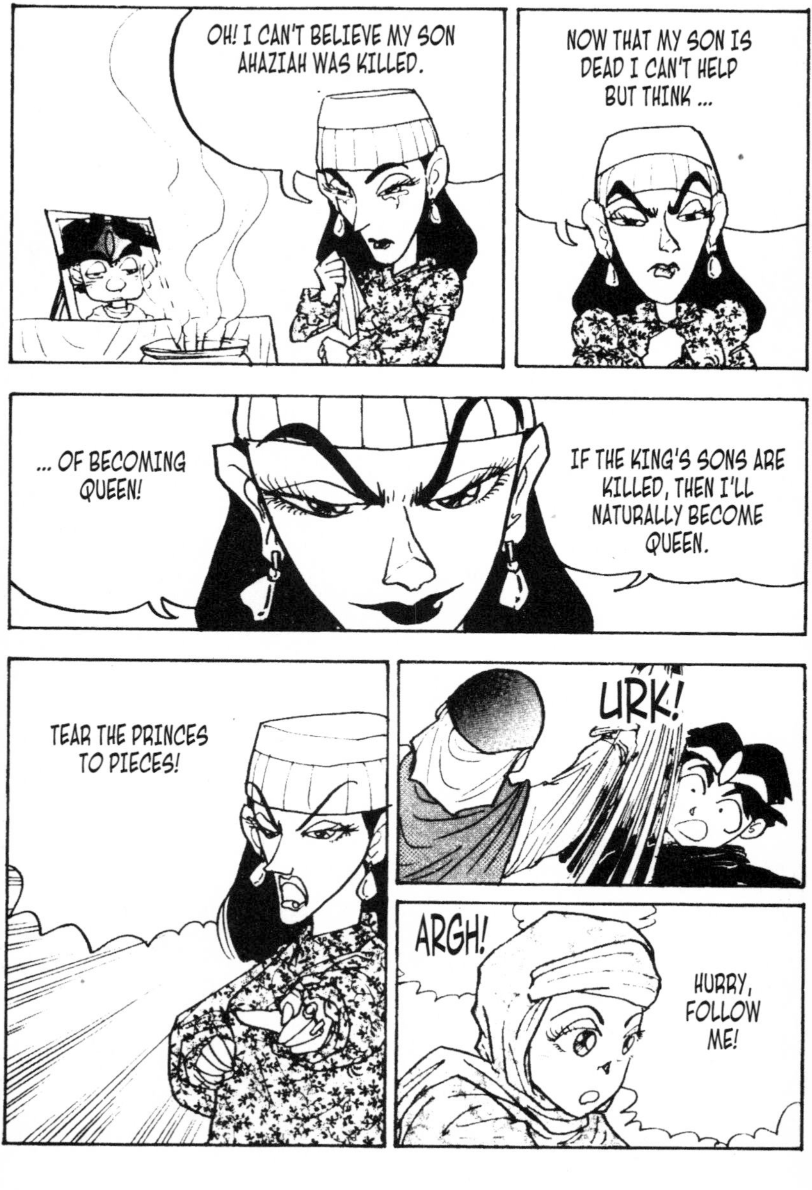
OH! I CAN'T BELIEVE MY SON AHAZIAH WAS KILLED.
NOW THAT MY SON IS DEAD I CAN'T HELP BUT THINK ...
... OF BECOMING QUEEN!
IF THE KING'S SONS ARE KILLED, THEN I'LL NATURALLY BECOME QUEEN.
TEAR THE PRINCES TO PIECES!
URK!
ARGH!
HURRY, FOLLOW ME!

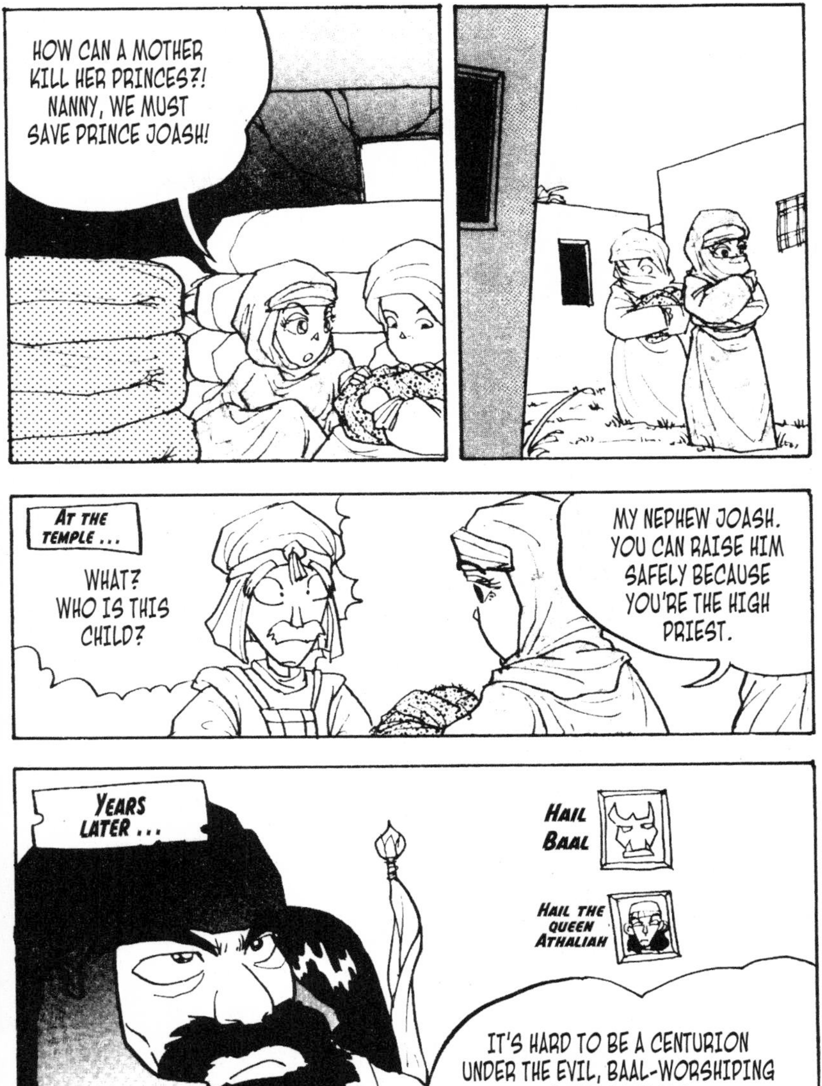
HOW CAN A MOTHER KILL HER PRINCES?! NANNY, WE MUST SAVE PRINCE JOASH!
AT THE TEMPLE ...
WHAT? WHO IS THIS CHILD?
MY NEPHEW JOASH. YOU CAN RAISE HIM SAFELY BECAUSE YOU'RE THE HIGH PRIEST.
YEARS LATER ...
HAIL BAAL
HAIL THE QUEEN ATHALIAH
IT'S HARD TO BE A CENTURION UNDER THE EVIL, BAAL-WORSHIPING QUEEN ATHALIAH.

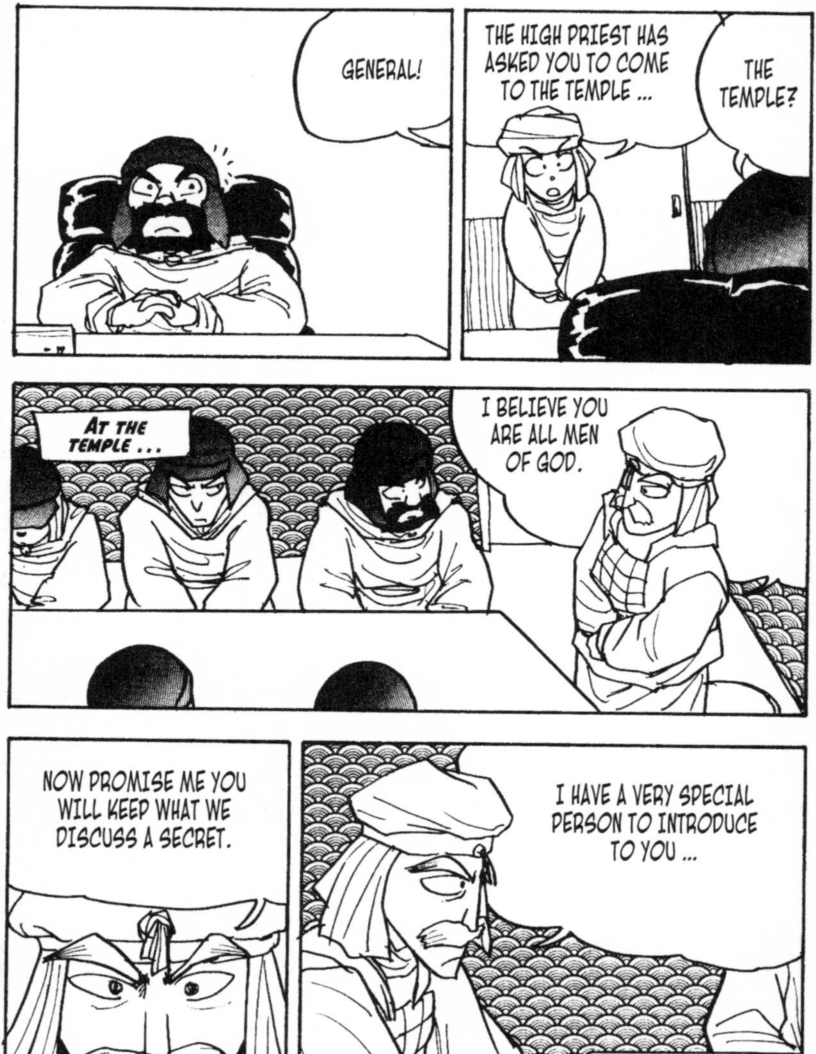
GENERAL!
THE HIGH PRIEST HAS ASKED YOU TO COME TO THE TEMPLE ...
THE TEMPLE?
AT THE TEMPLE ...
I BELIEVE YOU ARE ALL MEN OF GOD.
NOW PROMISE ME YOU WILL KEEP WHAT WE DISCUSS A SECRET.
I HAVE A VERY SPECIAL PERSON TO INTRODUCE TO YOU ...

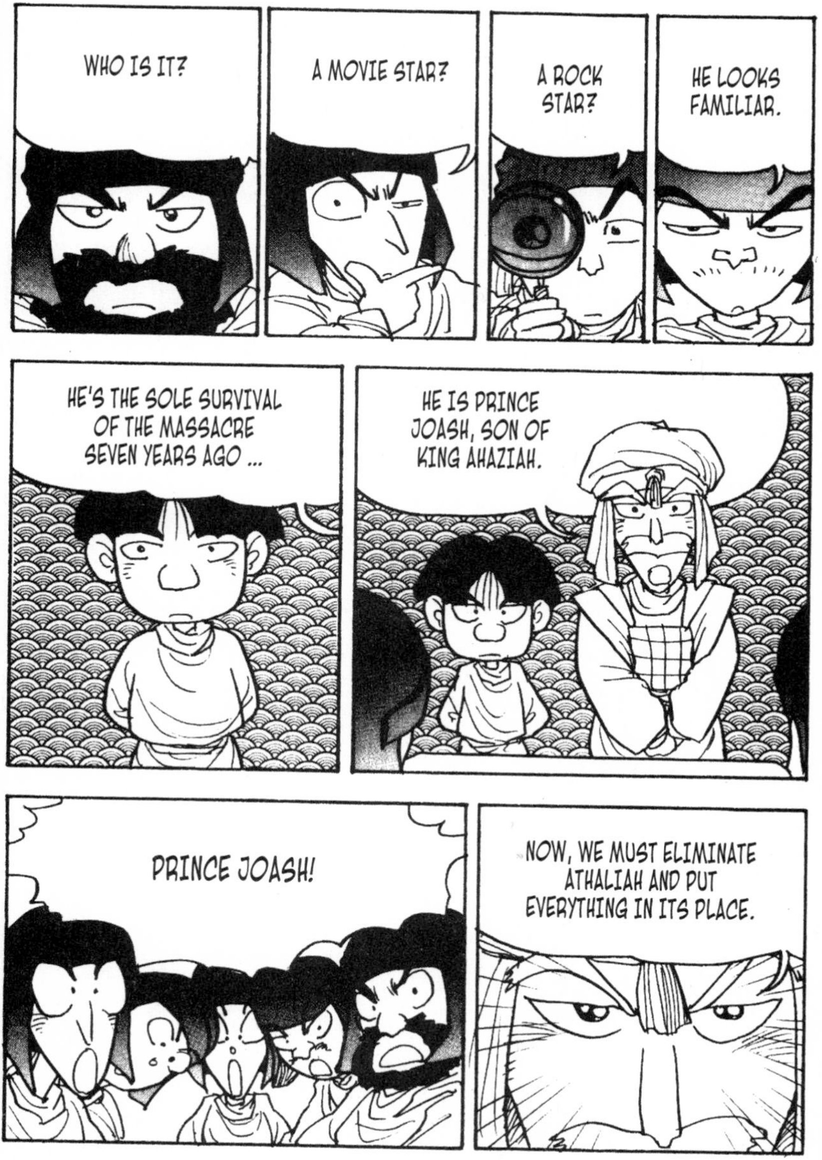
WHO IS IT?
A MOVIE STAR?
A ROCK STAR?
HE LOOKS FAMILIAR.
HE'S THE SOLE SURVIVAL OF THE MASSACRE SEVEN YEARS AGO ...
HE IS PRINCE JOASH, SON OF KING AHAZIAH.
PRINCE JOASH!
NOW, WE MUST ELIMINATE ATHALIAH AND PUT EVERYTHING IN ITS PLACE.

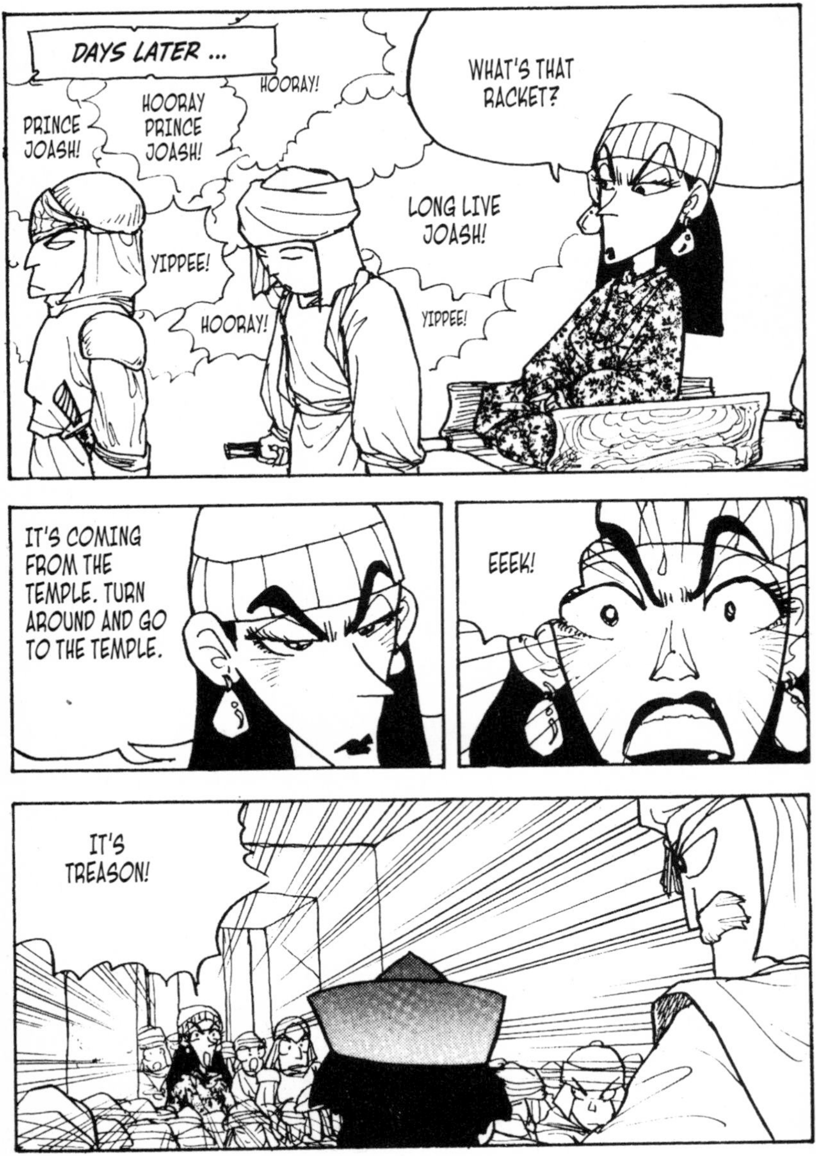
DAYS LATER ...
PRINCE JOASH!
HOORAY PRINCE JOASH!
HOORAY!
WHAT'S THAT RACKET?
YIPPEE!
LONG LIVE JOASH!
HOORAY!
YIPPEE!
IT'S COMING FROM THE TEMPLE. TURN AROUND AND GO TO THE TEMPLE.
EEEK!
IT'S TREASON!

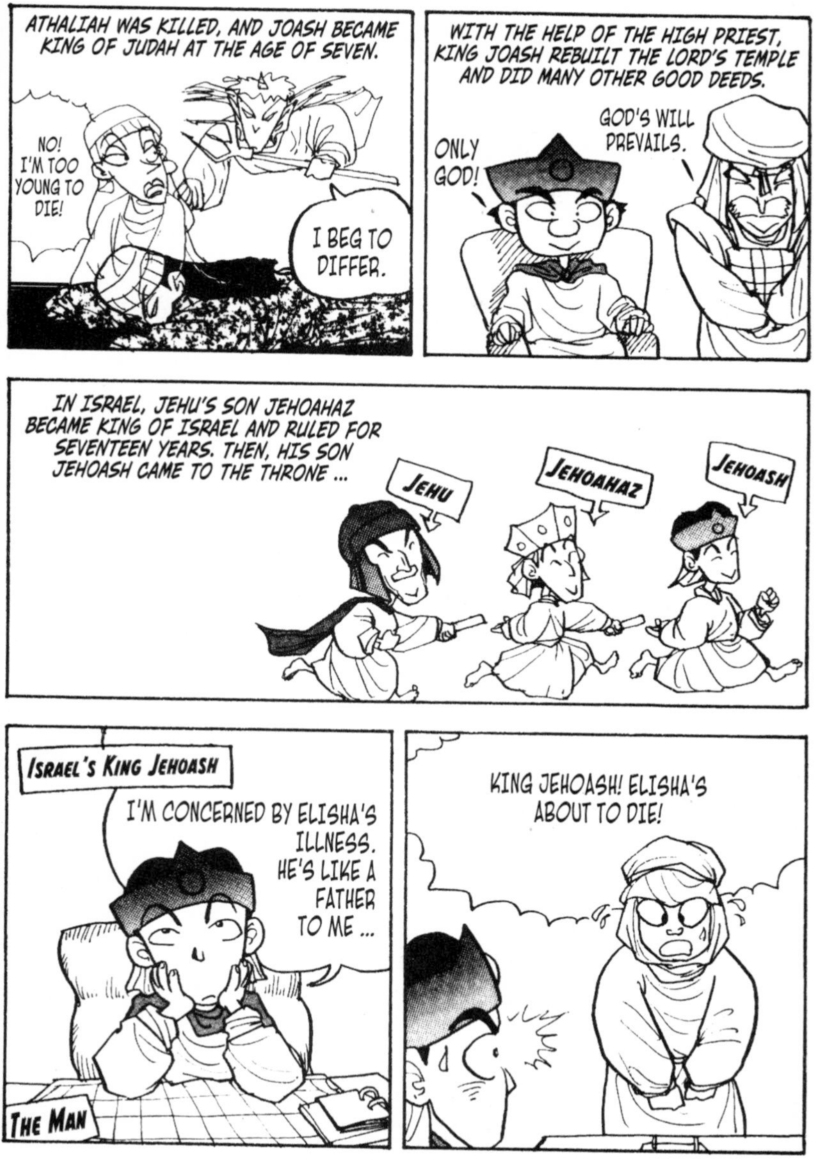
ATHALIAH WAS KILLED, AND JOASH BECAME KING OF JUDAH AT THE AGE OF SEVEN.
NO! I'M TOO YOUNG TO DIE!
I BEG TO DIFFER.
WITH THE HELP OF THE HIGH PRIEST, KING JOASH REBUILT THE LORD'S TEMPLE AND DID MANY OTHER GOOD DEEDS.
ONLY GOD!
GOD'S WILL PREVAILS.
IN ISRAEL, JEHU'S SON JEHOAHAZ BECAME KING OF ISRAEL AND RULED FOR SEVENTEEN YEARS. THEN, HIS SON JEHOASH CAME TO THE THRONE ...
JEHU
JEHOAHAZ
JEHOASH
ISRAEL'S KING JEHOASH
I'M CONCERNED BY ELISHA'S ILLNESS. HE'S LIKE A FATHER TO ME ...
THE MAN
KING JEHOASH! ELISHA'S ABOUT TO DIE!

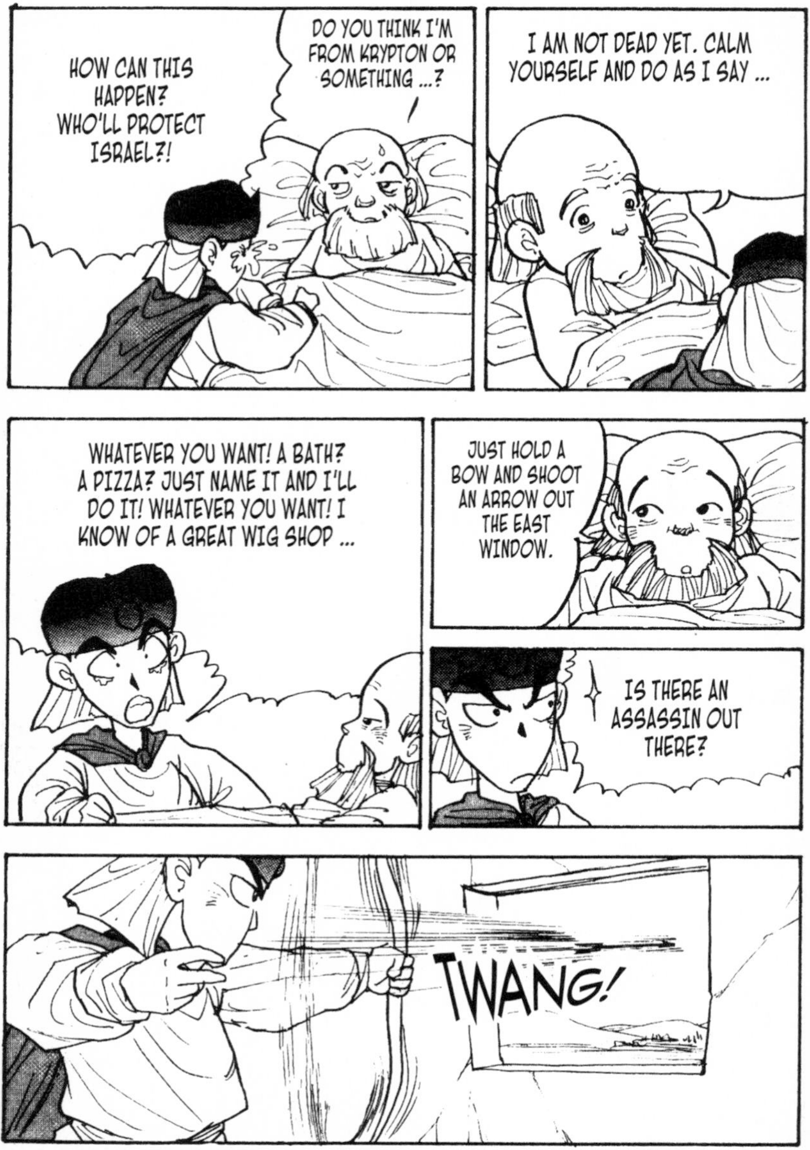
HOW CAN THIS HAPPEN? WHO'LL PROTECT ISRAEL?!
DO YOU THINK I'M FROM KRYPTON OR SOMETHING ...?
I AM NOT DEAD YET. CALM YOURSELF AND DO AS I SAY ...
WHATEVER YOU WANT! A BATH? A PIZZA? JUST NAME IT AND I'LL DO IT! WHATEVER YOU WANT! I KNOW OF A GREAT WIG SHOP ...
JUST HOLD A BOW AND SHOOT AN ARROW OUT THE EAST WINDOW.
IS THERE AN ASSASSIN OUT THERE?
TWANG!

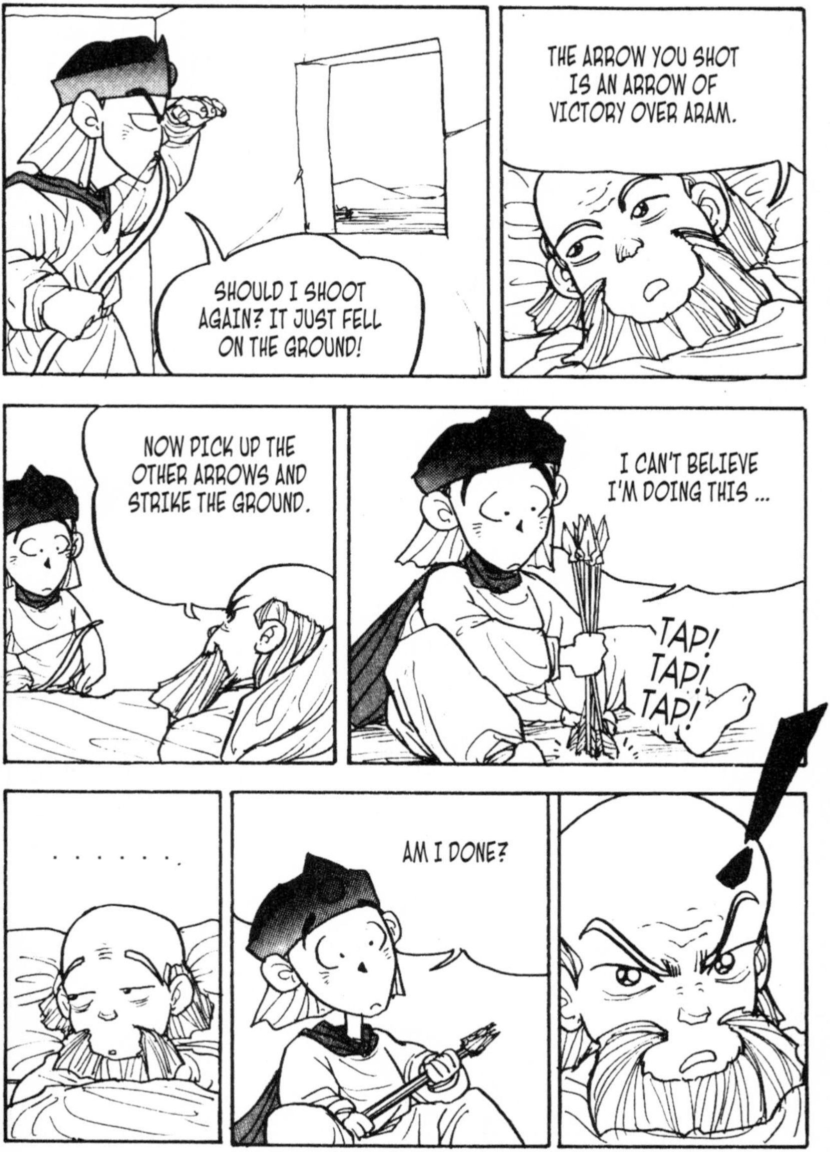
SHOULD I SHOOT AGAIN? IT JUST FELL ON THE GROUND!
THE ARROW YOU SHOT IS AN ARROW OF VICTORY OVER ARAM.
NOW PICK UP THE OTHER ARROWS AND STRIKE THE GROUND.
I CAN'T BELIEVE I'M DOING THIS ...
TAP! TAP! TAP!
. . . .
AM I DONE?
!

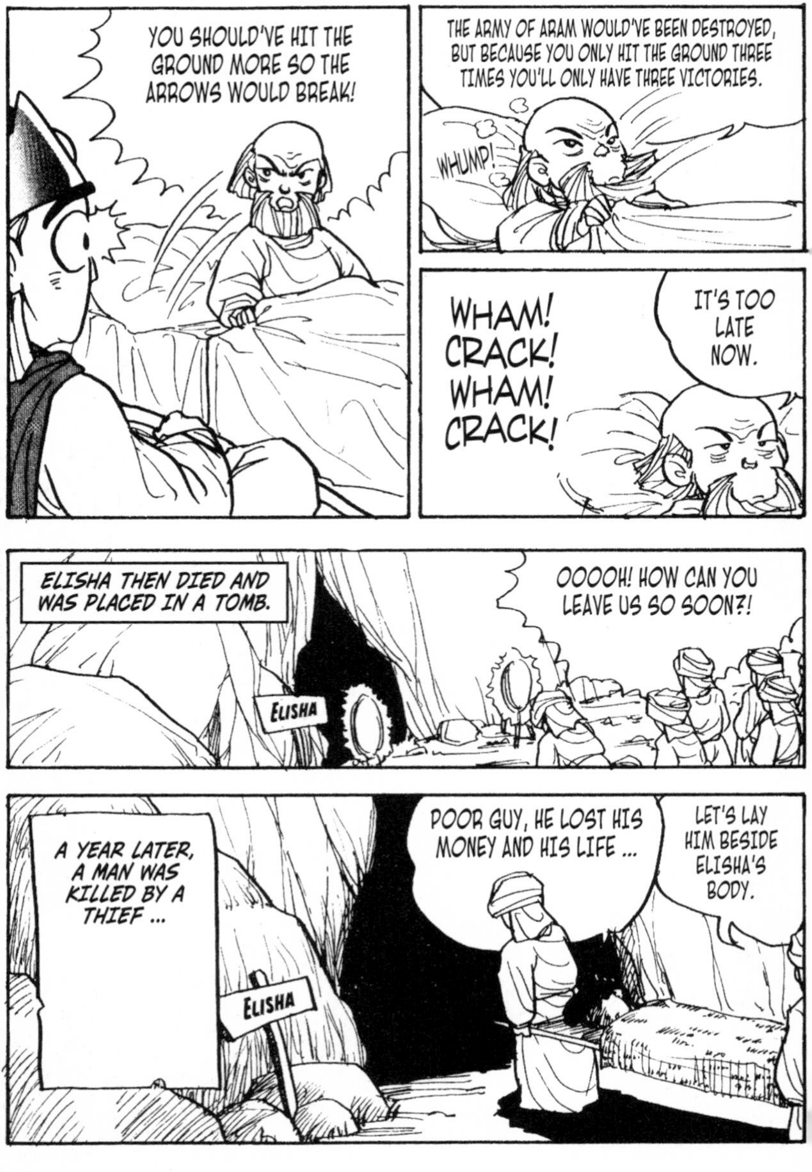
YOU SHOULD'VE HIT THE GROUND MORE SO THE ARROWS WOULD BREAK!
THE ARMY OF ARAM WOULD'VE BEEN DESTROYED, BUT BECAUSE YOU ONLY HIT THE GROUND THREE TIMES YOU'LL ONLY HAVE THREE VICTORIES.
WHUMP!
WHAM! CRACK! WHAM! CRACK!
IT'S TOO LATE NOW.
ELISHA THEN DIED AND WAS PLACED IN A TOMB.
OOOOH! HOW CAN YOU LEAVE US SO SOON?!
ELISHA
A YEAR LATER, A MAN WAS KILLED BY A THIEF ...
POOR GUY, HE LOST HIS MONEY AND HIS LIFE ...
LET'S LAY HIM BESIDE ELISHA'S BODY.
ELISHA

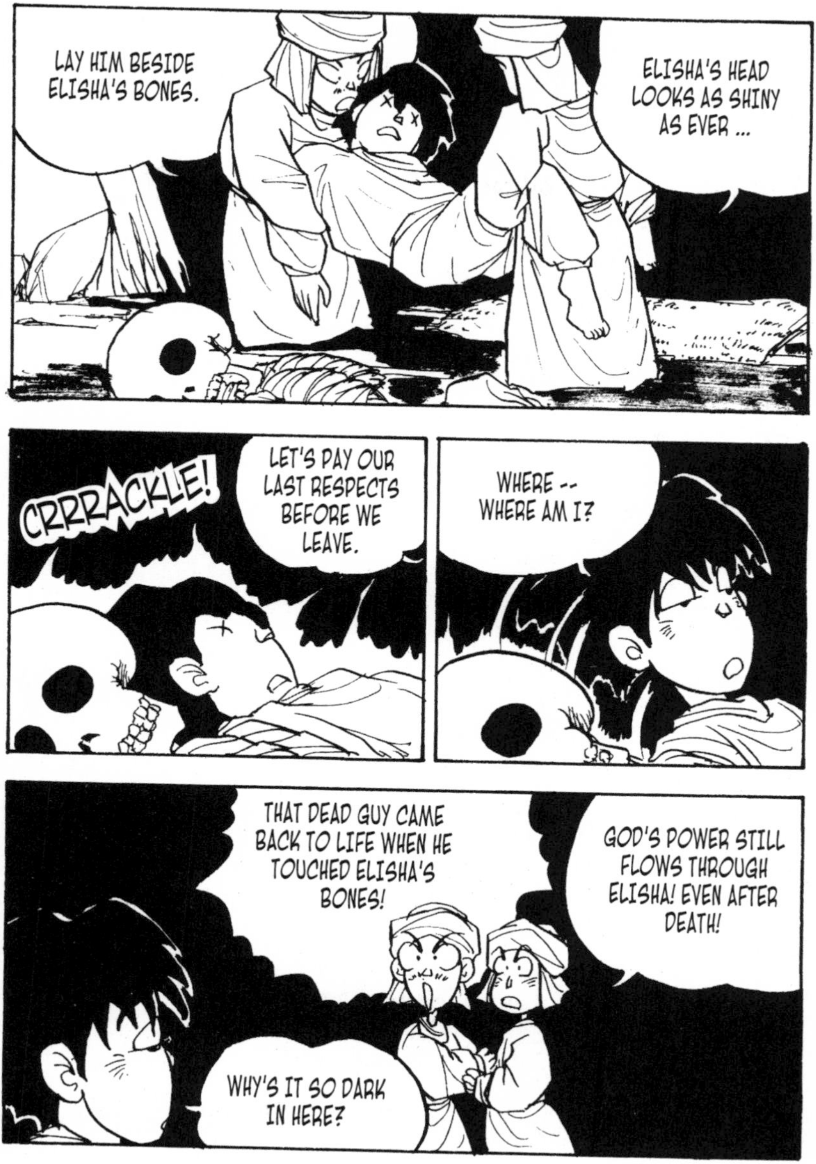
LAY HIM BESIDE ELISHA'S BONES.
ELISHA'S HEAD LOOKS AS SHINY AS EVER ...
CRRRACKLE!
LET'S PAY OUR LAST RESPECTS BEFORE WE LEAVE.
WHERE -- WHERE AM I?
THAT DEAD GUY CAME BACK TO LIFE WHEN HE TOUCHED ELISHA'S BONES!
GOD'S POWER STILL FLOWS THROUGH ELISHA! EVEN AFTER DEATH!
WHY'S IT SO DARK IN HERE?

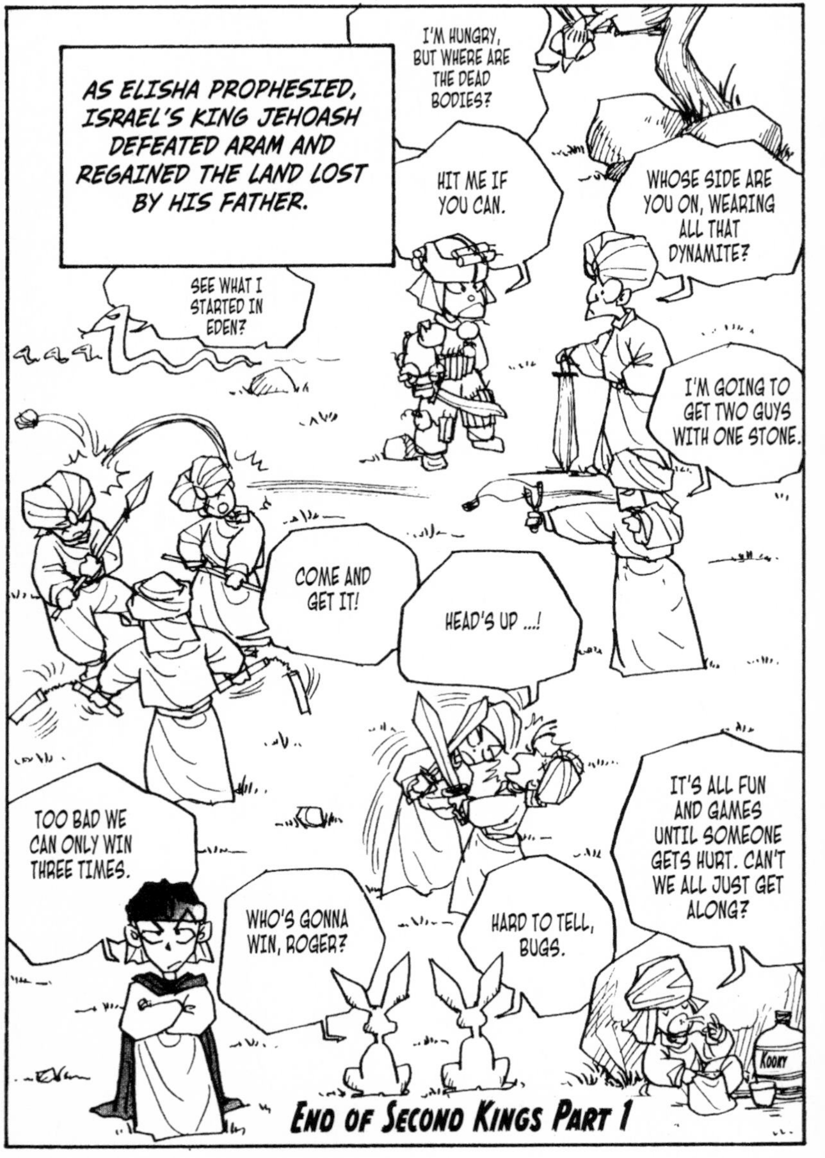
AS ELISHA PROPHESIED, ISRAEL'S KING JEHOASH DEFEATED ARAM AND REGAINED THE LAND LOST BY HIS FATHER.
I'M HUNGRY, BUT WHERE ARE THE DEAD BODIES?
HIT ME IF YOU CAN.
WHOSE SIDE ARE YOU ON, WEARING ALL THAT DYNAMITE?
SEE WHAT I STARTED IN EDEN?
I'M GOING TO GET TWO GUYS WITH ONE STONE.
COME AND GET IT!
HEAD'S UP ...!
TOO BAD WE CAN ONLY WIN THREE TIMES.
IT'S ALL FUN AND GAMES UNTIL SOMEONE GETS HURT. CAN'T WE ALL JUST GET ALONG?
WHO'S GONNA WIN, ROGER?
HARD TO TELL, BUGS.
KOOKY
END OF SECOND KINGS PART 1

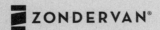